Deep Water

HE HAD an image, suddenly, of massacre sites like this one, scattered the length and breadth of the Domains. It had taken a thousand years, but Acton's people had killed, and killed, and killed again, until they owned the whole of the country, from cliff to cove, from sand to snow. His own village had been the last to live freely in the old way, and the last to be slaughtered. No doubt the invaders had thought themselves safe, then, thinking they had killed the last of the pure old blood. But they had overlooked him, and now he would bring about their ruin.

Saker looked greedily at the bones before him. Here was an army indeed, if even a fraction of those slaughtered by the invaders had stayed in the dark beyond the grave, yearning for revenge. He would give it to them, full measure and spilling over. They would take back their birthright and the land would flourish under its rightful owners. The people of the old blood – *his* blood – would live in freedom again, and he would be responsible.

By PAMELA FREEMAN

The Castings Trilogy
Blood Ties
Deep Water

Deep Water

BOOK TWO OF THE CASTINGS TRILOGY

PAMELA FREEMAN

www.orbitbooks.net

ORBIT

First published in Great Britain in 2008 by Orbit

A CIP catalogue record for this book
is available from the British Library.

ISBN 978-1-84149-702-0

Typeset in Sabon by M Rules
Printed in the UK by
CPI Mackays, Chatham ME5 8TD

Papers used by Orbit are natural, renewable and recyclable
products made from wood grown in sustainable forests and certified
in accordance with the rules of the Forest Stewardship Council.

Mixed Sources
Product group from well-managed
forests and other controlled sources
www.fsc.org Cert no. SGS-COC-004081
© 1996 Forest Stewardship Council

FSC

Orbit
An imprint of
Little, Brown Book Group
100 Victoria Embankment
London EC4Y 0DY

An Hachette Livre UK Company
www.hachettelivre.co.uk

www.orbitbooks.net

To Stephen and Robert

Foreverfroze

LAST
DOMAIN

NORTHERN
MOUNTAINS
DOMAIN

CLIFF
DOMAIN

Oakmere

Golden
Valley

LAKE
DOMAIN

FAR NORTH
DOMAIN

Baluchston

NORTH
DOMAIN

Sendat

CENTRAL DOMAIN

Pless **Mitchen**

THREE
RIVERS
DOMAIN

Sandalwood

Wooding

Carlion

N

THE ELEVEN DOMAINS

THE WELL OF SECRETS

'The desire to know the future gnaws at our bones,' said Safred, the Well of Secrets. 'Or so a stonecaster told me.'

Her uncle Cael grunted and kept cutting up the carrots. Carrots, beets, onion and garlic, lemon juice and oil. Delicious.

'Are you going to bake that?' Safred said hopefully. She wasn't fond of salad, but Cael loved it.

Cael grinned at her. 'The desire to know the future gnaws at our bones.'

She laughed, then sighed.

'They're coming. Send out the word. The girl is badly hurt.' She paused. 'They may not get here in time. It will be difficult.'

'Don't tire yourself out.'

'You'd rather I let her die? Besides, you'll like her, this Bramble. She's contrary.'

He grimaced at her but went out to the street to spread the word, as she had instructed. The Well of Secrets sat for a few moments more, wondering if she had the strength to bring the Kill Reborn back from her second death. The gods were silent on the matter, although she had asked them, a thing she rarely did. Prophecy was all very well, but sometimes things came to a tipping point, where the future could go either way, or they came to a person who held the future in her hand, and this was such a time and Bramble such a person. If the Kill Reborn lived . . . if the girl Bramble survived . . . which was more important? Safred thought that not even the gods knew. What would happen in the next day would shape the future of the Domains, perhaps of the world, and Safred was as blind to it as – as Cael was.

'Gnaws like a rat,' she said, and laughed so that she would not cry.

ASH

'ASH! CATCH HER!' Martine shouted.

Ash moved by instinct, kicking his horse towards Bramble's as she swayed and slid sideways, her eyelids fluttering. He grabbed her awkwardly, her shoulder hitting his and almost pushing him out of his saddle. He gripped with his knees, but that was a mistake, because the horse – what was its name? Cam? – took that as a signal to go faster. They started to pull away from Bramble's horse, with Bramble still half out of the saddle and Ash's reins caught up underneath her back. She was not quite a dead weight, and she struggled weakly, as though she thought Ash was trying to pull her off the horse. Her skin was as hot as though he were holding a cup of fresh cha.

Bramble's horse blew out through her nose in disgust and stopped dead, and Ash's horse stopped with her. They were still badly aligned, but now he could hoist Bramble back onto her seat. He brushed her wounded arm as he steadied her, and she made a sound halfway between a moan and a scream, and fainted truly.

He managed to push her so that she fell forwards, over her horse's neck. The arm that the wolves had savaged dropped and hung straight, and Ash could see for the first time just how swollen it was. The sleeve of her shirt, even pulled back as it was, cut deep into the puffy red flesh.

The wound, made by a wolf's claw, was starting to smell, the unmistakable sweet smell of decay.

Martine smelt it too. 'The Well of Secrets is her only hope of keeping that arm,' she said. 'We'll have to ride faster.'

They used a shift of Martine's to lash Bramble to the neck of her horse. Ash was nervous as he did it, because Trine had already tried to take a few bites out of him, but this time she waited patiently, occasionally turning her head to nose at Bramble's good shoulder.

Then they rode.

They had sighted Oakmere, where the Well of Secrets lived, from the top of the Golden Valley mountain pass just before sunset, and the town had seemed only an hour or so riding away. Ash had thought they would have plenty of time to reach it before the northern twilight ended. But as they went down into the valley, and then up the hill and down into the next valley, and the next, they realised that they had been deceived. They had stopped to rest the horses at a stream that flowed icy cold down from the mountains, but they didn't dare take Bramble off Trine in case they couldn't put her on again. They managed to get her to drink a little water, and Martine made a cold compress for the arm, but it was clearly useless.

'I don't know how fast we can go without risking the horses,' Ash said with frustration.

'The horses can be sacrificed if necessary,' Martine replied.

Ash's mouth twisted wryly. 'As long as you tell her it was *your* decision!' he said. He had met Bramble only that morning, but he knew already that her horses were like gold to her – no, not gold, but something more precious. He didn't want to be the one to tell her one of them was dead.

Martine returned the half smile. 'That's fair. Let's go.'

Even tied on, Bramble swayed in the saddle. By sunset, she was delirious, muttering about guilt and death and someone called Leof who had let her go from somewhere, against orders. 'Shagging pine trees!' she said suddenly, clearly, then moaned. Ash felt embarrassed and guilty, as he had when Doronit had made him listen to the secrets of the dead, back in Turvite. He tried not to listen, but his horse worked best with Trine, so he rode next to Bramble, supporting her, and he felt every word as well as hearing it.

Martine took their reins and led them both, to leave Ash's hands free. He trusted her to find the road and set the pace. All his attention spiralled down to Bramble. He was determined to save her. He had killed a warlord's man to protect her, back in the Golden Valley, and he didn't want that death to be for nothing. If Bramble lived, he would feel better about killing the man Sully. If she died – he didn't want to think about the waste of two lives, so he rode and rode and supported Bramble and prayed to the local gods.

The ride turned into a rhythm of canter and rest and canter. He was blind to the spring beauty of the mountains; deaf to the wind and the birds and the constant, rushing sound of the streams. All he knew was Bramble's back under his hands, his own back screaming in protest at the unnatural pose, his breath and the horses' drowning out hers. She was breathing in feeble gasps, as though each breath hurt.

Every hill forced her back in the saddle until she was supported only by the cloth under her armpits and by Ash's hands. Every downslope sent her sliding towards Trine's head, rubbing the inflamed arm and shoulder and making her cry out. She roused sometimes and blinked vaguely at Ash. He got her to drink whenever he could, but finally she didn't even react when her arm hit the saddlebow.

Ash raised his head and stared at Martine in despair. 'She's dying,' he said.

He became aware that it was growing dark. They had ridden through the long hours of twilight and into the night. The horses were labouring up another slope, a zigzag path that led to a high ridge. They were exhausted. Ash became abruptly conscious of the pain in his legs and back. His own tiredness almost overwhelmed him.

'It can't be far now,' Martine said, but her tone was doubtful. She looked pale and her face showed more lines than usual. She eased her backside in the saddle and winced. 'Let's hope she can cure saddlesores as well,' she said.

It was a good try at a joke, but Ash was too tired to laugh. They plodded up the rise, sure that there would be nothing but another empty valley in front of them.

There were lights. Below them in the valley, there were lights beginning to shine. One by one they sparked up, flaring gold and white and yellow until the valley seemed carpeted with stars.

Ash tried to say something, but his mind refused to work.

Bramble breathed more harshly.

'That's the beginning of the death breathing. It will get louder, and then the rattle will start,' Martine said, her voice tight. 'Go! Go! There's still a chance!'

They set the horses at the downslope as fast as they dared. Then, Ash gritted his teeth, took the reins back from Martine, and urged Cam and Trine even faster. If the horses broke a leg, so be it. Bramble's breathing was coming slower and louder. He put his head down and pushed the tired horses to their fastest pace. They couldn't do it for long, but he spoke to them, as he had heard Bramble doing back in Golden Valley.

'Come on, come on, you're her only hope! Come *on*!' he shouted.

Astonishingly, they responded, letting the momentum of the slope carry them, getting their legs under them by sheer luck and will, almost falling down the hillside. They left Martine behind.

Then the lights were around him, and people – people leading them to a house and saying things like, 'The Well of Secrets wants you to take the sick lass straight to her!' and 'Don't worry now, she'll fix her!' and 'Someone get Mullet!'

It was disorienting, loud, deeply reassuring. All his senses had come abruptly alive, so that everything registered sharply: the golden lights and the night chill, the shining eyes of the people milling in a group behind the horses. His own tiredness washed away in a surge of relief and warmth.

Then there was a house, with wide double doors lit by oil lamps, and an old man waiting for them, so old his back was bent half over and his eyes were milky with rheum. He helped Ash dismount painfully, who then set to loosen the cloth under Bramble's armpits.

'I'm Mullet. She sent me to take care of the horses,' the old man said, and reached for Cam's leading rein with the assurance of an ostler. Cam neighed in alarm and threw up her head. Ash couldn't believe it, but Bramble roused at that and looked at Mullet closely. He met her eyes and grinned, showing one tooth top and bottom on different sides of his mouth. 'She'll be right with me, lass,' he said. Bramble nodded and fell off the horse.

Before Ash could move to help, another man was there to catch her and cradle her. Ash assessed him. Tall, very strong, about fifty, with olive colouring and bright blue eyes, a neat beard that left his cheeks bare. Not a Traveller. He had come out silently, leaving the door wide open behind him, and now he simply turned and walked back inside with Bramble.

Martine arrived, scrambled off her horse and gave the reins to the grinning old man, who grinned even wider as he saw her limping. The man carrying Bramble didn't look back. Ash was annoyed that he and Martine were being ignored, but he reserved judgement. Saving Bramble's life was the important thing.

He stayed behind Martine as they went into the house. As they passed the threshold he shuddered, feeling suddenly edgy and dangerous with it.

'Remember, no killing the Well of Secrets,' Martine said in a whisper, reading his mood as she so often did. 'If she's really irritating, you can do it later.'

He grinned involuntarily and relaxed a little as they went through the doorway into a room that took up the whole ground floor. The kitchen hearth was at the back, fire blazing, with a table and chairs before it, and a door near the hearth led to a yard he could see through a window. There were lamps alight everywhere, making the room as bright as day. At the front was a big open space with another table covered with a mattress and coverlet. An ordinary mattress, not a featherbed, and a coverlet of homespun wool dyed dark orange. He had had a coverlet of the same colour in his room at Doronit's, when she first started training him to be a safeguarder. He was looking at the bed and thinking about coverlets because something in him did not want to look at the woman who stood on the other side of the table. To speak to her, to deal with her, would change life forever.

Every ounce of Sight in him had reared up and screamed the moment he had walked into the room. It was the first time he admitted how strong his Sight had become. If it were Sight. He didn't know if life would be changed for the better or worse. Just that it would be changed profoundly, irreversibly. The Well of Secrets caught the thought, Ash realised. He had *Seen* her catch it, seen the oddly bright green eyes smile a little, the head tilt up just a fraction, the short sandy eyelashes flicker.

'Nothing lasts forever, not even change,' the Well of Secrets said directly to him, then she turned to the table where the man had already laid Bramble. She took a small knife from her belt and cut Bramble's shirt off, revealing the arm, so swollen and red that it looked like it didn't belong to her pale body. The original wound from the wolf claw had almost disappeared into the swelling. Bramble roused a little and whispered, 'If I die, tell my sister. Maryrose. Carlion.'

The Well of Secrets nodded matter-of-factly, and Bramble fainted.

She was deeply unconscious, alarmingly pale, and still beautiful, her upper body covered only by breastbands. Martine glanced at Ash, clearly wondering how susceptible he would be to this display of female flesh. That annoyed him. He was keeping watch on both doors and on the big man who had carried Bramble in. He glanced at the Well of Secrets, but turned away immediately. He couldn't spare any attention for Bramble. In a strange place, even one that had welcomed them, his safeguarder training took over. He had to mind their backs. He would think about Bramble being beautiful later – if she lived.

The Well of Secrets took hold of Bramble's arm and began to sing softly, in the harsh, grating voice of the dead, but modulated by a living body. *His* voice. Ash whipped around and took a step forward, but the big man put out an arm to bar his way. Ash didn't notice. All his attention was on the Well of Secrets, his guts churning with disbelief and a wild hope that, somehow, he was about to find the answer to his own strange voice. She sang a chant from the burial caves, a lament from beyond the grave, horrible, spine-chilling, nauseating. As she sang, the flesh on Bramble's arm cooled, paled. The red streaks, which had stretched threatening claws up to her shoulder, now shrank back and disappeared.

A part of him almost, *almost*, understood what she was chanting. Stray fragments whipped past him before he could fully grasp their meaning. Something about coolness, and wholeness . . . but he couldn't really understand. What he could feel was the ebb and flow of power. He closed his eyes, and it was plainer, like water flowing into a stream and being turned back by a strong current. The water flow increased, but it made no headway. The current was too strong. Ash could feel the sweat break out on his back and forehead. So much power being poured out. So much that the vessel itself might be emptied, and they would be left with two corpses. Because it wasn't working.

Bramble's breathing stopped.

The Well of Secrets turned sheet-white and staggered. She grabbed onto the edge of the table to stop herself falling. The man sprang forward to support her. While she stood, breathing fast and weak, the red marks began to creep up Bramble's arm again, but the girl lay still as stone.

The healer released herself from the man. She faced the table with determination and placed her hands again on Bramble's shoulder.

Ash moved forward and stood next to her, and put his own hand over hers. He didn't quite know why, but he was sure that he had to do it, sure with Sight and with something more familiar to him than Sight, a fighter's instinct, solidarity.

This time the Well of Secrets' song was stronger, like a call to arms. Sweat stood out on her forehead and her hands began to shake, but she kept singing. The song rose in pitch and loudness until it was painful to hear. Ash began to tremble and feel weak, but he didn't know if it were just the noise, or if power was being taken from him.

He closed his eyes and saw that both were true, that it was the song itself that siphoned strength from him. He could feel himself getting weaker, but he knew that it wasn't going to work. That Bramble was dead.

The Well of Secrets stopped singing.

Ash almost fainted as the power drained away, and he thought he might topple backwards, but then he felt someone giving him a push in the back to steady him and he stood upright, firm on his feet. A surge of strength went through him and into the Well of Secrets. She began singing again, louder than before.

Bramble coughed and began to breathe again. Her eyes stayed closed, but she said, 'Oh Maryro-ose!' in the voice of a young girl complaining about having to do something she didn't want to do – clean up her room, perhaps.

The Well of Secrets began to sing again, her voice dropping suddenly to a whisper, a plea. The wound disgorged a great gout of pus and then began to close, weeks of healing before their eyes. But it was greater than healing, because the wound itself disappeared. Then the chant died away and there was no mark on Bramble's arm, not even a scar to show where she had been wounded.

'She'll sleep the night through and wake hungry,' the Well of Secrets said, her words blurred with exhaustion. She patted Ash's arm in acknowledgment and he almost fell. The big man guided her away, up the stairs. She only came up to his armpit. Not a tall woman, not beautiful, not commanding or elegant or motherly or any of the things that gave women power of various kinds in the world. Ordinary, except for those eyes. But there, thought Ash, lay Bramble whole and unmarked. And he himself was still trembling.

As they reached the bend in the stairs Martine found her voice. 'Thank you,' she said, her face showing that she knew the words were inadequate. The Well of Secrets smiled at her wryly, acknowledging the thought as well as the thanks, and continued up. The man stayed on the landing, watching until they heard a door close upstairs.

'Most people don't find their tongue so fast,' he said. 'She doesn't get many thanks.' It was not clear whether he thought this was a good or bad thing. He came back down the stairs and turned to Ash. 'She's not so good at giving them, either.'

'It wasn't me,' Ash said. 'Something else helped.'

The man looked at him sceptically and shrugged. 'I'm Cael,' he said. 'You'd be Ash and Martine, yes?'

They nodded. Ash was uncomfortable and wondered instantly what else Cael knew about him. Martine's mouth was set. She didn't like it either. She sniffed, and then motioned to the pool of pus on the coverlet. 'I'll clean that up, if you tell me where to find water.'

He smiled with his eyes. 'Most people don't think of that, either. Expect it to disappear by enchantment. Don't worry. There's someone paid to clean.' He looked at Bramble. 'Do you have another shirt for her?'

'Her pack is on her horse,' Martine answered.

'I'll get it,' Ash said, and he made for the open door, glad of the excuse to get out of the room, but still having trouble controlling his legs. Halfway to the door he had to sit down on a bench.

There was a crowd standing just outside. They had clearly been listening and matching. They looked at him with interest and his cheeks reddened.

'You, Little Vole, go and get the girl's pack from Mullet,' Cael ordered a young blond boy. The boy ran off and Cael closed the doors. Ash let himself sit for a moment to recover. He didn't have to prove anything to anyone.

'They were expecting us to arrive,' Martine remarked.

'She told them to keep the street clear so the horses could get through. She said there was no time to waste.' Cael's voice held a slight disapproval.

'We came as fast as the horses could bear,' Martine said. She shifted uncomfortably, aware abruptly of her own chafing and sore muscles. 'And that was a good deal faster than I found comfortable, I can tell you!'

He laughed, a booming laugh as big as the rest of him, and Martine smiled, but she wasn't as easily distracted as that.

'Are we allowed to know who you are?' she asked.

'I'm uncle to the Well of Secrets.' He used the honorific sarcastically. 'Her real name's Safred. She told me to tell you.'

'Why?'

He shrugged. 'Fools need the mystery. Those who have mysteries of their own need the truth.'

'Did she say that?'

He regarded her quizzically, head on one side and eyes bright.

'Nay. She's not one for turning phrases. She said other things, though. Like to find you lodgings somewhere cheap but clean, and look after the horses, and make sure the young lad eats well.'

Martine laughed. 'No fear there. He has the appetite of a wolverine.'

The door banged open and the boy, Little Vole, ran in with Bramble's saddlebags. The men left it to Martine to dress Bramble in her clean shirt, and when she was ready, Cael picked her up and led the Travellers to their lodging house, around the corner in the market-place.

Oakmere was not what Ash had expected. Although there were more inns and lodging houses than you would normally find in a town of middling size, there were no shanties on the edges, no crowds of beggars targeting new arrivals, no one selling souvenirs on the street, no one offering to guide them or cure them or sell them an underage daughter, guaranteed a virgin.

Ash walked behind, still guarding their backs. Oakmere had a thriving market, judging by the number of shuttered stalls and tents. As in Turvite, in Sator Square, the marketplace was alive at night, with eating houses and a few stalls still open.

Two Travellers and a third being carried attracted some attention, but not the black looks he had been braced for, the type Travellers normally endured in small towns. Here, there was curiosity but no hatred. A couple of stallholders and diners even smiled at him. It unsettled him more than open hostility would have. He wasn't used to a world where Travellers were welcomed.

There was a large inn on the southern side of the marketplace, but Cael turned into a much smaller lodging house near it.

Despite Safred's advice Ash wasn't interested in finding dinner. They had settled into their room and Bramble was sleeping deeply on a bed in the corner.

'You heard. She sang with – with the voice of the dead.' He sat on the edge of his bed, elbows on his knees, his hands hanging.

Martine looked at him with affection and some concern. 'Well, she's a real healer, a prophet, a conduit for the gods.'

'But the voice of the dead! That's *my* voice, the voice I sing in! Could – could I be a healer, too? She took my strength, she used it.'

'I think you would know by now if you had that gift,' she said gently. 'Apart from anything else, I think Doronit would have found it out.'

Ash flinched slightly at Doronit's name. She had trained him as a safeguarder, and he had planned to make his living that way since those were the only skills he had mastered, but now he had to ask, what was he? A healer? An enchanter? Or just someone with a bit of Sight that the Well of Secrets could use?

Martine reminded him, 'The Well of Secrets said you had to eat.'

'But why?' His voice rose like a young boy's and he flushed. Any message from Safred sounded portentous, threatening who knew what.

'I think just because she foresaw that you would be . . . overset a little, and wanted you to settle down.'

'Does that mean she saw what I'd do?'

Martine shook her head. 'No. I'm sure of that. She was surprised when you stepped forward. I don't think she's used to getting help, especially strong help.'

He reddened and bent to fumble at his bootstrap to conceal it.

'Come downstairs and eat,' Martine said as though she hadn't noticed.

The smell of fish frying was coming up from the kitchen. Saliva flooded into his mouth and he was suddenly hungry.

'I'm ravenous. Come and eat,' she said again, and this time he came.

It was full dark as they sat down to the table in the kitchen below, and the other lodgers had eaten long ago. But the woman of the house served them, a young squint-eyed red-head called Heron, wearing the brooch that widows in the Last Domain were given a year after their husband's death.

Heron sat down with them after she served their meals, with a cup of cha warming her hands. Ash ate without paying attention, food to mouth without looking and without tasting.

'Heron,' Martine said. 'That's an unusual name for a red-head. And we met a blond Vole earlier.' Ash was curious about that, too, but he hoped the woman wouldn't take offence.

'A lot of us in the Last Domain have Traveller names now,' Heron said easily. 'I was named Freyt, but my parents learnt Valuing a good twenty years ago and they renamed me.'

Martine showed her surprise.

'You didn't know?' Heron said, surprised in turn. 'We're most of us Valuers hereabouts. It's why she's safe here. She's one of us, you know. Raised as a Valuer, for all her father was a warlord.'

They nodded. All the Domains knew that the father of the Well of Secrets had been a warlord, although rumour varied about who, exactly. More than one warlord had smiled when he was asked. None of them wanted to deny it, even those who were reputedly happily married at the requisite time.

Ash realised this explained the strange normality of Oakmere. Only in a Valuer town would the extraordinary powers of a Well of Secrets be housed in an ordinary house. Only in a Valuer town would a true prophet have to pay to have her cleaning done. Because in Valuer philosophy no one person was fundamentally more important than another. All lives Valued equally. Even Travellers. To show they believed it, Valuers took Traveller names. In a Valuer town, charlatans and treasure-seekers would find little to pick over, because Valuers were rarely rich. The rich had no time for a way of thinking that meant they were no better than the nightsoil collector. What was the point of being rich, if that were so?

Martine was smiling and gestured at her bag of stones to thank Heron for her explanation. 'I could cast for you, if you like.'

Heron shook her head. 'Safred will tell me if there's anything I really need to know. But I give you thanks for the offer.' She collected the empty plates and went out to the scullery, leaving them to contemplate life in a town where their only valuable skill was considered worthless.

Martine shrugged and smiled at Ash. 'Maybe I'll have to learn to cook at last,' she said to him.

He looked at her blankly, realising that he had heard the conversation, but had immediately forgotten it. His mind was still full of the ebb and flow of strange powers; he wondered if he would ever feel such strength again.

Martine sighed. 'Come on, then. Time for bed.'

Ash lay in bed, looking up at the dark ceiling, and went over the healing again in his mind. He had done nothing, he realised. He had just stood there and let his strength be used. Just like he had let Doronit use him. It was why he had left her, because all she wanted to do was use his strength for death and destruction. But she had used him easily before that, because he had felt he had nowhere else to go, nothing to offer the world. She had used him again and again, and he had let her, out of fear and desire and a terror of being cast out into the world on his own. It wasn't like his parents had wanted him. A singer who couldn't sing, a musician who couldn't play – what use was he to his parents, who were consummate performers? That was an old grief, and he forced it away by thinking of that moment when strength had flowed out of him to Safred.

Was that all he was good for? Giving his strength away to others – to women? The thought profoundly disturbed him, but he couldn't find an answer. He tried to feel again the power Safred had so easily drawn from him, but had no sense of it within him. Perhaps she had drawn it all away. Or perhaps she had emptied him temporarily and when he was recovered, he would be able to find it again.

He slept uneasily and dreamt of a tall red-headed woman standing in a doorway, nodding encouragingly at him.

SAKER

OH, IT WAS so easy! There were so many bones here, and not buried, just thrust into the cave like garbage and the stone rolled across the cave mouth to keep down the smell. No laying out, no ceremony. There had been no sprigs of pine between these fingers, no rosemary under their tongues. Hundreds of bones, hundreds of skulls. So many names responding to his call.

He had an image, suddenly, of massacre sites like this one, scattered the length and breadth of the Domains. It had taken a thousand years, but Acton's people had killed, and killed, and killed again, until they owned the whole of the country, from cliff to cove, from sand to snow. His own village had been the last to live freely in the old way, and the last to be slaughtered. No doubt the invaders had thought themselves safe, then, thinking they had killed the last of the pure old blood. But they had overlooked him, and now he would bring about their ruin.

Saker looked greedily at the bones before him. Here was an army indeed, if even a fraction of those slaughtered by the invaders had stayed in the dark beyond the grave, yearning for revenge. He would give it to them, full measure and spilling over. They would take back their birthright and the land would flourish under its rightful owners. The people of the old blood – *his* blood – would live in freedom again, and he would be responsible.

To raise the ghosts of the dead, he needed to know their names. He had brought the skull of the man Owl from Spritford in case he could not See the names of the dead here, but that was not necessary. He could feel the presence of spirits already, and he was sure he would be able to sense them respond as he called a litany of Traveller names.

He placed Owl's skull at the entrance to the cave anyway. The man deserved to be recalled from death, and he was a good leader. Saker tolled the names with glee: 'I seek justice for Owl, Juniper, Maize (he thought briefly of his Aunty Maize, cut down by the warlord's man), Oak, Sand, Cliff, Tern, Eagle, Cormorant . . .' So close to the sea there were lots of seabird names, and even fish: Dolphin, Cod, Herring . . .

At almost every name there came the *flick* in his mind which meant that someone of that name was buried here, and in one out of ten a picture came to his head: men, women, grammers, granfers, all ages and conditions, with nothing in common but the fact that they were here, and angry. All of them, angry, and here in spirit, ready to take revenge for their deaths. It was the dark of the moon and he had used no light; they would be invisible to the inhabitants of the town below them. The brick houses of the harbour town looked more formidable than they really were. They would be upon the sleeping usurpers before they realised what was happening.

'I seek justice for Oak and Sand and Herring and all their comrades.'

Saker paused. He could feel their anger, the desire for revenge, building beneath him, here on the hillside overlooking the harbour. It was dangerous, that anger, to him as well as to the invaders. He remembered when the ghosts of Spritford had met two Travellers at the river. For a moment, there, he had feared that they would strike down the Travellers, not recognising their own. They had not. But because this was a night attack, when Traveller and invader would look alike, sound alike in the dark, he had made precautions. He entered the new part of the spell.

'I seek recompense for murder unjust, for theft of land, for theft of life; revenge against the invaders, against the evil which has come of Acton's hand . . . let no Traveller blood be spilt, let no brother or sister fall by our hands. Listen to me, Owl and Oak and Sand and Herring and all your comrades. Taste my blood and recognise it: leave unharmed those who share it with me and with you.'

The spirits of the dead were listening. The rest of the spell wasn't in words, but images in his mind, complex and distressing. Colours, phrases of music, the memory of a particular scent, the sound of a scream . . . When he had gathered them all he looked down at the skulls. He pressed the knife to his palm then drew it down hard. The blood surged out in time with his heart and splashed in gouts on the bones. He flung his arm wide so that the blood touched as many bones as possible.

'Arise, Oak and Sand and Herring and all your comrades,' he commanded. 'Take your revenge.'

This time, he had a sword ready to give Owl, symbolically making him the leader. The other ghosts accepted it. They looked to Owl immediately, and he pointed with his sword towards the sleeping town, his face alight with anticipation. Then he began to run towards the houses, and the others raced after him, each of them holding whatever weapon they had died with: scythe, hoe, knife, sickle. Not soldiers' weapons, but deadly enough.

Saker watched, smiling, as they streamed down the hill, towards Carlion, and then he went to follow.

LEOF

LEOF WAITED IN the cold before dawn for the signal to attack, hidden in the trees, calming his horse with a pat now and then. The still water of the Lake hid nothing, as Lord Thegan had said. Leof was sure that his lord must be right. The tales were nothing more than Lake people subterfuge.

'Perhaps there is a tricksy spirit,' Thegan had told his men the night before. 'Or perhaps the Lake People have some slight enchantment to call up illusions to frighten the cowardly. But remember, it is no more than illusion. It cannot be that the Lake has any real power.'

He was reassured remembering those words, spoken with the confidence which inspired others. It was no wonder his men had followed Thegan here to the Lake so willingly. They believed everything Thegan said: that the people of Baluchston were strangling trade between the Domains by charging exorbitant prices for ferrying goods and people across. And there was no real reason a bridge couldn't be built, that Baluchston was just using old stories about the Lake so it could keep its monopoly. Old stories, and their mysterious alliance with the Lake People. An alliance which needed to be broken, so Baluchston could be taught a lesson.

The fact that, if Thegan took over Baluchston – a free town, for Swith's sake! – he would hold the entire centre of the Domains, from Cliff to Carlion's borders, was never mentioned, but the men weren't fools. They knew and they approved. Their lord *should* be the most powerful in the Domains. They were sure he deserved it, and so did they. His power would be their power, and they would swagger and bask in it.

Leof checked the horizon again, but there were only whispering reeds and, far off, the sky starting to pale as dawn approached.

Thistle moved restlessly and Leof murmured softly to her. A good horse, Thistle, though not a chaser. He had left his chaser mare, Arrow, back at the fort.

Thoughts of Arrow inevitably made him think about Bramble; about their first race against each other, he and Arrow against her and her roan gelding; about the night that followed in his bed at the inn. That led him to memories of losing her, and losing her twice, when he had set her free to find her own way out of Thegan's territory, against the express orders of his lord. His unease over his disloyalty made Thistle shift beneath him, and he thought again of Arrow, burying memories of Bramble as deeply as he could.

When foot soldiers went against horsemen, they aimed to bring the horse down first, then deal with the rider. He had no mind to lose Arrow to a stray arrow or a spear thrust. His lord had scolded him about leaving her behind, but in that friendly, jovial way that meant he should not take it seriously. Leof had almost brought her, even so. Anything to show Thegan that he was loyal.

As though the thought had triggered it, the signal to advance rang out, a long horn call that echoed strangely through the pine trees. Leof urged Thistle forwards, followed by the small squad of horsemen and the much larger group of archers and pikemen that Thegan had put under his command. Their task was simple: the horsemen were to secure the shore of the Lake so that the archers could shoot flaming arrows into the reeds. Then the whole troop would protect the area until the reeds had burned down to the waterline and the Lake was exposed. Thegan had placed bands all around the perimeter of the Lake, in both Central and Cliff Domains. His aim was to lay bare the secret lairs of the Lake People, the hidden islands where they were protected from attack. With the reed beds empty, Thegan would be able to see right across the Lake, into the heart of its mystery.

Leof gave his men hand signals, but they weren't really needed. These were experienced men, at least half of them from the Cliff Domain, most of whom had fought with him on past campaigns. Thegan had mixed the Cliff men up with the Centralites, putting battle-hardened men side-by-side with those who had never fought, 'to make sure no one panics when the arrows start flying', he said, and

Leof had nodded. That had been the moment when Thegan had forgiven him and started treating him again as a trusted officer. Thegan
had smiled at him for the first time since he had stopped Thegan's
archer from shooting Bramble in the back as she escaped from Sendat
and said, 'Just as well I have experienced officers, too,' and clapped
him on the back. The relief had been enormous.

Leof put the thought away from him and concentrated on getting
this sortie right for his lord. The archers lined up a short distance back
from the shoreline and set arrows to their bows. Broc, a boy barely old
enough to fight, ran along the line with a blazing torch, setting each
arrow alight, then stood well back from the horses so that none would
be spooked by the flames.

Leof raised his hand and dropped it again, and the arrows flew,
bright as shooting stars, into the air and onto the reed beds. It was a
beautiful sight, the bright flame against the still-dark sky. They waited
with all senses fully alert for response, waited for the reeds to catch,
waited for the flames to rise, licking, into the sky.

At first it seemed that nothing was happening. The fire arrows
burnt among the reeds, throwing writhing shadows over them. Then
slowly, slowly, the reeds began to catch. Leof braced himself for the
Lake's response. Lord Thegan had warned him that they had to stand
firm against illusion. He had warned his men likewise and they
were ready.

A deep vibration came from the Lake and the still water between
the reeds began to whisper as though it were a quickly moving current.
Leof felt the ground shake beneath him. His horse reared and only his
long experience in chasing allowed him to anticipate the movement
and jump off safely. Thistle tore the reins from his hand and bolted.
Behind him, the other horsemen were falling as their mounts reared
and then raced away to the forest. The archers, confused, stepped
back, away from the Lake. Then, from beyond the reeds, there was a
rushing sound, loud, sibilant, like wind through trees, like breath
through giant lungs. It was moving closer, and it was nothing human.
The archers broke and fled into the trees, followed by the horsemen,
some limping, leaving only Leof standing firm; and Broc, behind him,
clutching his torch.

'What is it, lord?' he asked.

The sound grew too loud to make a reply. *Illusion,* Leof thought, *to
make us run away. I trust my lord. It's only illusion.* Before him, out

of the darkness, roared a wave mounting higher than a house, higher than a tree, a hill of a wave that loomed above them. Broc screamed and ran, dropping the torch.

Illusion, Leof told himself, just before the wave hit.

BRAMBLE

THE CEILING WAS dark green, with wooden beams. Bramble had never seen a green ceiling before. She was more tired and more hungry than she had ever felt in her life, and she was disoriented by waking in a room with a green ceiling.

Then she remembered, and her body of its own accord curled into a tight ball of misery, head on knees, trying to shut out the world. Maryrose. Maryrose was dead.

She lay and shook for a while, remembering. She had died again, only this time it was her body that had died. She remembered lying on the Well of Secret's table, body in flames, arm hurting almost past her ability to bear it. Then she had – fainted? Died.

But instead of being in the Well of Secret's house she had been in Maryrose's front room, and Maryrose was lying dead, with Merrick next to her, dead, and she knew it wasn't a dream. She had been glad she herself was dead, and she called out, 'Wait for me!' to Maryrose, so they could go on together to rebirth. She was glad to be out of it all, glad to be set free of whatever destiny the gods had planned for her.

She called out again, 'Wait for *me*, Maryrose!' in exactly the same way she had called out to her big sister when she was tiny and Maryrose walked too fast on her longer legs.

And just like then, Maryrose heard her and came back for her. She – her spirit – appeared somehow, as though she had walked in from another room through a door that wasn't there, and stood looking at Bramble with the same loving annoyance as when they were children.

'What are you doing here?' she asked.

Bramble felt a moment of surprise. Ghosts weren't supposed to be able to talk. 'I'm dead,' Bramble said.

'Nonsense.'

'I am so!'

'Well, you shouldn't be. Not yet. You've got work to do.' She pointed to her own body, lying limp on the floor. 'You're supposed to stop all this.'

She put out her hands and turned Bramble so that she was facing the door, although ghosts were not supposed to be able to touch anything, not even each other. 'Go on, then. Get back there.'

Bramble hesitated, looking back to her. 'Mam and Da? Granda?'

'They're fine. They went back to Wooding for Widow Farli's wedding to the smith. They missed all this.'

'Mare –'

'Oh, don't worry,' Maryrose said, the exasperated big sister. 'I'll wait for you. We both will.' Bramble smiled and she smiled back, exasperation melting into love. 'You do what you're told and go back.'

Then Maryrose pushed her between the shoulder blades and she took two steps and was through the doorway before she had finished saying, protestingly, 'Oh, Maryro-ose.' Then – nothing, until she had woken here, under this green ceiling.

She forced herself to uncurl. Maryrose was dead. Someone had killed her. It was Bramble's job to stop whoever it was. So. If that was the destiny the gods had in mind for her, she would embrace it. She would find the murderers, and disembowel them.

She lay for a moment, staring up at the ceiling, and then lifted her left hand, gingerly, to touch her shoulder. Her mind remembered the pressure, the pain, the burning and nausea and sheer *wrongness* of that swollen arm. But her body didn't. It was all gone. Cautiously, her head spinning, she sat up and examined her body. Not even a scar. She was starving, her body clamouring to replace the energy she had lost.

Suddenly, her hunger was gone, replaced by awe. What kind of person could do that, heal without leaving a scar? To heal was one thing, but to knit the flesh back to a state where it did not even remember being injured . . . that was tinkering with powers deeper even than the local gods.

The room had three beds, covered with green blankets matching the light colour of the walls. It was like being inside a forest. She should find that comforting. She should be happy to be alive. Again. Twice she'd been pulled back from death by the power of the gods; and this time, by Maryrose.

The first time, when the roan had saved her in the wild jump across the chasm outside Wooding, she had entered a living death, her spirit split from her body, her senses dull, her heart empty except for love for the roan. It had only ended when she became the Kill Reborn, truly reborn by some power in the running of the Spring Chase.

Would she go back to that death in life again? It didn't feel like it. All her senses were sharp. She could hear footsteps outside, climbing the stairs. She felt the bed linen under her thighs, the warmth of the late afternoon sun that slanted through high windows to fall across her shoulders. Saw each individual dust mote as it danced in the sunbeam. Each beautiful detail of the day filled her with grief and anger that Maryrose had been cut off from the world so viciously.

She was so weak she couldn't even stand up. And she stank with old sweat. At that realisation, her mouth twisted with amusement. At least the Well of Secrets couldn't bespell that away – she stank of the last few days and was glad of it.

Martine put her head around the door and smiled at her. 'Hungry?'

Bramble nodded. If she was going to live, and find out what had happened to Maryrose, she had to eat. Martine came in with a laden tray, followed by Ash who carried a basin and ewer, the water steaming from the top.

Bramble sniffed. 'It's true, I need that. One thing she couldn't take away was the stink.'

Martine's eyes crinkled with laughter and understanding as though she, too, found the Well of Secrets daunting and was glad to make a little joke about her.

'Food first, though,' she said, handing Bramble a warm roll dripping with butter. It disappeared in two bites.

'That was the best thing I ever tasted,' Bramble said, wondering, feeling guilty that she could enjoy food knowing that Maryrose was . . . she couldn't think about that now. Her body was ravenous, demanding food, and she had to feed it. She had work to do.

'Near death lends spice to living,' Martine replied.

'Not always.'

The young man, Ash, was busying himself tidying the two other beds. Bramble realised he was trying not to look at her in her breastbands. That was both endearing and a bit worrying. The last thing she needed was a youngling yearning after her. She pulled the sheet up to cover herself. He had, after all, saved her life. Both of them had.

'I have to thank you,' Bramble said, pausing before devouring a mug of soup. It was hard to pause, she was so hungry. She took a tiny sip. Asparagus and cream. Wonderful. 'I owe you my life.'

Ash turned at that and Martine shrugged. 'That's what happens when you travel with a safeguarder,' she said, waving her hand at Ash. 'People get safeguarded.'

Bramble looked at Ash with new eyes and he flushed. Under his shaggy black hair, he was a bit older than she had thought, and strong with trained muscle. He smiled at her tentatively and she realised that he was unsure of himself despite his strength and agility. She smiled back.

'Thank the gods, then, that you came at the right time.' And the Lake, she thought, that sent me there right then. She remembered leaving the Lake and being transported through time, late autumn becoming spring in a heartbeat. She shivered with remembered awe. That was true power.

'Mmm,' Ash said. 'It was their fault, all right.'

Ah, Bramble thought, so it's not just me the gods have been ordering about. I'm not sure if that's good or bad.

'After you've washed,' Martine suggested, 'we should go to see Safred. The Well of Secrets.'

'The Well of Secrets,' Bramble echoed. 'Yes. I suppose we must. After I've seen the horses.'

Fed, washed, dressed in clean clothes and with her horses well cared for in the rooming-house stables, Bramble walked around the corner of an ordinary looking street to meet the Well of Secrets. She didn't pause, or knock. If this Safred was a prophet, she should be expecting them.

As she pushed open the big double doors, they were met by a tall, good-looking older man.

'Ah, you're on your feet!' he said. 'Good, good.'

It was odd to meet someone who clearly knew her but of whom she had no recollection. Bramble forced a smile. 'Thank you for your help.'

He waved that away and moved back from the door. 'Come in, come in. I'm Cael, Safred's uncle. They're waiting for you.'

Sitting at a table were two women and a boy of about fifteen. The younger of the women, a girl really, had the dark lean looks of the Traveller and the flexible body of a tumbler or dancer. She sat with her legs drawn up on the chair, one arm around a raised knee. She reminded Bramble of Osyth, though Osyth would never have sat so casually. Pless, where she had worked for Osyth's husband Gorham the Horsespeller, seemed a very long time ago.

The boy had light brown hair and was taller, gangly with the swift growth of youth.

Then there was the other woman. Red-headed, older than her, around forty, stout but not fat. Bramble forced herself to look Safred in the eyes. Oddly, where she had expected to find something strange, something foreign, she found someone much like herself. Not an ordinary woman, but a woman nonetheless, beset by the gods and carrying a destiny unasked for. There was humour in the folds of her mouth and the lines around her intense eyes.

Bramble had no time for humour. 'My sister's dead,' she said. 'Who killed her?'

Safred sat up straight, astonished. 'How do you –' she began to ask.

Bramble cut across her. 'Never mind how I know. Who killed her?'

Safred's face sharpened with interest; with a kind of hunger. 'Tell me how you know,' she asked again.

'Tell me who killed her.'

The Well of Secrets wasn't used to being resisted. She swallowed and sat back in her chair, mouth tight. 'His name is Saker.'

'Saker?' Martine asked. Bramble had almost forgotten she and Ash were there.

'That is his name, the enchanter, the one who raises ghosts. Saker. A bird of prey. He has a flock of falcons at his command. Last night, he loosed them onto new victims. In Carlion.'

Martine and Ash looked shocked.

'Ghosts?' Bramble asked. 'Maryrose wasn't killed by ghosts. She was almost cut in two. Ghosts can't do that sort of thing.'

'These can.' Safred looked at Martine and Ash. 'Tell her.'

Martine described the attack on Spritford. The maimings, the deaths, ordinary people cut down in their homes and on the street by ghosts who could hold a weapon and use it against the living. An unstoppable force, because they could not be killed themselves.

The young man and woman listened with appalled interest, but it was clearly old news to the big man, Cael, although he asked several questions about the ghosts and the way they had looked and spoken. Bramble was astonished that anyone could make ghosts speak. Ash looked fixedly at the table at that point, as though he were not proud of the ability.

Bramble sat for a moment after Martine finished. 'What does he want?' she asked finally.

'He wants the Domains,' Safred said.

'Why?'

Safred picked up a jug of cha and began pouring out cups and handing them around. She gestured to Bramble and Martine and Ash to sit down, and they did.

'We don't know,' she said reluctantly. 'Yet. All we know is that the ghosts are those who have been dispossessed and are still angry. Perhaps they are taking back what was theirs before the invasion.'

'Do we know where he is, so I can go and kill him?' Bramble asked. There was silence. She looked around the table at the mixture of surprise and shock in the others' faces. 'What? It's the simplest solution.'

Ash nodded agreement, and then looked unsure. He took the cup of cha and sipped, staring at the tabletop.

Safred shook her head. 'The ghosts would still be there. Now they have been called up . . . the gods say that killing Saker will not end it. Others will learn how to call the ghosts. There are many who are angry. Now they have proof that an army can be conjured . . . even if Saker dies there will be others. Too many others, for too long. The Domains would be destroyed. Thousands would die.'

'Deal with the others one by one, as they arise. Stop this one now.'

'It seems to me,' the dark-haired girl said unexpectedly, her voice deep and pleasant, 'that the problem is the ghosts, not the enchanter. Without them, he's helpless.'

Safred smiled at the girl. 'That is true. It is the ghosts we must dispose of.' She looked around the table and gestured to the girl and boy, introducing them. 'Zel and Flax, Bramble, Martine, Ash.'

The girl nodded and the boy smiled at them. Zel and Flax, Bramble thought. So she *did* look like Osyth – these were Gorham's children. Bramble had never met them, but Gorham had talked about them often enough. And Zel's careful speech, with no trace of Traveller in it – that was Osyth's training. Zel was trying hard to fit in here.

'When ghosts quicken, they must be laid to rest,' Safred said.

They sat for a moment, thinking that through. Bramble remembered the last quickening she had seen, the warlord's man whom she had killed, rising three days later as ghosts did if they were not prepared for death. She had been ready to go through the ritual that would have laid him to rest, would have offered her own blood in recompense, but she had been prevented. She wondered, uneasily, if his ghost still haunted the linden tree near her home village.

Safred looked at Ash. 'You have done it,' she said.

He nodded. 'They need blood.'

'They need *specific* blood,' Martine said quietly. 'The blood of their killer.'

'They need more than that,' said Safred. 'The blood is just a symbol.'

'Acknowledgment,' Ash replied. 'The killer must acknowledge his guilt and offer reparation.'

'These ghosts are hundreds of years old,' Cael said slowly, his deep voice doubtful. 'Their killers are long dead.'

Safred nodded and placed her hands flat on the table. Ash noticed that they were not pretty hands, not the hands of a warlord's daughter. They were sun-speckled and the nails were cut short. Safred seemed to lean on the table for support, as though even she could not believe what the gods were asking.

'Yes. A thousand years dead. Like the one responsible. The one who can acknowledge what was done.'

'One?' Cael asked. 'Just one for all of them?'

Bramble went cold as she realised what Safred meant. 'Acton.'

Safred nodded. 'Who else?'

Acton had led the invasion of the Domains, leading his men from beyond the western mountains through Death Pass in the last days of winter, falling upon the unprepared inhabitants like a wolf pack. He was a legend, a hero to most people in the Domains, a name out of history. Hard to think of him as an actual human being who might have a ghost, just like anyone else. Bramble's Traveller grandfather had raised her to consider him as an invading murderer, the leader of the dispossession, but even she was used to thinking of him as larger than life. More evil than anyone. Treacherous. Greedy. Filled with the lust for blood. They said he had laughed as he killed.

It was one thing to hear that an enchanter had conjured up ancient ghosts and given them bodily strength, but it was quite another to think about conjuring Acton's ghost. For surely that was what she meant. Which was ridiculous, wasn't it?

Bramble was abruptly aware that the sun was setting and the shadows in the corners of the room were reaching out. She shrugged off the feeling of unease and looked around the table. Each face had its own kind of uncertainty and reluctance. Except Ash's. His was carefully blank.

'According to the song about the enchanter from Turvite who raised the ghosts,' Ash said quietly, 'you need the bones of the person who was killed. Acton's body was never found. Even if we *could* learn how to raise a ghost, we wouldn't be able to find his bones.'

'Why would he offer acknowledgment and reparation anyway?' Zel asked. 'He weren't sorry for what he'd done while he were alive.'

Bramble noted Zel's slip back into Traveller speech – it was a sign of how shaken she was by the idea of raising Acton. They all were. Ash's hand had gone to the little pouch on his belt.

'That is true,' Safred said slowly, sitting back in her chair. 'But the grave gives a different perspective.'

'And the bones?' Martine asked.

'There is a way to find the bones, if Bramble and Ash are willing.' She looked at Ash. 'You have something of Acton's.'

Ash already had it in his hand. He had been way ahead of the discussion, Bramble realised. He reached forward and placed a brooch in the centre of the table. A man's cloak brooch, ornate and beautiful. It sat in a pool of sunlight, looking pretty but ordinary.

'This belonged to Acton?' Zel asked, fascinated. She reached out as though to touch it, then pulled her hand back and stuck it in her lap. Bramble raised an eyebrow at her.

'It's not going to bite. May I?' she asked Ash, and when he nodded she reached out to pick up the brooch.

Safred stopped her with a hand on her wrist. 'No. To be used, the brooch must pass from its rightful owner to the Kill Reborn in the right time and place.'

'Oh, shagging hells!' Bramble said. 'Fight spells with spells, is that it?' She was very tired but sat in her chair with a straight back, determined not to show any weakness to Safred. The brooch seemed to draw her gaze. She felt a little dizzy, but that might have simply been from fighting the poisoning in her arm.

'Yes,' Safred said quietly. 'This is your task, Bramble. Not to kill, but to live.'

Bramble dragged her eyes away from the brooch. 'What do you mean?'

'Of all of us around this table, you are the only one with mixed blood. Cael and I are of Acton's people, the others are pure Traveller. You bring both together – the link to the gods through your Traveller blood, the link to Acton's people through your mother's line. You are the only one who can do it.'

Bramble fell silent. Martine asked the question for her.

'Do what?'

'Find Acton's place of death.'

'How, exactly?'

Safred looked uncomfortable. 'I know the steps to take, but I don't know what will happen. Will you do it? Will you let the brooch guide you?'

The others held their breath, waiting for her to respond. Bramble wanted to say, 'No. No, what I will do is ride to Carlion and make sure that Maryrose is dead and my parents are all right. Then I will find Saker and gut him.' But she hunched her shoulders as she drew breath to say it and felt the smooth way the arm moved in its socket. She remembered that her arm had no scar. Remembered that yesterday she had been dying and now she was whole and healthy. Because of Safred. She let out her breath, suddenly feeling very weary.

'Can't the gods just tell us where the bones are?' she asked instead.

Safred seemed almost embarrassed. 'They don't know.'

'I thought they knew everything.'

'They don't pay much attention to humans, you know. Only when something big happens, or when they take a liking to someone. Acton – I don't think they noticed much about the invasion in the early days. It was just humans fighting each other.'

Bramble understood. Humans did fight each other. Look at Lord Thegan preparing for war with the Lake People. She saw, vividly, in her mind's eye, Maryrose's blood on the floor; Merrick's arm cut to the bone. A human enchanter had been responsible for that. Oh, yes, humans killed each other.

'What about the stones?'

Martine immediately pulled out her pouch and cast, then shook her head. 'No. Nothing. They are not speaking to me.' She looked at Bramble. 'I'm sorry. It happens, sometimes, when the gods are involved.'

Bramble stared at the tabletop. Her heart pulled her to Carlion; her instinct said to obey the gods. This kitchen was a long way from any altar, but . . . In her mind, as she used to do in her home village of

Wooding, she asked them, Should I go to Carlion now? They replied, faintly, as they had done so often to keep her from Travelling, *Not yet.* Well, that was that. Safred studied her in shock, as though she had overheard the exchange. Maybe she had. Bramble returned her gaze blandly, enjoying her uncertainty.

'Will it take long?' she asked.

Safred hesitated. 'I'm not sure . . . but we can't do it here. We must go to the Great Forest. There is a lake there, the gods say.'

'So,' Bramble said, 'let me see if I understand you. I have to go to a lake somewhere, use the brooch in some way you don't understand to do something you don't understand to find out the death place of the biggest bastard who ever lived, who died a thousand years ago and whose bones may be irretrievably lost and who is unlikely to want to help us anyway.'

The silence was heavy with antagonism. Bramble and Safred stared at each other.

'It's the only way,' Safred said at last.

'Hmm,' Bramble said.

Safred looked at her. 'There is a risk . . . some who take such journeys do not come back.'

Bramble bared her teeth in a semblance of a smile.

'Don't worry,' she said. 'I'm good at coming back.' And *then* she would go to Carlion and find the enchanter and kill him.

ZEL'S STORY

MURDER'S AN UGLY word, don't never doubt that. But it's a solid one, like a stone in your hand. I went to a stonecaster, and she plucked that Murder right from the bag, and Necessity, too.

We was Travellers, my brer and I. We did the rounds, town to town, city to city. We scrounged off the land where we could, worked where we could, sang in the taverns every night for food, for a roof in winter, out in the stable. Sang till Flax's voice broke; ah, he had a voice could pierce right through your body and blood, sweet as first love. In the taverns, when Flax let out those high, quivering notes, even the rowdiest of them would calm on down and get sentimental; sometimes even throw coins. It weren't very often I had to shag for our supper.

Then his voice cracked and we knew he had to stop his singing or risk losing his voice for good and all.

We was in Sandalwood, then, on the outskirts near the tanneries. So we walked on to Pless, and we went on back to our parents' house.

They'd always been pleased to see us, before. They'd been Travellers, too, the both of them, roaming free all their youth, taking their knocks and their sweets, rambling all over the known world, my mam said once to me, even down to the sandy waste, and up to Foreverfroze, in the north. They'd met up on the road, my father a horsebreaker, my mam a juggler, like me.

They only settled down in Pless when my mam got the rheumatics and couldn't juggle no more, and my father found a fancy-woman there he'd a mind to keep. He set up as a horse trainer and it's true, it's a rare horse my da can't spell into manners.

We didn't want to Settle, so they laughed and let us go, but they'd taught us how to see trouble coming and my mam showed us a few sneaky moves with the knife. Since those days we'd come visiting every year, spend a week or so and back on the Road again, and there'd be smiling and hugging enough to last the year round.

This time it were different. It were a sharp, cold autumn already, with worse to come and the grandams saying it'd be a killing winter, graveyards fat by Winterfest. I thought we could rest out the winter there with Mam and Da, work on a new act, teach Flax some more juggling, maybe some tumbling or a mind-reading act. I could sing, but not like Flax, not with that clear, heart-aching sound that brought silver out of purses.

I didn't think they'd mind. I'd of worked for my keep, and for Flax's, if they'd wanted. I didn't realise they'd turned respectable. Da were setting his sights on the town council, and trying to forget his murky past; and Mam were pushing him hard as she could go. Me, I think it were the fancy-woman Mam had in mind; seems a town councillor got to be really respectable, and maybe the fancy-woman would of had to go.

It weren't the shagging that worried Mam; it were the silver that went to keep bread on that woman's table and clothes on her back. Mam'd stick to silver like it were her life's price to let it go; and maybe that were true, once, out on the Road.

So when me and Flax turned up, unexpected, at the door, with Flax half-grown out of his clothes and me none so clean, neither, with the track from Sandalwood coming through swamp as it do, well, they weren't exactly so pleased as we thought they'd be.

Maybe we shoulda turned and walked away right then and there, before that hurt got any deeper. Maybe we shoulda said the Traveller's goodbye, 'Wind at your back', and scooted along to the tavern and juggled and sang till we got our eating silver and our travelling silver, and just kept on going. But we didn't. No, we was cold and hungry and hoping for some hugs, so we walked straight on in and sat by the fire, and listened to the news.

They told us about the town council straight off, and if I'd been paying attention I'da noticed that new look on her face, that wary, not-welcoming look; but Flax had a cough from the damp swamp air and I were bustling him close to the fire and getting him cha. I just took it like a joke and laughed; my da the town councillor!

The next few days, I were too busy nursing Flax to think much of it. There was people coming and going all the time, with Mam serving them hot wine and spice biscuits, the smell drifting up to us and making me hungry as a waking bear, but Flax were so sick he didn't even notice. It were a bad fever, and he were coughing up blood.

The herb woman said he'd be safe if he stayed mostly in bed all winter. That were bad news for Mam and Da. They'd not told anyone about us coming back; and then I remembered that the last couple of visits we spent a lot of time at home, not visiting or going out. I realised that not many people here knew Mam and Da even had young ones, let alone that we was Travellers — and that's how they wanted it.

So they told the herb woman Flax were their stableboy, and they made me promise not to come down the stairs when there was visits going on; and I shrugged and said, 'If you want,' for I didn't see much harm in it, then.

Mam wanted us out, though, that were certain. She got this worried look back of her eyes every time the door banged, for fear it were some neighbour dropping in. Da turned quiet, and went to the fancy-woman's for his evening meal more often than not. And that didn't help Mam's temper – not at all.

Now if Flax'd been hale, I woulda just packed us up and taken the Road again, winter or not, but the herb woman warned me, quiet in the corner, that it were his life's price to go on the road before spring, and I believed her, he were that quiet and pale after the fever left him, and still coughing like an old man.

They knew I wouldn't leave without him. They wouldn't let me sing in the taverns, or juggle, in case anyone found out I were their daughter, and though I put in what I could of our Travelling silver, I had to keep some back for spring, to set us on the road again. I did what I could around the house but it weren't much compared to what we was eating, especially Flax, now the fever were over and his real growing time began.

Da got broody over his ale next to the fire, when he were home, though mostly he were out at the farm, working the horses.

Then Mam started muttering and counting her silver in the dark of night. Night after night I'd wake up and hear her, clinking and counting, all alone in her bed in the clear frost silence, with Da off to the fancy-woman. Maybe it shouldna been so much of a surprise when I came through to Flax's room and found Mam with a pillow over his face.

I fought her off him and it shoulda been easy, an old rheumaticky woman and a young one like me, but it weren't easy at all. She fought like it were her life she were fighting for, and I had to fling her down on the floor before she give up. Flax slept through it all, and I knew she'd given him a sleeping draught in his cha.

'Eating us out of house and home,' she said, staring up at me like a trapped rat. 'You're sucking us dry, sucking us dry . . .'

'Let me go out to juggle, then,' I said. 'I'll pay for Flax and me, both.'

'Nay, nay,' she said, shaking her head so hard her hair came out of its braid. 'You'll bring disgrace on us, and we're so close, so close.'

'Keep away from him, then. If you hurt him, I won't sit quiet and say nothing. I'll brand you up and down the town a killer,' I said. 'Here we stay till spring, Mam, and Flax can take the road again. Make your mind up to it, that's the way it is. If your council's so important, then Flax's keep and mine is the price you have to pay for it.'

She went away, but I knew that weren't the end. I'd have to keep an eye on her all winter, and I couldn't. I had to sleep sometime. To eat what she cooked and to drink what she brewed, like the others. It were too easy for her to slip something in.

I thought awhile on going to my father, but I knew him. He'd always gone along with her over everything except the fancy-woman, and now I thought on it, she'd never faced him down about that. If she had, I reckon he'da caved in, like he always did. If she'd managed to kill Flax, and me not knowing, he woulda asked no questions.

Now, I thought, she'd have to kill both of us.

That were when I went to the stonecaster, for, truth to tell, I couldn't see my way out of it. The caster pulled Murder from the bag, and Necessity. And I thought, her or me. Her or Flax.

Two lives for one, I thought. I did it that night, while Da were with the fancy-woman and Flax were sleeping deep, and Mam too, for I'd used her own sleeping powder in both their chas.

I broke the latch on her window, like a too-strong gust of wind had blown it open, then I closed her door behind me and left her to the killing frost.

It were a long winter, shut up in the house, me and Flax practising the new act, him getting stronger every day. Da spent more time with us, less with the fancy-woman, but he didn't seem too upset, apart from that. Before we left he asked us how we'd feel if he married the fancy-woman. Maude, he called her. We shrugged and gave our blessing. It were no skin off our noses.

LEOF

Leof woke with his mother's voice in his ears. 'Go home, child,' it said. 'Leave this place in peace and go back to one who will love you.'

He struggled up, murmuring, 'Mam?', half-expecting to find himself in his bedroom at home, half-expecting to hear his brother's snoring and the well pulley clanking in the yard outside as the stableboys filled the horses' buckets.

He didn't expect to find himself in the top branches of a pine tree, precariously wedged between a limb and the trunk, his head aching so badly that it felt like it would blow apart. The dawn light was not golden, but grey, and it was a long, long way to the ground.

Shivering with cold, he took stock. He was wet but not sopping, as though his clothes had been dripping for some time; they were clammy against his skin. He smelt of lake weeds.

Struggling to a more comfortable position, he sat himself in the fork of the tree and looked out. The wave had carried him a long way inland; he could only just glimpse the Lake through the trees, and then only because so many of them were broken in half, or their branches had been ripped away. Below, the forest floor was a mess of broken limbs and fallen trees. And bodies. Oh, gods of wind and storm, the bodies of his men. He could see three, four, at least five. They lay with the abandonment of death, limbs crooked, some buried under trees, some splayed on top.

He had had six horses and fifteen archers under his command; perhaps the others had been lucky too. Leof paused at the thought, remembering the voice which had spoken to him as he had woken. Perhaps luck had nothing to do with it. Perhaps the Lake had preserved those she wished to preserve. In which case, why him? Why him and not, as he could see as he climbed down towards the nearest body, why not Broc?

Broc lay on top of a smashed tree trunk, his back as broken as the tree. He looked older than he had the night before, as though he had tasted pain and despair before he died. Leof remembered his father, taking him to see what the Ice King had done to the villages he pillaged. Twenty-two years ago, when he was eight. The bodies had lain everywhere, cut down mercilessly, and for what? A few trinkets and some goats. Barely anything had been stolen. His father made him look at each body – children, women, men, granfers and grammers – all slaughtered and left in their blood. The flies had swarmed over the face of a little girl about the same age as he was, and he had vomited. He had been ashamed, but his father had understood.

'You will lose men in battle,' his father had said. 'It will be hard. But it is not so hard as seeing the bodies of the innocent folk who you have failed to protect.'

That had been the moment when Leof had sworn himself to be a soldier, to protect the people of his land from the raiders who had left not a single person alive in two whole villages. He had known then, and in the years since, when he had defended the Domain against the Ice King's raids, that he was doing the right work. No matter how hard killing was, it had to be done, to protect the innocent.

Now, he stared down at Broc, who was both a man he had lost in battle *and* an innocent he had failed to protect. Tears scalded Leof's eyes and he let them fall onto the boy's body. It was the only blessing he could give him, and a plea for forgiveness. He should have told Broc to run as soon as the ground began to shake. He should have run himself, as Thistle and the other horses, wiser than men, had done. He should have known the horses would not be affected by illusion. Lord Thegan had been wrong. This was his fault.

Leof banished the thought immediately. Commanders based their decisions on the information they had at the time. Thegan had not had the right information. The Lake was much more powerful than they had known. They would have to regroup and make new plans.

On that thought, his tears dried and he began to think again like an officer. He checked the other bodies, without trying to disentangle them from the branches and debris which lay over and under them like macabre winding sheets. Two archers, two horsemen. He would have to search further afield for the others. He sent out a halloo but heard no response, so he began the gruesome task of searching for more bodies, in case there was anyone left alive.

He found three more men dead and a horse he didn't recognise before the cold and dizziness made him stop. Although he didn't have any obvious injuries apart from bruising, his head was pounding and he was shivering in fits and starts. He needed to find help before nightfall, or he would become another of the Lake's victims.

Reluctantly, he turned towards the Lake shore. There would be searchers out, he was sure. Sooner or later, Lord Thegan would organise the remnants of his army. He would expect a report from his officers. There had been twenty of them, each with a troop stationed at intervals around the Lake, so they could attack it from all sides.

Leof approached the shoreline cautiously, wondering if he should call out to reassure the Lake that he meant no harm. Then he remembered the voice he had heard. It had not seemed violent or maddened, just sad. Somewhat reassured, he threaded through broken branches and climbed over fallen trees.

The Lake stretched before him, impossibly peaceful. The water was still and serene, reflecting a perfect blue sky – so still that even the reed beds were silent, their eternal whispering paused. This was how the Lake should be, not riven by war and death. Leof was overwhelmed by remorse. It came unexpectedly, so quickly that he was taken by surprise. We should not have come here, he thought. We have no right to invade these people. Then he wondered whose thought it was, his or the Lake's, and was frightened, truly frightened, for the first time since he was a boy, at the idea that the Lake could put a thought in his head.

To his relief, he heard a shout from his left and turned to find a search party of four men making their cautious way around the shoreline. Hodge led them, his grim face lightening as he saw Leof.

'My Lord Leof!' he called, raising his hand in greeting. 'Thank the gods!'

Leof went to meet them and clasped forearms with Hodge, although that was a gesture used between equals, not between officers and sergeants.

'I'm glad to see you alive, sergeant,' Leof said. Hodge nodded.

'Same with us, sir. You're the first we've found in this stretch.'

'How far did it go?'

Hodge stared at him, surprised. 'All the way around, sir. Wherever we had men, wherever the arrows caught the reeds. We've lost – I don't know how many, maybe a quarter of the men, a third of the horses.'

'My Lord Thegan?'

'Thank the gods, he's safe. He was ordering the attack from a lookout point and it was almost higher than the wave. He just got a wetting.'

Leof exhaled in relief. 'He'll be angry.'

'Cold angry, sir, and dangerous with it.' Hodge cleared his throat, aware suddenly that sergeants don't make comments like that about their lords. At least, not to officers. 'He wants all survivors to gather towards Baluchston.'

'Baluchston?'

'Aye.' Hodge spat to one side. 'The wave didn't touch the town. So my lord reckons they've turned coat there, gone native, like. He's going to raze the town, he says, to teach them a lesson.'

Leof went so still that he heard his heart thumping clearly, heard the blood thrum in his ears. He had to get to Thegan. Try to turn his anger away from the town. It was the Lake who had sent the wave, not the people of Baluchston. He knew that in his bones.

'Do you have horses, sergeant?'

'Aye,' Hodge nodded. 'We've been gathering up the strays. Most of the horses made it out. About ten minute's walk back that way, sir. We found your Thistle.'

Thistle safe. Leof smiled and clapped Hodge on the back. 'A silver piece to every man in your group, sergeant, when we get back to Sendat. That's the best news I could have had.'

He started off towards the horses with a light step, but turned back sombrely as he remembered. 'You'll find eight men and a horse that way,' he said, pointing back to the forest. 'I couldn't find anyone alive.'

'Aye, sir,' Hodge said, nodding to his men to continue their search. 'I think this section had the worst of it, by the numbers dead.'

'The wind was at our backs,' Leof said. 'The Lake had only one chance to stop us.'

'She only needed one chance, sir,' Hodge said. Leof noticed that 'she'. He wondered if Hodge, too, had heard his mother's voice telling him to go home. He wished, with all his heart, that he could follow that advice. Instead, he kept walking around the shoreline, trying to think of arguments which would convince Thegan that no good would come of massacre.

SAKER

SAKER FLUSHED EVERY time he remembered throwing up after the battle at Spritford. If he was to take back this land for its rightful inhabitants, he had to get over his squeamishness. So he followed his ghosts, his little army, down into Carlion determined to be detached; to be strong.

What he saw tried his resolution. The people of Carlion were mostly asleep, although a few late drinkers were on the streets, making their way home. They died first, Owl and his followers smashing into them before they realised what was happening. They didn't even have time to raise the alarm.

Owl gave the first blow: a backhanded sweep with a sword which cut open a man's neck to the bone. There was no scream, just a gargling sound as the blood spurted on the street, covering Owl. He grinned and spun to strike at a woman. But he stopped in mid-stroke and pushed her aside, moving on swiftly to another target.

Ah, Saker thought, noting her dark hair as she ran, sobbing with fear, into an alleyway. The spell is working. It protects those of Traveller blood. He concentrated on the feeling of satisfaction that gave him, so he didn't feel sick at the terrible noises coming from the battle around him; so he didn't feel at all for the man who had just died. That man was an invader, he reminded himself. Living off the profits of murderers. Deserving of death.

Then the ghosts went to the houses. Carlion was a peaceful town. It had its share of robbers and tricksters, but they tended to concentrate on the country visitors and traders who passed through. The residents left their doors on the latch, except during the big Winterfair. That was why Saker had chosen it as the first city, instead of Turvite, where crime flourished and householders put good stout bars across their doors before they went to bed.

The ghosts simply walked in for their slaughter. They disappeared from the silent, moonlit street into houses all along the main street and a few moments later the screams started.

Saker began to tremble, but he breathed deeply and admonished himself, imagining what his father would say if he could see him. Just standing still wasn't enough. He had to be part of it, to see it.

So he followed Owl into the next house.

It was a brick house, well-to-do. The front room was used as a carpentry workshop but there was a big standing loom there, too. Stairs led up to the sleeping chambers. As the door crashed back and Owl rushed in, a voice was raised in question from upstairs. A young auburn-haired man ran down, staring blankly at Owl and Saker. He was tying his trousers as he came; he had no weapon. Behind him was a red-headed woman in a nightshirt: tall, with a strong, attractive face.

Owl raised his sword and the man, quicker than he looked, jumped the last few steps and caught up a long piece of wood which lay on the workbench. He brought it up in time to block Owl's stroke, but the wood shattered.

'Merrick!' the woman screamed. She grabbed Owl and pulled him back, giving the man time to recover and find another weapon. All he could find was a chisel with a long point. Sharp enough, but no use against a sword. As the woman grabbed him Owl turned and raised his sword to strike at her, then stopped as he had done with the woman in the street. He pushed the red-headed woman away. Saker couldn't believe it. This red-head was one of the old blood? No, surely not!

'Maryrose!' the man cried, and slid around Owl to her side, helping her up.

Owl grinned, satisfaction on his face as he prepared to strike the man. As the sword came down, knocking aside the chisel, the woman threw herself in front of the man. The sword almost cut her shoulder off and she dropped straight down, dead already. Merrick screamed in anguish and launched himself at Owl, but two more strokes stopped him. He fell beside her, but he wasn't quite dead. His blood flowed out across the woman's hair, turning it dark, like a Traveller's. He tried to turn himself towards her, but only managed to slide his hand along the floor to touch her face. Her eyes stared blindly, green as grass. The man's fingers slid, shaking, along her cheek and fell.

'Maryrose,' he whispered. 'Wait for me.' Then he died.

Owl smiled and turned to the door. Saker was shaking, but he reminded himself that this was necessary. This was no more than the invaders had done to his people.

He followed Owl outside.

There were people on the street now, rushing out to see why their neighbours were screaming, some men already armed, as though they had been expecting trouble. There was confusion, shouting, men trying to form groups to fight, women collecting children who had wandered out in their nightclothes, yawning.

Many died. Mostly it was quick. But sometimes it wasn't. Even the men who had come ready for fighting were soon overcome. Those with swords didn't know how to use them. They did better with the tools of their trades: knives, hoes, scythes, axes. They fought with desperation but could not do well enough to save themselves. Not when a ghost could take a stab to the heart and still keep fighting.

Yet Saker was astonished to see how many the ghosts passed over. Traveller blood must account for it, because there was no visible difference – the ghosts slashed down at one man but merely shoved another aside; they ripped a scythe across a woman's throat and leapt over her almost identical neighbour.

No matter what the people of Carlion did, they could not defend themselves against his army.

The only house untouched was a stonecaster's house with a big red pouch hanging outside, which Saker's Sight could tell had a spell on the door against ghosts. So. Something to think about.

He had seen enough. He walked through the dying and the dead, past people cowering behind carts and children bleeding over the bricks of the street. Dawn would come soon and he suspected that the ghosts would fade, then. He had to be ready to leave as soon as they faded.

When he stood by the burial site and looked at the bones laid out before him, he had a revelation. He had raised Owl's ghost by simply using his skull. He didn't need to go from place to place, raising the local dead against the living. He could take them with him. A bone, just one bone from each, was enough. If he used fingerbones instead of skulls, he could carry an army in a sack!

Frantically he began to collect fingerbones, laying them on the sack he had wrapped Owl's skull in. He sent out his Sight so that he could feel the spirit of the person who had owned the bone – when he felt the tingle that said the ghost was walking, he put the bone on the pile. In the end, he had a pile of bones which would fit into his smallest coffer. He pulled out the scrolls he kept there and put them in the sack. They weren't as precious, now, as the bones.

By the time the sun edged above the blood-red horizon, Saker was ready, horse harnessed, reins in hand. As he felt the spell dissolve and the ghosts fade, he started off, leaving behind a carpet of bones cast across the disturbed earth.

ASH

SAFRED POURED OUT another round of cha while Cael lit a lamp, making the shadows sharper and the dark outside the windows seem more threatening. She looked at Ash.

'There is more needed. Once we have the bones,' Safred said, 'we have to raise Acton's ghost. The gods say you must sing him up.'

Ash felt as if someone had punched him in the stomach. He stared down at the table, his hands hidden but his shoulders hunched tight. Was *this* why he sang with the voice of the dead? To sing spells of resurrection? It had a nasty logic about it. But he couldn't sing up a ghost.

'I don't know how,' he said.

'You'd better find someone to teach you,' Bramble said. He looked at her sharply and then nodded, once, abruptly. Many things made sense to him, all of a sudden. If such songs existed, he knew where to find them. It was even the right time of year – and, of course, that was why the gods had told them to stay in Hidden Valley until the spring. So he would be able to go straight to the Deep and demand answers.

Unexpected anger swept over him. This was a matter of *singing*. Of *songs*. He was supposed to know all the songs. His father had said he had taught Ash all the songs there were. Then he paused, his anger faltering. That was not exactly what his father had said. He'd said, 'That's the last song I can teach you, son.' Ash had just assumed that meant his father didn't know any others. Because he had also said to Ash, 'You must remember *all* the songs.' He had remembered them all, but apparently he had not been trusted with every one. He felt sick, and angry enough to take on even the demons of the Deep.

'Yes,' he said to Bramble. 'I should. I should be able to . . . can I take a horse?'

Bramble nodded. 'Yes, but you don't know how –' she started to say.

'Do you want me to come?' Martine asked.

Ash hesitated, and then shook his head reluctantly.

Safred chimed in at the same moment. 'Martine comes with us.'

'Really?' Martine's voice was dangerously calm. She clearly didn't like it. Her mouth was tight.

Safred put up her palms in the traditional mime of good faith. 'Not *my* idea,' she said hastily. They were all silent. It took some getting used to, this idea that the gods were organising their lives. 'Your destiny is here,' Safred said in a small voice.

Then she sat up, regaining her confidence, turning to speak to Ash. 'After Bramble finds Acton's death place, you and she can go to find the bones together.'

'Did the gods say that, too?'

'No, but isn't it obvious?' Safred was becoming annoyed. She wasn't used to people questioning her.

Ash shook his head. 'No. I have to go somewhere else first.'

'Where?'

He just stared at her. 'Set a meeting point,' he said. 'I'll join you later.'

'You must be at the lake, to give the brooch to Bramble at the right time!' Safred insisted.

Ash wondered why Safred didn't simply take the brooch from the table.

Safred flushed. 'To be used, the brooch must pass from its rightful owner to the Kill Reborn in the right time and place,' she insisted.

Ash nodded, picked up the brooch and weighed it in his hand for a moment. Then he held it out to Martine. Her lips twitched, but she took it respectfully enough.

'I give you this brooch,' Ash said. 'You are now the rightful owner.'

Martine nodded and slipped the brooch in her pocket. Safred frowned. She opened her mouth to speak, but Ash forestalled her, as though everything had been settled.

'If I'm Travelling alone . . . I don't really know how to look after a horse,' he said to Bramble.

'Take Flax or Zel,' she said. 'They'll know more than I do. They're Gorham's children.'

Ash had no idea who Gorham was, but the dark-haired girl's head came up.

'Flax stays with me,' she said. 'We'll both go.'

There it was, a flat statement leaving no opening for discussion. Stone. But Ash was stone, too. He had to be.

'No. You can't come. I'll go alone.'

Safred looked curiously at Ash, her eyes unfocused. Ash suspected she was listening to the gods. If so, they didn't tell her anything she wanted to hear. Her face tensed.

But she put her hand over Zel's.

'We have need of Flax. He should go with Ash.'

'I look after him.' Zel's voice was almost pleading.

'Yes,' Safred said. 'Perhaps it is time to share that privilege.'

Zel's eyes were dark with internal struggle. Safred patted her hand gently.

'You have done enough.' Again, there was a layer of meaning that Zel seemed to understand.

'I'm a safeguarder,' Ash reminded them. 'He can look after the horses, and I'll look after him.'

Zel stared at him intently, trying to read his soul. 'Do you promise to look after him? As though he were your own brer?'

Ash nodded. 'I promise.'

Zel let out a long breath. 'All right then. He can go.'

'Anybody planning to ask Flax what he thinks?' Ash asked.

Safred looked startled, which was satisfying. Ash was tired already of people who arranged other people's lives as though they were gods themselves.

But Zel laughed bitterly. 'Oh, he wants to go,' she said.

It was true. Flax's eyes were alight. No surprise, Ash thought. What boy wouldn't rather travel with another young man than with his sister?

'We must decide where to meet,' Safred said. 'But I think, not now. Tomorrow, at the altar for the dawn prayers. Let the gods guide us.'

Ash felt a little uncomfortable at the thought, remembering two black rock altars – the one in Turvite, where the gods had called to him, and the one at Hidden Valley, where they had commanded him to come here, at this time. Or perhaps they had set the time so he could save Bramble's life by killing the warlord's man, Sully. The thought of Sully pierced him with regret. He hadn't meant to kill; his training had taken over. He hadn't been able to stay, as he should have, and attend the quickening of Sully's ghost. He should have been there, three days later, waiting, ready with his knife, to admit his guilt, cut his own flesh and offer blood to Sully's ghost as reparation for his death. He sat for a moment at the table as the others got up. To lay one ghost to rest, that he understood. That was personal, immediate, necessary. But to lay an army of ghosts, who had died perhaps a thousand years before . . . he shook his head and pushed back from the table, following the others towards the door. He couldn't imagine how that might work.

Flax was cock-a-hoop as Bramble led him and Ash to the stables so that she could check on the horses and introduce him to Cam and Mud. She wouldn't dare lend Ash Trine, she said. Besides, she liked the cross-grained animal the best.

Flax chattered happily about getting back on the Road. 'I can't stand it in towns,' he said. 'They close in around me.'

'Me too,' Bramble said. 'You've always Travelled?'

He nodded. 'When our mam and da Settled, Zel and I took the Road together. Six years ago now.'

Ash revised his estimate of Flax's age upwards. He had to be at least seventeen, although he talked like a much younger boy.

Flax knew horses, all right, and he soothed them with his voice. Bramble relaxed about letting her precious horses go to someone else. After he had finished grooming them, Flax left with a cheerful 'Wind at your back!'

After that, Bramble spent some time with Mud and Cam, teaching Ash about their grooming and feeding, telling the horses that she was sure they would meet again. Of course they would. They nuzzled her and whickered gently as though trying to comfort her against the coming separation – until Trine got jealous and nipped them away from her. She laughed, and dusted her hands off. She seemed revived by her contact with the animals, but she still looked very tired.

'Enough for one day,' she said. She turned to Ash and raised her eyebrows. 'Have you wondered, if we're going to lay all these ghosts to rest, who's going to give the blood the ritual needs?'

He had wondered. To set a murdered ghost to rest, the killer had to acknowledge guilt and then offer his own blood to the ghost. Ash shivered, remembering the touch of ghostly tongues on his own flesh, when he had offered his blood as reparation to two men he had killed – men, he reminded himself, who had been trying to kill Martine. No need to feel sorry for those two. But the ritual was specific. Each ghost needed blood. Although, he remembered, those ghosts had refused blood from Martine. 'Blood's just a symbol,' they had said. 'Didn't you know?'

There was too much they didn't know, he thought, and that might be the death of them all.

After dinner at Heron's, he went out to the garden behind the house for a breath of air, then stayed, sitting on a bench, looking up at the clear sky. A big lilac bush shed its petals over him as the night breeze stirred its branches. The scent reminded him of another night, camping by an abandoned house whose garden was full of lilacs. His father had taught him the love counting song that night:

> There are ten white flowers my lover gave to me
> Here are the petals of those sweet sweet peas:
> Honesty
>   That's one!
> Verity
>   That's two!
> Poetry
>   That's three!
> And Lo-o-ove
>   Ch: Love can't be counted
>   Love can't be caught
>   Love must be given
>   Never sold or bought

It was a sugary, sentimental song and he'd never liked it, but his father, Rowan, had enjoyed playing it on the flute, giving it lots of trills and flourishes. Ash didn't want to think about his father, so he concentrated on identifying the northern stars he had heard about but never seen before. There was the white bear, there was the salmon . . . a noise behind him made him spin around, knife springing from his boot to his hand as if it had a life of its own.

Martine stood there, holding a cup of cha, her pale face showing clearly in the moonlight but her eyes unreadable. She raised an eyebrow at the knife.

'If I'd wanted to kill you, you'd have been dead long since,' she said.

He flushed. He was so on edge that he'd almost welcome a good fight. 'Sorry. But . . . I don't like it here much.'

'Mmm. It's not a comfortable time, I'll give you that.' She smiled suddenly. 'Have a cup of cha, lad.'

He took the cup with as good grace as he could and Martine sat down beside him, bringing her feet up to sit cross-legged.

'Do you want to tell me where you're going?' she asked.

He paused, not entirely sure what to say. 'To find my father,' he said finally.

'Do you know how to find him?'

He looked down at the cha and nodded. 'I know where he'll be at this time of year.'

'You're going to Gabriston?' Martine asked carefully.

His head whipped up in astonishment. She should not know. No woman should know.

'How . . . ?'

Martine shrugged. 'I'm a stonecaster. We get to know lots of things we shouldn't.'

He relaxed a little, but he was worried, all the same. He didn't know how much she knew, and so couldn't risk talking about any of it. He thought, instead, of the fact that his father had not taught him all the songs. Not all.

After so long away from his parents, after so much doubt and betrayal with Doronit, after taking on responsibility from the gods, who would have thought two words could hurt so much? They knifed into Ash's stomach, into his heart. It had been the one certainty of his life, that his father had trusted him with all the songs, *all* the songs, so they could be preserved as they should be, voice to voice.

How could he go back and ask? If his father had wanted him to know – had *trusted* him – he would have taught him the songs already.

'How are you planning to pay your way?' Martine asked.

He'd been worried about that, too. He had nothing – and the only thing he owned of value, the brooch, had been commandeered.

'I thought, Cael might . . .'

'I'm not sure they have much to spare themselves,' she said thoughtfully. 'I think you might need these.'

She pulled a pouch out of her pocket. For a wild moment, he thought she was giving him her own pouch of stones, but then he saw it was the stones she had taken from the stonecaster's son last autumn.

It seemed like years ago that they had helped the stonecaster's ghost to find rest. He had made the new pouch for these stones himself last winter, sitting by the fire at Elva and Mabry's, the month before their baby was born. Just the thought of little Ash warmed him. Having a namesake who was being raised Settled, a loving family around him, strong walls to protect him, made Ash feel stronger himself. Older and more competent. Not enough to make him take the stones, though.

'You'll know them,' Martine reassured him. 'They speak loudly, at first. They want to be known. And remember, just answer whatever question you're asked. Don't make my mistake and tell people more than they ask for.'

'I'm not a caster,' he said hastily.

'You could be. You have the Sight. You know it.'

He didn't *know*. Just suspected. He didn't *want* to know. He was strange enough already; able to see ghosts, to compel them to speak, speaking himself with the voice of the dead. Having the Sight would just make him even odder.

'Stonecasters aren't thought of as freaks, you know,' Martine said, seeming to read his thoughts as she so often did. 'We're just part of the furniture of the world, really.'

He laughed unwillingly. It was true, stonecasters were accepted everywhere. When she offered him the pouch, his hand seemed to rise of its own accord to take it.

The heavy softness of the leather, the stones within it, fit into his palm as though he had held it a thousand times before.

'So,' Martine said. 'So.' She sounded disappointed, and reached to take the pouch back.

'What?' Ash said, startled. His fingers tightened on the pouch. Martine paused.

'They are not in harmony,' she said.

He had no idea what she was talking about. She was surprised in turn. 'You can't hear them?'

Ash shook his head. Martine's face was unreadable, as it had been the first time he met her. It was as though she had withdrawn from him. As though he had failed her.

'The stones sing. Well, not exactly. Not like humans. But when they do not have a caster, they sing constantly, out of tune, out of rhythm. It's unpleasant. That's why I rolled this pouch up in a blanket. So I wouldn't have to listen to them.'

'And?'

Martine hesitated. 'When they find their caster, and he or she takes them in their hand, they come into tune.'

Ash stared down at the pouch, which seemed as silent as the grave to him. 'I can't even hear them,' he said. 'So I suppose they didn't come into tune.'

'No,' she said gently, resting her hand on his shoulder. 'I was sure you were a caster. I even cast the stones about it, and they said yes, definitely. I don't understand –'

'What's to understand?' he shot back, suddenly angry. He tossed the pouch into her lap. 'I can't do it. Just like I can't sing. Or play the flute. Or *anything* to do with music.'

'That may be,' Martine said slowly. 'But my casting was quite clear. I've never known the stones to be completely wrong. I'll cast again.'

'Don't bother,' he said. 'I still won't be able to hear them.'

He strode off and walked the streets of the silent town until the salmon star had swum its way below the horizon. Then he went back to the lodging house and lay in the green-ceilinged room, trying not to think of all the things he was useless at – all the people he had failed. Perhaps his father had been right not to trust him. The only thing he seemed to be good at was killing.

BRAMBLE

FIRST LIGHT WAS early so far north, even in spring, and they were all yawning and shivering as they met outside Safred's house and followed her through the alleys and streets of the town to a small wooded area on its outskirts. A score or so of townsfolk came with them, and they greeted one another with nods and yawning half-smiles so simply that Bramble knew they took the walk to the gods' wood every morning.

The wood was surrounded by fields and some houses, and it was clear that the town had expanded around the altar, but had left enough space to keep the gods happy. They didn't like being crowded, it was said.

Bramble could feel them, lightly, in her mind. It was not the uncomfortable pressure they used when they wanted her to do something. This was almost companionable. It was the first time she had felt this way, going to greet them. At home, in Wooding, she had hated the dawn prayers, surrounded by those afraid of the gods, or of life, by the pious and by those who wanted to be thought pious, like the Widow Farli. But here, she sensed nothing from these people but simple devotion. No doubt it was harder to pretend to be pious with the Well of Secret's eyes on you.

The rock was in a clearing, surrounded by old beech trees, huge and knotted and twisting overhead so that their branches met and the altar seemed to be at the centre of a domed room. Moss and young grass covered the ground and Bramble could hear the trickle of a stream which the gods always liked to have nearby. Although they were close to the town, she felt as though she were deep in a forest, perhaps even the Great Forest that she had dreamed about so often. The hairs on the back of her neck raised, and she knew that the gods had turned their attention to all of their followers, not just her.

They came to the altar in the silver light just before dawn, and knelt together, in silence, as the winds of dawn began to blow. Safred bowed her head; Martine and Ash looked down at their hands, which was not quite the same thing. Zel was praying, her mouth moving silently, her hand clasping Flax's. His face was blank. Surprisingly, Cael was also praying fervently, hands clenched against his chest.

Bramble's mind was empty of prayers. All she could do was feel: grief for Maryrose and a dark scouring of blame and anger for the gods, because they hadn't protected her sister. They gave her no reply in words, but she had a strong sense of their regret. It wasn't enough to ease her grief, but her anger cooled a little, and turned towards Saker. I will kill him, she thought. The pressure on her mind increased with the thought, but for the first time ever, she had the sense that the gods were undecided. *Should I kill him?* she asked them, but she heard no answer except, *Not yet.*

As the first light touched the tops of the trees, throwing shadows down onto the altar, the other townsfolk stirred and got up, backing away respectfully until they were beyond the circle of trees. But Safred motioned to their group to come closer. She laid a hand on the altar.

'Today we part. But we'll meet again, to bring the parts of the answer together.'

'Aye,' Cael said. 'But where, and when?'

They looked at Safred, who hesitated. Bramble could tell there was no answer from the gods.

It was Martine who answered. 'Turvite,' she said.

'The stones?' Safred asked. 'The stones say so?'

'Common sense says so, which is worth more,' Martine replied briskly. 'It was Acton's last big battle. It's the biggest city in the Domains. Sooner or later this Saker will go there, and he will bring his army.'

'Oh, yes,' Bramble said, feeling Martine's words ring true. 'He'll want Turvite. He'll want to succeed where the old enchanter failed.'

'Yes. He will want to surpass her,' Safred said slowly.

'So,' Cael said. 'Turvite.'

Ash flinched, just a little, as though Cael's voice had been a prod to his memory. 'Um . . . Turvite might not be so healthy a place for Martine and me,' he said.

Martine laughed. 'True,' she said. 'Perhaps we should meet just *outside* Turvite. There's a village a few miles up the river, called Sanctuary. We could meet there.'

'As soon as we can,' Safred said reluctantly, and it was an irritant to her, they could all see, that she did not know the time and date.

'Where will you go to find the songs?' she asked Ash.

His face closed down. 'South,' he said.

'But I need to know –' Safred began, and at the same moment the gods roared into Bramble's head, forbiddingly. *No!* they ordered. Safred jerked as the command hit her. Ash shook a little, as though he had heard them too, but his face stayed stony.

'No,' he echoed the gods.

Safred stared at him, her eyes burning and her face pale, but at last she nodded and the pressure in Bramble's mind eased off. Bramble could see the effort it took her not to ask more. She waited for Safred to say some final exhortation or blessing, but she just stepped back from the altar and walked away, her back to the altar. That unsettled Bramble, who always backed away, out of a mix of respect and caution. It seemed to her that Safred took the gods for granted, and that was not quite safe. She shrugged. None of her business. She had to see to the horses for the journey.

They walked back to the town and Bramble went straight to the stables instead of to Safred's house with the others. She led the horses around to the house, trying not to think about being separated from Cam and Mud. There was no choice, really, but she took a few moments as she led them to talk to them, telling them they would meet again, soon, soon. Trine got jealous and bumped her head against Bramble's side. Instinctively, she braced for a lance of pain from her arm, but of course there was none. She was healed. She wasn't sure she would ever get used to that.

Bramble had bought provisions for a few days' journey from Heron and had insisted on paying for the room as well, over Ash and Martine's protests. 'Least I can do,' she said. She never had liked being in someone's debt and only the knowledge that the gods had sent Ash and Martine to her at the right time allowed her to bear the gratitude she owed them. She grinned at Ash. He was still walking stiffly from the long ride. She remembered how much learning to ride hurt.

'Think you can manage another ride?'

He looked at Cam with some doubt. 'If I have to,' he said, then laughed with her. There was something false about the laughter, though, as if he was trying hard to seem light-hearted. Bramble felt a little protective of him, which was stupid, considering it was *he* who had saved *her* life. Zel brought a sack out from the house and dumped it next to the doorframe.

'Another journey,' Martine said. 'Maybe Acton was right when he sent us on the Road. It seems like we can't get away from it no matter how we try.'

'No rest for the Traveller,' Ash said. 'Not this side of the burial caves.'

'I guess we must be Travellers, then,' Martine said wryly. Zel went back in for another load, leaving the door open behind her. Martine said quietly to Ash, 'I cast again, and the stones said the same thing.'

He went very still for a moment, then shrugged. 'Doesn't change anything.'

'It may be that you need to find different –'

Ash cut her off. 'Forget it. I can't do it, and that's all.'

Bramble busied herself with checking the girths on the horses. No business of hers. They had the right to their own secrets. But she noticed distress in both their faces, although they tried to disguise it with the blank face so many Travellers seemed to develop. A protective face, that gave nothing away.

Safred's voice reached them, murmuring quietly. Then the sound of a man sobbing uncontrollably. One of the pilgrims, no doubt. Bramble was uncomfortable with this side of Safred's power. To heal flesh was extraordinary enough. To heal the spirit – something in her rebelled against that idea. To be so vulnerable to someone who was, after all, only another human . . . although at one time she had intended coming to the Well of Secrets for exactly that kind of healing, now it seemed inconceivable to her. There was no way she was baring her soul to Safred.

Safred's voice came again. Martine, Ash and Bramble exchanged glances. After a few moments the sobbing stopped and Safred appeared in the doorway, Cael behind her.

'Sorry to keep you waiting,' she said cheerfully.

Bramble looked at Ash and smiled. 'Parting of the ways. I guess we're not meant to travel together, lad,' she said half-regretfully. He nodded, half-regretful himself.

Zel and Flax emerged from the house, Zel talking in a big-sisterly tone.

'You help as much as you can. Stay out of the inns. Wait until we're together again.'

Flax bore her advice patiently; more patiently than most younger brothers would have. His mouth was crooked up a little at one corner, as though he found it amusing, but he listened and nodded and said, 'Yes, Zel,' in all the right places.

Mullet came around the corner leading four horses, three skittish chestnuts who looked like they had the same breeding and a much older, steadier bay. The old man nodded familiarly to Bramble. She nodded back and smiled. They had met already that morning to groom and saddle the horses. That had been the best time since she'd come to Oakmere, going quietly about the familiar tasks in the warm, lantern-lit stable, working companionably with Mullet as she had done so often with Gorham, the comforting smell of horses surrounding them.

She had been surprised to find the horses in such good condition after their frantic race to get her to Oakmere, but Mullet had grinned.

'Well of Secrets, she gave them a visit,' he said.

'She *healed* them?' Bramble asked, astonished. It had not occurred to her that Safred would care about animals. Animals had no secrets.

'Said you'd need 'em,' he confirmed. Yes, that made more sense. Safred might be a seer, but she was practical, too. She wouldn't let anything get in the way of the task at hand.

Now, as Safred swung up on the old bay, Bramble could tell that she had been right. Safred didn't care about the animal; it was just a way to get to where she was going. Bramble was trying hard not to dislike Safred, out of gratitude, but she suspected that it was a losing battle.

'Let's go,' Safred said. 'May the gods go with you.'

'We might have less trouble if they didn't,' Cael said softly to Bramble, and she chuckled.

Safred jammed a battered old leather hat on her head – all those freckles, thought Bramble, still amused, glad in some way to notice any weakness in her. They mounted their horses. They paused for a moment, exchanging glances: Zel and Flax, Ash and Martine. Then they rode away, Safred, Zel, Cael, Martine and Bramble to the north; Ash and Flax to the south.

Cael laughed openly at the look on Safred's face as she twisted in her saddle to watch the young men ride away.

'That boy has a secret,' she said, her eyes hungry.

'And the right to keep it,' Cael said.

Reluctantly, Safred nodded and started her horse off again. 'For now,' she said.

They rode out of the town towards the north, passing through streets which led to houses with large vegetable gardens and then a narrow strip of farmland, just showing the first greeny-purple tips of wheat above the soil. There were oats, too, in strips among the wheat, and cabbages, onions, beets – all the staples that would get a northern town through the long stretch of winter.

Not far from town they skirted a lake fringed with willows.

'Oakmere?' Bramble asked.

Cael grimaced. 'They cut down the oaks to build the town, then someone brought a willow up from the south and they just took over.'

Bramble pursed her lips. 'Yes, incomers do that.'

He gave her a look that showed he understood that she was talking about more than trees, but made no comment. She found herself liking him. He reminded her a bit of her own uncle, her father's brother, who was a chairmaker and woodcarver. She hadn't seen him often in her childhood because he lived in Whitehaven, where there was a bigger market for the intricate and expensive carving he loved, but she always enjoyed his visits. He was far more jovial and light-hearted than her parents, and took Bramble's daily explorations of the woods in his stride, unlike every other adult she knew. Cael had the same acceptance of life, the same good-natured easiness and enjoyment. But her uncle had been no fool, and neither was Cael.

Soon the farmland gave way to scrub and heath and then to sparse woodland, mostly birch and beech and spruce. It was clear that the trees were harvested by the townsfolk. There were stumps and coppiced trees, cleared areas where young saplings were springing up, the remnants of charcoal burners' fires.

The road was bordered by hedgerows – hawthorn, in flower, and wild white roses, which sent thorned canes onto the track and forced them to ride single file, Zel leading, ahead of Safred. Gorham must have thrown Zel up on a horse before she could walk; she rode as if she were a part of the animal. Safred was competent enough on a horse, Bramble had noted, but mounted clumsily, and she used reins and a saddle, which somehow surprised Bramble. She herself was riding Trine, not trusting her to anyone else, and as usual went without a bit. She had given Trine's saddle to Ash, for Mud, and rode Trine with just a blanket and saddlebags. The bags Merrick had given her. A torrent of grief broke over her at the memory and her chest felt painful, as though her heart was being squeezed. She forced herself to pay attention to where they were going. Ahead of them was a line of darker trees. Bramble couldn't see what they were – pine or larch or oak, maybe elms. There was no sense of a specific colour green, just a wall of darkness which grew as they rode closer.

They reached a crossroads where a much larger road led off to the north-west. Safred dismounted and the others followed suit and stood by their horses. Martine and Cael thankfully stretched their legs.

'Ahead is the Great Forest,' Safred said. She paused and took off her hat, pleating its crown without looking at it. 'When we get to the altar we'll be safe, I think. Until then, be careful. Don't leave the path.'

'They always say that in the stories,' Bramble said involuntarily. 'The old stories about children lost in the Forest always say, "Don't leave the path," and the child always does.'

'Yes,' Safred said. 'Remember what they meet when they do.'

They rode on.

The Forest began abruptly. There was a small slope covered with a dense thicket of wayfaring trees, not yet in flower. The greyish branches and rough leaves almost barred the path, but Cael pushed through, and they were suddenly among pine trees. Huge, straight, ugly. It was a little like the forest near the Lake, but *more*.

The enormous trees made Bramble feel as though she and the others had been shrunk to child size, or smaller; that they were toys pretending to be human, like the dolls Maryrose used to play with. She wondered if anyone or anything was playing with them, and what the game really was.

Under the high, intertwined branches, they rode in an artificial dusk that pressed heavily on them. The ground was covered by a carpet of browned pine needles so thick that the horses' hooves made no sound and Bramble was for the first time glad of the chink of bits and bridles from the others' horses. Far above them, patches of orange lichen spread like disease on the trunks. The smell of pine was so strong that after a while Bramble's nose blocked it out and she could smell nothing. See nothing except the gloomy brown and tan of the forest floor. Hear nothing except the faint sough of wind in the branches high above them. There were no stumps, no clearings. No one came here for wood or charcoal or pine, Bramble suspected. No one came here unless they had to.

Back at her home in Wooding, she had wanted so badly to come to the Great Forest, but this was not what she had hoped for. All her life, she had imagined herself running free here, but in her imagination it had been a wilder, more isolated version of her woods at home, filled with familiar, beautiful greens: oak and elm and alder and willow, holly and rowan and hazel, each a different shade, each taking its proper place in the burgeoning life of the wood.

This Forest's life was the opposite of that simple kitchen table they had sat around yesterday, of the daylight life of eating and drinking and talking and being. The opposite of the familiar stable where the horses' breath had showed misty in the chilly morning. Even the opposite of the gathering in the dawn around the black rock altar, where their own breaths had billowed out like steam. This was a place where breathing was foreign. Unwelcome. She felt the pressure of the Forest in her mind, like the pressure from the gods but with a different flavour. There was no voice here, as the gods had voices. There was nothing here but time, endless tree time, where a single heartbeat took a whole year and a thought might last the length of a human life.

Bramble remembered her panic in the forest by the Lake and how the presence of the horses had saved her from it. She saw that the others were starting to feel the same panic now. Picking up on their riders' anxiety, their horses were growing increasingly nervous, especially the two skittish chestnuts that Zel and Cael were riding. Bramble did not give into it so badly this time – perhaps because she had found a way through it before, and now kept her attention on Trine's warm hide and the way her muscles moved.

'Concentrate on your horses,' she called to the others, her voice dropping flat and harsh into the silence. 'Feel their warmth. Smell them. They'll comfort you.'

Her companions turned back to look at her in surprise, then they nodded and moved with more confidence. Safred leant down in her saddle to lay her face against the bay's neck. Zel dropped her hands so that they rested on the saddle bow, where she could feel the shift of her horse's muscles.

Bramble saw them relax a little and was pleased. Whatever they had to face in this forest, they weren't going to be in a panic when it found them.

Then they reached a stream, bubbling over flat round stones, no more than a hand span deep but too wide to jump across. At least, it was too wide for these horses. If the roan had been with her, they would have made it easily. She pushed aside a sharp pang of grief at the thought, but the memory of the roan lying in a stream much like this one, bleeding, his head in her lap, returned implacably. Guilt, as well as grief, welled up in her. It was her fault he had died. If she hadn't made him run in that last chase, he would never have fallen. He would still be alive. Concentrate! she told herself, and looked up and down the stream, searching for a crossing place.

The stream was wide enough that a shaft of sunlight made it down through the bordering trees, and bushes and grasses grew along its banks, their sharp green shocking in the gloom of the pine forest. It was the most cheerful place they had come to in the Forest, but the horses refused to cross. Bramble dismounted and walked to the front, leading Trine. There was a flat space on either side of the stream, but it was bare of any marks. Not even animals came here to drink. Trine snorted and backed away from the water.

'Water sprites?' Bramble asked Safred.

Safred shrugged, but Cael answered. 'You can see water sprites, usually.'

'What, then?' Bramble asked.

Martine bent to sniff the water. 'It smells of something I've met before,' she said thoughtfully, 'but I can't quite place it.'

In turn, they bent and sniffed the brown water. For all of them, it brought up an almost memory, a feeling that they knew the scent if only they could remember. It was neither pleasant nor unpleasant, but it was not pine or fruit or flower or bog or anything else that you would expect to find in a forest.

'If the horses don't want to cross it, I don't think we should,' Cael said. The others nodded and Bramble was relieved. She trusted the horses' instincts more than the humans'.

The stream crossed the path at a right-angle and there seemed no other way over it. The path clearly continued on the other side.

'Don't go off the path, children,' she said wryly.

'Bramble's right,' Zel said suddenly, not seeming to notice the wryness. 'This might be a trick to get us off the path.' She swung down from the chestnut and sat on the pine needles to take off her boots.

'Zel?' Martine said. 'What are you doing?'

'I reckon I can make it across there,' Zel muttered, pulling her boots off with a strange ferocity. 'This is something *I* can do.'

Bramble nodded. She'd feel like that, too, surrounded by people who can speak to ghosts and tell the future. Hells, she *did* feel like that, and she was the Kill Reborn. But although Gorham had told her that Zel was a tumbler, it was a very long way across that stream. She said nothing. The girl knew her own business best.

Cael wasn't so sure. He measured the stream by eye. 'It's too far!' he said. 'You'll fall halfway.'

Zel jumped to her feet and began to do some limbering exercises, swinging her arms and legs. The horses edged away, the white of Trine's eyes showing. Bramble went to her head and soothed her.

'We'll see,' Zel said. 'If I get over we can string up a rope and you can slide across.' She paused. 'Do we have rope?'

'Aye,' Cael said, his voice deep and comforting. 'We've got rope. But that won't get the horses over.'

'We'll have to leave the horses,' Safred said, her voice tight. 'We have to get to the lake by sunset.'

Neither Bramble nor Zel liked that idea. Bramble didn't want to leave Trine in a strange place with who knew what hiding in the shadows. Zel, it was clear, had anticipated who would be left behind to look after the horses. She prepared for the jump with her mouth set.

Bramble found it hard to believe there was any danger. She remembered jumping the chasm near Wooding. *That* had been dangerous. This was just a shallow stream which, as the sun rose above the trees, began to sparkle in the sunbeams. But the horses wouldn't cross it. Bramble shrugged. Nothing was ever shagging easy.

Zel backed up the path and motioned them to move out of the way. Bramble and Cael took the horses off a little; Martine and Safred went to the other side of the track. Bramble expected Zel to run, instead, she took a couple of long paces and then started to do flip-flops, hands to feet to hands, building up speed. At the very edge of the water she jumped high and curled into a ball as she spun in the air, across the stream: once, twice, three times . . .

Her feet came down only a foot from the bank. She splashed heavily into the water, landing on hands and knees. The water flew up and doused her and the smell, whatever it was, immediately grew much stronger.

Zel knelt in the water, silent. She seemed frozen. Petrified.

'Zel?' Bramble called, but she didn't respond. Bramble edged down the stream, still holding the bridles, so she could see her face side on, but Zel's expression was fixed in a grimace of surprise.

'Turned to stone?' Cael wondered, voicing all their thoughts. He picked up a pine cone from the track and threw it at Zel's back. She twitched in response. He did it again and she scrambled up to her feet, her face changing gradually from surprise to fear, her eyes following something to her right, her head turning as she tracked something that wasn't there.

'Zel, keep going!' Safred called, but Zel remained still, breathing hard. Cael threw another cone, and another. Zel's back shrugged and involuntarily she took a half-step. Then she screamed, the scream of a child who has seen a monster. Bramble bent and grabbed a cone and threw it, too. Then they were all throwing cones, some landing near Zel, some hitting her legs and back, and one bouncing off her head.

'Aow!' she said, and took one more step. Enough to bring her out of the water. She stood looking down the track and shook her head as if to clear it. Then she turned, her flexible tumbler's body seeming heavy. Her feet fell solidly with a thwack into the mud.

'Are you all right?' Martine called.

Zel nodded and looked around again, clearing her throat as though she hadn't spoken for a long time.

'I'm fine.'

'What happened?' Safred asked.

Zel shrugged. 'I dunno. Everything . . . changed. Like I were somewhere different. There was elk. I think elk, but they was *huge*. A whole herd of 'em. And the trees was different – oak, I think, maybe some elm, and grasses and . . . and there were this *thing*, like a giant cat, shagging enormous, chasing the elk and they was running and running and the ground were shaking and then that thing, that big cat, it had these *teeth* down to here,' she gestured to below her shoulders, 'it stopped running and it turned to me and started to come. It were going to jump, like a wolf jumps – it were going to take out my throat, I could *smell* it. Then something hit me on the back of my head and I took a step and it – it was gone. All of it were just *gone*.'

She sat down heavily, as though talking had exhausted her.

'You were right here,' Cael reassured her. 'You never left us.'

Zel bit her lip. 'If that thing had landed on me, I'd be dead,' she said with certainty. 'Here or not, there or not. I'd be dead.'

'Mmm,' Safred said. 'Better not to take the horses through it, then.'

'How do we get over?' Martine asked.

'We tie a rope high on one tree over this side,' Cael said, 'and then throw it to Zel. She can fix it lower to a tree on the other side and we slide down the rope. We can use one of the leading reins to hold onto.'

Safred looked doubtful. 'I'm not so good at climbing trees,' she admitted. Bramble was amused to hear that the Well of Secrets had any flaws. 'There's an easier way,' she said. 'It's simple. Just tie a rope around your middle, toss the other end to Zel and let her drag you across. Or if she's not strong enough, she passes it around a tree over there, throws it back and we all haul on it. Doesn't matter what you see or what you smell while you're going over, you'll be across in a moment and back to your senses.'

'It's a risk,' Cael said thoughtfully. 'That cat thing might be waiting for the first one over.'

'I'll go first,' Bramble said.

'No,' Safred said. 'We need you. We can't risk you.' She looked at Cael.

Silently, he took rope out of his saddlebags and prepared to throw it to Zel. Safred's eyes clouded for a moment and then she shook her head as if to clear it. Asking the gods? Bramble wondered. If so, she hadn't got an answer. Her face was hard to read. This was her uncle, after all, Bramble thought. She had to be worried, even if she didn't show it. Or was she so used to being controlled by the gods that she didn't fear anything they didn't tell her to fear?

Zel pushed herself to her feet and caught the rope Cael threw over easily, then passed it around a nearby pine at waist height and threw both ends back. He caught them and tied one end securely around his waist. They took hold of the other end and held the rope taut. Zel positioned herself at the tree to make sure the rope didn't catch on anything.

Cael walked back a few paces from the stream.

'I'm going to take a run-up so I'm moving fast when I hit the water,' he said. 'Ready? Pull!'

He ran at the water and they had to haul quickly on the rope to keep it tense. As his feet splashed into the stream his steps faltered. Unlike Zel, he kept going, but he slowed down and put his arms out in front of him as though warding something off. Bramble was closest to the stream and she hauled hard on the rope, jerking Cael forwards.

'Pull!' she commanded and they pulled together, leaning into the rope and walking backwards up the path. Cael was drawn forwards across the stream but he went in staggering paces, arms frantically trying to clear something from in front of him as he went. He grunted with effort as he swept his arms from side to side. A couple of times he jerked as though he had hit something. He stepped sideways and the rope went slack. He was only a few steps from the bank. Zel was shouting at him, waving her arms near his face, balancing precariously on a rock at the water's edge, all her tumbler's agility called into play. He didn't react to her at all.

'Pull!' Safred shouted and they pulled more desperately, tightening the rope and dragging him face-down into the water. The smell of the stream became much stronger, making them gag. Then he was flung up in the air, his arms flailing, by a force none of them could see, although they felt the strength of it as the rope was jerked through their hands, burning as it pulled. Cael was thrown up and forwards, as dogs who are gored by a boar fly through the air from the boar's tusks. He landed heavily on the side of the stream. His shoulders were above the stream and Zel grabbed them and hauled him as they pulled the rope. As though aware of her for the first time, he rolled to his hands and knees and shuffled himself out of the water, then collapsed on the ground, his hands shaking as he tried to undo the rope.

There were scratches all over his face and his clothes were ripped across the chest. A long, shallow gash cut across the width of his body. It looked much like a tusk wound, Bramble thought, widening as it went from a narrow point. He had been very lucky.

'Are you all right?' Safred called. He nodded and touched his face. Blood was welling in a dozen scratches.

'Uncle? Can you talk?'

'I always told you to get outside and play more when you were little. You should have listened to me and climbed a few trees while you could because, niece, I think you should climb one now.' Cael was trying hard to speak light-heartedly, but long tremors wracked him, the aftermath of terror.

'What was it?' Martine asked, but he shook his head, shuddering at the memory.

'Tell me,' Safred said urgently, her eyes intent.

He smiled shakily at her. 'At last, I have a secret that you want! But this is not the time, niece.'

'Tell me,' she said again, pleadingly.

He shook his head. 'Never mind about it now. Just rig up that rope and hold on tight.'

Safred's face was a mixture of exasperation and thwarted desire. Bramble realised that knowing things, being *told* things, was as necessary to Safred as breathing. She was called the Well of Secrets because once told, the secrets were never spoken of again, disappearing as if into a deep well; but she drew those secrets to her more like a whirlpool than a well. She sucked them in as though they were air to breathe. Martine was staring at Safred, too, as though comprehending the same thing. She saw Bramble looking at her and raised an eyebrow, as if to say, 'Interesting, isn't it?'

Cael tied off the rope around the pine tree they had used as a pulley and Martine pulled the rest of it back to their side. She looked doubtfully at the nearest tree. Bramble took the rope from her, exasperated, then took a rein from Zel's chestnut and tucked it into her belt.

'Don't tell me *you* didn't climb trees when you were a youngling either?' she said as she swung up onto the lowest branch. Fortunately, near the stream the pine branches grew close to the ground and were relatively easy to climb.

Martine didn't respond, but Zel answered for her.

'Travellers don't, mostly,' she said. 'You get yelled at if anyone sees you. Sometimes they throw rocks.'

Bramble sniffed. She had been yelled at more times than she could count, climbing other people's trees, but no one had ever thrown rocks at her. Because she wasn't really a Traveller, just Maryrose's wild little sister. Gods she hated that whole way of thinking about Travellers! It stank like rotten fish. She put her anger into her climb and ignored the scratches from the pine twigs and bark. At a point where a branch had broken away, leaving a gap they could swing through, she attached the rope firmly to the trunk, making sure it was lodged securely on the stub of the branch. The line stretched tight right across the stream. She would have to bring her legs up at the end, though, to stop them splashing in the water as she landed.

She balanced on the branch below and doubled the rein, then flipped the doubled length over the rope and caught it with her other hand. She understood the theory. You were supposed to hold onto the rein and your body weight would slide you down the rope to the other side. From here, the rope looked frayed and the rein too thin. Break your neck, or simply fall into the stream and be ripped apart by whatever had attacked Cael. She grinned, feeling her blood fizz with the familiar excitement of danger, and launched herself from the tree.

The rush through the air was dizzyingly fast. Bramble tried to bring her legs up in time so that they did not hit the water on the far side of the stream, but just as she began to lift them, something invisible grabbed her ankle and yanked. She fell into the water with a flurry and splash that blinded her.

Scrambling to her feet, she blinked the water from her eyes and found that the something was not invisible after all. It was a man – no, a woman – no, a *something* almost human which stood, lounging, on the bank, laughing at her dishevelment and her astonishment.

Everything around her had changed, and she was caught in a surprise so profound that it left no room for other emotions.

Movement caught her gaze, and the being on the bank looked with her, still laughing. Fleeing through the trees was a herd of brown deer, but of a kind she had never seen before, with a broad white stripe down their back and black legs. They bounded over bushes and fallen trees, through undergrowth which masked the rest of the Forest. What had been pine trees were now elms. There were birds singing. Thrushes. The stream was narrower, and clearer, the water less brown, the stones rougher under her feet.

Her companion had a long knife in its hand. A stone knife, the kind that never dulls. It looked sacrificial. As she thought it, the laughter stopped. The person on the bank looked at her and smiled a kind, terrifying smile. It was thin, and no taller than she, and beautiful the way a hunting cat is beautiful, the way a hawk is beautiful as it hovers, waiting for the kill. There were hawk's feathers woven into its hair, so that she could not tell where the feathers stopped and the hair began, and its eyes were gold and slitted like a hawk's. Behind her, the undergrowth rustled and she wondered how many of them there were, and why she was still alive. Astonishment gave way to acceptance. If it was her time to die, so be it.

'Will you not run, as the deer run?' it asked. Its voice was warm and oddly husky, as though it spoke little.

Bramble shook her head. 'I have done running,' she said. 'If you want to kill me, go ahead.' She knew the edge of the stream would get her back to her own people, her own – what, time? place? world? She also knew she couldn't get to the edge of the stream before that wicked blade took her throat. She wasn't inclined to run for its amusement.

Concern filled its eyes but it came a step closer. Its bones moved oddly under its skin, more like a cat than a person. Another step. It raised the knife to her throat but did not touch her.

'There must be fear to cleanse the death,' it whispered.

Bramble knew that she should be shaking in terror, but the feeling refused to come. She wasn't good at fear, never had been. With the roan and Maryrose both gone, there was nothing in this life she would mind leaving. It would take more than the threat of death to make her afraid. As though it recognised the thought, the hunter frowned.

'There must be fear,' it repeated. It increased the pressure on Bramble's throat until she felt a runnel of blood make its way down her skin.

'I've been dead,' Bramble said. 'There are lots of things worse than a clean death.'

It began to shake, its face crumpling with uncertainty. 'Without fear, the death is tainted. The hunter becomes unclean.'

'Then don't kill me.'

'But the Forest requires it. All who see us must die.' Then it cocked its head as though listening. 'If I do not kill, I betray . . .'

Bramble listened too. Around them, everything became quiet. The thrushes stopped their trilling, the wind died, the stream itself seemed to pause. Then a shiver came through the trees, not from the wind but from the earth, a shiver that passed *up* the trees and lost itself in the grey sky above. Bramble felt that a message had been sent, but in a language she could not hear. The golden eyes filled with tears which trickled slowly down its face, as though the message had been one of great grief. It lowered the knife and slowly slid it into a belt sheath.

'I may not kill you now. The Forest knows you, Kill Reborn. You may travel safely here.'

'And my friends, too,' Bramble demanded. 'And our horses.'

It nodded. 'If you will it. But the Forest says, move swiftly. The time is almost ripe.'

It drifted back towards the undergrowth, and as it went, the scent from the stream intensified.

'Wait,' Bramble said. 'What *is* that smell?'

It laughed bitterly. 'Memory,' it said. 'Memory and blood.'

She took a step forwards to follow it, to ask it more about the Forest, but the step took her from the elms back to the pines, to a blue sky above and Cael grabbing her hands, hauling her out of the water.

'How long was I there?' Bramble said. Safred and Martine, on the other side of the stream, opened their mouths to ask questions but Cael waved them silent.

'Only a moment. How long was it for you?' he answered.

Bramble considered. 'A few minutes, maybe. Hard to tell. Long enough to almost be killed.'

'What did you see?' Safred called. Her face was intent.

'Later,' Bramble said. 'There was a message from the Forest. Travel swiftly, it said. The time is almost ripe.'

'Aye,' Cael said grimly. He called to Martine. 'Keep your legs well up, lass, when you come over.'

Bramble shook her head. 'No, it should be all right now. The Forest has given us leave to travel.'

Immediately, Safred plunged into the stream, crossing in a few strides without incident. She reached the other side and Cael took her hand to haul her up. He grinned at her.

'Should have gone first if you wanted to know what was out there, girl,' he said. She looked sideways at him, annoyed.

The smell had gone from the stream. Martine led the horses to the water and this time they ambled across willingly, snatching mouthfuls as they went.

Safred laid her hand on Cael, her eyes closing. Martine said quietly to Bramble, 'Healing him,' and Bramble nodded. Safred opened her mouth to sing and Bramble felt a shock go through her when the song came: grating, horrible, somehow familiar. She turned to Martine.

'Is that how she healed me?'

Martine nodded. 'With a little help from Ash.'

Knowing how horrendous her own injury had been, Bramble expected Safred to deal with Cael's scratches easily. But the song continued, louder, and Safred was frowning. Cael looked down at his chest, where the long gore mark stood out livid against his skin. It began to bleed. Sluggishly, then faster and stronger. His face paled and he reached up to grip Safred's wrist. She stopped singing and her own face was so white each freckle showed up clearly.

'They are not there,' she said. 'The gods are not there.'

There was such desolation in her voice that Bramble went to her instinctively and put a hand on her shoulder.

Safred looked at Bramble's hand. It was scratched and bleeding from climbing the pine tree. Safred touched it lightly and closed her eyes.

The scratches disappeared, fading away completely, just as her shoulder wound had. Safred didn't even need to sing.

Her eyes opened full of relief, but as she looked at Cael, she was at a loss. 'I don't understand. They were there, easily, then. For Bramble.'

'But not for me,' Cael said. His face was unreadable.

'You said,' Bramble reminded Safred, 'that whatever guides you is weak in the Forest. Perhaps a wound that the Forest has inflicted is beyond their power here.'

'You got that scratch from the Forest.'

Bramble shook her head. 'Not from the Forest. Just from a tree. There's a difference.'

Cael shook his head as though it were too hard for him. He went to his horse, pulled a kerchief out of his saddlebag and mopped the blood from his chest.

'Enough,' he said. 'If the Forest wants me to bleed, then I'll bleed. Let's get going.'

Safred studied him with a worried face, but eventually she nodded.

In silence, they mounted up and followed the trail before them.

'Me first this time, I think,' Bramble said and Safred nodded agreement.

'Quickly, then. The lake is not far now.'

THE HUNTER'S STORY

I WAS THE FIRST the fair-haired invaders killed here, but of course I did not die. I think the blue-eyed people did not understand what I was; where I was; when I was. I have heard that there was no Forest where they came from; only trees, here and there, lonely and longing for the Wood.

So perhaps they did not understand about me; us; all of us who are the Forest. They were surprised when I did not fall as they hacked at me; they became afraid and ran. Their running became part of me, as the running of the aurochs is part, and the running of the deer. All the hunted are part of me, because how else can I be a hunter?

Only the hunter who knows the fear of the chase can feel the true, pure victory; only the hunter who pays for his prey with terror is washed clean of guilt. To feel what they feel; to run as they run; to die as they die is the only way. If you hunt without it, you too will die in turn, as the humans do.

It is not hard to kill. The hard part is to do so while feeling all that the prey feels, and yet keep the clarity of purpose that allows the killing stroke, the slash of the knife to the perfect spot which will cause the least pain.

I remember my first kill. Who does not? It was so long ago that the Forest itself was different. I remember the cycads and the ferns. I remember the big lizards, which were never hunted, because they did not fear as we did. Their feelings were so far from us that it was never clear if we were clean after, so the flock leader ordered us to leave them alone. To prey only on the warm-blooded ones, who were enough like us, social and grouping together and fearing sharply the rustle in the bushes which said the killer was hiding, waiting, watching . . .

Blood is good when it is warm. Just one sip is all we need. Blood is life and more than life – the knowledge of life, which is what the animals lack and we provide for the Forest. Only those who kill understand life completely; only those who witness the eyes as they dull know the value of what leaves the body with the last breath.

Predators are the cull: we keep the bloodlines clean, the herds healthy, the memories alive. All the memories. None we have killed is forgotten. None we have killed truly dies. Each of our hunts lives forever in the Forest, in the special places of remembrance. We live there, also, alive at once in a dozen times, alive only at the times of the hunt, feeling again each kill: the aurochs, the deer, the boar, the humans. The humans feel fear the most vividly and are hardest to encompass in the moment of death, but we can do it. We must. The Forest requires us to kill all those who see us, so we have learnt how to kill men.

I know how to kill humans, but not the Kill Reborn. She had no fear. In all the untold years I had never met prey that had no fear of me. It changed me, that moment. To look into a human's eyes and see only calm, acceptance, interest – that is not what a hunter sees. But I had seen it. So what was I now? If I were not a hunter, did that mean I was a mortal, like her, subject to death as she was? I feared so. I knew I had to follow this Kill Reborn until I could taste her fear, until the Forest allowed her death. For all humans die. Then I would be a hunter again, and cleansed, and the memory of her death would join the other memories of my hunts.

Memories of death are eternal, kept in the Forest until the sun becomes ripe and is eaten by the gods. The Forest itself is smaller than it was; the places of remembrance fewer and busier than they were, with memories circling through them faster than in the past. This is due to the fair-haired men. But the Forest has withstood much in the past: fire and flood and ice. What is a thousand years? Nothing. Always it has recovered, and it will recover from this. Because we know, we hunters, that if necessary, we could take back the Forest land from the newcomers. I alone culled those first fair-haired men, and we could kill the others. We have had practice.

Although holding their fear and their pain would stretch us, we could do it, if we had to. If we were asked to. If the Forest woke.

LEOF

WITH THISTLE UNDER him and seeming to have taken no hurt, Leof felt steadier, more competent. His clothes were mostly dry by now, which also helped. He followed the directions the horse detail had given him and found the road to Baluchston only ten minutes' ride south. He swung onto it, joining the remnants of Thegan's army, all of them looking bedraggled and quite a few still dazed.

Wherever he could as he passed, he identified sergeants and told them to organise the men into squads so that by sunset, as they approached the outskirts of the town and could see the Lake again on their left, he was at the head of a reasonably well-ordered force, although the men were marching slowly and showed the tell-tale signs of exhaustion, shuffling feet and hanging heads.

'Fire and food in camp,' he encouraged them and was as glad as they were to see the tents and campfires which marked their goal.

He coaxed a canter from Thistle and went ahead to alert the sergeants-at-arms who would be responsible for billeting the men. Several men hailed him boisterously as he entered camp, comrades from both Sendat and Cliffhold. He greeted them with a similar relief. Not all gone. Not all dead.

In fact, looking around he realised that the Lake had been remarkably merciful. There were far more men gathered here than he had expected. He had been stationed almost at the far end of the Lake, and his rag-tag assortment of men were the last in. Although their numbers were much diminished, Leof reasoned that at least half the survivors were still on the other side of the Lake, the Cliff Domain side. If what he saw around him represented the other half, then they had not been as badly hurt as Hodge had suggested. Perhaps he and his men had, indeed, taken the worst beating.

He dismounted and handed Thistle's reins to a young ostler with a nod of thanks.

'Where's my lord?'

'In his tent,' the boy said. Leof was reminded for a moment of Broc, but put the thought aside. There were always casualties in battle.

He found Thegan's tent easily enough. It was placed in the centre of camp. It looked just as it always did on campaign, the brown canvas with gold ties at the corners both workmanlike and impressive, just like my lord Thegan. Leof hesitated at the door flap, then went through.

Thegan was seated at his map table, three of his officers behind him. Leof recognised them and was relieved to see them. They were older than he was, and sensible. He was sure they would see the folly of razing the town.

Thegan looked up as he entered and jumped to his feet.

'Leof!' He strode around the table and clasped Leof's upper arms. 'Gods be blessed!' He smiled with real pleasure and Leof smiled back, warmed and thankful in turn. This was the Thegan who had earned his loyalty.

Since that disastrous night when he had stopped Horst from shooting Bramble in the back, Thegan had been distant with him, particularly when he returned empty-handed after searching for her. He thrust down his guilt that he had in fact found her but let her go. That had been true disloyalty to his lord, and there was no arguing it away. He had wondered, uncomfortably, for weeks afterwards, if he had acted merely to show her that he was not the killer for hire she thought. That her distrust of warlord's men was unfounded. But he thought, bleakly, that it was more likely that he was just too soft to take a woman prisoner. Particularly Bramble, so wild and reckless. It would have wounded his heart to bind her hands and force her back to serve the warlord.

Well, if he couldn't serve his lord by giving him Bramble, he would have to serve him some other way.

'My lord.'

'How many did you lose?'

'I think about half my squad,' Leof answered, sobered.

Thegan clicked his tongue and let go of his arms, moving back to the table and looking down at the map of the Lake that lay there.

'That's the worst we've heard so far,' he said quietly.

'The wind was at our back, my lord,' Leof explained. 'The Lake needed to make sure we were knocked out.'

Thegan looked at the other men, as though Leof's words were significant.

'You think it was the Lake, then?'

'Well, of course . . . what else could it be?'

'The town wasn't touched.' Thegan's tone was grim.

'But, my lord, isn't it known that the Baluchston people have an agreement with the Lake? That it leaves them alone?'

'We know that they, unlike everyone else who settled this Lake, live in safety. The Lake is dangerous, I grant you that. So is the sea, and the storm. But to plan and execute an attack like last night took intelligence, and I do not believe that the Lake has that. Any more than the storm does.'

'Perhaps that is so,' Leof said slowly, wondering for the first time why he had assumed that the Lake was acting on its own behalf, without guidance. Was it just the voice he had heard, or was it all the stories that were told about the Lake, stretching back centuries? Stories about attacking forces befuddled, turned around in the middle of battle so that they were fighting their own side, or gone missing altogether only to turn up weeks later, swearing they had no memory of the time in between. Those stories were part of every child's upbringing in the Domains, and so were stories about the mysterious Lake People, the only original inhabitants who had successfully resisted Acton's forces. And still did.

'Why should it be the Baluchston people who planned it?' Leof said. 'Why not the Lake People?'

'The Lake People are nothing but Travellers who do not travel,' Thegan said impatiently. 'Do you think if they had power like that they would skulk in the reeds like water rats? Do you think they would let Baluchston stand and the ferries run across their precious Lake?' He shook his head. 'No, if the Lake People controlled the Lake they would have taken it back from Baluchston long since. As they haven't, the control must reside in Baluchston.'

'But what would they gain from attacking us?' Leof asked. He wasn't convinced, but he knew Thegan in this mood. No argument would change his mind.

'They hope to maintain their freedom.'

'They have freedom. They're a free town.'

Thegan looked at him, an amused twist at the end of his mouth.

'They *had* freedom. They are clever enough to realise that if I hold both Central and Cliff Domains, and cleared the Lake, their freedom would mean very little.'

Leof paused. The other men were carefully not reacting to that statement. Now was not the time to argue for the continued liberty of the free towns. Towns outside the warlords' control had always been a sore point with Thegan, despite the fact that Acton had established them himself to encourage trade between the Domains. Better to cut to the core of the debate.

'My lord, what if no one controls the Lake? What if it *is* intelligent?'

There was silence in the tent for a long moment. Thegan seemed to think about it, but Leof realised with a shock that he was only pretending.

'If it *is* intelligent,' he said eventually, 'then it will be pleased that we are ridding it of Baluchston. If it is not, then we will destroy those who control it. Each and every one of them.'

Leof felt forced to protest. 'What if it was only a few, or just one enchanter working on his own?'

Thegan did pause at that, then shrugged. 'We'll give them a chance to surrender the enchanter and swear their loyalty. If they don't, we fire the town.'

But if there is no enchanter, if the Lake is intelligent, then you have just invented the perfect reason to destroy a free town, Leof thought. He felt colder than he had when he woke that morning. Because he didn't know if Thegan really believed what he was saying, or if he had just seized the chance to take control of a free town without protest from the other warlords.

'Come, you look like you need some food and a sleep,' Thegan said to him, once again the commander concerned for his men. 'The men need a rest, too. Tomorrow will be soon enough to march on Baluchston.'

SAKER

OR THE FIRST few miles out of Carlion, Saker was surrounded by
other carts, riders and people on foot. The roads, caught between dry-
stone walls, were so clogged that the walkers were faster than the carts.

His disguise was perfect, except that he was travelling alone. So he
stopped and offered a lift to an old couple carrying a baby. They
accepted with relief. The old man climbed into the back of the cart
with some help from Saker; the woman clambered up next to Saker
with more agility. She carried the baby in a shawl tied around her
chest. It was not a newborn. Its curly yellow hair waved in the breeze
as it popped its head up out of the shawl and looked around. Saker
hated it. It was the inheritor of Acton's brutality. With hair like that, it
would never be treated like an animal. Never be spat at, or cursed, or
refused service. He set his heart against it.

Then he wondered, why were they alive? Had they run away so fast
that the ghosts hadn't got to them? He asked his passengers.

'Ghosts? No bloody ghosts, sir, they were demons from the cold
hells! Ghosts can't do what they did!' the man shouted over the noise
of the wheels on the rough road.

'They killed our daughter's husband, they did, right in front of us,'
the woman confirmed.

'And your daughter?'

'Oh, she's been dead these ten months, birthing this one,' she said,
smoothing down the baby's curls.

'They didn't attack you?'

'It was strange, it was,' she said, thinking hard. 'It was like we
weren't even there. Like they only saw him. As though Lady Death had
sent them specially to get him.'

She sounded as though she didn't mind that idea. Saker gathered that the baby's father had been disliked. It worried him, though, that three blond people had been overlooked by the ghosts. Surely they couldn't be Travellers in disguise, too? He thought of the red-headed woman. He would have sworn she was one of Acton's people, but Owl had thrust her aside; protected her, until she threw her life away to protect the man. Useless sacrifice. But if she had old blood, if the blonds beside him had old blood, if so many of the inhabitants had that blood running in their veins . . . where did that leave his crusade?

Perhaps he could refine the spell. Set the barrier higher, so that only those with *enough* old blood would be protected. But how much was enough?

All day, he pretended to be a kind young stonecaster who had been caught in Carlion unawares. He delivered the old couple and the baby to the woman's brother's cottage in a village on the boundary of Three Rivers Domain, left amidst their effusive thanks, and found a room for the night at the local inn.

He sat in a corner of the common room and listened to the talk around him. It ranged from disbelieving to hysterical, from terrified to belligerent. No one spoke of anything but the stories from Carlion. They didn't realise where he had come from and he kept silent rather than be deluged with questions. Halfway through the evening the door opened to let in a family: parents and two young girls, just out of childhood, both with light brown hair like their father. They were carrying bundles of cloths, with oddments sticking out of them: a candlestick, a tinderbox, an empty waterskin. He knew instantly that they were from Carlion, and as soon as the innkeeper realised it, too, she bustled them off into the corner next to him and interrogated the parents.

'We don't know what happened,' the man said. 'We were sleeping, and then the door banged back and these . . . these *things*, like ghosts but real, burst in on us. They had swords, just like warlords' men!'

'I screamed,' one girl said.

'It was like they didn't see us,' the mother added. 'They looked us over but they didn't see us. Thank the gods!' She began to cry, taking off her headscarf to mop up her tears and revealing, not the black hair Saker had expected, but pure gold. 'They killed our neighbours. Both sides. Just slaughtered them in their beds. Half the town's dead!'

The older girl started to cry, too, but the younger set her mouth and sat closer to her father.

'We're not going back there!' the mother said wildly, and the younger girl nodded decisive agreement.

'It's shagging cursed,' the girl said. The mother immediately scolded her for swearing. Saker saw the satisfaction on the girl's face and realised she had planned it that way, to stop her mother crying. She was of Traveller blood through her father, he was sure, even if her mother wasn't. But then why did the ghosts ignore the mother? He would have to smooth out any inconsistencies in the spell next time.

He wondered where to go next. He wasn't ready for Turvite. He would be, soon, but not yet. For Turvite, his army needed better weapons. Mostly they had scythes and sickles. They needed swords. He wouldn't find those in a free town. Inevitably, he thought about a warlord's fort. Fighting a warlord's force would garner many weapons. His army wasn't big enough to do that yet. But if he moved through Central Domain, gathering bones, he could take his force against Sendat, and get all the weapons he wanted.

Saker nodded, forgetting for the moment the red-headed woman who had betrayed her blood. Central Domain. He would stay here and aim for Sendat before autumn.

Then Turvite. He would succeed where the old enchanter had failed. He laughed to himself in the inn chamber. No one had ever been as powerful. His head swam. Loss of blood, he thought. Yes, a time quietly collecting bones would be good for him as well as for his plan. When they attacked Sendat, he would need lots of blood to raise his army.

BRAMBLE

ONCE THEY CROSSED the stream, the horses splashing through the shallow water, the Forest changed to a mix of trees, elm and oak and beech. Now, Bramble felt, she was moving in the Great Forest of her imaginings, the complex, vivid forest alive with bird calls and insect humming and the rustle of small animals and lizards. The trees were giants, particularly the beeches, a kind she had never seen before reaching huge arms to the sky. It could take minutes to move from one side of their canopy to the other. Here, the leaf fall from last winter was soft under the horses' hooves, and the heady, fragrant scent of damp spring earth was enough to make her light-headed.

As they went further along the track, there were more oaks and fewer other trees. Eventually they were riding through a forest entirely made up of oaks – vast, ancient trees that shaded the forest floor almost as thoroughly as the pine trees had. But this part of the Forest wasn't gloomy. The green of the oak leaves and the way they shifted in the breeze let little pockets of light dance across the ground between the trees, which meant there was grass and small plants covering the ground. There were snowdrops, primroses and daffodils.

Her surroundings should have filled Bramble with happiness. But underneath the surface, she could still sense – something. The sense of being *listened* to was very strong. Not exactly watched, the Forest had no eyes. But it was paying attention to them, and the sensation was not pleasant. Somewhat like the pressure of the gods in her mind, but far more alien. The sense of time – endless, unchanging time – was very strong, and made her feel like a mayfly, so short-lived that her life was worth nothing. She and her companions were there on sufferance, and only because she was the Kill Reborn.

The Forest respected killing and its aftermath. The flutter of birds above, the buzzing of insects, the rustle of animals in the undergrowth, these were all sounds of death as well as life. Each of those animals was hunting and being hunted. Bramble had always accepted that she was part of a great intricate web of life and death, of prey and predator, but she realised now that she had accepted it so easily because she had always been the predator.

She would stay that way, she decided. The prey fears, and she had learnt already from the hunter that, in the Forest, fear was dangerous.

Before them the track ended, in a wide circle obviously cleared so wagons could turn, although shrubs and saplings were springing up across the clearing. Beyond, there was only forest.

'Why would anyone bring a wagon all the way out here and then just turn around and go back?' Zel wondered.

'Not a wagon,' Cael answered. 'A sleigh. In winter, the trappers organise for supplies to be brought out. They meet the sleigh, and then it goes back.' He spoke with a little effort, his chest wound still pain-ing him. Safred looked concerned, but said nothing.

'So,' Bramble said. 'Where to now?'

'The lake is east of north from Oakmere,' Safred said uncertainly, her eyes unfocusing as they did when she listened to the gods. Then she shook her head in disappointment. 'That's all I know.'

Bramble pointed ahead and to their right. 'That's that way.'

'That's not east of north,' Cael objected.

'No. We've swung around a bit, following the trail. But it's east of north from Oakmere.'

'How do you know?' Zel asked. The question surprised Bramble. She had thought that a good sense of direction was a gift all Travellers had. She had certainly inherited hers from her Traveller grandfather. It had only ever let her down once, in the pine forest near the Lake, and even there she had been mostly on the right heading. Explaining her certainty was curiously hard.

'I just know,' she said.

Cael shrugged. 'All right, then,' he said. 'Let's go that way.'

Threading through the forest was much slower than riding on the track. There was more time to imagine eyes watching them. Ears lis-tening. Noses smelling. The sense of being listened to, being observed, was getting stronger.

But at least the trees here were centuries old, and beneath them only ferns grew, and mushrooms, so the going was easy. They walked the horses under trees so tall that they were unclimbable, so densely leaved that the sun was invisible. The air grew close and hot, smothering. Bramble found herself becoming more and more tense, ready for an attack that never came.

They reached a stream where she thought they should water the horses, so she dismounted and turned to face the others as they came up. Then she saw that the attack had been going on all the time. Cael, who had been immediately behind her, was shaking with pain and weakness, his face clammy white. His shirt was stained with blood. She went to help him down, and he came heavily into her arms, leaning on her shoulder.

'Why didn't you *say* anything?' Safred said, helping Bramble to sit him down on the grass. Martine grabbed a cup from her saddlebag. She went to the stream to get water while Bramble eased the shirt away from the wound. It didn't look good: red and puffy and still bleeding sluggishly from the tip.

'The Forest is keeping the wound fresh,' he said. 'I can feel it. Nothing to be done.'

Martine came back with the water. 'I think it's safe,' she said. 'It doesn't smell of anything.' Cael drank it gladly and held out the cup for more.

'If Safred can't heal him, we'd better get the Forest to do it,' Bramble said. 'Wait here.'

She knew what she needed, and the edges of a stream were a good place to find them: feverfew, comfrey, heal-all, greenwort. It took her only a few minutes to find them all.

When she came back, Martine was tearing up a shirt for bandages and Safred was washing Cael's wound, but in an unpractised way that made Bramble's mouth twist awry. Never had to learn simple healing, she thought. Just a moment with the gods and it all went away. Live and learn, cully.

'Make a compress of the heal-all and comfrey,' she said to Safred, handing her the leaves. Bramble picked up the cup and crushed some of the feverfew leaves into it, then filled it from the stream and set it to steep on the ground beside Cael. 'It won't be as good as a tisane, but I think we'd better not light a fire here.'

He nodded with an effort.

'It's an odd wound,' she said. 'What made it?'

Safred paused as she wrapped some linen around the plants. Listening hard.

'I cannot name them,' he said slowly. 'They were big. Flying. But not birds. Not bats, either. No fur. Huge. Clawed. One almost took me as a hawk takes a chicken, but I twisted and –' He gestured to his chest. 'Then *I* flew, for a moment!' He tried to smile, turning to Zel. 'Then this little one dragged me out of there.' She reddened a little and mumbled something inaudible.

They managed to get Cael back on his horse and he seemed a little better for the feverfew. Bramble gave the rest of the herbs to Safred and told her to make him a tisane tonight from the feverfew and greenwort.

'I have willow bark,' Martine offered.

'Good. That, too, then. It will help him sleep.'

'How do you know so much about healing?' Safred asked.

Bramble laughed at her. 'Safred, almost every woman in the Domains knows what I know. When you have a sick baby or an accident happens, not everyone can run to the Well of Secrets to be cured!'

Safred flushed and let her horse drop back until she rode next to Cael. Bramble thought she should have felt worse about teasing her – Safred was genuinely worried about Cael. But she didn't. She was too caught up in wondering what would happen when they got to the lake. Surely there would be an altar?

She yearned towards it. She imagined a clearing. The black rock, the familiar presence of the gods. They would be safe there, and Cael could rest – perhaps Safred would find the strength there to heal him.

The light shifted to gold, even through the oak leaves, and the few shadows there were began to lengthen. The sun was setting. The land tilted sharply upwards. They climbed a ridge and they were at the edge of the trees, as though the Forest had been cut off abruptly.

Beyond them there was water, surrounded by a ring of oak trees and then grass that sloped steeply up to the edge. After the darkness of the trees, the water shone brilliantly. Still as ice, it reflected better than any mirror, doubling the rose and pink and gold of the light, the small reddened clouds, the darkening sky. Not quite a lake but more than a pool, it was perfectly circular, and it was the strangest thing Bramble had ever seen.

At the margin, instead of mud or reeds or pebbles, a sheer edge rose up out of the ground, so that the whole lake looked like a big dish which had been almost buried and then filled with water. The edge caught the dying sun and glinted sharply.

In the very centre of the water was a small island, with a black rock altar at its heart. Much larger than most altars, Bramble thought it would be at least chest high on her; perhaps higher. Coloured the normal flat matte black, the rock it stood on gleamed darkly green.

Bramble swung down from Trine and patted her absently, then walked forwards over close-cropped grass, down to the water. The rim around the lake was rock. Or glass. A mixture of both? She had never seen anything like it. A green so dark it was almost black, on the western side, facing her, it reflected every bit of light from the dying sun. She went closer, carefully, and squatted down to study it.

The rim came up above her knees, and the level of water within it was higher than the grass outside, as if the lake truly was a dish. She reached out, waiting to see if the gods would warn her not to touch, but although she could just feel their familiar presence in her mind, they exerted no pressure on her. The rock was mostly smooth – smoother than river stones, as smooth as glass – but cut across with rougher streaks like the darker stripes in marble. It narrowed to a thin edge at the top. She leaned over the edge to look at the inside of the bowl, and found herself staring into water so clear that she could see her own reflection and the bottom of the bowl at the same time, so that it looked as though she were lying on the floor of the lake, looking up. Like a water sprite.

That unsettled her. She pulled back and her wrist grazed across the top of the rim. The edge was so sharp that she didn't realise she had been cut until the blood started to drip; some on the grass, some on the rock rim, some into the water.

As the first drop hit the lake, a wind seemed to shiver across the surface, ruffling the perfect reflection. Bramble shivered, too. Whatever this place was, it was not the home of her familiar gods.

'How are we going to get out there?' Martine asked from behind her.

Bramble stood up, wiping the blood on her breeches.

'Look,' she said.

As the sun dropped lower and the reflection paled, they could see that there were rings of rock leading to the island, like the edge around the lake, just under the surface. They weren't very thick, but they were each no more than a pace apart.

'Stepping stones?' Martine said doubtfully. 'What if we fall?'

Bramble shrugged. 'We get wet. And worse, maybe.'

Safred, Zel and Cael joined them. Cael was pale but looked a little better now he was out of the trees. He bent down to peer at the rock rim.

'Obsidian,' he said.

'Obsidian?' Martine repeated. 'This is *Obsidian Lake*?'

'What's Obsidian Lake?' Bramble asked.

'It's where the first black rock altar fell from the sky,' she replied, her voice faltering a little. 'It's a place from Traveller legend. Not a place for people, they say. Only for the gods.'

Martine was hesitant, and that was so unlike her that Bramble frowned.

'But the gods have brought us here, right?' she asked Safred, who nodded.

'Yes. We are where we are meant to be. We must do the work set out for us.' Her certainty reassured them all, but Bramble made a face.

'You sound like my grandam.'

'I'm sure she was a very wise woman.'

'Wise enough,' Bramble said, 'to know the signs of the Spring Equinox.'

'You have a good sense of time,' Safred said thoughtfully. 'That may be useful. Perhaps it's just as well you became the Kill Reborn instead of the one who was meant to.'

'The one who was meant to?' Bramble felt something tighten in her, but not unpleasantly. It was as though she were about to have a question answered that she had wondered about for a long time. She didn't know what the question was; but the answer was important.

'The gods didn't tell you?' Safred seemed surprised. 'You were supposed to die, you know.'

'At the chasm?' She knew the answer. Of course at the chasm. She relived that moment: the men chasing her, the roan making that extraordinary, impossible jump, and halfway over, her own fall and the roan's shift in mid-air to save her. Then, afterwards, the death-in-life existence she had led. The stonecaster in Carlion had told her – she had died, truly, and her spirit had left her, but the roan had saved her body. She would still be dead inside, if he had not run so fast in her first Spring Chase that she overtook the Kill, snatched his banner, and became the Kill Reborn, symbol of new life. Unlike the other Kill Reborns of history, who just won a race by a big margin, she had been truly reborn.

'Yes,' Safred said. 'The gods helped the roan make the jump, not you. The roan should have gone to Beck, so he could become the Kill Reborn.'

'*Beck*?' The face flashed before Bramble's eyes – a thin, older man with brown hair and a small beard, the face that had led the pack which hunted her to the chasm. She remembered, too, the scars and marks on the roan's hide that Beck had laid there. 'They were going to give him to *Beck*?'

'He was a good rider. Good enough to be a Kill Reborn. He had mixed blood, too, and was certainly a killer. He was suitable for this task.'

Bramble was furious. 'And too bad for the roan, given to a cruel master!'

'Yes,' Safred said quietly. 'Too bad for the roan. But the roan loved you and saved you, to have you instead. So we are here.'

'"Love breaks all fates",' Cael quoted, a slight rebuke in his voice. Bramble knew he was trying to turn her anger away from Safred, and knew that he was right. This wasn't the Well of Secrets' fault. Nor, really, was it the gods'. They were doing the best they could to restore balance to chaos. It was Saker's fault, and he would pay.

She scowled, but looked out at the lake, watching as the ripple of wind died away and the surface returned to pure reflection.

'What did you mean,' Martine asked, '"he was certainly a killer"?'

Safred looked at her wryly. 'Haven't you wondered why you were chosen by the gods? It is because you are all killers, and have deaths to expiate.'

Zel hung her head, but Martine met Safred's gaze coolly.

'I have killed only where I had no choice, to protect my life or the life of another,' she said. 'I have no regret and no guilt.'

Safred nodded. 'That is the attitude of our enchanter,' she said. 'It is good that you share it.' Martine went still for a moment. Safred looked at Zel, then covered Zel's hand with her own. Zel's head came up.

'I did what I had to do,' she said. 'I must pay for it.' Her mouth was firm and Bramble was reminded even more of Osyth. Zel was like stone, as Osyth had been, a person who could not be turned from her course by anything.

Then Safred looked at her.

'I didn't mean to kill him,' she said. 'I don't think I have reparation to make.'

Safred kept looking at her, drawing her somehow so that all she could see was the bright eyes.

'I was not talking about the warlord's man,' she said softly. 'He was not the only one who died because of you.'

Abruptly Bramble was back in the field outside Pless, the roan's head in her lap, the stream flowing past them, guilt and grief and pain pounding her in waves. It had been her fault, and she would live with that forever. She dragged in a deep breath and pulled herself back to the present. 'I have made my apologies for that,' she said angrily. 'It has *nothing* to do with you.' She was furious that this – this *woman* would use her love and grief for the roan to manipulate her. Let her rot in the cold hells, she thought. She doesn't own me.

'"No one wilt ever tame thee",' Safred whispered.

Bramble breathed in sharply in shock, then was strengthened by her anger. 'Shagging right,' she said. 'Get another lackey.' Then she thought about Safred's claim that they were there because of being killers. It made some deep sense that she couldn't quite puzzle out. If the gods needed a killer, she would be a killer indeed; and Saker would be her victim. 'After I do this thing with Acton,' she said, 'can I kill Saker?'

'Who knows?' Safred said wryly. 'No one's told me.'

The black rock stood glinting sharply with light, bright where before it had been dark. It beckoned to Bramble, and to the others, too, she could tell. Martine shivered whenever she looked at it, and Safred completely avoided looking at it. But it won't go away, cully, Bramble thought. Not on your life, or on mine. Or on Maryrose's.

They had only minutes before it was time to walk out to the altar, but setting up camp seemed too mundane a thing to do when the lake shimmered in front of them, reflecting the darkening sky, the first evening star.

Bramble looked after Trine, glad to have something to do to keep her mind off those sharp ridges of rock and the clear water that seemed, somehow, so threatening. Trine was perfectly happy under the trees, but she would not move out onto the short grass that ringed the lake, and Bramble did not try to persuade her. Cael had already tethered the other horses to a tree.

'I'll set up camp while you do whatever it is you have to do,' he said.

'When I come back, I'll try again,' Safred said to him and he nodded before gently shooing her away to join the others.

Safred, Martine and Bramble walked slowly down to the rim almost an hour after sunset, moving towards darkness, with a sky of red and gold and purple clouds behind them. The evening breeze had picked up and whipped the water into small waves. It was chilly but not cold, breezy but not windy, dim but not dark, although the pale spring moon was hidden behind the clouds.

Bramble felt her spirits rising as the night grew wilder, felt a lifting of the heart that was as familiar to her as the beginning of a chase. She went first. She thanked Gorham for making her wear tough boots as her feet would have been cut to the bone at the first step up onto the rim. She found her balance and then stepped towards the next rim of rock. If she fell, she would die. She was quite certain of that, sure beyond words or reason. The gods confirmed it: *Walk carefully*, they said. *Come to us.*

Each step was precarious, and each grew harder as the light faded away. After a handful of steps, she looked back. Safred and Martine were poised on the ridges behind her, reminding her of the Wind City legend, the Sea Woman who walked on water. Bramble shivered a little. The Sea Woman was a nasty spirit, no friend to humans. She shook off the thought and started to enjoy herself, enjoy each moment her foot found the next stepping place and the quick excitement of shifting her balance with a hop so that she moved firmly onto the ridge and still kept her balance. The water was cold in her boots, and her feet began to go numb.

Halfway across, the moon emerged from the clouds and the lake became a bowl of silver, cupping them, the Forest beyond a dark wall. She had the sense that the water itself was curved upwards, that the island truly lay in the bottom of a bowl. It felt dangerous, and Bramble was glad of it. The promise of danger gave her relief from mourning.

She was only three paces from the island, then two, and one – she stepped onto the darker surface of the island expecting to find dirt and grass. Instead, she slipped and fell as her feet slid out from under her. The island was made of the same smooth dark green glass as the lake bowl. She looked up at the altar; it was fused into a spire of the rock so that she couldn't tell where the lake rock ended and the altar began. That felt unchancy. Wrong. She struggled up and planted her feet firmly on the rock, then helped Safred and Martine across safely.

She began to move towards the altar, but Safred stopped her with a hand on her arm.

'I don't know what will happen,' she said, her voice low. 'You will see the past, the gods say, but they don't say how.'

Bramble shrugged. 'Guess I'll find out soon enough.'

Safred smiled tightly, and motioned her towards the altar. Breast-high, it was larger than any Bramble had seen. She came towards it with another familiar sensation. The gods were waiting. The pressure on her mind was there, as it always was at an altar; the hair-raising, spine-chilling stroke along the skin, *beneath* the skin. She took a breath with difficulty, like breathing under water, but before she could lay her hand on the rock, mist began to rise from the altar's surface.

Gentle wisps at first. Then deepening to fog, swirling upwards in a column which flattened out to spread in a dome over them, coming down onto the water and moving outwards, until the sky was blocked, and the land was invisible, and they were encased in a brilliant, moon-lit cloud. Bramble shivered with a simple chill as the mist droplets settled on her skin.

The mist was unchancy, no doubt, but the gods were there, solid in her mind, and she knew the fog was to protect her. She just didn't know from what. They could hear the wind in the Forest, and the waves on the lake, but inside the mist everything was still. Gradually, the stream of mist died away and the altar was left bare, not even damp. She reached out and placed her hand on it.

'Martine,' Safred said quietly. Safred had her listening look on, and Martine's face mirrored hers. She placed the brooch on the altar next to Bramble's hand. It clinked, softly, as she set it down and immediately the wind died in the Forest, the waves subsided, the trees ceased to whisper. There was complete silence as she spoke.

'This is mine by right, by gift. I cede it to you, to the gods of field and stream, of fire and storm, of earth and stone, of sky and wind.' She paused then, and as though prompted further, added, 'I cede it to the gods of water and memory, that good may come of evil, that life may come from death.'

She took Bramble's hand and placed it over the brooch.

For a moment Bramble's hand was caught between the warmth of Martine's hand and the cold of the brooch, then Martine lifted her hand and Bramble's fingers curled around the heavy circle.

'Gods of water and memory, aid your daughter,' Safred said, her voice very gentle. Then she began to speak in the guttural, screeching voice of the dead.

The world grew darker and the land rocked beneath Bramble's feet. The waves were rising. The mere was turning against them. In her head the pressure of the gods intensified. She didn't feel fear, because the pressure didn't leave any room for fear, but it did leave room for action. She turned from the altar and tried to warn the others but as she opened her mouth to tell them to run the waters rushed over them and she was drowning.

LEOF

—

IN THE VERY early morning, Leof woke in the officers' tent with his mother's voice whispering in his ear: 'Go home, little one, go home . . .' His face felt surprisingly cold; when he raised a hand to his cheek he found that he had been crying, but he didn't know for what. His drowned men? His mother? He scrubbed all traces of the tears away, as embarrassed as a child might be, and rolled out of bed. The men around him were still asleep.

Even so early in the morning the latrine pits were busy. He made his visit and went to stand by the edge of the camp, looking towards the Lake, where the houses of Baluchston showed their roofs as black triangles against the paling sky. It was going to be a beautiful spring day. A good day for attacking a town, he thought wryly. A good day for destroying a thousand years of tradition. A thousand years of freedom.

He knew he had to talk to Thegan, and knew also that it would make no difference.

As a rider in the chases, he had loved it when the chases were held at the free towns, because they brought competitors from all over the Domains, all keen to see if their horses were the fastest. That was how he had met Bramble, at a chase in Pless. One of the most prestigious chases, because Pless was a horse-breeding area and had a strong local field as well as the riders like him who brought their horses from far and wide.

He liked the free towns. He liked the sense of purpose in them, even if the purpose was mostly about making silver. He liked the casual warmth of their people, the way they walked with heads high, unafraid. Since he had come to Central Domain he had noticed how few people looked up, in case they met the eyes of a warlord's man and were –

what? Beaten for insolence, perhaps? It was not like that in Cliff Domain, where the warlord's men were a disciplined fighting force, respected for protecting their people against raids by the Ice King's men.

Perhaps my lord Thegan is right, he thought with a kind of despair. Perhaps what this country needs is to be brought together under the rule of one overlord, someone who knows how to keep discipline among his men, someone who could protect the rights of the ordinary people. But whether Thegan was the right person to do that, he did not let himself consider.

Leof knew that no matter what he said to Thegan, Baluchston's freedom was over. The best he could do was prevent the sacking of the town. There were lots of stories about the sacking of towns from earlier wars between Domains – Leof didn't want to be part of one.

He left the gradually lightening sky and went to Thegan's command tent. Dawn was usually a good time to catch Thegan alone.

Thegan looked up from a pile of papers as Leof entered, and smiled at him.

'Just the man I need,' he said. 'I want a thorough tally of who we have lost so that the families can be informed. You know most of the men, don't you, even the Centralites?'

'Yes, my lord,' Leof answered by rote. Then he took a breath and plunged in. 'But there is another duty I would prefer.'

Thegan leaned back a little from his table and pushed the papers away, his eyebrows rising. He looked mocking and suddenly older, as if Leof were an importunate child.

'Prefer? I don't remember asking your preference, officer.'

There was a lump in Leof's throat, which he had to swallow down.

'My lord, I would ask that you let me parley with Baluchston. Let me convince them to surrender.'

'To surrender the enchanter?'

Leof paused. He had to say this just right, or Thegan would take offence. 'My lord, if I were that enchanter, I would have left the town long ago. The town may not be able to produce him.'

'Then –'

'Then they must surrender to us, to prove their good faith,' Leof said hurriedly. 'It seems to me that no matter what they do, only the surrender of the town will prove their good intent.'

Thegan smiled slowly. 'That is very well thought out, Leof. Yes. Good. You may put that argument to the Baluchston Voice. I think they have kept the custom of a Voice, rather than a Mayor.' He paused for a moment, considering that. 'In fact, it could be argued that Baluchston is not, and never has been, a free town. It was not founded by Acton or his son. It keeps the customs of a village. It has no charter with any warlord.' He smiled with genuine pleasure, seeing potential problems with other warlords disappear with that argument. 'It has no claim on anyone's protection. Go and tell them so, and tell them that they have until noon to make up their minds.'

Leof nodded and turned to go, his stomach churning. But he should have known Thegan would not let him go so easily.

'Leof?'

He made sure his face showed nothing as he turned back. Thegan was smiling, but it was the dangerous smile, the one that tightened the corners of his mouth but didn't reach his eyes.

'After you have parleyed, I want that list of the dead by noon.'

Leof nodded. 'Of course, my lord.'

He left the tent with a sense of overwhelming relief, and realised that for a few moments he had been in as much danger as Baluchston.

'Hodge,' he called as the sergeant went past. 'My lord wants a tally of the dead. Get three of the men who can write to make a list. Then come to my tent with an honour guard. We're going to Baluchston.'

He rode in on Thistle, with Hodge and three others on matching bay geldings, Thegan's honour guard horses which had somehow escaped the wave. Men and horses were as polished as a quick brush-up could make them and the Baluchston people stopped in the street to look at them. Their expressions were odd: a mixture of fear and surety, as though they believed that, though the soldiers could try, nothing could hurt them. But the trying would be painful.

Leof had been an officer of one kind or another since he was eighteen, carrying the burden of ensuring his men's safety, but he had never felt responsibility weigh so heavily before. Not soldiers but townsfolk at risk . . . Riding through the town with everyone looking was like the beginning of a chase, when the competitors lined up in front of the crowd. He tried to feel some of the same exhilaration chasing brought, but the stakes were much too high.

Leof knew, theoretically, how to handle this. He could not stop and ask for directions to the Voice's house. Thegan would say that would show weakness. So they rode to the market square, which led directly onto the Lake shore and the ferry wharves. It was disconcerting, to have an open side to a town square, a side which moved and glinted as the current sent the Lake water downstream towards the high, impassable falls that plummeted to the Hidden River. The open side made him uneasy, as though the Lake were watching, as though the ground were shifting under his feet.

He stopped the small troop in the middle of the square and simply waited until, some minutes later, a fat old lady tramped out of one of the shops and came to stand in front of him.

'I'm the Voice,' she said simply. 'My name's Vi. What can we do for you?'

Her voice was dark and somehow comforting, the voice of the wise old women of the fireside stories. Wise old women are sometimes enchanters, Leof reminded himself. He gave the signal to dismount, swung down from Thistle and handed her reins to one of the men, patting her absently on the flank.

'I speak for the Lord Thegan,' Leof said formally, bowing. 'I would have speech with you on his behalf.'

She nodded and led him towards the draper's shop from which she had emerged. A number of other townsfolk watched. Vi looked at them as though to invite them to join the discussion, but they shook their heads.

'Best you handle it, Vi,' one called. She nodded and ducked into the dark interior of the shop.

Hodge began to follow them, but Leof signalled him to wait with the horses. Hodge didn't look happy but he obeyed. Leof relaxed a little. Better to have no witnesses to this.

'We don't bother with a Moot Hall,' she said as she threaded her way past bolts of fabric, skeins of wool and a pile of cured sheepskins. 'We generally have our meetings in here.'

The room beyond was a light-filled kitchen, smelling of fried fish, centred around a large pine table, scrubbed white. Leof stood, unsure. The protocol of a warlord's fort he understood, but not that of a kitchen!

'Sit you down, lad.' Vi smiled with real humour, as though enjoying his uncertainty.

Suddenly Leof laughed. Solemnity wasn't natural to him, and Vi's casual welcome suited him much better than it would have suited any of the other officers. Better to parley with humour and wisdom than with protocol and hostility. He sat down, not at the head of the table, but in the middle, and Vi, as though appreciating his tact, sat opposite him and poured them both some cha from a jug standing ready. Equals. His mouth twitched, imagining Thegan's reaction to that. That sobered him.

On the way into town, Leof had practised a dozen different ways of beginning this conversation, but he discarded them all. It was clear to him that Vi knew why he was here.

'Well, now, my chickling,' she said in her deep, comforting voice. 'Here's a pretty pickle.'

'He wants the town,' he said simply. 'And he'll take it, however he needs to. If you resist, he'll kill every one of you. Not one warlord will object. He'll make it sound so *inevitable* that they won't be able to.'

Vi nodded. 'So?' she prompted.

'So you should surrender. Save the lives of your people.'

Vi's eyes were hooded as she looked down at her mug of cha, nodding. Then she looked up challengingly. 'Might be that the Lake will have something to say about that.'

Leof paused, not sure how to reply. Truth, perhaps, was all the weaponry he had.

'He doesn't believe in the Lake. He . . . he *can't* believe in it, I think.'

She nodded. 'Doesn't mean the Lake will ignore *him*.'

'He says it was an enchanter who called the waters up.'

Vi sniffed with contempt, reminding Leof vividly of his aunty Gret. He paused, then said delicately, 'The question is, *when* would the Lake act, and what would she do? She can't just inundate the town – that would cause more deaths than Thegan. What can she do to protect you?'

'You don't know?' Vi seemed surprised. 'Hmm. Well, best not to tell you, then, I think.' She thought it over. 'I'll go talk to her. This is a decision best left to her.'

'You only have until noon. After that, he attacks.'

Vi drank her cha slowly, deliberately. 'Better if he doesn't,' she said just as deliberately. 'Best if you stop him, lad. Or the Lake might do more harm than she has already.'

The cha was good, and brought him a clearer head than he'd had since the Lake had risen.

'You're Acton's people,' he said. 'Are you sure she'll protect you?'

Vi laughed. 'Oh, lad, we stopped being Acton's people a long time ago. We're Baluch's children. Baluch's and the Lake's. She'll look after us, don't you worry.' She reached across the table with some effort, and patted his arm. 'Looks to me like you might have stopped being one of Acton's people yourself.'

He pushed back from the table and stood up, appalled. 'I am my lord Thegan's man,' he said furiously. 'My loyalty is to him and to my comrades. I came to warn you, to convince you to surrender so that lives would not be lost needlessly. Do not impugn my honour!'

'Oh, lad,' Vi said, sympathetically. 'You've got more honour in your little finger than Thegan has in his whole body.'

'Until noon. You have until noon by the grace of your lord Thegan.'

She shook her head. 'He's no lord of mine, lad, nor ever will be. But I'll talk to the Lake and see what she says. Won't be back by noon, though. I'll have to go out to the deep water and that takes time. Sunset, say. I'll be back by sunset. Do what you can to stay his hand until then.'

Leof turned on his heel and walked out without replying. Stay his hand? Might as well try to stop a storm. Baluchston was doomed.

ASH

RIDING SOUTH OUT of Oakmere felt wrong to Ash. For one thing, he wasn't comfortable on a horse, and the chafing from his last ride was already making itself felt. For another, it felt disloyal to send Martine off with the others, even though he couldn't take her where he was going.

He had woken and gone through the process of leaving Oakmere with a fragile shell of normality carefully built around him. He pretended that nothing was wrong, but he knew that Martine wasn't fooled. Maybe not Bramble, either. But what could he do about it? He couldn't change who he was, no matter how many people he disappointed. Now, as he rode, it felt like there was an empty place on his belt, where the stones should have hung.

They had reached the beginning of the ascent to the Quiet Pass by the time he came back to himself.

'Um, south?' Flax asked hesitantly. 'Just "south"?'

Flax had apparently been waiting for his attention to return. The lad, it was clear, was good at reading moods.

'I couldn't tell her more. We're going to the place that is not talked about,' Ash said, reluctant to say even that much. He shot Flax a glance and then looked more closely as he realised the words meant nothing to him.

'Where'd that be, then?' Flax asked.

'Your father must have taken you there?' Ash was astonished. Unless he had misunderstood, Flax had been on the Road all his life, and so had his parents until recently. But Flax shook his head.

Ash didn't know what to say. It wasn't his job to tell Flax about the Deep. It was his father's. In fact, it was forbidden to speak of it.

'Your father was a Traveller?' He had to make sure, before he said anything.

Flax nodded. 'Aye, he were.'

Flax was certainly talking like a Traveller, although back at Oakmere, he had chattered to Bramble as though he'd been born a blond. Ash shrugged that away. He spoke mostly like one of Acton's people himself, after intensive training by Doronit. Lots of Travellers spoke with two voices. But he had to make sure Flax had the right to go to the Deep.

'And your grandfather? Your father's father?'

'He died when Da were a baby. Da were brought up by his mam, Radagund the Horse Speller.'

Even Ash had heard of Radagund. Flax was very proud of his famous grandmother. But it explained why he didn't know about the Deep. His grandfather had never taken his father there. But surely other Travelling men could have?

Delicately, he asked, 'Was your grandam friendly with other Travellers?'

Flax shrugged. 'I suppose. She worked mostly for Acton's people, though. Travellers don't have horses, much.'

So, here he had a young Travelling lad who hadn't heard of the Deep. Well, there was no doubt he had a right to know, even if Ash wasn't the perfect person to tell him. But there was the prohibition against speaking of the Deep outside. He had to respect that.

'Before I tell you where we're going, you have to promise not to repeat anything I say. To anyone. Especially women. But not even to other male Travellers. If you do . . . you will die.'

'What, you'd kill me?'

Ash looked down at the ground, then straight into Flax's eyes, mouth firm. 'If I had to.'

Flax's eyes widened, and then he grinned, as though it was an adventure.

'I promise.'

Ash wasn't sure he trusted any promise from Flax, but he *was* sure that after the demons at the Deep had him, he would keep the secret.

'We are going to a place . . . a place where men go. Men of the old blood. Only men.'

Strongly interested, Flax leant forward in his saddle to stare more directly at Ash. Cam increased her pace in response, but Flax pulled her back to a walk.

'What for?'

Ash hesitated. 'That depends. It's a craft thing. What they do depends on who they are . . . how they make a living. What do you do?'

'Me? Oh, I sing,' Flax said.

Ash felt like he'd been thumped simultaneously in the stomach and the head. Why hadn't anyone *said*? Because Martine didn't know and the others didn't know it mattered.

'A singer?' he forced himself to ask, thinking, Please, gods, make him bad at it.

'Mmm,' Flax said. He launched into a cheery song about a summer's day.

> *Up jumps the sun in the early, early morning*
> *The early, early morning*
> *The early dawn of day*
> *Up wings the lark in the early light of dawning*
> *The early light of dawning*
> *When gold replaces grey.*

Ash remembered his mother singing that song. He remembered learning it. Flax's voice rose as clear and full as a nightingale's. His tenor could have been designed to match with Ash's mother's soprano. Ash could hear his mother singing the words in his head, and they blended so perfectly with the beauty of Flax's voice that it brought tears to his eyes.

Ash knew, sickeningly, what would happen at the Deep. His father, finally finding the son who would complete their music, who would enable them to perform all those songs that needed two strong, perfect voices as well as the flute and drum. All the descants, all the harmonies, all the counterpoints. They could even sing the sentimental duets that the inn crowds so loved, because Flax wasn't their real son, so there was nothing unnatural about him and Swallow singing love songs together.

No doubt he would teach Flax *all* the songs.

'Come on, sing along,' Flax said cheerfully, and started the second chorus.

For a long moment, Ash battled red rage: the desire to smash Flax's face, to leap upon him, drag him off the horse and slam his head against the road until there was no voice left to torment him. He shook

with the desire, and the only thing that stopped him was the memory
of promising Zel that he would look after Flax. Mud stopped in the
middle of the road and shivered, too. Ash's hands clenched on the
reins. It wasn't Flax's fault, he told himself. But he had to find someone to be angry with. The shagging gods! he thought finally, seizing on
the idea with relief. They don't care who they hurt, what they do.
They're the ones who brought us here. It's *their* fault.

With an effort, Ash took a breath and let it out, hearing Doronit's
voice in his head saying, 'Control. A safeguarder must have control.'
He took a second breath, a third, a fourth, and then felt calm enough
to say, 'I don't sing.'

'Everybody sings!' Flax said, but his voice was uncertain as he
looked at Ash's face.

Ash shook his head. 'Not me.'

Flax looked oddly at him, hesitating about whether to ask more
questions. Ash felt both irritated and protective of him. The boy was
his responsibility. He had promised Zel. Although she couldn't have
known what it would require of him, he would keep his word.

'It's good that you're a singer,' Ash said, with an enormous effort.
'My father will be able to teach you what you need to know.'

Flax nodded and stayed, blessedly, silent. As they continued up the
long slope that led to the mountain ridge, passing the occasional cart
or rider, Ash wondered over the fact that most people would think that
fighting Sully and his friend when they were trying to capture Bramble
was hard. That was easy, so easy, compared to *not* hitting Flax.
Compared to handing Flax over, safe, to his father, and saying, 'I have
found a singer for you.'

Which he must do. Because he had promised Zel. Then he wondered if Zel would thank him for that, if Flax found a way to Travel
without her.

FLAX'S STORY

THAT NIGHT TWO years back it all changed, we were down the road apiece before I spoke up. 'Sure you don't want to go on back?' I asked her.

Zel shook her head. 'Never no more,' she said, so quiet-like I could hardly hear. 'Never no more in that place.'

Well, we'd been Travelling together long enough for me to know when to keep my mouth tight closed, so I just hoisted the pack higher on my back and fell in step beside her.

It were a fine night, at least, and no suffering to be walking the roads under the new moon. I wished I could sing, but there were still three months to go then till my year was up. They say if a boy sings within a year of his voice breaking, it's gone for good. I wouldn't risk it, not for nothing. It's hard enough being without a voice for a whole twelvemonth — I couldn't keep me in my right mind if I lost my music for good and all. So we just walked.

After a few leagues, Zel stirred herself. 'There's a good stopping place near the stream in the withy hollow,' she said. 'We'll lie there.'

It were always Zel who decided where we stopped, where we went. When I were littler, I used to stravage her about it, but I know better now. 'Tisn't a thing in the world can push Zel from the path she's chosen. Earthquake wouldn't do it, nor death, neither, I reckon. Truth to tell, it were just being the little brer what made me tickle her about it anyway. I didn't know enough to make any choices. Now, I know more than she did then, and that's enough to know she chooses better'n me, most times.

Maybe not this time, though.

Maybe this time she were turning her back on a good thing, and maybe it were for me.

See, there were this man in the last town, in Gardea, and he were head over ears taken with Zel. Hanging around the tavern every night, digging in his purse for silver, clapping hard after we finished juggling and tumbling. Oh, he were smitten, hovering like a honey wasp over fallen fruit. Aegir, his name was. A cobbler.

Well, she's never one to turn a good-looking man away, not our Zel. So she went off with him one night, two, then three, but always came back before morning, grinning like a cat.

On the fourth night she came raging in, kicked the straw into a heap and threw herself down onto it loud enough that I knew she wanted to talk. We didn't have a lantern – not many tavern keepers let us have a lantern in the stable, for fear of fire – but my eyes were dark-ready, and I could see she was fuming.

'He wants to *marry* me!' she said, fierce and low, like it were an insult, like our own parents wasn't good and married before they had us.

'I said to him, "You don't know me," and he *laughs*. He laughs and says, "Sure I know you, lass, inside and out." Thinks he's so clever!'

'So what'd you say?'

'I didn't say. I just got on up and walked right out of there.'

She settled down to sleep as though she'd finished even thinking about it, but I couldn't. I could see that cobbler, not understanding, lying bewildered in the dark somewhere.

Next night he were there, waiting for her after the act. But she pushed on past him like he were thin air, and we grabbed our packs and took the road, with him following like a duckling after its mam, shaking his head and trying to get her to speak with him. Zel kept her mouth tied up and her eyes down until he dropped back, still bewildered.

Myself, I think if he hadn't said he knew her, she mighta stayed. She don't like being known, our Zel. She don't like strangers knowing her business, she don't like family, even, knowing what she's thinking. Much less a cobbler from a tavern. She mighta stayed a bit, if he hadn't said that.

Not for long, 'cause she's a Traveller; or maybe she thinks she has to be one, because of me. There were no room in that cobbler's life for a brer who can't earn his keep 'cept by juggling in the taverns.

She knows I couldn't live in a town year round. It were hard enough the winter before, living with Mam and Da because I caught a killing

fever, and couldn't take the road. I couldn't survive a spring indoors.
But I think she were walking so hard away from that place 'cause some
part of her wanted to stay, wanted that cobbler and that nice featherbed instead of straw in the stable with me. I thought, maybe some
day that part'll be stronger than the part that wants to take the Road
with me.

When we got to the stream near the withy hollow, there was
Travellers already there. But it were near moonset, and we was tired,
so Zel just went on down and said the Travellers' greeting, 'Fire and
water'.

There was three of them, a mam and two brers, twin men fully
grown. They had a fire going well, and they was roasting turnips and
hedgehogs.

They nodded at Zel, and then at me. 'Fire and water and a roof in
the rain,' the mam said, very polite. 'Share our fire.' Which were nice
of her, for, say what you will, there are Travellers on the Road I
wouldn't sleep easy near, let alone opening the fire circle to.

Zel looked sideways at her and at me, but we sat down and spread
out our food: waybread and dried apples and ewe's cheese. We all
shared and ate merrily enough, then Zel got out her little balls and juggled a time or two, for thanks.

They were tinkers, they told us. The mam was Aldith, and the twins
were Ber and Eldwin. They were like as the two wings of the one bird,
both dark-haired and dark-eyed, but the one, Eldwin, was a tad more
heavyset and looked after Ber, passing him food like Zel did for me.
The mam, too, fussed over him some, though he seemed hearty
enough, and laughed a lot.

We sat, staring at the fire, like you do after a long day and a hard
walk. It were peaceful, for a time. Then a cold shiver passed right
through me and I looked up. It were quiet, suddenly. The mam and
Eldwin was watching Ber, holding their breaths.

Ber shook his head, his eyes gone blank and wide in the firelight. I
felt behind me for a heavy bit of wood, for I've seen men's eyes go like
that in a baresark fury, but he didn't move. The fire dipped down to
embers, like something was eating the light.

Eldwin said, 'Oh, protect us from demons.' The mam just moaned
a little and rocked to and fro. Zel was tense beside me, ready to run or
fight. Then Ber spoke.

'This fire circle,' he said, 'is closed to murderers.' His voice were quiet and pleasant, like you'd say 'morning to a friend. Like he didn't know what he were saying. 'There is a murderer here,' he said. Next to me, Zel had her hand on her boot knife, easing it out of the sheath.

'A kin murderer,' Ber said, or maybe it wasn't Ber, 'cause he were foaming a bit at the corners of his mouth, and the mam were rocking hard and stuffing her shawl in her mouth to stop herself from screaming.

'Why didst thou kill thy mam?' Ber asked Zel. She'd let go the knife and were staring at him like he were the entrance to the cold hells itself. I had no breath in my body, and my heart pounding were like a wind in my ears.

'Why didst thou kill thy mam?' the thing inside Ber asked again, its eyes fixed on Zel. She were sweating and shivering, both, as she resisted that voice.

'Why didst thou kill thy mam?' it asked, and no living being coulda denied it an answer.

'She was going to kill Flax!' Zel shouted suddenly. 'She had the pillow over his face, smothering the life out of him. It was her or him.' She quieted. 'Her or me,' she said. 'Her or both of us.'

'This fire circle,' it whispered, 'is closed to murderers.'

Then it left Ber, as swift as it came, and the warmth came back to the night air and the fire sprang up high again. Ber closed his eyes and fell sideways. Eldwin leapt to catch him. They laid him down on the grass and poured water into his mouth and patted his cheeks until he stirred.

The mam looked at Zel and me, sitting frozen in our places.

'Wind at your back,' she said. The Travellers' farewell. So we took our packs and we walked out of the hollow and onto the cold road without another word.

We walked along in silence.

'It were true, Flax,' she said finally. 'It were her or us.'

'Because of me,' I said. 'Because you wouldn't leave me.'

'She were mad on silver, you know that. Having us both to stay all winter, it were too much for her. Eating them out of house and home, she said we was.'

'Because I were sick,' I said. 'If I'da been well we coulda taken the Road.'

'That's so.'

There's nothing on Earth or under it can sway Zel once she's made

a choice. She made up her mind a long, long time ago that I were hers
to look after, hers to guard. This were no different.

But I'm not the little brer I were. Already I'm taller than her.

Walking down that road, all I could think on was, sometime or
other, my choice and Zel's choice would go different ways.

And what then?

BRAMBLE

BRAMBLE BECAME AWARE of a light. A candle floating in a small dish of water. Darkness around it, and everything blurred. She tried to look at the candle, but her eyes wouldn't obey her. They looked up, instead, to the horse that was standing quietly before her. Bramble assessed it automatically, the part of her mind that Gorham had trained noting its points: a short, stocky bay mare, a pony, really, but with heavy bones and a thick coat, bred for endurance in a cold climate. Her hands, of their own volition, rose to fasten the strap of the bag attached to the front of the saddle, but her eyes remained fixed on the saddle, as though she could do this job without thinking about it. As she could, normally.

It was a strange saddle, with a high pommel that formed two horns at the front and a matching pair of horns at the back. The stitching was large and it had a single girth plus a breastband and a breech strap which went around the rump. This saddle was clearly designed so the rider would find it hard to fall off. It was well-made and solid and would be reassuring to the rider. But Bramble knew there was no saddle like it anywhere in the Domains.

The saddlebag attached, her eyes dropped to her hands. A man's hands. Abruptly she was aware of her private parts. Oh, gods, that felt so . . . *wrong*.

She never allowed herself to be afraid, but now she was, even while she recognised that what she was seeing and feeling was the result of the spell. She was *inside* someone – maybe one of her ancestors? Seeing what he saw. The pony moved with a slight jingling of bridle. I'm hearing what he heard, she thought. She could smell, too, the familiar scents of a stable with another odour underlying it. The tallow candle, maybe, made from an unfamiliar animal.

Not only sight and smell and hearing, but everything else, too. Bramble realised that 'her' heart was beating fast. The man was excited, or anxious, or happy. She didn't know which. Couldn't guess. Couldn't, thank the gods, hear his thoughts. All she could do was observe.

She tried hard to make him drop his gaze to the floor. But no matter how much she concentrated, her will had no effect.

Like a familiar embrace grown suddenly too tight, she felt the presence of the gods. Were they warning her to make no changes, to leave everything as it was? She stopped trying to control the man, and the pressure eased immediately.

Instead, she felt the gods' attention turn to the doorway, which opened to let a woman enter. She was bundled up, with a baby in a sling across her chest, and Bramble couldn't see her face within the hood made by her shawl.

The woman came forward into the small circle of light, skirting the horse casually, with a hand on its rump. It flicked its ears at her and whoofed a great breath out in a friendly fashion. She moved towards where the man stood.

'Gris,' she said, putting back her shawl. She was very young and beautiful in that corn golden way of Acton's people, eyes like a summer sky and cheeks as pale as milk. Bramble had always disliked girls like that – they were often stupid and flighty, too obsessed with their own good looks to notice anyone else. But this girl was staring at the man with great concentration. Oddly, it felt like she was staring into Bramble's eyes, yet couldn't see her.

'Asa,' he replied. Bramble felt sick to her stomach. It was a horrible thing, to feel one's lips move and words come out without any control. She remembered for a moment the Traveller boy in the inn in Sandalwood, who had been taken over by a demon. Had it been like this for him? She tried to pull back from the man's body, to reduce her awareness of him to what he saw, just what he saw. She was a little successful. The feel of rough cloth against his back receded. The sense of his genitals faded a little. At least he wasn't attracted to the woman. As soon as she had come in his heart had slowed, and her beauty made no impression on him at all. Asa, Bramble thought. That was the name of Acton's mother. She was reliving the past.

For the first time, she wondered if perhaps she could *change* history. If Acton died now, the Domains would never be invaded. The original inhabitants would be safe. Perhaps Acton's people would die instead, she thought. They are both my people. At that thought, the pressure from the gods increased, as though they were agreeing with her. She relaxed. I will make no changes, she promised them. I will merely watch, and discover what we need to know. The pressure diminished immediately, but didn't disappear.

Bramble concentrated on what Gris and Asa were saying.

They were speaking a language she did not know. Some of the words were almost familiar, but pronounced oddly. The pressure of the gods increased in her mind, sending the voices fuzzy and warbling, then they steadied and she could understand what was being said. The gods had given her the ancient language as though it were her own.

'It's all ready,' Gris said. 'There's enough food to get you home. Do you have the things?'

From beneath her shawl, Asa produced some clothing and swaddling bands.

'Will they believe it?' she asked with intensity.

He nodded. 'The cliff is an ancient sacrifice place. If they find your clothes and the baby's swaddling there, they'll assume you readied yourself for sacrifice and jumped.'

'Naked?' she said doubtfully.

Gris smiled. Bramble could feel the face muscles moving, but she couldn't tell what kind of smile it was. It didn't feel happy.

'That is the way for sacrifices. They won't question it once I tell them about our conversation. How you couldn't bear to live with Hard-hand anymore. How the baby reminded you too much of him. And how I suggested you make a sacrifice to the gods in reparation for his murder.'

She looked doubtful. 'Make sure they don't blame you.'

His mouth set firmly. The cheek muscles clenched. 'I will,' he said. Bramble could hear the determination in his voice. So could Asa. She nodded, then looked down at the covered baby. She drew the shawl away from his face and Bramble saw that he had inherited his mother's gold hair. He was not very old; no more than a month, maybe younger. Gris touched the baby's cheek softly with the back of one finger.

'Look after Acton,' he said. 'He is my heir.'

She smiled then, a sweet smile, and nodded. Bramble tried to get a better glimpse of the baby's face, but Gris was looking at Asa.

'I will see you some other day,' she said, and kissed his cheek. Bramble felt a flush creep up his face, but there was no response in his loins. He boosted Asa into the saddle and held the door open for her. She and the baby rode out into a windy, cloudless night and waters rose up around Bramble, as they had at the altar. This time she didn't fight them, but it was still unpleasantly gut-wrenching, the sensation of being overwhelmed, of actually dying, as strong as it had been the first time. She could easily be afraid, she thought, though she had given herself to the gods and had to trust in them. But it was hard to trust when the waves seemed intent on drowning her, on thrusting her down into darkness.

The sensation of goosebumps on her skin woke her. She was cold. She could tell she was thickly clothed, but she was still cold. She badly wanted to shiver, but her body wouldn't cooperate. Vision came slowly. She was in a big hall, with a fire in a circular fireplace in the middle of the room. There was no chimney. The smoke from the fire streamed upwards to a hole in the roof. There were shuttered windows without any chinks of light. Either they were wadded against the cold or it was night.

Bramble noticed all this with difficulty, as though the person whose body she now observed from saw dimly. The body felt vaguely unwell and sluggish. But at least it was a woman. She was sitting at a table on a backless bench or stool.

The fire was too small to heat more than a tiny circle around it, but the people in the hall didn't seem to notice. There were twenty or so men sitting at long tables and eating from bowls. They were full-bearded and long-haired; their blond hair tied in plaits on either side of their face or loose down their back. They were dressed in leather and homespun and boots with the fleece left on the inside. Some women were sitting with them but more were serving. They wore long dresses, to the ground. That must make it hard to get around, Bramble thought. Although she habitually wore breeches herself, most women in the Domains wore loose trousers under a full knee- or calf-length skirt. It was a good combination of modesty and practicality, she'd always thought, though she didn't bother much about modesty herself. Those long dresses were an invitation to trip.

The women carried bowls and spoons and bread on wooden plates from another room. The kitchen, Bramble supposed. There were children of all ages everywhere, the older ones sitting at the table, the younger ones running around and shrieking as they chased each other. Bramble had an impression of metal glinting above her head, but the woman she inhabited was too used to this room to look at the roof.

Then a woman with gold hair in two thick plaits came into view, carrying a bowl which she put down in front of the woman. It was soup and it smelled good, of lamb and barley.

'Here you are, Ragni,' she said.

'Thanks, lass,' Ragni replied. Out of the corner of her eye Bramble could just see the golden-haired woman. Yes, it was Asa. She looked much happier now. Then a toddler with her own bright gold hair ran up to her and grasped her by the legs. Ragni looked at him and her face creased in a smile.

'May the gods bless him, he's getting so tall!' she said. Her voice was quavery and when she reached out a hand to touch the child's cheek, it was wrinkled and spotted with age. Bramble was again conscious of how weak she felt. I should remember how this feels, she thought. I should have been more patient with Swith and his cronies when they complained about getting old.

'He's getting so cheeky!' Asa said, but she smiled as she swung the little boy up into her arms.

'Food!' he demanded. 'More!'

'You've had your dinner, Acton, and there's no more until the men have finished eating,' Asa said firmly.

'Acton man!'

Ragni, Asa and a couple of men sitting nearby laughed.

'Aye,' one of them said, 'you're a little man already, aren't you? Here, have some of ours.'

Asa smiled at the man, the only red-head in the room. He held another toddler on his knee – an even paler blond than Acton – and was feeding him soup from his own bowl.

Asa put Acton down on the bench and the little boy on the man's lap wriggled down happily to sit next to him. Acton grabbed the piece of bread the young man held out. The other child held out his own hand for some.

'Share with Baluch, Acton,' Asa said. Acton stuck his lip out and shook his head. Elric laughed and handed another piece of bread to Baluch.

'You're too soft on him, Elric Elricsson,' Asa said with mock severity. Elric ducked his head and smiled and continued to share his soup
with both boys. Acton swung his legs and grabbed for the spoon.

'No, Act'n,' Elric's child said. 'Da's spoon!'

'That's right, Baluch!' Asa said, and made Acton give it back to Elric.

'Let me know when you've had enough of him,' she said to Elric,
and went back to the kitchen.

'Wooing the babe so you can woo the mother, eh?' Ragni chuckled.
'Well, your own wife's been in her grave long enough, I'll grant you.
It's not a bad idea, lad, but you'll have to do more than share some
soup. She's still the chieftain's daughter, and she's covered herself in
glory these past years.'

Elric was bright red with embarrassment. 'Aye,' he said. 'I know.
That's why I'm off in the spring.'

'Trying to cover yourself in glory, too? Make sure you don't cover
yourself in your own blood and guts instead. Glory costs too much,
sometimes.'

'I don't care what it costs,' Elric said, looking towards the kitchen.
'Whatever it costs will be worth it.' Bramble felt the shiver that meant
the gods were listening and grieved for the young man. Nothing good
ever came of an oath like that.

Then the waters rose again and washed away the sight of the little
gold-haired boy putting his face down into the soup bowl and slurping
loudly. Somehow, although she was not conscious of having a body of
her own, she felt herself smiling. It was hard to believe that this little
scamp would grow up into the murderer and despoiler she knew him
to be. The man who would slaughter thousands, and laugh while he
did it, and then set up the whole system of warlordship which still
tyrannised her country. Bramble felt her smile begin to fade, and then
all sensation was swamped, as wave after wave broke over her until
she felt nothing, saw nothing but the black of bottomless water.

Hearing came first. Panting, the thud of feet on the earth, and a swish-
ing sound Bramble couldn't identify. She was moving, fast, shifting
from side to side. The panting was her own breath, loud in her ears.
She was holding something.

Her sight cleared as a sword came down towards her head, just like
the sword that Thegan's man had aimed at her, but there was no Ash

here now to save her. She had no time to feel anything, not even fear. Before she could react, her body swung its arms up and blocked the stroke with its own sword. Wooden, not steel. It was not a warlord's man attacking her, but a boy, aged eight or nine years old. A boy with shoulder-length golden hair caught in two plaits at the front.

'Hah!' he shouted, and lunged forwards. The tip of his sword hit Bramble – hit the boy Bramble was inhabiting – just under the chest bone. He was wearing a padded jacket, but even so it hurt. She felt the pained exclamation making its way up his throat, and felt him bite it back. She understood that. Show no fear. Show no reaction to those trying to hurt you. Don't let Acton the bully scare you.

Then Acton grinned and clasped his opponent around the shoulders. Although he was not much taller, he seemed far sturdier.

'Baluch, that was a great match!'

The boy smiled, widely. Bramble became aware that they were surrounded by an audience of other boys and a few men, who were all stamping their feet and clapping with enthusiasm.

Baluch raised his hand in acknowledgment.

'How long did I last, Da?' he asked one of the men. Elric Elricsson, a few years older – and with only one arm. The right sleeve hung empty. So glory had had a high price, Bramble thought. I wonder if it got him what he wanted?

'A count of ninety,' Elric said, smiling. 'Well done, lad.'

'That's better by fifteen than anyone else,' another older man said approvingly. All the other men were greying or bald. Old men. Where were the young ones?

The old man turned to Acton. 'You'd better watch yourself, little rooster, he might knock you off your perch.'

Acton laughed heartily, but not in mockery. It was simple enthusiasm, Bramble saw. He was brightly, vividly alive and everyone there seemed to turn towards him, to angle themselves so they could see him. The other boys began a scuffle, looking out of the corner of their eyes to see if Acton was watching. Showing off for him. He didn't notice.

'Baluch could be better than me, *I* think,' he said. 'He thinks faster. He just needs to practise more.'

Elric nodded. 'That's what I keep telling him.' He cuffed Baluch lightly on the back of the head. 'Practice. That's the secret. But he's always off with his harp and his drum.'

His voice was both faintly accusatory and proud. Bramble knew

that tone. Her mother had used it whenever she talked about the food that Bramble brought home from the forest.

Acton let go of Baluch's shoulders and slapped him on the back.

'He makes the best songs,' he said with admiration. Elric laughed.

'Maybe so, maybe so. But songs are for after battle, and you won't survive to get to the songs unless –'

'Unless I practise more. Yes, Da,' Baluch said, with humour and resignation.

It still felt very odd to Bramble, to have someone else use her mouth and her tongue, to feel her body move and speak, it seemed, without her volition. But she was becoming accustomed to it, to distancing herself from the sensations so she could study Acton and her surroundings.

The group of boys was breaking up, allowing Bramble to see past them to the horse yard and the countryside beyond. Despite the summer-gold grass which covered its bones, it seemed barren to her, devoid of trees except for a few birches on the leeward side of hollows and small ridges. It was easy to tell which way the wind blew here – always from the snow-covered mountains, stunting and bending the trees until their top branches almost swept the ground. The mountains curved around, setting a barrier against the sky, the snow glowing orange and pink with the sunset. She had never seen mountains like these before – in comparison, the peaks near Golden Valley were mere foothills. She wanted Baluch to stand and stare at them, but he turned and followed Acton and the others towards a long building which she supposed was the hall she had been in earlier.

There were outbuildings beyond it – stables and byres, houses and animal enclosures. As she meshed her senses more fully with Baluch's, Bramble could smell the animals – horses, pigs, the wet-wool reek of sheep. She heard cows in the distance, saw hides stretching on drying frames. The frames were made from bones lashed together with leather strips. Timber was scarce, then. Valuable. As Baluch's eyes skimmed across the darkening grasslands, Bramble longed for the trees of home.

Baluch pulled a small wooden pipe from his belt and put it to his lips as he walked. He played a quick, flickering melody which made everyone increase their pace until they were striding along fast. Bramble wished that she could make music like this. She could feel his delight at the effect the tune was having. Then Acton halted, suddenly, and turned to look sideways at Baluch. It was a glance full of mischief and amusement and it made him seem older than he was.

'Stop it!' he ordered, half-laughing. 'I'm not marching to anyone's tune!'

Baluch smiled. Bramble was beginning to get a sense of this boy's feelings. He was half sorry that his trick had been recognised, but also pleased that Acton was asserting his independence. He didn't really want to control people. Or at least, he didn't want to control Acton. Bramble knew that feeling, too. It was how she had felt about Acton the stallion, back in Pless. Famed for his wild strength and impossible to ride, the stallion had been a symbol to her of something she felt in herself. She had been glad every time she looked at him that something, some fellow creature, had refused to be tamed, as though that was a promise of equal wildness for herself.

Baluch stared at Acton, smiling, and Bramble stared too. He didn't look like a mad killer. He looked like a friendly, energetic boy who was used to being very, very good at things, better than anyone else, with a touch of the arrogance that that brought. He's a chieftain's grandson, Bramble thought, remembering the old woman's words to Elric Elricsson. Her resentment at warlords rose up in her at the thought, but it was hard to sustain when Acton punched Baluch lightly in the arm and said, 'Race you to the hall.'

They sprinted off together, Acton in the lead, while the waters rose up and covered Bramble once again.

SAKER

THE NEXT DAY, Saker turned north from Three Rivers Domain and headed upriver towards Pless, into Central Domain. He had consulted his scrolls at length the night before, and had mapped out a wandering course that would let him visit all the massacre sites in the songs Rowan had shared with him. It would take him weeks, but that was all right. He had time.

He would not mention to anyone that he had come from Carlion. He was just a stonecaster, travelling the roads looking for customers, as he had been so many times before.

He considered raising the ghost of his father, Alder, to tell him the good news about Carlion, but he was so tired. Too much blood had been needed for Carlion. He would raise his father next time, so Alder could watch the invaders die, and be proud of him.

It was a fine day, and Central Domain was pretty country. Saker hummed as his horse ambled along the dusty roads, and did not admit to himself that he was glad there would be weeks before the next deaths.

MARTINE

'DO WE MOVE her?' Martine asked Safred.

Bramble lay sprawled across the rock at the base of the altar, her face scowling in concentration although her eyes were closed. She moved, twitched, frowned again.

The mist surrounded them still, spreading the moonlight into a blanket of silver around them. Martine didn't trust it, even if it did come from the gods.

Ever since Bramble had cried out in some kind of warning and collapsed at their feet, Martine had been fighting a sense of outrage, a feeling that no human should go through what Bramble was enduring. Her Sight told her that it violated more than time and space; it hacked at Bramble's identity and the centre of who she was. Who knew what this experience would do to her?

'I think we must,' Safred said, with the look on her face that meant she was listening to the gods. Martine listened, too, but although she could sense their presence they had never talked to her except through the stones. She was not like her daughter Elva, whose mind was taken over by the gods as casually as she might slip on a coat. She sent a prayer to whatever gods were listening for Elva's safety, and the safety of her husband Mabry and the baby Ash, back in Hidden Valley. Their home there had seemed a bastion of warmth and security, but nowhere was secure when ghosts carried weapons and used them for dark revenge.

As they stood, trying to decide what to do, the mist vanished as rapidly as it had come, leaving Martine feeling defenceless and exposed. It was growing dark rapidly, and the moon went behind the clouds. Martine dreaded the journey back across the sharp-edged rings of rock that were the only stepping stones. She wasn't even sure it was possible.

'How can we?'

Safred gnawed at her lip. 'The gods say, her spirit is in the water now, and the water knows her blood. We can float her back.'

'Put her in the *lake*?' Martine shivered with a deep reluctance. 'I think I'd rather wait with her here.'

Safred looked puzzled, but shook her head. 'The gods say that she is not safe here. That . . . that she might be *burnt*.'

So. Martine let out a long breath. Yes. That was possible. On the night of the Spring Equinox, at a black rock altar, that was very possible. But she couldn't explain that to Safred.

'You know what they mean,' Safred said accusingly.

'If she lies out here all day in the full sun, she *will* get burnt.' Not a lie, but not the truth Safred wanted. Martine went on before Safred could ask another question. 'Do the gods say whether *we* can float back, too?'

Immediately, Safred shivered. 'No. No. They say on no account. We must walk. But she will float.'

Martine untied her belt and strapped it around Bramble's chest. She held out her hand and Safred, after a moment of confusion, took off her own belt and gave it to her. Martine tied the two together and then took Bramble's shoulders while Safred took her legs. They slid her down the glassy rock to the edge of the water. Every bit of Sight Martine had told her that the water was dangerous, but they were here because of the gods, and it was a bit late to stop obeying them now.

'One, two, three,' she said. They slid Bramble into the water. An expression of panic came over her face, but then it cleared and she floated easily, more easily than she should have, as though the water itself was supporting her, high enough to pass over the rock ridges which lay just under the surface. Her head floated easily, her mouth well clear of the water.

Martine gestured for Safred to go before her, and then she took hold of the two belt ends and stepped onto the first rock ring. As though the movement had caused it, the moon came out from behind the clouds and the lake burst into brilliant reflected light. Martine tugged at the belt and Bramble spun slowly, moving gently until her head bumped Martine's foot. It was as though she towed a corpse.

The journey back lived in Martine's memory as the strangest time of her life. Bramble lay as though dead, and it seemed to Martine that she towed death itself, life itself, memory and courage and grief, all in one package. The lake was calm, the small waves caused by Martine's steps soft against her boots. The moonlight cast long shadows so that she seemed to be a giant, striding across the face of the ocean, pacing not from rock to rock but upon some elemental power beyond her understanding. Although she had faltered and swayed on the journey out to the altar, now she walked with ease, each foot finding the perfect resting point on the next ring of rock. It seemed that the shore approached *her*, grew larger and wider until she lost all sense of size, until the trees seemed as big as mountains and the rim of the lake bowl was like a cliff, shivering with light under the moon.

Another sense, an older and more familiar sense, told her that it was wrong to walk away from the altar on the night of the Spring Equinox. That she still had work to do. *Later*, she told that voice, and on the thought everything returned to normal size, she took the final step over the knee-high rim, and brought Bramble safely to rest against the obsidian edge.

Cael was there, although she hadn't seen him waiting. She wondered if she had seen the real lake shore or some other country, some other time, but put the thought away. Cael went to lift Bramble out, but Martine stopped him. She gave him the belt, and he used it to drag Bramble half-upright, so he could grasp her without putting his hands in the water. Then he lifted her, with a grunt of effort that made Martine remember his wound, and carried her to the camp he had set up on the slope under the trees, where Safred was already warming herself by a fire. Through it all Bramble never opened her eyes, although her body was tense and her face set.

When it was approaching midnight, by the stars, Martine checked Bramble once again and gave her some water. She drank with a faint smile on her face, though there were dark circles under her eyes. Zel and Martine had stripped off her breeches and put a cloth under her, so they could give her water regularly without fearing that she would soil her clothes. They had laid a blanket over her for modesty, but now Martine tucked it in for warmth as well.

Martine gathered her flint, handstone and tinder. Spring Equinox. She hadn't celebrated it since Elva left; it needed at least two Traveller women, one to hold the flint and the other to strike. Three was better, but tonight they had only two, her and Zel. And a black rock altar.

Perhaps tomorrow night, or the next, Bramble would be with them. She hoped so. It was good to have three women for the third night, to represent the three sisters.

She really didn't want to walk out again on those precarious rock rings, but her Sight had been clear. The altar was waiting for the ritual, which was precise and demanding. No steel to strike fire from. Steel was too new a thing. The ritual went back far past the time humans first made steel. Fire must be made from stone and flint. The handstone must be old, the flint new, the tinder natural, not charred. That meant special tinder, because sparks from a handstone were not as hot as sparks from a firesteel. Birch tree fungus was the only tinder that caught readily. Martine, like all Traveller women, collected the fungus when she saw it, for any future need. She had gathered some in Hidden Valley, where the birch trees grew thickly on the upper slopes. She and Elva had gone out one clear winter day, saying only to Drema and Gytha that they were collecting firewood. Which they did, as well.

She went softly to where Zel was curled up in a nest of blankets, then paused. She didn't know how devout Zel's mother had been – perhaps Zel didn't know the rituals. But as she hesitated Zel's head came out of its nest, eyes bright in the starshine, and she slid to her feet without words, then reached down to pick up a small pile of kindling she had hidden under the blanket.

They walked towards the water.

'I have one new flint,' Martine said quietly.

'I only have one, too,' Zel said.

That was a problem. Each night of the ritual there must be a new flint, to call the wildfire. Three nights, two flints.

'We'll have to go looking for another,' Martine said.

Zel nodded, but she looked anxious. 'What if we don't find one? What happens if the ritual isn't completed?' Her voice rose with worry. It was odd to see her normally calm face twisted with concern. Zel didn't like not being in control of things, Martine knew. Something about Zel made her feel very old and not as wise as she should be. Like the fake grandmother she was. She wondered if she'd be wiser if Elva had been a true child of her body, not just her heart.

'What if he isn't pleased?' Zel insisted.

'Shh,' Martine said. If Safred were to wake now, she'd sniff a secret and they'd never reach the end of her questioning. What could they tell

her? She had no old blood at all – she'd said so. Martine handed Zel
the birch fungus tinder.

Traveller women had tried to introduce women of Acton's blood to
the fire once before, and Martine didn't want to be part of a disaster
like that. Even the Well of Secrets wouldn't be safe from the fire. He
didn't like strangers, they all knew that.

'I don't know,' Martine said softly. 'We'll worry about that if we
need to.'

Zel swallowed hard before she took the first step onto the seemingly blank face of the water, but she had a tumbler's balance and made
the next step more easily than Martine. Martine was overwhelmed by
the sense that the lake was watching. Not antagonistic, but ready to
react to anything it deemed a threat.

They paced out, side-by-side as the ritual demanded, and stood at
the altar. Martine stretched her senses, but the gods were not here.
They were never here at the fire's time. She always wondered why –
was it fear, or respect, or had some kind of deal been done? Then she
reined in her thoughts. Cynicism had no place on this night.

Zel made a small nest of the tinder and kindling on the smooth face
of the altar and stood back. Martine placed her striking stone and the
new flint side-by-side on the altar next to the tinder, and stood next to
Zel.

'We are daughters of fire,' they said together, 'daughters of Mim the
firestealer, Mim the firelover, Mim the fire's love. The fire must never
die.'

Martine felt, as she always did in rituals, a mixture of self-
consciousness and exaltation, of silliness and awe. There were tears in
Zel's eyes. Together they took a pace forwards.

Zel picked up the handstone and placed it close above the nest of
fungus, bark and pine needles. Martine took the flint. She had to get
the angle of the stroke precisely right, which was always harder when
someone else was holding the stone, and harder still because of the
height of this altar. But it wasn't the first time either of them had done
this, which helped.

Zel braced herself, and nodded. Martine struck down cleanly into
the shallow groove on the handstone and sparks flew down the groove
straight onto the tinder. Immediately, it caught. They waited a moment
for the spark to grow. It glowed in the darkness, a ring of light that
gradually expanded. Zel folded the rest of the kindling over the top of

it, and both of them crouched down so that their mouths were on a level with the kindling nest.

'Take our breath to speed your growth,' Zel whispered. They blew softly, very softly, into the nest, and then there was flame as well as spark. They stood up and moved back a pace, waiting.

As the fire grew, licking at the kindling, Martine felt his presence. As always, it manifested within her body, not her mind, completely different from the presence of the local gods. Heat flooded her, spreading out from her solar plexus and her loins, making her nipples tight. Zel's head dropped back, her eyes closed and her breath quickened. It was worse – or better – when you were younger, Martine thought, but on the thought another wave of heat swept over her. Her body took control of her thoughts and filled her mind with images of fire, flames, burning gold. Each image brought a sense of touch, too, of stroke and probe, of caress and tease. She ached, deeply, for the fire's touch. For fulfilment.

Her body began trembling. She made the final step of the ritual, the one that was always hardest for her, and surrendered to him, although, always, always, there was a small part of herself she did not give; could not give. Her eyes closed and the fire filled her mind.

And died.

Martine opened her eyes slowly, gasping with disappointment and frustration. The kindling had burned away, cleanly, leaving nothing behind. No ash, no charcoal. Nothing to show there had been a fire at all. Of course. It always did, if the ritual had gone well.

It had been quick, but this was only the first night. Foreplay, nothing more. Heat drained away from her but left some things behind. Frustration. Readiness. A sharpening of her senses, so that everything made an impression: the cool breeze from the mere, the murmur of the trees, the dense blackness of the altar in the moonlight.

Zel wiped sweat from her face and shivered.

They looked at each other to make sure the other was ready to speak, and then said, together, 'The fire will never die.'

Then they turned and slowly, carefully, made their way over the water and back to camp. The campfire had flared up, as fires always did in the vicinity of the ritual. They banked it again and checked the area carefully. This close to the forest, every spark was a potential catastrophe.

Thank the gods – or the fire – that Safred was still asleep in her tent.

'After Bramble wakes up,' Zel said quietly, as they paused before going to their blankets, 'we is heading back to Oakmere, right?'

Martine nodded.

Zel grinned. 'Good. Lots of likely lads in Oakmere! I love the week after Equinox!'

They stifled their laughter behind their hands. Martine knew she was acting like a silly girl, but she didn't care. That was part of the ritual, too. Zel was right. Traveller women who didn't have their own men came from the three-night vigil with the fire ready and eager for the first good-looking man who crossed their path. It was one of the reasons they had a reputation for being free with their bodies. But it was worth carrying that reputation for the rest of the year, to have the week after Equinox.

Martine took her blankets and stretched out next to Bramble, who was moving her legs restlessly. She straightened the blanket so Bramble's legs were covered, and checked the cloth they had laid under her. It was still dry, so she gave her more water. She had sweated a great deal already, and lack of water would kill her if they weren't careful.

Martine found it hard to sleep. Her body thrummed still with desire and arousal. She remembered past Spring Equinoxes, especially the ones after Elva was fully grown, when she had felt free to go out looking for pleasure. She smiled into the darkness. Shagging in the week after each Equinox, when all the senses had been brought to singing life, was like nothing else. It had been a long time since Martine had let herself enjoy it, though. Too long, she thought. Too long.

BRAMBLE

HER MOUTH WAS full of ashes. She was choking on them, smothering in them, coughing convulsively to clear her throat. She was coughing so hard that her eyes were streaming and she could see nothing, but she could hear a man shouting at her in a voice which showed he expected to be obeyed, a voice like a drum.

'The gods do not talk to children! They do not talk to half-grown boys too big for their boots! The gods talk only to the chieftain. So it is. So it will be.'

Like an echo, other voices confirmed, murmuring, 'So it is, so it will be.'

The voice dropped lower, but became more menacing. 'Do you understand, Baluch?'

Baluch could barely respond, his body was so wracked with coughs, but he nodded.

'A mouth full of ashes is the price for lying to your chieftain. It's a small price. If you were a man full-grown, I would have cut off your hand.'

Baluch's eyes cleared at last. The speaker was a balding older man, fifty or so, with a bushy grey beard and bright blue, angry eyes. He was dressed as the men at the practice fight had been dressed, in baggy leggings and rough-spun tunic, but he had a great cloak of rabbit skins slung from his shoulders. With a shock, Bramble saw that the brooch which held the cloak was a larger version of the one she had laid her hand over on the black rock altar. For a moment she wondered how long she had been travelling, washed on wave after wave of ancestral memory. What were the others doing, there by the dark mere? The image of trees, water, the rising mist flashed across her mind and was swept away by the immediate sensation of Baluch spitting and spitting again, trying to get the ashes from his mouth.

'Enough, Father,' Asa's voice came. 'He understands.'

She handed Baluch a horn of water and a basin. He grabbed at it and swilled his mouth over and over again.

'Hmmph,' the chieftain grunted. 'Very well. We will start the search for the child at first light.'

He turned and walked away and only then was Bramble aware that they were in a corner of the large hall, where the shuttered windows showed a faint purple twilight. Outside, the wind whistled around the building and the walls radiated cold. The hall was packed with people, men, women and children, most of them moving uneasily, talking to each other, avoiding the central fire where a woman Asa's age sat rocking back and forth, her hands to her face, another woman patting her on the back.

Baluch had used up the water in the horn and his mouth felt almost normal, although puckered and sour. He stared into the grimy water in the basin. Bramble felt his despair and heard a faint dark music, deep notes sonorously played – a dirge. She knew it was from Baluch's mind, but he seemed unaware of it.

When a hand landed on his shoulder he didn't look up, as though he knew who it was. 'I know where she is,' he whispered.

The hand lifted and Acton came into view, looking about thirteen, perhaps less. 'Where?'

Baluch gestured with the hand which held the drinking horn. 'A cave, under a ridge. I can't describe it well enough, but I could find it.'

'Mmm,' Acton said.

Baluch raised his head. 'I *could*. Your grandfather thinks I'm lying, but I'm not!'

'Shh,' Acton cautioned him. 'If he hears you say it again you *will* lose a hand. The gods talk only to the chieftain.'

'But my mother had the Sight –'

'Athel was a woman, and under his control. No threat to him at all.'

'But *I'm* not a threat. Everyone knows you'll be the next chieftain –'

'So,' Acton said, ignoring him, suddenly cheerful, 'maybe it isn't the gods. *Maybe* it's a friendly spirit.'

'Uh, he won't believe that.'

'No. But if we bring her back alive he'll pretend to believe it. Come on.'

The music in Baluch's mind died away, changed to something warmer, deep notes still but with hope at the centre of them. He followed Acton dumbly, out the back of the hall to a small chamber where Asa and a couple of women waited, holding candles.

'You'll get lost yourselves,' one of them muttered, casting a dark look at Baluch.

Acton grinned at her, and kissed her cheek. 'I know these hills like my own hands, Gret. Don't you trust me?'

She smiled despite herself. 'I don't trust the weather. It smells like a blizzard to me.'

Acton nodded, solemn, his gold hair glinting in the light of the candles.

'That's why we have to go now. A blizzard will be the death of her.' As one, the women shivered and made a sign with their little fingers, clearly a ward against evil chance.

'Harald should –'

Acton cut her off firmly. 'My grandfather is right. To go out now, not knowing where Friede is, would be foolhardy. More would be lost. But to go out knowing where she is, that is different.'

'The gods –'

'Not the gods,' Baluch said hastily. 'A friendly spirit, that's all. Only the chieftain speaks with the gods.'

Asa nodded approval. 'Yes,' she said. 'A friendly spirit. Good. Go find her. But . . .' her voice faltered a little and she put out a hand to smooth Acton's hair. 'Don't take stupid chances. One life is not worth two.'

He smiled at her, but was clearly preparing to ignore her advice. His eyes sparkled with pleasure at the thought of the risks he was about to take. Bramble couldn't help but understand that. She had felt the same often enough herself, before a chase.

The women helped them into heavy winter clothing: shaggy sheepskin coats and leggings, felt hats with earflaps and long neck pieces to wrap around their throats, gloves. They took a pack with candles, tinderbox, dried apple, water, bread and another coat for the girl when they found her.

'She won't need boots,' Baluch said dreamily. 'We'll have to carry her back.'

They went out into the sharp wind. It was almost full night, the sky a scudding mass of clouds flickering across a sickle moon. There was a thin layer of snow across the ground. Acton led until they were in the lee of the last outbuilding. Already Baluch's nose was red and sore. His ears were aching. The buffeting of the wind, which would merely have been uncomfortable to Bramble, was painful to him because of the insistent whuff and whine. It was as though his ears were more sensitive to the noise than to the cold. His inner music died under the clamour.

'Well?' Acton asked. 'Which way?'

Baluch stilled, his head down. Bramble noted that the toes of his boots were scuffed like a little boy's, and was filled with a sudden maternal affection for him. This was, of course, the Baluch who had founded Baluchston. The one who had struck a deal with the Lake for a town and a ferry. The first ferryman. She had never quite understood why the Lake had made that agreement, but from inside Baluch's mind it made some sense. This boy would understand the Lake. So why was he best friends with Acton the warlord?

Bramble could feel the presence of the gods around Baluch, but the pressure on her own mind was light. All their attention was concentrated on him.

Then Baluch's head came up, and he pointed. 'Up the northern flank,' he said. 'Over the sheep stream, beyond Barleyvale, and farther up.'

Acton nodded. 'You follow me,' he said, 'until we're there.'

Baluch bit his lip as though not liking the instruction, but followed closely in Acton's footsteps. Bramble realised that Acton was taking the force of the wind, sheltering Baluch and making it easier for him. That made sense. Baluch was smaller, slighter – more likely to founder in the wind and cold. He was the one who could take them to the girl. It was a good tactical decision. Or perhaps it was simply a boy sheltering his best friend from a harsh wind. She didn't know which. The fact that she couldn't tell from Acton's manner annoyed her. What was to decide? He was Acton, warlord and murderer. So he had a friend. Even the worst of men may have friends.

But not, part of her mind suggested, friends like Baluch.

There was no room for further thought in the next two hours. The buffeting of the wind and cold took thought away, even though Bramble withdrew her senses as far as she could from Baluch's. She had wandered winter forests, been caught out in a snowstorm or two, but the temperate south had nothing like this, not even in the dead of winter. There was nothing in this harsh land to protect them except the occasional ridge or clump of rocks. They crossed thin, half-frozen streams, careful to keep their boots dry, and started on a steep upwards slope.

The footing was treacherous: loose scree that shifted and tripped them time and again. Without the gloves, Baluch's hands would have been slashed and scored. Acton fell less often. From time to time he would put a hand back to help Baluch over a rough patch, or to pull him to his feet after a fall.

They had wrapped their scarves over their faces, leaving only their eyes visible, but even so Bramble could see that Acton was enjoying himself. At first it made her cross. She was *not* enjoying having to endure Baluch's struggle through wind and freezing cold, climbing a shagging mountain in the middle of the night. Then she thought, but I might, if I were really doing it. Not enjoy the physical discomfort, but the wildness of it, the sense of being on the edge of things, the knife's edge between joy and despair, success and failure. I might enjoy that.

They came to a sharp defile between two ridges, where they were protected from the wind. It felt almost warm by comparison and they pulled back their wraps so they could talk. Despite the shelter, they had to shout over the sound of the wind wuthering outside the defile.

'How far now?' Acton asked.

Baluch considered, again looking at his boots as the gods concentrated upon him.

'We have to climb the next ridge and then go around the rocks to the cave. Not far, but hard.'

'How in the name of Swith the Strong did she get up here anyway?'

Baluch shrugged. 'You know what Friede's like. It was a nice day this morning. She probably wanted to explore.'

Acton shook his head, with some admiration. 'More like a boy than a girl!'

Baluch grinned. 'Asa's son should know how strong women can be.'

Acton made a face but underneath it was pride for his mother. 'Strong enough to tan our hides if we don't bring Friede back safe.'

Baluch nodded, serious again. They wrapped themselves and started off, reluctantly leaving the shelter of the defile to climb the ridge before them.

'You go first, here,' Acton said. Baluch looked quickly at him, as though surprised, but went willingly enough up the uneven slope.

The ridge was so steep that they had to go on all fours, grabbing at

harsh rocks that cut through their gloves, and sending stones skitter-
ing down the slope beneath them. It was soon clear that Acton had the
worst of it, as he had to avoid the rocks that slid from beneath Baluch's
boots. The way broadened at one point so they could climb side-by-
side and when it narrowed again, Baluch motioned for Acton to go
first. Acton shook his head. Baluch pushed him, gesturing, Go on!
Acton studied him for a moment, then shrugged and began to climb.
They couldn't talk; the wind made speech impossible. It felt as though
the wind wanted to pluck them off the ridge and cast them down onto
the rocks below. Perhaps it did. Perhaps the howling was wind spirits,
not just air streaming through gaps in the rocks.

Bramble forced her mind away from that disquieting thought and
wasn't sure if it were hers or Baluch's. His breath was coming faster as
they climbed and his legs ached and burned, but only from the knees
up. Below that he was numb with cold. The clouds finally covered the
moon when they were halfway up and the rest of the ascent was in the
pitch dark, fumbling for handholds and footholds, grasping unseen
outcrops, not knowing how securely they were anchored in what was
now more cliff than ridge.

Baluch's attention narrowed to the feel of his hands, the rock beneath
his feet. Occasionally he flinched as a rock dislodged by Acton's feet
bounced past him. One stone the size of a fist thudded into his shoulder
and made him lose his grip. His heart beat wildly as he lunged for another handhold, scrabbling until he was grasping the rock face securely.
Bramble felt him begin to quiver deep inside, but he dragged in a great,
gulping breath, the cold needling his lungs, and began to climb again,
ignoring the quivering and the beating heart. Not long after, they reached
a ledge and Acton squatted with his back to the cliff. Baluch joined him,
both of them taking long breaths. Acton was tired, too.

Then Baluch stood and pointed, not up, but along the ledge. He
edged towards a large whitish boulder which blocked it. Bramble was
puzzled, at first, that she could see it. The night had been so dark
before. Where was the light coming from? Then she realised that it was
snowing and what she saw was the snow on the top of the rock,
reflecting what little light there was. It had been snowing for a while,
it seemed by the amount of snow on ledge and rock, but Baluch had
been so concentrated on the next handhold, the next step, that he had-
n't noticed, and so she hadn't noticed either.

There was a gap between the boulder and the rock face, and they edged between it, Acton having more trouble than Baluch. Beyond, the rock face the ledge curved around and ended in a cave mouth, darker by far than the surrounding rock. It was quieter in the lee of the boulder. Baluch went up to the cave mouth and unwrapped the neck piece from his mouth. It was stiff with snow and ice. He cleared his throat.

'Friede?' he called. 'Friede?'

'Shhh!' a whisper came furiously from the dark cave. 'Shhh! You'll wake her!'

Scrabbling noises were followed by a head appearing from the cave. Bramble could barely see, even though Baluch was standing close. It could have been any age child, boy or girl, from the voice and the hat, but Acton had that expression on his face that Bramble had seen so often from others when she herself had been young; the one that meant 'this girl doesn't act as she should'. Despite the fact that Friede was responsible for them having to make that horrible climb, she found herself liking her.

'Wake who?' Baluch said.

'Shh! The bear.'

Both boys took an involuntary step backwards and Friede made a reproving noise. 'It's all right, she's in the winter sleep. But she'll wake up if you make too much noise.'

'You're in trouble,' Acton said. 'What's worse, you got Baluch in trouble.'

Friede emerged fully from the cave and stood awkwardly on the ledge. Astonished, Bramble saw that she was lame, with a crutch under her left arm. She was small; perhaps seven or eight.

'How did you get up here in the first place?' Baluch asked, exasperated.

'I fell from up there,' Friede said, gesturing towards the top of the cliff. 'It's not a bad walk if you take the long way around. And then I couldn't get down. Obviously.' She seemed irritated rather than scared or upset, and Bramble adjusted her estimate of Friede's age upwards, but she wasn't sure how far.

'So you just found a bear's cave?' Acton said. Bramble couldn't make out his face but his voice was amused.

'It was warm,' Friede said dismissively.

'It may have to be warm,' Acton said. 'We'll have to stay in it tonight, all of us.'

Immediately, Bramble felt the pressure of the gods grow greater around Baluch, and he shook his head.

'No, we have to go now, before the snow gets too deep. This blizzard is setting in for a long visit. Days, maybe weeks. We won't get home if we don't make a move right now.'

Friede stared at him curiously.

Acton grinned. 'The gods are leading him, girl. They must like you.'

Friede took in a long breath. 'The gods talk to you?' Her voice was full of wonderment and she looked at Baluch with a simple admiration which was clearly unusual in her.

'Sometimes,' Baluch mumbled, head down.

'*So*,' Acton recalled them back to business, 'we'd better go up rather than down.'

'I can't climb up,' Friede reminded him impatiently, back to her usual self.

'You can't climb down, either,' Acton said. 'If we have to carry you all the way home, I'd rather do it down a nice soft slope instead of the way we came, through the rocks.'

'But to get to the slope . . .'

'Come on,' Acton said, cheerful as though they were off for a picnic. 'Climb aboard.'

'Get her past the boulder first,' Baluch advised. 'The climb isn't as steep further down the ledge.'

'Fine. Let's go.'

They went back past the boulder, Acton leading, Friede edging along cautiously, Baluch behind ready to catch her if necessary. Once they were through, Baluch got the extra coat out of Acton's pack and helped Friede put it on. She sighed as she felt the warmth envelop her.

The ledge went back for another forty paces before it petered out, and the cliff was definitely at a less worrying slope at that end. Still, over the next half-hour Bramble wished that she could just withdraw from Baluch's mind altogether. She didn't understand why she had to live through this part of Acton's life.

Friede climbed on Acton's back without a word, as though she were used to this particular indignity. Baluch had to find their way up the ridge, and clear any loose rock or pebbles from their path. Acton stayed well back so that Friede wouldn't be hit by the debris, but followed Baluch's path faithfully. Baluch's hands were bleeding inside his gloves and only the warmth of the blood kept them from freezing, but Bramble knew that as soon as the blood stopped flowing it would freeze and cause frostbite. Baluch knew it too. He kept muttering, 'Spare gloves, I should have known we'd need spare gloves,' all the way up. Bramble could feel the burn and tremble of his legs and arms, the deep exhaustion which he kept back purely by will. She could only imagine how hard Acton was finding it with Friede on his back.

The climb didn't end suddenly, but slowly. The ridge folded back in a series of small summits, so that it seemed Baluch had reached the top several times before he actually did. Each time his heart leapt as the ground levelled out, and each time he set his mouth and kept going as he realised that the top was still above him. Finally he took three steps on level ground; four steps; five, and collapsed in gratitude. A moment later, Acton and Friede collapsed next to him.

They sat shoulder to shoulder, breathing hard.

'Well,' Acton said. 'At least that warmed me up.'

Baluch choked with laughter and punched him on the arm. Friede stood, hoisting herself on her crutch.

'We'd better go,' she said.

They were standing, Bramble saw, at the top of the ridge. On the other side, the ground sloped gently away, in a long hill that seemed endless in the darkness. She had no sense of direction without her own body to orient her, but Baluch seemed confident that they could find their way home.

'It's further, but at least we won't get lost,' he said.

The snow was not so deep on the summit of the ridge, but as they moved down the long slope it lay thicker, and further down it had already shifted into drifts. On the upland, Friede had struggled with the crutch. Here, she had no chance. She fell three times before she would admit she couldn't cope.

'Told you we'd have to carry her,' Baluch said. He presented his back to Friede and she climbed on with much less resignation than she had shown at the cliff face. She was slight, but any extra weight at all was a burden in these conditions. Baluch set his teeth and struggled on, with Acton going ahead to break the snow where it lay thickly, using Friede's crutch as a shovel where he could. The snow was falling more thickly now, the wind not as strong but still cutting.

Their exhaustion had moved past the point of physical pain. Bramble could feel that Baluch's arms and legs were protesting at each movement, but he seemed unaware of it, and unaware, too, of the music coursing through his mind, horns and fifes playing marching music, a steady, insistent beat. He and Acton both had settled into an unthinking, deliberate plodding that was like sleepwalking. Bramble worried that they would become lost through sheer inattention, but Acton seemed to be heading towards a particular goal. Often they had to skirt boulders or cracks in the rock, but always he would turn back to the same direction, like a sunflower turns towards sunlight.

The snow fell even more heavily, so they paused to tie themselves together with Friede's neck piece. She hid her face in Baluch's back and he could feel her breath, warm in the middle but cold on the edges, on the back of his neck. He couldn't feel his hands anymore, although Bramble knew they still supported Friede's legs.

After an interval that seemed to go on forever, they stopped to swap positions, with Acton taking Friede and Baluch going forward to tramp down the snow. Although Friede had been heavy, this was the more difficult task, requiring sheer dogged strength. Baluch couldn't sustain it as long as Acton, and they swapped twice more before, finally, they saw lights in the distance through the falling snow.

The snow was lying chest-deep and it needed both of them working together to force a way. But the sight of home filled them with energy and Baluch's steps were lighter even as he struggled through drifts.

They came back to exactly where they had started from, the back entrance to the hall. Acton banged on the door with a fist and Asa opened immediately, calling out loudly.

'Marte, she's here, she's here, they've brought her back!'

The woman who had been rocking by the fire, her face red and blotchy with crying, pulled Friede from Baluch's back, sinking down to the floor and stroking her hair, laughing and crying and shaking her. Baluch's legs shook. His face burned in the sudden warmth. His father, Elric, rushed over to support him. Baluch gladly grabbed onto his arm and tried to smile.

Acton unwrapped his face and shook himself free of snow, as energetic as if he had never left the room. He threw his hat and gloves onto a bench and hugged his mother with one arm.

'I need something warm to drink!' he declared. 'It's as cold as the hells out there.'

Asa laughed. Baluch was watching his father, whose eyes rested on Asa with appreciation, but without longing. He's given up trying to win her, then, Bramble thought, and wondered if his empty sleeve was to blame for Asa's lack of interest.

'I should beat you for this,' Elric said, returning his attention to Baluch, but it was clear from his smile that he didn't intend to.

Other people crowded around them, exclaiming and shouting to others in the hall. Baluch felt overwhelmed by the noise. He tried to fumble his gloves off, but they were stuck to his hands by blood.

Acton noticed. He reached out and stopped Baluch. 'You'll have to soak them off in warm water,' he said gently. Elric took Baluch by the arm to lead him into the hall. As they turned towards the door, the chieftain appeared in it, rubbing his eyes.

'What in all the hells is going on?'

Silence fell, except for Friede's mother's quiet scolding. The chieftain looked at them for a long moment. Friede looked up and met his gaze.

'You are in trouble,' he said. 'I'll deal with you tomorrow.' She nodded and yawned, which sent her mother and several of the other women into a scurry, saying, 'Let's get her to bed, she's exhausted, tomorrow's soon enough to worry about tomorrow . . .' They took her out into the hall, leaving the chieftain staring at Acton and Baluch. Mostly, Bramble noted, at Acton. Elric tensed as though getting ready to resist any attempt to punish his son.

'It wasn't the gods, Grandfather,' Acton said. 'It was a friendly spirit.'

'Hmph,' his grandfather said. He turned to Baluch. 'Is that so?' Baluch nodded silently. 'No more to be said, then.'

Elric relaxed, and so did Baluch. Moving back into the hall, Harald spoke over his shoulder, seemingly casual. 'But you'd better have mulled wine to warm you. It's a man's drink, I know, but just this once . . .'

Acton smiled blindingly and slapped Baluch on the back. 'Told you it'd be all right,' he said. 'Swith, I'm hungry! Mother, any meat left from dinner?'

Baluch followed him into the hall smiling, his internal music changing to triumphant horn blasts as the waters rose up and Bramble floated on their tide.

ASA'S STORY

THE WOMEN STAY in the women's quarters. Yes, of course. So the men think, if they think about it at all. But when the men venture away after the spring sowing, what do they think the women do? The ewes must be milked, the cows tended as they calve, the wheat weeded, the vegetables hoed, the barley malted and the ale brewed, and the women do it as they always do. But the sheep must be shepherded too, and the birds kept off the crops, and the horse yoked and the cart loaded for market. The wool is mostly spun in winter so the looms can be busy all through the long evenings of summer – but with the men away the wood must be chopped and the animals slaughtered and the meat butchered – yes, and the wolves chased away from the young lambs, too. The boys do some, of course, but without the women the men would find a cold hearth and an empty steading when they returned with their wounds and their tales and their glory.

So the women stay in the women's quarters, of course. But in the soft summer evenings after the light has faded too much to use the looms and the children are asleep, the women sit in the long hall and sing and laugh and drink small ale and make jokes about the men. As women always have.

So it was in our steading until the raiders came. For our men had sailed off, as they always did in summer, taking the pelts and the hides and the precious inkstone to the trading towns down south, sometimes all the way to the Wind Cities, and there was no one to protect us from the raiders.

The men came not from the sea, where we had a lookout placed, but over the mountains from the east. Not in the morning, when mostly they attack, but in the cool evening. So it was that the women were in the long hall, and that was the saving of us, because Eddi, Gudrun's son, called out loud enough from the stable before they killed him so that we had warning, and we could bar the doors and drag the tables across them. I thought they might burn us out, but it had been a long march and they wanted beer, and knew there would be barrels in the hall. So they battered the doors down. But we had time, Haena my mother, Gudrun and Ragni and I, to take down the ancestral shields that hung along the walls, and the spears that went with them.

My mother Haena was the oldest, white-haired and bent, but she straightened herself and faced them first, as she should, being our chieftain Harald's wife. The rest of us lined up behind her, hoping that by fighting we were dooming ourselves to die, and a quick death was what we prayed for, the best we could have, we thought.

They burst through the doors and came at us, but stopped in surprise when they realised it was only women facing them. Their leader was a tall strong man, sandy-haired and green-eyed, so green I saw it even in that moment of dread. I will not say his name in case his ghost seeks me out and takes revenge, but his use-name was Hard-hand, for indeed his hand was very hard on those he punished. He looked at us – and no doubt we looked ridiculous enough to his eyes – and laughed so hard he brought tears to his eyes. His men began to grin, then laugh, and lowered their weapons. Then Haena threw her spear and got one of them in the arm. He swore and pulled the spear out. The rest laughed even louder. Their leader had to prop himself up against the wall.

'Serve you right, Os!' he howled.

'Pierced by love's arrow!' said another, who looked to be the most intelligent of them. I found out later that he was their skald, their poet, and his name was Gris the Open-handed, for he was the most generous of men, even to strangers and women. He was Hard-hand's brother.

Then Gudrun heard her son Eddi's death cry come from the stable and grief took her and made her berserk. She ran screaming and struck at the leader. He swiped her aside with a casual blow with his sword, but such was his strength that the single blow near cut her in two and she fell, her scream turned to pain and then to silence before she lay full-length on the ground.

Hard-hand smiled, still, but his eyes were cold as he looked us over. He looked longest at me, and lingeringly. I knew that look and I hefted my spear higher. My mother Haena took a step back and rested her hand on my shoulder, giving me strength, because she knew that look too. Athel, my cousin, who was younger than I but had the Sight, dropped both spear and shield and put up a hand.

'Remember the strength of women,' was what the men heard her say, but the women heard her voice, or perhaps the voice of the goddess, speaking under her words, saying, 'Remember the strength of Haena's line.'

We all remembered that the women of my mother's line had a power over men, only one kind of power, and only to be used once in a woman's life. My mother had used it to bind the man of her choice to her and so married my father Harald, and he was faithful to her life-long. My grandmother had done the same with my grandfather, Sigur. So it went back for generations, and for the men concerned there was no shame, for to be chosen by a woman of our line was an honour-gift, and the power bound the woman as much as the man, to be faithful forever. We remembered that now, and I began to shake as I understood what was needed of me.

To bind this green-eyed man to me for life, for his life or mine, and to have no other man. I was very young and had not even exchanged courting glances at the Summer Gatherings. It seemed hard to me, too hard, to give away all that: all the possibilities of love and marriage and children and happiness. I felt I would rather die. But then I looked around the hall. There were nine of us, counting Gudrun, and I had the lives of seven other women in my hand. Women of our steading, for whom my family was responsible. My mother's hand on my shoulder tightened and then dropped as she left me to make the choice alone. I thought, I will make this choice, but my life will be short.

So I looked at that green-eyed man, and I looked with the eyes of power. They say the power came from the gods originally, and I believe it. At that moment I was more than a woman in her hall; more than a girl facing her enemy. I was greater, impossibly strong, impossibly desirable, impossibly desiring. I saw his face change, and I exulted.

'I will go with you,' I said, in the trading language that my people and his shared. 'If you and your men leave this steading and all its people in peace.'

One of his men laughed. 'You'll go with us if we choose and we'll all have you until you're –' Hard-hand smote him with the flat of his sword right across the mouth so that he fell to the floor, bloody, his teeth falling out into his palm, and he was called Bloody-mouth forever after. Hard-hand never took his eyes from mine.

'Willingly?' he asked. There was so much yearning in that question it made me both exultant and sick to my stomach with all it implied.

'If all are safe. Willingly,' I said slowly.

'So be it,' he said. 'I will come in the morning and escort you to my home, where you will be my wife.' At that his men almost fell over with astonishment, but they said nothing.

He turned slowly, reluctant to take his eyes from me, but once that contact was broken he whirled into action, ordering his men outside to retreat, to set up camp by the stream in the sheep meadow, to leave all their plunder behind them. They complained loudly, as such men do, but Gris quietened them. He looked strangely at me, Gris. Later, when I knew more of Hard-hand's life I understood why, for giving mercy to defenceless women was not something anyone who knew him would have expected.

I spent the night collecting my belongings and crying in my mother's arms. But in the morning I rose up and put on my travelling clothes. My mother pinned my cloak with her best brooch, that had been made by Elric the Foreigner in her youth at the behest of my father Harald, as a betrothal gift.

'You are a worthy daughter of a great line,' she said formally. 'May the gods protect you and bring you safe home.'

'My mother, live long and die blessed by kith and kin, by wealth and weal, by fame and fortune.'

'Fame I shall garner from your actions, fortune you have already been to me, kith and kin shall live here safe, remembering your name with praise.'

She was proud and stately but her eyes were full of tears, as were mine. Tears of grief and fear, for who knew what waited for me over the mountains in the strangers' land?

Customs differ, but work is the same everywhere. What I found over the mountains was a strange life, yet in essence it was the same life I had left. There were no women's quarters or men's hall. Families had their own quarters and women lived with their own men and children, all in one small house. It is not a good system, for the children annoy the men and the men annoy the women and no one ever gets a moment to sit quietly alone. Women are kept apart from the other women who would give them comfort and advice and share the child-rearing and the cooking and the endless scouring of pots. That was different. The herbs they used for cooking and preserving were sometimes strange to me. But the work was the same: they had goats, not sheep, but though goats are cleverer than sheep they still need to be fed and milked and delivered of their young. The wool was softer but a little harder to spin; the blankets lighter but warmer. Small differences.

The great difference was Hard-hand. On that first morning, when I left my mother, he had given me a horse to ride, a pony that carried me sure-footedly over the mountain trails, even past a great chasm that reached so far down into the depths of the earth that the bottom could not be seen. Hard-hand had ridden beside me all the way, but there he got off his horse and led my pony. He remounted and I thanked him, and then he tried to talk to me, although he had trouble finding something to say. He was not a clever man. In the end he told me about his land, his manor as he called it, and the people who owed him fealty. He had been elected a chieftain, at least, and so I would not be shamed in lying with him.

The gods' power worked strangely on me. In my heart I hated him – not so much for his attack on our steading, for such things are to be expected – but for forcing me to make the choice I had made, for taking me from my family and friends, for stealing from me my right to choose my husband. For turning the great power of my mother's line, which should be used to create strong families living in joy, into a weapon. Yet his person was not distasteful to me. When he reached for my hand I did not feel the urge to snatch it away.

We came to his farmstead with its cluster of small buildings in the late evening after a long, long ride. I was swaying in the saddle and he looked at me with concern as he lifted me down.

'Siggi!' he yelled. A woman came out of his house and went to greet him, to kiss him, but he pushed her back roughly.

'This is –' It was then he realised that he did not know my name, that he had ridden beside me all day without asking. Gris laughed.

'Asa,' he said. 'Her name is Asa.' I learnt later that it was typical of him, to learn what others did not know, did not think worth knowing.

'Asa,' Hard-hand said, his voice caressing. The woman Siggi heard it, and her face went hard. 'She is to be my wife,' he said. 'Treat her well. Tonight I will sleep in my mother's house and in the morning we will be hand-fasted.'

Siggi hated me from that moment, and I did not blame her. She had

been his concubine for three years before I came, and had borne him
two daughters. Now he looked at her as though she were no more than
a servant. She wanted me dead, but she did not dare disobey him.

She took me inside and showed me a room to sleep in, for in this
place they slept in separate rooms, alone or with their husbands and
children, instead of all together as we did.

I slept well through exhaustion and rose to wash and ready myself.
Hard-hand came at sunrise, as the custom was there, and we were
hand-fasted over a holy fire struck from flint that had never been used
before. Unlike us, where the chieftain is the go-between to the gods,
these people had a seer to perform all the ceremonies, a man who
could always hear the gods' voices, as Athel sometimes could. I discovered, after, that their gods are smaller than ours but much more
approachable, and anyone could go to their black stone altar and
speak to the gods, ask for favour, beg forgiveness. I never dared, being
a child of different gods, but Siggi gained great comfort when the gods
told her I would be gone within a year.

She told me that the morning after my wedding, when I rose from
my marriage bed bruised and shaken. Hard-hand was bound to me,
but that did not change his nature, and it was his nature to take what
he wanted when he wanted it. And I was bound to be faithful to him
until death.

Siggi taunted me, 'The gods have promised me, you will be gone in
under a year! He will tire of you and kill you and I will have him back.'

'Is that what the gods say?' I asked, looking her straight in the eyes.

She shrugged, uncomfortable. 'They say you will be gone in under
a year, and *I* will be the chieftain's wife.' Then she smiled maliciously.
'You thought you had stolen him but he will come back to me when
he tires of you.'

I nodded. 'Until then, I am his wife and the mistress of this steading.
Fetch me water to wash in.'

She glowered, but she obeyed. I washed slowly, thinking about her
message from the gods. 'Gone' they had said, not 'dead'. I would have
been an honourable wife to him if he had treated me with honour. But
he did not. I rinsed the blood from my thighs and decided, at that
moment, to kill Hard-hand.

He was not an easy man to kill. He slept lightly, with his hand on
his weapons. He ate no food that I had not eaten first. Although he
wanted me nightly and the power of the gods meant that I did not

resist, he never trusted me. Nor should he have. But when two months went by and we realised I was with child, he relaxed a little.

That was a hard moment for me. I had planned to kill Hard-hand and then myself, but a child changed everything. I could not take the life of an innocent. Which meant I had to live. To live with Hard-hand until the child was born and I was well enough to travel. The day I realised I ran down to the goatfold and sobbed into the side of a nanny as she suckled her twins. I raged against Hard-hand's gods, because I thought they had caused this as a punishment for not worshipping them. Now I think I was wrong, but then I felt caught in a trap from which there was no escape. Except one.

So I played the part of the willing wife. I worked hard. I joked with the other women and with his men. I pretended to have fallen in love with him at first sight and the only one who did not believe me was Gris, who had looked at my face in my father's long hall when all the other men were looking at my body. There was a reason for that. Gris did not lie with women. Nor with men, so far as I could discover, but then men lying with men was scorned in that place and he would have been dishonoured by it.

As it was, his brother taunted him about his refusal to marry and advised him to get a woman from the far north, one of the Skraelings, who were so hairy they looked like men and might thus satisfy him. Hard-hand talked like this only in private, and I think did not understand that he was heaping dishonour on his brother. A joke, he thought it. But to Gris it was no joke, and his heart hardened against his brother day by day. The taunting became worse after my pregnancy started to show and the seer pronounced the child a boy. Hard-hand bragged that he was founding a dynasty and that his brother would never have descendants. That, I believe, truly hurt Gris, and I was sorry for him and tried to turn the talk away to other things. We became, in a sense, allies.

I began, through the winter, to squirrel food away against the time I had borne the child and recovered enough to travel. I would have to kill Hard-hand and try to escape over the mountains. Steal a horse. I did not ride well, but I could manage. Again, no one noticed except Gris. He came to me one afternoon in late winter. The rest of the men were out searching for missing cows. That day my back protested at every movement, I was so gravid. It would be only a matter of days before the child came. Gris handed me a travel pouch filled with dried meat.

'It is a hard journey even in summer,' he said. 'It will be early spring when you are fit to travel and you will need to keep your strength up on the road.'

I nodded. I felt that more was needed, that this man and I were bound together in a great undertaking. 'My son will be your son,' I said. 'When he is grown and you have need of an heir, send for him, and he will come.'

He stood very still for a long moment. 'He will unite our peoples,' he said finally. 'And rule with justice.'

I nodded formally, accepting his words. I expected to have many sons, then; to marry again and have a family with a man of my choice. Later I found that the gods exact a price for every boon. Never again did I look on a man with desire, no matter how well favoured he was, nor how kind. I would have married Elric Elricsson otherwise, because he was a good man and a kind father, but it would have been a poor bargain for him, getting a wife with no passion in her. I think the gods would have resented it.

The lying-in was hard, but then all are. The women did everything right and with gentleness, even though I was a stranger, even Siggi. She took the mattress from the bed-box and laid in the straw thick and deep, which was just as well for there was a deal of blood as well as the birth-waters. Well, no need to talk about it, maybe. Once it is over, birth is a private thing, a memory of darkness and pain and piercing joy.

Perhaps they were kinder to me than I expected because my pains started on the night before the first day of spring, as all were readying for the holiday, and spirits were light after the bleakness of winter. My son was born at sunrise the next morning, an omen among those people that he would achieve greatness. His father had been felling an oak sapling for the Springpole when he was called to see the baby, so he announced the child's name would be Acton, which means place of the oak tree. I was content with that name. The oak tree is strong and long-lived, and gives food and shelter generously to birds and beasts. Yet I have never understood why those people kill a tree to celebrate spring, the season of birth. Among my people, we use a living tree to wind the ribbons on and dance around.

I recovered quickly from the birth, but I pretended to be weaker than I was. I think Siggi suspected, but as it kept Hard-hand from my bed she said nothing. I put off the baby's naming ceremony as long as I could, until my strength returned, for I knew that Hard-hand would drink long that night and it was my best chance to escape. The baby was strong, too, and did everything lustily – yelled rather than cried, sucked eagerly at the breast, kicked and waved his little fists against the binding clothes. He would not go to sleep unless his hands were free. The other women scolded me for giving in to him.

'His arms will grow crooked if they're not strapped tight to his sides in the night,' said one.

'He'll be untameable as a boy, if you don't bind him now,' said another.

Well, she was right about that. But I was so tired that I left his hands free so he would sleep and I could sleep with him.

When it seemed we were due for a few days of good weather, I set the naming day for the next day. Just before dawn, I took off Acton's clothes and wrapped him in a shawl, as Siggi advised me. She was smiling, which concerned me, but she was often smiling now as the year passed and it came time for her gods' prophecy to come true. Hard-hand carried the child to the black altar stone and laid him on it, then took the shawl away so that my baby lay naked on the stone.

'Gods of field and stream, hear your son. Gods of sky and wind, hear your son. Gods of earth and stone, hear your son. Gods of fire and storm, hear your son. I bring you a new son: Acton, child of the spring. He is your sacrifice.'

Then he drew his belt knife. I couldn't believe it. I started forward, but Siggi held me back, laughing nastily. Hard-hand lowered his knife to the altar. Then, at the last moment, as I dragged myself out of Siggi's grasp, the seer brought forward a young fawn and laid it over Acton so that the knife slit the fawn's throat and the blood spurted over both stone and child. My boy cried out, but not in fear, and tried, I swear, to grasp the knife. A great shout went up from everyone at that and Hard-hand swept the fawn aside and picked up the baby, holding him high above his head. The sun came over the mountain at that moment and lit him red, so that the blood showed black against his skin.

'My son is a man already!' Hard-hand shouted and everyone cheered.

Every one of them, men and women both, drank deep throughout the day and by dusk Hard-hand was almost snoring. When Acton was fed and asleep I went to Hard-hand, took him by the hand and led him to our room. His men made lewd jokes as we went and Hard-hand belched and laughed with them.

I lay with Hard-hand for the first time since Acton's birth. But this is the strange thing – for the first time, he was gentle with me. He had never come to me drunk before and I wondered, and have wondered many times since, was it his real nature coming through because he was disarmed by the drink and by happiness, or was it an aberration caused by the liquor? I killed him in his sleep with his own belt knife, driving the blade deep into his neck because I was not sure exactly where to strike to reach his heart, and he died never knowing I had betrayed him. Yet it would not have felt like a betrayal if he had not been gentle with me. Did I do wrong? Still I do not know if what I did was murder or something else which has no name, because the need of women to kill in silence has no name. But I left that room weeping, which I had not expected.

The men outside had fallen asleep where they sat, except for Gris. I picked my way through the snoring men with Acton in my arms and made it safely to the stable where Gris was waiting. He had a good pony already saddled for me, a map, and my saddlebag packed full of food and clothing. I gave him some of my clothes and Acton's swaddling bands. We had arranged that he would take them to a cliff which was used for sacrifices, and make it look as though I had killed myself and the baby.

'Go the long way I have marked on the map,' he said.

I nodded and kissed his cheek before I left him. He flushed, and covered his embarrassment by boosting me into the saddle, baby and all. Then I left that place behind me without a backwards glance and rode into the night. Going home.

ASH

Flax led the way through Golden Valley.

'We've been this way a hand of times, back from Foreverfroze to see our grandam. It's always best to take the back roads, yes? We don't sing here, or tumble. It's too small a place, Zel says, and they don't like foreigners much. So. East or west?'

'East,' Ash said.

They veered off the main road and went by smaller paths and back lanes, avoiding the towns and the big horse farms that filled the valley bottom, and by mid-afternoon Ash was sick and tired of hearing 'Zel says'.

Away from the rich river flats the valley was rocky and wooded with spruce and birch as well as the poplars which gave the valley its name. The eastern trail wound up and down foothills that were surprisingly wild for such a settled, prosperous valley.

'We should be all right,' Flax reassured him. 'In the daylight it's a nice ride, Da says. A chance to get off the roads and into the woods.'

Rowan and Swallow, Ash's parents, stuck to the well-worn roads, the roads dotted with big inns where silver could be earned. The idea of taking a 'nice ride' in the woods was alien to Ash. The only time he had been 'off the roads' was when his father took him to the Deep.

Just thinking about the Deep felt wrong. That's what he had been taught, what all the boys had been taught: once you leave, wipe it from your thoughts like chalk from a slate. It doesn't exist. Don't talk about it to each other, don't even think about it. If Acton's people found out, heard even a whisper of Traveller men meeting in secret, there would be massacres. Ash knew that was right. He had passed enough crossroads with full gibbets and pressing boxes leaking blood from the executed.

That was what warlords did to all wrong-doers, even to their own people. For Travellers suspected of plotting, there would be no mercy.

Boys, or men, who talked about the Deep were shunned their whole lives, cut out of Traveller society as though they had the plague. They didn't last long, Rowan had said seriously. 'We of the old blood need each other, and without that contact . . . we sicken and die, or worse.' Ash remembered one man, a dry-stone fencer, who wandered through the Domains like a ghost, talking to no one except the shopkeepers who served him reluctantly, as they served all Travellers, until he stopped even going into shops. He had jumped from a quarry cliff and broken his neck, or drowned in the deep green water, but before that he had thinned down to a wraith with haunted eyes. Ash had been sorry for him, but his father had said, 'Leave him be, Ash,' in that tone which could not be disobeyed, because it was used so rarely. 'He spoke too much,' his father explained quietly, and it was the year after Ash's first visit to the Deep, so that he understood, and his eyes grew round with astonishment, that anyone would – could – disobey the demons.

In the old days, those who talked, even to each other, were hunted down and killed by the demons. That death might have been kinder, Ash thought. At least it was quick.

Ash couldn't question the prohibition. It was what had kept the Deep safe for a thousand years, and the Deep was all they had left.

They met no one all morning, not even charcoal burners.

'Zel says the valley lot don't come up here much. Scared of bears and wolves, she says.'

Ash kept a better lookout after that, and did see bear scat in a clearing. There were wolf tracks by the small pool where they stopped to water the horses. Cam and Mud didn't want to drink there, shifting nervously and showing the whites of their eyes. Flax gentled them and again quoted his father.

'Da says they'll never settle within scent of wolves.' So they moved on quickly, eating in the saddle. Heron had made bacon rolls for them, and packed more food that would keep for a couple of days: hard cheese, dried apples, flat biscuits.

They had reached well into Golden Valley by sunset, and found a camp by a stream edged by birch trees. Ash had almost ridden past it, but realised in time that it was up to him to name the camping place.

This was the first time he had been the oldest member of a Travelling party, and it was both unsettling and pleasant to take responsibility. Because Flax was certainly not going to.

Over the course of the day, Ash had passed through intense dislike to a simpler annoyance. Flax was so *young*. He rode along with a sunny smile, a song constantly on his lips. He didn't even realise he was singing, most of the time; it was as normal as breathing. His singing irritated Ash intensely.

At first he thought his irritation was because every pure note reminded him of his own inability to sing. But eventually he realised that it was because he carried his own songs with him, in his head, all the time, and Flax's singing cut across that internal music.

He had never thought about the music in his head before, except on odd occasions when he was particularly relaxed, as he had been the first night at Elva and Mabry's. But now, in competition with Flax's simple songs, he discovered complex layers of melody and harmony, the sounds of flute and drums and pipes and human voice, intertwining and shifting as the day lengthened and his mood changed.

The realisation was disturbing. As though he had been living all this time with a stranger in his head; a stranger who could actually make music, even if it were music no one could hear. He wondered how he had remained unaware of it all this time. The question forced him back in memory to the days when he Travelled with his parents. He remembered days of intense concentration as his father taught him the songs; nights of intense listening as his parents performed. There had been no room in his head then, for any other music.

There had been one day, a lovely, calm summer day when they were in Carlion, staying down near the harbour. He and his father had sat side-by-side on the dock, watching the fishing boats go out at sunset. Ash couldn't remember how old he had been – ten, maybe, or eleven. The evening sky had started a phrase of flute music in his head. He remembered wanting to share it with his father, and not knowing how. He couldn't sing it, he couldn't even hum. He had tried to learn flute the year before and had done badly, and at that moment he had wished intensely that he had persevered, so that he could at least share this fragment of melody with his father, even if he would never be good enough to play for customers. Then he had had a wonderful idea.

'Is there any way to write down music?' he asked his father. If he

could write it down, he could teach his father the melody and then his
father could play it!

'No!' his father said sternly. 'Never! Music must never be written
down. From mouth to ear, from fingers to eye, from heart to heart,
that is how music must be shared. Do you understand?'

Sternness was so rare for his gentle father that Ash had nodded,
startled, the melody vanishing from his mind. He had known that
songs mustn't be written down; but hadn't understood that the prohibition included all music. Looking back, Ash realised that that was the
moment he had stopped paying attention to the music in his head –
because what good was it, if it could never be shared with anyone?

As he and Flax put up their tents – separate, thank the gods and
Cael – Ash wondered about that prohibition for the first time. He
knew it was all of a piece with the philosophy of the Deep, but he did
not really understand what purpose it served. He had followed his
father's teachings with blind loyalty until now – but if his father had
truly withheld songs from him, that loyalty had been . . . mistakenly
given. The thought made him feel sick, but it stayed with him. And,
ignoring a guilty sense of doing something shocking, he started once
more thinking about writing down music.

They did without a fire – Ash felt that the less attention they called
to themselves the better. So they sat beside the stream to eat their cold
beef and bread and dried apples. Flax pitched a crust into the chuckling water and asked, 'Where are we going?'

Ash's first thought was that he shouldn't say, but Flax would know,
sooner or later. He remembered asking his father the same thing, the
first time they had left his mother with her sister near the Lake and
taken the Road by themselves. His father had stared at him, as though
weighing his words, and said, 'I am going where I must go, and you
are going with me. That is all you need to know.'

From father to son, that was reasonable. From man to man, it
would be intolerably arrogant. But he couldn't tell Flax *what* they were
going to. Or exactly where.

'The wilds near Gabriston,' he said reluctantly. Gabriston was on a
bluff downstream of the Lake. The Hidden River, which ran from where
the Lake plunged into a gorge just below Baluchston, came out at
Gabriston. The many streams which fed the Hidden River had carved the
local sandstone into innumerable canyons and gullies. The place was as
wild as still existed in the Domains, and it had a bad reputation.

Flax's eyes widened. Although it was just past sunset, Ash could see him clearly enough. He looked like a little boy being told a story.

'Zel says that place is haunted by demons and ghosts!'

'Well, *real* ghosts are nothing to worry about. And as for demons – I'll introduce you to a few when we get there.' Ash grinned. He couldn't resist the temptation to scare the boy a bit. Just a bit. But while Flax was young, he wasn't stupid.

'So they aren't real?'

'Oh yes, they're real. But they're probably not what you expect.'

Frowning, Flax took up the napkin his dinner had been wrapped in – probably by Zel. She had trained him well. He shook out the crumbs, folded it carefully, and tucked it back into his pack.

'What path will we take?'

'I'd rather not go into Thegan's territory,' Ash said, reluctant to explain why. The man he had killed to protect Bramble had been one of Lord Thegan's men. He remembered the man's friend, Horst, saying, 'You've made yourself a bad enemy today,' and knew that he'd spoken the truth. Thegan was a very bad enemy to have made; but there was nothing he could do about that now, except avoid him. 'So when we reach the mouth of the valley, we'll ride east into Far North Domain and swing around to come to the wilds below Baluchston.'

Flax nodded. He glanced at Ash quickly, as if gauging his mood.

'What's wrong with Thegan?' he asked.

As they were Travelling together, Flax had the right to know. Slowly, Ash explained, 'When Martine and I first came into Golden Valley on our way to the Well of Secrets, we found two of Thegan's men attacking Bramble. So I stopped them. One of them got killed.'

'You *stopped* them? You killed a warlord's man?' Flax's voice was high with excitement and his eyes were round. '*How?* What happened?'

At first, Ash misread his reaction for that of a youngster wanting an exciting story, and it annoyed him. Then Flax continued, 'I didn't know you could *fight* them!' and Ash realised that the wonder in his face was because a Traveller had stood up to a warlord's man and survived. Conquered. He looked at Ash with complete hero-worship, which made Ash feel sick.

'Don't you try,' he said. 'I've been trained as a safeguarder. You haven't.' He'd meant it as a dismissal of his own skill; to imply that that skill was nothing special, just an outcome of training, but Flax took it the other way. He nodded solemnly, even more impressed.

'Can you teach me?'

Could he teach Flax? Well, he *could* – but whether he *should* was another question.

'We have too far to ride and you have too many other things to learn when we get there,' he said, not wanting to refuse outright. 'Maybe later.'

'Is it a long way?' Flax asked, disappointed but philosophical about it.

'A few days' ride.'

'Zel told me not to sing for my supper,' he said. 'How will we eat?'

'Don't tell me you always do everything Zel tells you?' Ash said.

Flax grinned and got up. 'Not always,' he said. His smile was an invitation to share confidences, but Ash wasn't in the mood.

'Let's go to sleep,' Ash said.

Flax nodded and moved to open his tent flap, but paused halfway inside. 'You could sing with me,' he said. 'There are some good drinking songs that need two voices.'

Gods, that boy was annoying. 'I don't sing.'

Flax shrugged and disappeared into his tent. Ash lay in his own tent and deliberately didn't let himself think about the stonecasting he could not do, which might have paid their way. Instead, he sent his thoughts out to Bramble. Tonight was the Spring Equinox; whatever journey she was going on would start tonight, he was sure.

'Gods of field and stream, shield your daughter,' he whispered into the night, and felt better for it.

MARTINE

'SHE LOOKS UNCOMFORTABLE,' Martine said.

'I daresay she is,' Safred answered, smoothing back a strand of Bramble's hair.

Bramble lay curled up on her side, twitching slightly. Her black hair shone in the early morning sun, her skin pale, sweat beading her forehead and making stains on her back and under her armpits. Wherever she was, whatever she was doing, it was taking a lot of effort.

Every little while they would support her head and tilt water into her mouth. She swallowed reflexively but her eyes stayed closed. She made no sound, although sometimes she seemed to mouth words. Sometimes she smiled. She did not look like she was asleep, because there was no relaxation of her muscles. She stayed tensed against – something.

What was happening to her was horrible, worse somehow in daylight.

'She agreed to do it,' Safred reminded Martine, reading her thought, as she so often did. 'This was her task, and she knew it.'

'That doesn't make it right,' Martine responded.

Cael and Zel were off in the forest, hunting or foraging or perhaps just walking. No doubt Zel was searching for a new flint, too. They had struck up an odd friendship, speaking little but attending briskly to all the practical things that had to be done: setting up tents, seeing to the horses, cooking. Martine could see that there was a comfort in doing ordinary, necessary jobs, but she couldn't pull herself away from Bramble. She was in danger, Martine was sure. She felt that conviction deep in her bones, although she had no idea what threatened her. Obscurely, she felt that she owed it to Ash, who had risked his own life to save Bramble's, to make sure that the girl was all right.

'Is there danger?' she asked Safred abruptly. While it went against the grain to ask someone else instead of the stones, if you had a prophet handy, you might as well use her.

'There's always danger.'

'From what?' she demanded and then, remembering the ghost of the girl Ash had killed in Turvite and her warning, she added, 'From whom?'

Safred spread her hands. 'I don't know.' She was embarrassed. 'But the Forest has said Bramble will be safe, and we must trust to that. The gods are guiding her, no doubt.'

As so often with Safred, Martine felt that she meant more than she was saying, that she intended her to feel in need of guidance. She remembered Bramble's attitude to Safred, defiant and challenging, and smiled. Perhaps she needed some of Bramble's defiance in order to protect her. Perhaps she should trust her own annoyance, and let it guide her.

'It's the Forest that's hurting Cael,' she said harshly.

Safred paled. 'He's better this morning.'

'When he comes out of the Forest, he'll be worse,' Martine predicted. 'You should keep him out of the trees.'

She was right. When Cael and Zel emerged, he was leaning on her arm, shaky and pale, but he waved aside Safred's offer to try to heal him.

'I'll last until we're away from here,' he said. 'You can try again then.'

'Stay out of the Forest,' Martine said. 'It will do you no good.'

He nodded sombrely and then smiled, as if he couldn't help it. 'Caught between flint and striker,' he said, gesturing from the trees to the lake. 'If one doesn't get me, the other will. But we found a stream a little way back, where we can water the horses and fill our skins.'

'Don't trust it,' Martine said. 'Check it every time, in case it has the smell of – whatever that was at the other stream.'

Zel nodded. 'Hell'll melt before I trust any stream in this place,' she said. She looked at Bramble. 'How's she?'

'Fighting something,' Martine said. Bramble did, indeed, look as if she were fighting some internal battle, her face tight, her arms twitching, like a dreamer in a nightmare.

'Protect her, then, if you feel you must. She may be glad of it,' Safred said.

Martine sat down next to Bramble. She doubted that the threat to

Bramble would come from the outside, but she loosened the knife in her belt and the one in her boot and sat with her back to Bramble and the lake, scanning the Forest edge. But although she tried to put all her attention into her eyes, she was aware of Bramble, twitching slightly behind her, all her muscles taut as though she wanted to run, far away from here. Martine wanted to run, too. Her body was still keyed up from the ritual, and she was feeling unsettled and nervy.

She also didn't want to think about what 'destiny' of hers required her to stay in the Last Domain instead of Travelling with Ash. She had seen many people meet their destiny, and it had mostly been very unpleasant, often deadly. She shrugged. Well, if it came, it came. Elva was safe, and that was all that mattered. Elva and the baby.

LEOF

H E HAD LET his anger at the Voice doom the town. He should have swallowed the insult and kept her talking, convinced her to surrender and *then* consult the Lake. Buy some time.

Leof rode back to the camp in a foul mood, angry with himself, Vi, Thegan, even the Lake itself, ignoring the glances Hodge and the men exchanged behind his back. What was the point of this? Fighting the Ice King's men when they had attacked the Domains, that had been *necessary*. This was just politics.

Thegan was overseeing the making of fire arrows, checking that the men didn't wind so much linen onto the arrowheads that they would go wildly off course when fired. Leof knew the drill. The arrows would be dipped in oil and lit just before they were shot into the air to rain down destruction on Baluchston, as they had tried to do to the reed beds. The Lake doesn't like fire, he thought. She won't be pleased about this. At noon, they won't even be spectacular. The thought gave him a thread to follow when he spoke to Thegan.

'It's a shame to fire these things in broad daylight, my lord,' Leof said. 'They're much more frightening at night. Sometimes you only need one or two before they surrender.'

'So they're going to fight?' Thegan rested one brown boot on a barrel of oil and gazed sharply at him. The spring sun picked out the lines on his face, but it flattered him; he looked sharp as well, sharp and ready for action, ready for battle.

'The Voice has gone to "consult with the Lake",' Leof said deprecatingly, as though 'consult with the Lake' was a euphemism for something else, something more political. 'She says it will take until sunset. I don't

think she – the Voice, I mean – will let her people be killed. She would surrender before that.'

'So she will surrender as we approach the town.'

'Mmm. If she's there. She said the consultation had to happen in
deep water. That she – and perhaps others, do you think, my lord? –
would be out on the water all day. If we attack when she's not there –'

'Then she will be spared the sight of her town being put to the
flame,' Thegan said briskly. 'Order the men up for noon. Tell them to
have their farings early, and to eat lightly. We don't want them weighed
down and sleepy for the fighting.'

Leof bowed. 'My lord.'

He knew Thegan well enough to accept that any attempt to
sway him was useless. The only thing that could stop the sacking of
the town was Thegan's death. Perhaps the Lake would accomplish
that. Half of him was appalled at the thought, while the other – the
part that had been well taught by Thegan, he recognised – knew
that it was the simple truth. And although he winced at the thought
of Thegan's men descending on the townsfolk, angry at the Lake's
destruction of their comrades, and believing Thegan's claims about
the enchanter from Baluchston, still he was Thegan's man, and would
follow his orders. What else could he do? Set his own will up against
that of the warlord? Claim some right to command, a right that didn't
exist in any form? Nor would walking away, giving up his position,
help. The town would still die. Perhaps he could keep the men under
some control once the town was fired: keep the rapes and looting to
a minimum. He wondered if Acton had ever faced a moment like this.
But Acton had laughed as he killed, a thing Leof had never understood.

He called the sergeants together and gave them Thegan's orders. As
they left, he called Hodge back, knowing that Thegan had been testing
him all day, and would continue to test him.

'Get those lists of the dead ready for me. My lord wanted them
before noon.'

'Aye, my lord,' Hodge said. He hesitated. 'The old lady . . . she was
the Voice?'

Leof nodded. 'She's gone to consult the Lake. But my lord Thegan
wants their surrender by noon, and if he doesn't get it . . .' Leof
shrugged.

Hodge pulled at his lower lip, considering. 'Seems like someone should have told her my lord doesn't like to be kept waiting. Saving your presence, my lord.'

Leof chuckled without humour. 'Perhaps someone did, sergeant. And perhaps she ignored it.'

Hodge spat in the dust. 'More fool her, then,' he said dismissively, and went to follow his instructions.

The sun was climbing. Hodge brought back the list of the dead – too long, much too long, no wonder Thegan was angry, Leof thought. A waste of men, of time, of training – of sorrow and loss.

He presented it to Thegan in his tent.

'What a waste,' Thegan said, frowning blackly. 'When I think of all the training we put into getting the Central Domain men into shape!'

Leof said nothing. He was an experienced commander; he'd thought the same thing. It just sounded colder said aloud. He nodded and went back to readying his men, lecturing them about discipline and orderly occupation of the town, hoping to fend off the worst behaviour.

'Kill only those who resist,' he said. 'Remember, we don't know how many were involved in the enchanter's plot. Most of the towns-folk are probably as innocent as you or I. No breaking into homes without orders. No rape. If a woman fights, kill her cleanly. No destruction. My lord Thegan wants this town intact for his own use, and I'd remember that if I were you.' He said it with a smile and there were a few chuckles from the older men.

'Sergeants, you will be held responsible for the behaviour of your men.'

The sergeants turned as one to glare threateningly at their squads.

'We're like Acton's men,' Leof concluded. 'We don't want to destroy everything, because we'll have a use for it ourselves. Understood?'

The men nodded, but Leof doubted that, in the thick of it, amid the noise and the heat and the shouting, they would remember to control themselves. He'd done what he could.

The sun was climbing. Less than an hour to noon, and no word from Baluchston. Leof found himself checking the road to town every few moments, hoping to see a messenger bringing the surrender.

At noon, Thegan emerged from his tent and came to stand before his troops. The sun lit his fair head and reminded Leof of the old songs about Acton marching into battle with a head of shining gold.

'The town has defied us. The town has killed our comrades. The town will be taken. You have your orders. Kill any who resist.' He paused deliberately. 'There will be pleasures afterwards, for those who fight well. But I want order and I want discipline.' He smiled, that miraculous smile that no one could resist, and the men smiled back, even the crusty old sergeants. 'Those who fight well today will be rewarded. Are you ready to avenge your comrades?' He raised his voice to a shout on the last words.

'*Yes! Aye!*' they shouted back.

Thegan nodded and turned to his officers.

'Tib, take the lead –' he began but a scuffle behind the men attracted his attention and a quick frown.

'What's toward?' Leof shouted at the rear.

'A messenger, sir,' someone shouted back.

A stir went through the men, half of relief and half of disappointment. Leof sent a quick prayer of gratitude to the gods and shouted again, 'Take his horse and let him through, fools!'

But the man who struggled through the troops was clearly not a messenger from Baluchston. He had ridden hard and long; ridden to the point of exhaustion. He was an older man, completely bald, wearing a dark robe and carrying a stonecaster's pouch at his belt.

He was staggering as he walked, and almost fell as he passed Leof. Leof supported him the last few steps to Thegan.

'My lord,' the man said. His voice was hoarse with travel dust and he tried to clear it. Leof grabbed a waterskin from a nearby sergeant and gave it to him. He swallowed a mouthful and waved the rest away.

'Later. My lord, Carlion is attacked.'

Thegan straightened, his attention like an arrow finding its mark.

'Who? Not old Ceouf?'

The man shook his head.

'Not by the living, lord. By the dead.'

A stir ran through the men.

'To my tent,' Thegan said, nodding to his officers to follow. Leof supported the man until he sank onto the bench before Thegan's work table.

'Now,' Thegan said.

'I tried to warn the Council,' the man said in a flat voice leached by exhaustion. 'I'm a stonecaster, I saw disaster coming on us and I warned them. Every stonecaster in the city warned them, but there was

no way we could read the truth in the stones and no way we could prepare for such an attack.'

'The dead,' Thegan said. 'An attack by the dead?' His voice was
carefully noncommittal.

The man smiled. An intelligent smile. 'It sounds mad, I know. You
remember the enchanter who tried to raise the ghosts against Acton?
To give them strength and body?'

Thegan nodded. Everyone knew that story. After Acton's men had
taken Turvite, a mad enchanter had tried to raise a ghost army against
him, the ghosts of those he had killed. The story said she had wanted
to make them solid so they could fight again, but when that failed, she
tried to use the ghosts to frighten Acton away. Acton had laughed at
her, asking why he should fear the dead when he had already defeated
them alive? He wanted his people to live with a reminder of their victory. He laughed as he said it, and she cursed him with the loss of the
only thing he held dear, that he should never have what he most wanted, but he shrugged and said he already had it, and gestured to the city.
Then she jumped off the cliffs.

'Someone has found a way to do what she could not. Someone has
given ghosts a strong arm.' He paused, coughing, and Leof handed him
the waterskin again. This time he drank deeply and sighed afterwards.

'They came at night, maybe a hundred of them. Only a hundred,
but nothing could stop them. We had been warning the town for a
week and most men slept with their weapons by their bed, so the
ghosts found resistance, but it was a slaughter anyway. How can you
kill someone who is already dead? How can you stop someone who
feels no pain, who does not bleed?'

Leof imagined such a battle and felt himself pale. The other officers
clearly felt the same. Thegan's face was unreadable, but familiar to
Leof. It was the face of his general, a battle-hardened officer who had
faced fierce enemies many times, and had found solutions where others had seen only disaster. The ability was one of the reasons his men
followed him blindly – Thegan could always see a way clear even
when they could not.

'Cut off their arms,' he said. 'Cut off their legs.'

The man nodded. 'Yes,' he said. 'That might work. But lord, it
would take a trained fighting man to do that, and we were just merchants! They killed . . . they killed so many . . .'

'So you ran.'

'I fought,' the man said bitterly, and pulled his sleeve up to show a long wound, barely crusted over. 'Then I realised that perhaps no one would survive, and what we needed was an army. So I came to you. I have been riding for . . . I don't know how long. Three horses have foundered under me. But it was the night after the full moon when we were attacked.'

Thegan nodded. 'You did the right thing. Go and rest now.'

Tib went to the tent flap and called a solider to support the man and take him somewhere he could sleep.

'Wait,' Thegan said. 'Your name?'

'Otter,' the stonecaster said. He hesitated. 'Lord, when I rested a moment or two, I cast the stones. Carlion was just the beginning.'

Thegan nodded, his face as grave as Leof had ever seen it.

'Rest,' he said, his hand on Otter's shoulder comfortingly. 'We will manage it from here.'

Otter smiled, a startlingly sweet smile. His eyes were strange, not one colour or another. Right now they reflected Thegan's brown uniform and shone dark with flecks of gold.

'I knew I was right to come to you. The stones told me so.'

Thegan smiled at him and clapped him on the shoulder in farewell.

Thegan addressed his officers. 'Strike camp. We march to Carlion. The nature of the attackers – that stays between us until the men need to know. We must avoid panic.'

There was nothing else to be said. As Leof turned to go, Thegan stopped him with a hand on his arm.

'A wave from the Lake here, on the same night as the attack on Carlion. No coincidence. Which means this was meant to weaken us so we could not aid the fight against this ghost army.'

'So,' Leof ventured, hoping to rescue something from this new development, 'perhaps it was not a Baluchston enchanter at all? Someone who could raise the dead like this could certainly control the Lake . . . ?'

Thegan looked sharply at him, but nodded. 'Perhaps. Still, if one attack has been aimed at us, so may others be. I want you to ride immediately for Sendat and take control there. The reserves we left there must be trained up fast and hard; call in the oath men from the villages and begin training them too. We are going to need every spear, I think. As the stonecaster said, Carlion was just the beginning.'

Leof nodded slowly. Every village owed the warlord men to fight in times of war – the men took an oath to come when called, and were given weapons and some training in return. But they weren't soldiers, and they would need much more training before they could fight effectively.

'I will send out messages from here to the other warlords,' Thegan said. 'We must all be prepared. Perhaps other things have happened elsewhere.'

'Yes, my lord.'

Thegan picked up a knife from the table and studied the way the light fell on its blade. 'Protect the Lady Sorn,' he said softly. 'At all costs.'

'With my life, my lord,' Leof said immediately. Thegan shook his head and smiled – not the miraculous smile, but the real one, the one he kept for people he trusted. It was, as always, like being let into a secret room, a treasure house. Leof couldn't help but smile back.

'Not with your life, Leof. I need you to stay alive, too. Let others die for her.'

The combination of intimacy and callousness left Leof not knowing what to say. Thegan threw the knife down onto the table so that the blade stuck in.

'Get my fort ready for war, Leof. You know what we'll need.'

Leof nodded. 'Train them how to cut off someone's arms while they're trying to kill you,' he said dryly.

'Exactly,' Thegan said and smiled the miraculous smile. He handed Leof a sheaf of papers. 'Take the list of the dead with you and inform the families. Ride well.'

Leof hesitated. 'Do you have any word for me to take to the Lady Sorn?'

'No time. Just tell her the truth, and that I think of her.'

Leof saluted and left; gathered Thistle, his two remounts, his groom and their gear and was on the road before the last of the tents had been struck.

Riding out of camp, he couldn't stop himself wondering why he had been chosen to guard Sendat. Thegan was on his way to give aid to a free town. To protect it. From inside its gates, no doubt. How long would it need that protection? Forever? Carlion's days as a free town were over, it seemed to Leof, and he wondered if he had been despatched to Sendat in case he developed any inconvenient scruples about taking over a free town.

The only free town with a harbour near the Central Domain.

'From cliff to cove,' he said aloud, and encouraged Thistle to a canter as they passed the last of Thegan's pickets. 'He'll have it all.'

Part of him was proud of his lord's success, his intelligence and
strategy. That was the loyal part, the part that believed that Thegan's
plan to unite the Domains would bring lawful prosperity to everyone.
He concentrated on that part, on thinking those thoughts. Because
that's who he was, even if he had let Bramble go against Thegan's
orders. He was Lord Thegan's man, or he was no one.

BRAMBLE

THE SWORD IN her hand was heavy, but it was the smell that roused her: the acrid smell of fear-sweat on her own body. That smell was so unfamiliar to her that she reached out her other senses urgently, only to recoil when she found herself in a man's body, full grown. Full grown, but with only one arm. Elric? He was standing on a ledge a small way from the steading, looking out over the undulating landscape. She judged it was summer, and there was a band of men riding towards him, appearing and disappearing as they rode over the ridges and into the dales. They were moving fast. Elric was trying to still his quick breath, so he could shout. He turned half towards the steading.

'They're coming!'

An indistinct shout of acknowledgment came from the hall, and men with shields and spears ran out. They threw themselves flat on the ground, taking cover behind rocks and wedging shields in front of them. They held one spear in one hand and a couple more in the other, and waited, staring intently towards the riders.

A raiding party. A war party. Bramble didn't want to live through a raid. If Elric lived through it. She didn't want to die again. If Elric died while she was with him, what would happen to her? Don't think about it, she thought. There's nothing you can do, so forget it. Where is Acton?

Then she realised that Acton was one of the men – the very young, or old men – who were readying their spears. He was still only around thirteen or so, and he was smiling. There were other boys, who looked even younger. One of them was probably Baluch, but she had no idea which one. It was a strange thought, that she could know someone so deeply from the inside but have no idea what he looked like. The boys were all so young. Bramble supposed that most of the men were off raiding someone else's steading, and felt a stab of contempt for them.

Elric cleared his throat. 'Wait,' he ordered. 'Make every shot count.'

The band approaching them numbered about twenty men, all riding the short, stocky ponies Bramble had seen before. They wore leather fighting gear, with helmets of what looked like dark wood but which was probably leather. Oddly, they carried no shields. She was used to seeing the warlord's men riding, as Thegan's men had done, with shield on the left arm and right hand free for the sword. As though her thought had sparked the action, each rider reached for something slung across his back. A bow, short, curved, lethal-looking. They nocked arrows in unison and let fly. Elric dropped to the ground and Bramble heard the arrows whistle over, heard some thuds and swearing from his left. Someone had been hit. Elric lifted his face from the ground.

'Shields, ho!' he shouted, and jumped to his feet, letting go his sword and picking up a spear in one movement. Unlike the other men, he had no shield to cover him. He knew it; it was why he was sweating fear, she realised. He threw the spear, aiming not at the men, but at the horses. Of course, Bramble thought bitterly. They always suffer first.

Elric had no time to see if his spear had gone home. The raiders let loose another flight of arrows and one took him in the shoulder, a sudden thud followed by burning pain. She heard Acton shout, 'Elric!' and then the waters came up and tumbled her away.

'There'll be more before they've finished,' Asa's voice roused her. Bramble was back in a woman's body, thank the gods, looking down at Elric this time, swabbing blood away from his shoulder in the hall next to the fire. He looked very pale. With his shirt off, Bramble could see the scars of earlier fights, and the seared stump of his arm, the skin shiny with the burn marks of cauterisation.

'You were lucky,' the woman she looked through scolded him. It was old Ragni's voice. 'You shouldn't have been out there at all, with no shield and jumping up just so they could get a good shot at you.'

Elric bore it silently. 'How many?'

Ragni quietened for a moment, spreading leaves – comfrey, from the smell – on the wound. 'Two,' she said softly. 'Old Weoulf and that boy of Dati's. A few wounded.'

'Baluch?'

'He's fine, he's fine,' Ragni said, her voice back to normal. 'He's off with Acton and Sebbi, burying the villains. No fire for them. They can rot in the cold hells.'

A groan interrupted her. She looked over and spat on the floor next to a man lying flat, with no pillows or blankets under him as there were under Elric. He was bleeding slowly from a stomach wound. The enemy, Bramble presumed. He looked much like the people from the second wave of the invasion of the Domains, with Merrick's colouring, auburn hair and hazel eyes. Just another one of Acton's people, as far as Bramble was concerned. But not for Acton.

Acton then came in, followed by Asa and a stocky boy with wiry blond hair – Baluch? Bramble wondered – and stood staring at the man on the floor.

'Water,' the man begged. Bramble understood him, but saw that neither Acton nor Asa did. The gods' gift worked for this man's language too, it seemed. But Ragni had seen a lot of men die in her time, and she knew what he needed.

'Wants water,' she said, her voice cold.

'Give it to him,' Acton commanded.

'Won't make any difference,' Ragni said. 'Gut wound like that, he's not got long.'

'I want to talk to him,' Acton said, his jaw set. 'Give it to him.'

She grumbled under her breath but she filled a drinking horn and handed it to Acton.

He squatted next to the man and lifted his head enough so that the man could drink. Half the water dribbled out the corners of his mouth. Bramble, too, had seen enough people die to know that Lady Death was standing close by.

'Why do you come?' Acton demanded. 'Why do you attack us?'

The man understood. He smiled thinly and muttered three words, 'The Ice King.'

His speech was gibberish to everyone except Elric, who twitched on his blanket. 'That was my father's tongue,' he said. 'It means the Ice King.'

'Your king sends you?' Asa asked. 'Why?'

The man smiled again, bitterly. He had to force the words out. 'Ice King takes everything.' That was all. His face paled and his eyes closed. Acton eased his head back onto the floor and turned away to talk to his mother. The stocky boy lingered a little longer, staring at the dying man.

'Don't waste your pity on him, Sebbi,' Ragni said, venom in her voice. 'Dati's boy is dead, and it might have been you.'

Sebbi looked at her with shock but the waters came in a wave, a breaking wave, and threw Bramble backwards into the dark, so she didn't hear his response.

The water trickled away and kept trickling, an intrusive and yet pleasant noise, a small stream over rocks. She was dabbling her fingers in it, sitting on grass beside the water and looking up. For a moment, that was all she knew: the sound and the feel; then her sight cleared and she found herself looking up at Acton. Not her, of course. Baluch. This time she recognised him immediately, the feel of his mind, with a faint pipe music interplaying with the sound of the water under his thoughts, the feel even of his body, was familiar.

Acton was standing by a small cliff where a spring issued from the rock and trickled down past Baluch. The contrast to the last time they were on the mountainside was striking. Now it was summer, warm and fragrant, the sky blue, the sun mid-morning high. The grass Baluch sat on was springy and bright green. Almost too green. Bramble smelt flowers – lilies of the valley, she thought, but she couldn't see them because Baluch was staring at Acton.

'Can you tell us *now*?' he said, his voice half-amused and half-exasperated. He glanced to his left where the stocky boy – Sebbi, Bramble remembered – was sitting. They exchanged looks of exasperation.

Acton grinned at them. He had grown a bit, was maybe a year older, fourteen or fifteen, as big as most men already, but she could see he hadn't come into his full growth.

'All right. We are going –' he paused for effect, but he looked a little hesitant as well '– to the Ice King.'

'*What*? Are you insane?' Baluch jumped to his feet. Sebbi followed.

Acton grinned more widely, then sobered. 'You remember that man who died? He said the Ice King had sent them.'

'Of course I remember, but –' Sebbi said.

'We don't know enough! We don't know if they come willingly, what he wants, why he attacks us – we just don't know enough.' Baluch regarded Acton. Bramble could tell that he was measuring him, weighing his words.

'So this doesn't have anything to do with Harald refusing to take you on the trading expedition?'

Acton scowled, for once looking like a typical boy. 'I'm bigger than most of the men already!' he complained.

'Yes, yes, we all know that,' Sebbi said, his tone mocking. 'You're bigger and stronger and a better fighter, too.'

'Well, aren't I?' Acton challenged him.

Sebbi paused and Baluch held his breath. Bramble realised that there seemed to be some tension between Acton and Sebbi which made Baluch uneasy. But neither of the others was tense, just concentrated. 'In the practice yard, yes,' Sebbi said. 'You're good. But there is more to battle than skill. You've never killed.'

'I have. I threw my spears. They fell.'

Shrugging, Sebbi replied, 'The horses fell. The men – some were killed by the fall, the hooves. Some by the second flight of spears. But who killed whom . . .' His tone was challenging.

Acton smiled, rejecting the challenge. 'Only the gods know.'

Sebbi laughed bitterly. 'You're not the only one who missed out. They wouldn't let *me* go because it wouldn't have been fair to *you*. Even though I'm a year older. Even though *my* spear took one of them down cleanly.'

'That's true. It was a fine cast,' Baluch said quietly.

Acton nodded and the strain went out of Sebbi's face. Baluch sat again and plucked at the grass, avoiding Acton's eyes. Acton sat down beside him, hands hanging between his raised knees.

'We're ready, Bal. You know it.'

'You're Harald's only heir. He doesn't want to risk you when things are so uncertain.'

'I want to go to sea!' Acton said, yearning naked in his voice. 'I've always wanted to.'

'There may not be battle. It's just a trading journey.'

Acton laughed. 'Oh, yes, just trading. How many times have they come back from trading without having fought? Once, maybe, in our lifetimes? There are brigands on the dragon's road as well as on land. Besides, it's the sea itself I want, not just the fighting.'

'The dragon's road itself is as dangerous as any battle,' Sebbi remarked.

'Exactly!' Acton said, eyes shining.

'So if Harald won't let you risk your life there, you'll do it here?' Baluch's tone was dry.

Acton looked sideways at him, smiling, mischief in his eyes. 'We do really need to know more, Bal. I'm not planning for us to fight. Just to scout. To see what we can see of this Ice King's country and his people. We've traded with them for generations and now suddenly they have nothing to trade and begin to attack us. This Ice King is driving them, but we don't know why. If we knew more, we might be able to make a truce. But right now, we're snowblind.'

'Why now, when the men are away? Why not stay and help protect the steading?'

'This is more important.' Acton had a stubborn look, but there was something underneath it. 'The chieftains will meet at the autumn Moot.'

'That's what you're planning! You're going to stand up in front of everyone and boast –' Sebbi accused.

'Not boast!' Acton protested. 'Report back. To everyone, not just Harald. All of us.' He avoided Baluch's eyes. 'Decisions must be made by all the chieftains, not just my grandfather.'

'What does your mother think of this?'

'Well, she said she'd leave our packs behind this rock . . .' Acton said, getting up and ferreting out three packs as he spoke. He dangled them from his hands, his eyes alight with mischief and excitement. 'So I suppose she thinks it's a good idea!'

'Hmm,' Baluch said, taking his own pack.

'Sebbi's mother helped. And if *your* mother objects,' Acton added to Baluch, 'she would have told the gods and they would tell you. But they haven't, have they?' There was a note of real anxiety in his voice.

Baluch shook his head.

'No. They haven't told me anything,' he said reluctantly. Bramble could feel the gods listening, watching, but they exerted no pressure on either her or Baluch. For a moment, she seemed to catch one of Baluch's thoughts, a memory of his mother, dead in childbirth with him. The memory was sharp with long regret. She pulled away from it, not wanting to share his mind any more deeply than she did already.

Acton whooped exuberantly, sounding much younger than he actually was. 'So let's go!'

Despite themselves, the other boys smiled with excitement. 'We're not in this for adventure,' Baluch cautioned. 'If we get caught . . .'

'No,' Acton agreed immediately. 'We mustn't be caught.' His face became determined, and much older. 'The chieftains need to know.'

'So which way do we go?' Sebbi asked, settling his pack.

Acton shot Baluch a mischief-look. 'I was hoping the gods might guide us.'

'So that's why you brought me!'

Acton clouted him on the shoulder. 'I wouldn't have gone without you, you know that!' They smiled at each other. 'But it would be helpful if the gods –'

Baluch shook his head. Bramble could feel no pressure from the gods in either his mind or hers. 'We'll have to make our own way.' Almost in apology, he added, 'They don't talk often, you know.'

'Mmm. Well, I did bring a map, just in case you weren't feeling holy.'

Baluch threw a pebble at him and they laughed. The trickle of the water became a flood and moved Bramble, tumbling, through the darkness.

She was singing, a kind of singing, a kind of calling out, calling something. Her throat tightened and relaxed rhythmically and the notes came out, not words but sounds, clear like bells, and underneath it a clicking sound, rhythmic too but uncoordinated with her calling. It was both musical and very irritating at the same time. Her sight cleared as the waters subsided, and she saw what she was calling. Goats. Goats with small blocks of wood tied around their neck, which clicked together as they moved. In Wooding, which seemed further than a thousand years away to Bramble, they had bells for their goats, at least for the lead wether and a couple of others. She wouldn't have thought the wooden blocks would make enough noise to keep track of the flock if they got lost in the forest.

Then she saw that they were on a steep hillside, with no trees, just low bushes and grasses covered with low-growing flowers. The girl stopped her singing–calling as the goats crowded around her, nuzzling at her hands and sides, one of them trying to eat her apron. She laughed and pushed the animal away. Bramble felt herself relaxing. This was known territory, at last. Animals, womanhood, the smell of goats and wild thyme, the bright blue of crane's-bill peeping from the rocks, all of it was familiar. Her mother used crane's-bill to make a blue dye. Bramble relaxed a little, but wondered why the gods had brought her here.

The girl clucked to the goats and sat down on the grass as they wandered nearby to graze. She pulled an apple and some cheese from her apron pocket and began to eat, her fingers teasing the blue crane's-bill flowers. From her hand and bare arm, she was quite young, and red-headed with freckles. Bramble was reminded of Safred jamming her old hat on her head. This girl apparently accepted her freckles.

The black nanny goat which had tried to eat her apron came over to see if she could cadge come of the girl's lunch, but the girl laughed and pushed the goat's inquisitive head away.

'Not enough for me, let alone you, too, Snowdrop,' she said. 'At least you can eat grass.'

Bramble wondered at that. The season was high summer; there should have been enough crops ripe by now.

The girl plucked a flower and threaded it into her hair by her ear.

'You know, Snowdrop, they say if you sleep naked, wearing crane's-bill in your hair, on Mid-Summer's Eve, the Wise One will send you a dream of your future husband. Do you think it's worth a try?' Laughing, the girl lay back on the grass and closed her eyes. Taking advantage of her inattention, the goat came closer and stretched its neck to reach the cheese inside its cloth. The girl sat up, still laughing.

'I can't trust you for a second, wretched thing!' She pushed Snowdrop away firmly, the flesh warm and comforting under her hands.

The language the girl was speaking sounded different to Baluch's. Bramble could understand it, but the difference made her wonder just where she was. Over Snowdrop's back she saw three figures come into view around a curve of the mountain. Three young men. Acton and two others. One of them was Sebbi.

Bramble had seen Sebbi through Baluch's eyes; now she could see Baluch through the girl's. He was even fairer than Acton – a tow-headed, pale-eyed youth who next to Acton looked slight but who had a rangy strength of his own.

She watched his face as he looked at the girl and saw his hesitation, and then the pleasure and desire in his eyes. But the girl was looking mainly at Acton. Sebbi noticed that, too, and his mouth tightened. The girl didn't notice. She was smiling at Acton.

Oh no, Bramble thought. Not that. She could feel heat flowing through her, the quick heat of the young who want things immediately, right *now*. This girl was smitten with Acton at the first glance. He

was worth looking at, Bramble admitted grudgingly, if you liked that
tall blond muscly type. The girl obviously did. Bramble thought wryly
that the gods were having a joke with her. The only person she'd felt
comfortable being since this began was an empty-headed girl who
wanted the man she hated most.

The boys hesitated as they saw her, but she had clearly seen them
and there was nowhere to go on the bare hillside. Bramble could see
Acton make the decision; let's pretend we're just harmless travellers,
boys out for a lark. He'd noticed that she was pretty, just as Baluch
had, but without Baluch's hesitation and reserve.

Acton smiled. Bramble wanted to think that it was a smile calculated to charm, like the way Thegan smiled, but even she had to admit
that it wasn't. It was simply pleasure: a sunny day, a pretty girl, a
chance to stop hiking and chat. And get information. Oh, yes, that was
in his eyes, too: determination.

'Greetings,' he said easily, in the girl's language. Bramble suspected
that Acton had learnt some of the foreigners' tongue from Elric.

The girl dimpled and played with one long red plait. 'Greetings,' she
said. She flicked a glance at Baluch and Sebbi but returned immediately
to Acton's face. 'You're not from around here . . .' It was both question
and invitation. Acton moved closer and sat down on a nearby rock.

'From a couple of valleys over,' he said easily. Was that a lie or a
simple understatement? Bramble glimpsed Baluch's face and realised
he was undecided about the morality of lying to this far too trusting
young woman. The girl wasn't interested in interpreting Baluch's
expression, just Acton's, which was one of pure admiration.

'We thought we'd take a trip and, maybe . . . catch a glimpse of the
Ice King.'

His statement was daring, Bramble thought, said so straightfor-
wardly, but perhaps it was safer than making up excuses.

The girl pouted. The movement was unfamiliar to Bramble, and she
instantly hated the sensation. I am not like her! she thought defiantly
to the gods. I just like goats. Her own emotions almost distracted her
from what the girl was saying.

'Well, that's not hard. He's only one more ridge over. It's not like
you can miss him.'

Acton frowned, puzzled as Bramble was by the girl's tone, which
was both resentful and dismissive, as though Acton had spoiled the
afternoon by mentioning the king.

'Plenty of time for that later,' Acton said, sliding down the rock so that he was sitting next to the girl. 'There are more interesting things here.'

She smiled and leant back on her hands, tilting her head so that she looked at him from under her lashes. Her breasts were bigger than Bramble's and it was a strange sensation, to feel them move and shift under her dress. Acton smiled back and trailed one finger down her cheek. The girl's body came alight, on fire instantly. Acton's thumb rubbed against her lower lip and her tongue came out reflexively, licking both her lips and his skin. He leaned closer. The girl's eyes closed.

No, no, no! Bramble thought to the gods. Get me *out* of here! Now! But they didn't listen to her.

Baluch and Sebbi had disappeared from the girl's sight and thoughts, but just as Bramble felt the warmth of Acton's face next to the girl's and was bracing for his kiss, Baluch shouted loudly, 'Acton! Get over here!'

Acton jumped to his feet immediately and ran, leaving the girl flustered and furious.

She jumped to her feet and turned on them. 'What do you think you're *doing*?'

They were standing on the ridge, looking down into the next valley. Acton's hand had closed on Baluch's shoulder as if for support. The three stood silently, staring.

The girl advanced on them. 'What's so important . . . ?' Then she realised what they were staring at, although it was still out of her sight. Bramble impatiently willed her to go forwards so that she could see.

'Oh, gods! Is that all?'

Acton turned to her. '*All*?'

She tossed her head, another action which Bramble immediately hated. 'Oh, I know, he's destroying everything, he's wiping out all our farmland, we're all going to starve –' There was a sob in her voice and Bramble realised she was genuinely upset. 'But there's nothing we can *do* about it and I thought we were going to have a nice day, just for once, just one day when I didn't have to think about disaster.'

She moved a step forwards, sank down and began to cry, but not before Bramble had seen what was in the next valley. Or rather, what was filling the next valley.

Ice.

The Ice King. Not a person, but a river of ice.

It filled the valley and covered the hills beyond. There were some

peaks that stood out in the far distance, but each of the valleys between
had been overrun. The ice stretched, white and blue and deep black
where fissures broke the surface, as far as she could see. At its leading
edge it showed as a striped cliff of blue and darker blue and white on
top. It was too big to comprehend, too beautiful to be anything but terrifying.

As the girl's sobbing quietened, Bramble found that she could hear
the crunch and screech of ice breaking, of rocks being slid along with
force. The river was moving. Acton heard it too. He crouched down
next to the girl.

'How fast does it move?' he asked gently.

She shrugged, still crying.

'How long has it been in that valley?' Baluch asked, not looking
away from the ice.

'Since three days after the Springtree dance,' the girl said, sniffing
and wiping her nose on her sleeve.

'It's Mid-Summer tonight,' Baluch said. 'That means it's eaten the
valley in less than two months.'

'He eats everything,' the girl said. 'My gran says it's a punishment
sent by the Wise One because we haven't been sacrificing enough.'

'What do you think?'

She hauled herself to her feet as though she were as old as her gran.

'I think the world is coming to an end, that the ice giants are eating
the world like the old stories say, and we'd better enjoy ourselves while
we can.' She looked at Acton and Bramble could feel, finally, the desperation under the coquetry. 'What do you think?'

He came closer and framed her face with gentle hands. 'I think you
are beautiful, that you have eyes the colour of the sea,' he said, and
Bramble could tell that there was no lying anywhere in him and perhaps never had been. So what changed him into Acton the invader?

He bent to kiss the girl.

Get me out of here *now!* Bramble screamed to the gods and at last
they responded, sending the waters to tumble her away, to swirl her
and shake her and land her somewhere, anywhere, but in Acton's arms.

ASH

THE NEXT DAY, a day of high white clouds and breezes, they rode through winding trails along the side of the mountain, heading south towards the pass into the North Domain. Ash considered all the different kinds of trouble they could get in, down in the populated parts of the valley. It was a truism among Travellers that two young men, Travelling together, were the most likely to attract unwanted attention.

'Bullies, bastards and bashers,' his mother had warned him when he was only eleven or twelve. 'They all go for the young men on their own.'

He couldn't see any way around it, though. They had to head down to the river flats, to make their way around the eastern spur of the Northern Mountains that fenced in the valley. The bluff reared up in front of them, growing taller as they rode through the next day, a sheer cliff bespeckled by stunted trees clinging to ledges and crannies.

'Do you know any way *over* the bluff?' he asked Flax.

'I'm not going up there!' Flax retorted, alarmed. 'That's wilderness!' Cam skittered a little, picking up on his fear.

Wilderness. Ash shivered. In wilderness, the old agreements with the wind and water spirits were void. Humans were prey, easy prey. The wilderness wasn't like the Great Forest, which had its own laws. There were no rules, and no help. Acton's people avoided the canyons near Gabriston because they believed them to be wilderness like that: fatal for humans. They were fatal, too, for anyone without Traveller blood in them. But the bluff ahead, that must be real wilderness, without demons, and no place for them. The valley was a haven in comparison. But they were likely to meet problems there.

Imagining all the problems, and planning how he'd deal with them

if they arose, took enough of Ash's concentration – along with the riding, which still didn't come easily – so that he could mostly ignore
Flax's incessant humming and singing.

He was so concentrated on the threats ahead that the shouts behind
them took him by surprise.

'Oi! You! What do you think you're doing?'

They both turned in their saddles to see three men riding up behind
them, on bay horses that even Ash realised were beautiful. The three
men were all red-heads, brothers by the look of them, and they sat
their horses in the same way that Bramble and Zel did, like they'd been
born there.

'We'll never outrun them,' Flax said quietly. 'They're chasers.'

Ash nodded. Better make sure they didn't have to run, then.

He raised a hand in greeting.

'Gods be with you,' he said politely.

The greeting surprised them. But then they looked at his dark hair
and dark eyes, and their own eyes narrowed. Flax moved forwards a
little and their expression lightened as they saw his fairer hair and
hazel eyes. Ash dropped his gaze. Let them think he was a servant, if
it made them feel better. 'Pride gets you killed,' his mother had taught
him, and she was right.

'Greetings,' Flax said, friendly and casual.

'What do you think you're doing, riding through our land?' The
eldest of them spoke belligerently, but as though he always spoke like
that, not with any especial malice.

'Sorry,' Flax said. 'I'm on my way to Mitchen, and I thought this
was a public road.'

'Why not take the main road, then?'

Flax waved his hand. 'It's so pretty here, I just wanted to enjoy the
ride.'

They frowned. Ash thought it was probably a bad excuse. But the
youngest man, a boy really, was looking at Flax with undisguised
admiration. Flax smiled at him.

'It is beautiful,' the boy agreed, pushing back his hair with one hand
and smiling for all he was worth. His brothers shot him looks of
annoyance, though clearly they knew all about his predilection for
young men, because there was no puzzlement or disgust, just that look
that brothers get when their younger siblings do something stupid. But
the eldest wasn't minded to let it go that easily.

'What's *he* doing here?' he said, staring at Ash.

'He's my safeguarder,' Flax said. It was an inspired idea. They looked taken aback, but not disbelieving.

Eyes still down, conveying no threat, Ash added, 'Young master here likes to wander around. His father sends me to take care of him.' He lifted his eyes and risked a conspiratorial smile. 'Make sure he doesn't get into bad company.'

The second man's mouth twitched, but big brother wasn't cozened so simply.

'A Traveller who can fight. Seems to me I've heard something about that recently . . .'

Ash shrugged, and Flax cut in.

'We've been up in Foreverfroze.' He addressed the younger brother directly. 'It's so beautiful up there. Have you been?'

'No, I always wanted to go but –'

His brother cut him off. 'You're that one who killed the warlord's man.'

Each man was suddenly still, staring at Ash. Except Flax.

'Oh, don't be silly. Why would he do that? And when, anyway? He's been with me.' His manner was perfect, and the men relaxed. Ash was impressed by the quality of his lying. That had to come from practice. He wondered how much truth Flax told Zel.

'Off our land,' the eldest brother said.

Flax and Ash both nodded, and turned their horses towards the river flats.

'Del, why don't you go with them and make sure they do leave?' the second brother said, amusement in his voice.

'Good idea!' the youngest said and didn't wait for endorsement from the eldest. He kicked his horse to move ahead and led them down a steep, stone-covered trail with the confidence of someone who'd done it all his life. Flax followed, just as flamboyantly. Ash came last with much more caution, finding another source of annoyance at Flax. It was all right for these boys who rode before they walked . . .

Del kept turning around in the saddle to flirt with Flax, who gave back smile for smile. Ash wasn't sure if it were acting or not. He suspected not, and wondered. Men shagging together was frowned upon among Travellers and it was one of the other differences between them and Acton's people. 'We all have to do our duty to the blood,' the boys had been told on his first visit to the Deep. 'The blood must survive.'

And they were also told: no more than two children who needed to be carried. Children must be spaced so that, if necessary, parents could pick up one each and run. This was the man's responsibility, to refrain from sex so that there were never more than two young children at a time. Many Traveller families had grown-up children and then a new batch, young enough to be their siblings' children.

'Oh, there's no room at our house. My grands all live with us and my brother's brood and I've got four sisters, too, and none of them married yet,' he heard Del say with mock outrage.

The prohibition against having more than two children at a time, combined with the Generation law, which for hundreds of years had forbidden Travellers to move in parties containing more than two generations – parents and children – meant that there were no large, happy, dark-haired families full of siblings who complained about each other and squabbled and borrowed each other's things and backed each other up in fights. Ash wondered what it would be like to live like that, in the middle of so many kin. But neither he nor any child of his was likely to find out.

They reached a ridge from which they could see the fertile valley, with wooden fences and houses looking like toys.

'This is the edge of our land,' Del said with clear reluctance. He pointed south. 'Follow the trail down that way and it brings you to the main road.' He edged his horse closer to Flax and Cam. 'Sure you can't stay?' he asked, resting a hand on Flax's shoulder. Flax looked a little downcast, too.

'I wish I could,' he said. 'But we have to get on.'

They both sighed. Ash envied them for a moment: the quick solidarity, the easy friendship. Their ease together wasn't just being attracted to each other; they were the same kind of person, spoiled and cosseted and sunny-natured as a result, expecting the best from the world. But in Ash's experience, the best didn't happen often, if at all.

He coughed politely, as a servant might to remind his young master of the time.

'Yes, we have to get on,' Flax repeated sadly. 'Thanks for your help.'

'If you're ever back this way . . .' Del touched Flax's cheek gently, and Flax nodded, then gave a cheeky grin.

'Oh, I'll pay a visit, don't you worry about that!' They both laughed and Del was still laughing and waving as they headed down the trail he had shown them and turned a corner, hiding him from sight.

'He was nice,' Flax said.

Ash made a noncommittal noise of agreement, and Flax grinned at him.

'Not your type? You don't know what you're missing!'

For the first time they laughed together, so they were not on guard as they rounded another curve in the trail and found themselves on one of the roads that criss-crossed the valley floor. Ash hadn't realised how far down they'd come and it made him nervous. This road was used. He could see a cart in the distance to the south, coming closer, and to the north was a man on foot, with the heavy pack of a hawker. At least he was moving away from them.

'Look for a way to get off this road,' Ash said. 'We need to go the back ways.'

Flax grinned. '*You* could always go over the bluff instead of around it. You're the one they suspect. I'll meet you on the other side.'

Ash shuddered involuntarily, and Flax laughed.

'Very funny,' Ash said sharply. He forced himself to look unconcerned, but the very thought of wind wraiths made him shake. Doronit had made him confront them – to tame them, even – but the memory of their long claws and sharp, hungry eyes still troubled his dreams.

He was so caught up in the memory of the night on the cliffs of Turvite when he had met the wraiths that he barely noticed the bullock cart coming towards him. His instincts kicked in at the last moment and he assessed the driver, a middle-aged man . . . someone he knew. Frantically, he tried to place the face, but it wasn't until the man spoke that he recognised him. This was the carter they had met, he and Bramble and Martine, on their journey out of Golden Valley to the Well of Secrets.

'You!' the man said accusingly, pointing at Ash. 'You're that Traveller they're looking for! I saw you before, with the two whores.'

Ash froze, caught between two equally strong impulses. The first, the oldest, was to run. The other was to kill. If they let the carter go, he would raise the valley against them. They would be tracked, captured, probably executed. Even the Golden Valley executed murderers. He thought fleetingly of the pressing box, and hoped it would be a quick hanging instead. But if he killed the carter now, it would buy them enough time to get out of the valley. Particularly if they hid the body and let the bullock loose . . . He found that his hand had moved to his boot knife without him willing it. He could hear Doronit's voice, teaching, 'Assess the threats against you and then remove them.'

It was good advice, and might save their lives. It might even save the Domains, because if they didn't complete their task and meet up with the others, there would be no one to stop the ghosts . . . One life against two. One against many . . . The time seemed to stretch out endlessly as he sat, poised between the two choices. The carter pointed his whip at them and almost snarled. Ash's fingers took a firmer hold, a throwing hold so he could draw and flip the knife right into the man's throat in one movement.

'You're scum, all of you!' the carter said. Ash's hand twitched, wanting to throw the knife.

'Death of the soul,' he heard Martine's voice say quietly, and remembered another ghost, a girl he had killed, who had warned him against this path. His fingers loosened on the knife hilt.

'Say nothing. Just ride,' he said to Flax quietly, and they swung around the man and pushed the horses to a canter. Once they were out of sight, they found the next path up into the hills and took it as fast as the horses could safely go on the steep ground.

They went fast and silently for an hour or two, cutting between tracks, heading back up the hillside, and then behind them they heard the belling note of hounds on the scent.

They looked at each other in alarm. The horses picked up on their nervousness and tossed their heads, Cam dancing a little sideways, which almost knocked Ash and Mud off the path. Ash recovered with difficulty and nodded his head to Flax to lead the way.

They came to a brook tumbling down the hillside in a mist of white spray, so they headed the horses upstream through the rocky flow and picked their way past two obvious trails until they came to a large stone jutting out into the water. Flax swung down from Cam and cajoled the horses into scrambling up onto the stone and stepping from there to a patch of thick grass, so that once the wet hoofprints had dried there would be no sign they had left the stream.

The sound of the dogs grew fainter behind them.

Ash felt as though he moved in a dream. After all, this was the stuff of Traveller nightmares: Acton's people on the hunt, dogs, a wilderness with no refuge, and he himself as guilty as he could be; no defence possible. He *was* a killer. Sully *was* dead. That thought made him wake up.

'They're after two of us,' he said to Flax. 'And you haven't done anything. If we split up, you should be all right.'

Flax shrugged. 'That carter saw me with you. He won't forget.'

That wasn't quite true. The carter had stared at Ash the whole time.

'You know what the grannies say,' Ash reminded Flax. 'It's our duty to survive.'

'Survive and breed?' Flax grinned. 'Not likely to happen with me, anyways. Never saw a girl I'd give a tumble to. Come on.'

He led the way up a narrow track, barely a deer trail, threading through the byways as quietly as they could. On the stony paths they had to move more slowly than Ash would have liked, but a lame horse would be the death of both of them.

Twice more during the day, in the distance, they caught the sound of baying hounds, and sweat broke out all over Ash. But the belling notes became no louder, and they found another path which took them further south.

'I just hope we don't go too far up,' Flax said, giving the bluff ahead of them a worried look. They were much closer, but they wouldn't reach it that day.

Just before night they found a hollow in the cliff which trickled spring water down into a small pool. It was as good a stopping place as they could hope for on the hillside, screened from view from both sides. They couldn't risk putting up the tents, so they slept on the ground, rolled in a blanket, cold and uncomfortable, and they kept the horses tethered right next to them. Ash took the first watch. He was more used to going without sleep, and Flax was tired out. Waiting in the dark, danger lurking in every rustle of the bushes, he blessed Doronit for her relentless training. He and Flax might not get out of this alive, but at least he wasn't sitting here panicking and feeling helpless. If the hunters came, they'd get a fight.

BRAMBLE

THE DIRGE OF pipes being blown slowly filled her head. The sound was almost torture, but saved from that by the gradual change of tone in the music. There was melody there, if she could only concentrate enough to follow it. She strained through the darkness and found that, although her sight cleared, she was still in the dark.

All she could tell was that she was in a room, somewhere inside. The darkness pressed in on her as strongly as the sound of the pipes, droning outside. The dirge was a sound that remembered grief, or promised it. She, he – Baluch, she thought, from his reaction to the music – was sitting on the ground with his back to a wall, his knees drawn up in front of him. The air was hot. Too hot, but the only comfort in the place was the warmth of another body next to his, and he didn't move away. Acton, perhaps? Or Sebbi?

Without the sound of the pipes she would have believed them benighted in a cave. She was fairly sure that the pipes were real, not just in Baluch's head, but she couldn't be certain.

Then the pipes outside mounted in intensity and a door was flung open, letting in a blinding light.

'Come on, then,' a voice boomed, echoing off the walls. Baluch turned his head. It had been Acton sitting next to him, with Sebbi on Acton's other side. They looked tired and Sebbi was trying not to look scared. Baluch's heart had started to beat wildly. Whatever was happening, Bramble thought, it's not good.

The voice belonged to a shortish, heavy-muscled man with red hair. His shoulders were huge and he wore only a length of undyed wool wrapped as a skirt. The rest of his body was warmed by a thick cover of hair. His beard obscured most of his face, and his head hair reached in many plaits down past his waist. There was so much hair on his face that it was easy to miss the sharp intelligence in his eyes.

'Out!' he ordered.

The three boys stood and walked slowly out the door, Acton first. They were all taller than the man, but Baluch, at least, didn't feel as if he were looking down on him. Bramble could feel the real fear that curled inside his stomach.

Outside, in pre-dawn light, there was a large circle of people, men and women and children, all with red hair. Bramble noted one girl with eyes red from crying, and thought, that's the one from the mountain, I reckon. Lost her lover. She couldn't feel much sympathy.

The hairy man took a knife from his belt – a black stone knife, the kind that never lost its edge. A knife from the gods.

'The Ice King has been sent as a punishment by the gods!' he declared, deep voice booming over the silent gathering. 'And why? Because we have been lax in our worship! We have foregone the ancient sacrifices! We have turned from the old, true ways and followed the ways of greed and easy living. So we are being punished!'

He pointed to the north. As one, the crowd turned to look and a moan broke from every lip. The Ice King towered over the village, less than an hour's walk away. Around the houses, Bramble could see carts laden with household goods. Ready to leave.

'It is time to return to the old ways!' the man announced. His eyes shone with fervour. 'We do not even have to give up one of our own. The gods have sent us their sacrifice!'

He raised the knife and a roar went up from the crowd. He shook the knife in the air and they roared louder. Then he lowered the knife and they quietened.

'But the sacrifice must be chosen. I have inspected these gods'-gifts and all are fit. So we will leave it to the gods.'

He gestured to a woman standing nearby, a thin-faced woman with eager eyes who reminded Bramble of the Widow Farli in Wooding. She handed over three straws. One was short.

The hairy man turned away from the boys and put the straws in his fist, then turned back and offered it to them.

'What happens if we won't choose?' Acton asked.

The man looked hopeful. 'Then you all die.'

Acton looked at Baluch, and then at Sebbi. 'If one of us is chosen, will you let the others go?'

The hairy man stilled for a moment, then nodded. 'Aye.'

'It doesn't matter who dies,' Acton whispered. 'What matters is that the others tell the chieftains about the Ice King.'

Sebbi laughed shortly. 'Hah! Easy to say.'

The hairy man thrust his fist towards Baluch.

Bramble could feel the pressure of the gods suddenly descend. He hesitated. They were telling him which one to choose. He could perhaps save his comrades by choosing a different one, but then he would be disobeying the gods. She could feel him think it through. What if the hairy man was right, and the gods had chosen their sacrifice? Perhaps the one they wanted him to choose was the short straw. How could he know? He yielded to the pressure and closed his fingertips around the straw the gods insisted on, and drew it out slowly.

It was long.

Bramble found that she was almost as relieved as Baluch. Don't be ridiculous! she thought. You know he doesn't die here. He founds Baluchston. But somehow it didn't feel like that to her, as though they were living a history already laid down in stone. It felt as though Baluch had made a real choice, could have chosen differently, could have died here.

Acton nodded to Sebbi to choose. Giving him a better chance. Sebbi glared at him, but reached for a straw. Short.

'Hah!' the hairy man shouted. 'The gods have chosen!'

The crowd roared again. Acton put his arm around Sebbi's shoulder. 'I'll take your place.'

Sebbi shrugged him aside. 'The gods chose *me*, not you. It's my death will save these people.'

Acton nodded respectfully. 'Your choice.'

He and Baluch both pretended not to see the sweat standing out on Sebbi's forehead.

In the crowd beyond, the men were assembling weapons. Spears, knives. No swords.

'I will be killed like an animal,' Sebbi said, his face pale. 'Without a warrior's death, how will I be reborn?'

Baluch moved to him and put a hand on his shoulder. 'You will go straight to the gods, Seb. You are their chosen. Of course you will be reborn.'

'Unless the sacrifice is not just this life, but all the lives I might have had,' Sebbi said.

Neither of them knew what to say to that. They stood quietly, waiting. Baluch was fighting both grief and a kind of horror that life could go so quickly awry, so badly. Bramble could feel his longing for home. For once, there was no music in his mind. Then the pipes began again and he shuddered.

Sebbi noticed. 'Thinking of music even now?' he mocked, his voice tight. 'What's the matter, isn't it in tune?'

Baluch looked him straight in the eye. 'I will write a praise-song for you and they will sing it until the end of time,' he said.

Sebbi's eyes grew bright. 'Yes,' he said. 'Give me life that way, Bal. If they take away all my rebirths, make sure I live in the memory of our people.'

'I will,' Baluch swore.

The hairy man approached them and took Sebbi by the arm, not unkindly. 'It's time, lad,' he said. 'Come, you must be blessed.'

He led Sebbi over to the space in front of where the men stood with their weapons.

'Can we do anything?' Baluch whispered to Acton.

Acton shook his head, his eyes fixed on Sebbi. 'I'm not sure we should even try. Maybe this is what the Ice King needs. Besides, what's important here is that at least one of us gets back to the Moot.'

His voice was implacable. There! Bramble thought with a strange relief. That's the invader. Ready to let others die for his own purposes.

The hairy man moved to strip Sebbi of his clothes, but Sebbi forestalled him and undressed himself quickly. Baluch mourned over him, but he was also noticing the details so he could work them into the song later: the way Sebbi stood tall in front of the crowd, the respect that had awoken in those watching as he had undressed, the way the light seemed to gather over his wiry golden head. The hairy man raised his knife and started to speak but Sebbi cut him off, shouting: 'I come as a willing sacrifice, to help the peoples of this place. I take your message to the gods: Save us! Curb the Ice Giants and let us live in peace and plenty!'

The crowd erupted in acclamation. The men shook their spears in the air, the women cried out and called as the goat girl had called the goats, ululating.

The hairy man pointed to the horizon, where the sun was just about to appear. 'Be ready!' he cried.

As the first gold edged over the mountain, he pushed Sebbi in the back. 'Take our evils, take our lacks, take our contrition to the gods and beg them to hear our plea!' he said. 'Run!'

Sebbi ran. As soon as he started, the men began to chant while the women sang a two-note hymn.

'Blood cleans, blood binds, blood scours, blood ties, blood washes, blood pulls . . .' they sang. The gods gathered, their pressure building, filling both Baluch and Bramble with holy terror. The gods' attention was stronger than she had ever known it.

Then Bramble realised the men were chanting numbers. They were counting. Counting as she had so often counted before a chase. But this was summer, not autumn. *After Mid-Summer*, the gods told her, absently, with only a part of their attention. *Any time after Mid-Summer, the sacrifice can be made.*

The Autumn Chase, Bramble thought, appalled. This is the real Autumn Chase. She was expecting them to count to fifty, but at forty-nine the men sprang away, led by the hairy man, and the gods went with them, leaving she and Baluch stunned.

The women followed the band of men, and the children ran beside them.

Acton turned to Baluch. 'Let's go.'

'We can't just leave!'

'We have to.'

'But –'

Acton dragged him away. 'He's going to die. Do you really want to watch?'

'Yes!' Baluch shouted. 'I promised him a praise-song. I have to watch!'

He pulled his arm from Acton's grasp and ran after the crowd as fast as he could. He was much faster than the women with their long skirts and he passed them easily, although his legs were cramped from sitting so long in the dark.

The men were loping after Sebbi. Bramble could see him, going up a rise in the near distance. He was running smoothly, his bare legs flashing pure white in the early sun. The men increased their pace and Sebbi turned, curving his flight away from them towards the Ice King. Bramble could guess his reasoning: if he was to die to banish the Ice King, then the best place to shed his blood should be on the ice itself. The men agreed. They let out a howl of approval and quickened their pace. Baluch pushed himself to run faster. He angled across the grass-land so that his path would intersect theirs close to the ice.

The ice had pushed boulders, soil and rubble before it. Collapsed houses. Precious spars of wood. Sebbi faltered as his foot landed on something sharp. Then he straightened and ran on, limping just a little. He left a clear trail of blood behind him. The chasers yelled in triumph. The blood heat was taking them over, the thrill of chasing. Bramble felt sick. This was what she had felt, chasing the Kill. This was her ritual, her greatest pleasure – her salvation. She realised that she had been truly reborn in the Spring Chase because somewhere, sometime, perhaps a thousand years before, a man had died in autumn. Life sacrificed, life returned, that was the bargain. It might even have been Sebbi's life that had given hers back to her.

He was at bay, now, standing bravely before the ice cliff. The men came within spearshot and howled triumph again. The spears flew. Baluch was counting them: ten, twelve, fifteen . . . Blood blossomed on Sebbi's chest and legs. He flung his arms wide, his jaw set, determined, then took the pain and used it to scream to the heavens: 'Hear our plea! Save us!' Then he fell.

The men crowded around so that Baluch could not see, then broke apart as some of them picked up the body and hoisted it onto their shoulders, its arms and legs dangling. They were all smeared across their faces with Sebbi's blood. Bramble's gorge rose, but Baluch was calm now, all his grief transmuted into an arrow of concentration aimed at the party of men.

Acton appeared at Baluch's shoulder.

'Time to go,' he said. The women came up, tearing at their faces and grieving for the young life cut down. But this, too, was part of the ritual and mostly their eyes were dry and bright with hope. Baluch put out a hand and stopped one of them, an older woman.

'What will happen to him?' He had spoken without thinking, in his own language, and she did not understand. Acton repeated it in her tongue. She hesitated.

'I do not know,' she said finally. 'In the old days, he would be torn apart and scattered on the fields to ensure good harvest. Now we have no fields . . . perhaps he will be scattered on the ice.'

They could see, when they turned back to watch, that the chase party was following the line of the ice, stopping at intervals for prayer. Acton and Baluch watched long enough to see that the end of the prayer was followed by some part of Sebbi's body being cut off by the hairy man and thrown onto the ice.

'Will it work?' Acton asked Baluch in an undertone. 'What do the gods say?'

Baluch shuddered. 'The gods say nothing. But I think it will take more than one man's blood to satisfy the Ice King.'

The men howled as Sebbi's hand was thrown high onto the ice cliff.

'Enough,' Baluch said, turning away as the waters descended on Bramble like ice crashing down from the king.

LEOF

LEOF COULDN'T BITE back a smile when he saw the roofs of Sendat appear, and Thistle picked up her pace as she scented the stables of home.

'Good to be back, my lord,' Bandy, his groom, said.

'Good and bad, man,' Leof replied, waving to a few townsfolk as they made their way up the winding road to the fort.

He assessed it with new eyes as he came near. Although it was reasonably well fortified against normal attack, it would be helpless against an enemy which could not be killed. The walls needed to be much higher, giving defenders the chance to isolate and deal with individual attackers. The top of the walls needed to be sharp, rather than wide, and the defenders should be armed, not with spears, but with axes. Meat cleavers, even, lashed to poles, would do until they could get proper halberds made. The smithies would have to work overtime. Halberds were the best weapon, he was sure. The long blade fixed firmly to a long pole – it combined sword and spear, with the advantage that it kept your enemy at more than arm's length. A broadsword could hack off a limb, but it needed luck as well as strength and judgment. A good whack with a halberd, on the other hand, had so much leverage behind it that it frequently sent limbs flying. The weapon wasn't used much in close-quarter work because of the danger to your own troops, but a line of defenders, trained to work together . . . The plan was all Leof could think of, and he was miserably aware that it was full of flaws.

They rode into the muster area to shouts of welcome from the stables and the smithies. Leof dismounted thankfully and gave Thistle to Bandy, patting her and murmuring gratitude for her hard work as he did so. He ordered another groom to help Bandy before heading straight to the smithies, walking the kinks and aches from his legs and telling himself he was not at all tired.

The chief blacksmith, Affo, was a surprisingly small man, though with the massive arms of his trade. Leof didn't tell him the details of the attack on Carlion, just that the town had been attacked, and the warlord's men would be marching to give aid.

'We have perhaps a day before they march past us. And in that time . . .' he paused, unsure of how to phrase the order, then shrugged the problem aside. No good way to say it. 'I want as many axes as you can produce.'

'We're doing that already, lord,' Affo said, surprised. 'Battleaxes, halberds, even choppers.'

'What?'

'The Lady Sorn ordered it, after that mad – after that messenger from Carlion came. She said,' he added, clearly fishing for information, 'that my lord Thegan needed them. She said not to worry about finishing them off, no decoration or such, just make them sharp?'

'If your warlord wanted you to know why, his lady would have told you, no?' Leof said severely.

'Aye, lord,' Affo said. His expression plainly said, 'All lords are mad.' Leof hoped he'd keep thinking so, instead of wondering what kind of enemy needed to be attacked with axes. The thought hadn't occurred to Leof, but of course Otter would have come to Sendat first. Lady Sorn had reacted as befitted a warlord's lady. He breathed more easily. The men would not be going into battle badly armed, although they would only have enough axes for the forward guard.

He turned towards the hall and the Lady Sorn. He half-expected her to be waiting for him in the muster yard, but of course she would not do that. Not the Lady. She never intruded on the public spaces – the men's spaces. The hall, the residence and the gardens were her domain and she kept to them. Leof had approved of that when he first came to Sendat. She acted the way women should, modest and refined. Then he had met Bramble, and his ideas about what a woman should do had undergone considerable change.

Sorn was waiting by the fire in the hall, sitting in a pool of sunlight from one of the high windows. The light turned her auburn hair into fire and made her skin glow, enriched the deep green of her dress and sent flickers of light from her earrings into the corners of the room. She seemed, for a moment, a creature of flame and leaf, like the embodiment of a forest, caught on a tapestry of the seasons between autumn and spring. Then he saw her face, calm as an iced-over pool, and thought, between autumn and spring is winter.

Normally, Sorn was surrounded by her maids and ladies, but now she was alone, except for the small hunting dog that was always at her side. She was waiting to hear her lord's message in private. Leof wished he had something better to tell her.

He bowed and saluted. Composed, Sorn rose and bowed back, protocol strictly observed, no trace of anxiety on her face. The little silvery whippet – what was its name, something odd, he couldn't remember – stood at her side, shivering as whippets do in the presence of strangers. She quieted it with a touch and it lay down again, head raised.

'My lady, I bring greetings from the Lord Thegan,' Leof said.

'You are welcome, Lord Leof.'

She gestured to him to sit beside her and he eased himself into a cushioned chair thankfully. Sorn poured him wine from a glass jug.

'You have heard the news, I gather, from Otter the Stonecaster?' He took a long swallow of the wine; it was a winter red from down south, full and comforting.

Sorn nodded. 'I did what I could to prepare.'

Leof smiled at her. 'I've just come from the smithies. You did exactly right, my lady. My lord's men will be marching through here on the way to Carlion by tomorrow sunset, and it will . . . it may make a great deal of difference, having the axes ready for them to take.'

She nodded, serious. 'My lord?'

He hastened to reassure her. 'He will be with them. He bids me to tell you that he thinks of you. He is well, although . . .' he took the sheaf of papers Thegan had given him from inside his jacket, 'not all will be returning with him. The Lake – or, my lord thinks, some enchanter controlling the Lake – raised a great wave against us. Many were killed.'

Sorn looked at the papers and went very still.

'How many?' she whispered. The whippet sprang to its feet and nosed her hand. She patted it absently. 'Shh, Fortune.'

'About a quarter of our forces,' Leof said. 'My lord has charged me with letting the families know.'

Sorn reached for the papers. 'This is my responsibility,' she said, her voice low. 'You will have enough to do.' She hesitated. 'And the Lake People?'

Leof sighed. 'We never laid eyes on the Lake People,' he said. 'My lord blamed an enchanter from Baluchston for the wave and was about to punish the town when the messenger from Carlion arrived.'

Sorn took a deep breath and let it out slowly, still looking at the list of names. 'Baluchston is a thorn in his side,' she said absently. 'He will have it out one way or another.' Then she looked up with anxiety in her eyes, as though he might hear that comment as disloyal. It was the first real emotion she had shown. The whippet stood alert, regarding him warily.

Leof smiled reassuringly at her. 'One way or another,' he agreed. She relaxed a little although, as always, she sat very straight. Fortune sat down again.

'Go to your quarters, my lord, and rest. Tomorrow will be soon enough to begin your work.'

He smiled at her ruefully. 'I doubt my lord would think so, I have a few hours' work yet before I can rest. But I would be glad of some food.'

She smiled back, her face lighting with a hint of mischief. 'I confess, I ordered a meal sent to the officers' workroom. It should be there by now.'

He chuckled. 'Too predictable, obviously. Thank you, my lady.' He rose, bowed and went out, leaving her sitting quietly. The sun had moved past the window while they talked and she sat now in a pool of shadow, studying the lists of the dead, her dog at her side.

ASH

THERE WAS A trail, Flax said as they changed shifts at midnight, which skirted the upper bluff well above the road used by carts and riders. 'Clings to the mountainside, like,' he said, 'about halfway up. It's *supposed* to be below the wilderness.'

There was a silence as they both considered that, weighing dangers.

'Can we use it without being seen?' Ash asked.

Flax was only a patch of deeper darkness against the hillside, but somehow Ash knew he was pulling at his lip, considering.

'If we start early enough. Maybe.'

So they started well before dawn, as soon as there was enough light for the horses to find their footing. The most dangerous part was where they had to descend a way into the valley, towards a larger road past a prosperous horse farm, from where the upper trail branched. Coming down the hillside was one of the hardest things Ash had ever done. He pulled up the hood on his jacket, just in case. He felt completely exposed in the dim light, as though a thousand eyes were watching him.

But they turned onto the trail without incident and continued quietly past the farm. It was so early that the dogs were still asleep, but as they passed the farm one woke and barked, waking the others until there was a chorus of barking. The door of the farmhouse crashed open to show the farmer, axe in hand, silhouetted in the opening. Ash stiffened, but Flax raised a hand.

''Morning,' he shouted genially. 'Sorry if we've woken you!'

Hesitantly, the farmer raised a hand in reply. Ash willed himself to keep Mud to a walk, matching Cam's gait. He didn't turn his head – with his hood up, the farmer couldn't see his hair or eyes, and wouldn't

know he was a Traveller. Flax's light brown hair was clear in the growing light, and he hoped that would be good enough.

The farmer stood, scratching his head. He watched them until they
were well past the boundary of the farm and the wild scrub started, but
that was fair enough. Any farmer might do the same to strangers. Yet . . .

'Look back,' Ash said. 'Can you see him?'

Flax flicked a glimpse back over his shoulder. 'Dung and pissmire!'
he swore. 'Someone's riding off the other way.'

'They set a watch, in case we came this way,' Ash said. His heart
was beating faster and he felt fear coil in his gut.

They urged the horses to a canter and kept the pace up as long as they
dared, until the trail became too steep and winding for it to be safe. There
was no sense cutting across the trails they found. Now it was a race – they
had to be around the bluff before they were caught. Had to be out of
Golden Valley by nightfall, or they would not be leaving at all.

All morning they climbed up and southwards into scrubby forest
where rocks broke through the ground like warts on a toad. They
stopped only to spell and water the horses. There was no food left and
they filled their bellies with the cold stream, which only made Ash feel
emptier. He allowed himself to hope, just a little. If they could just keep
far enough ahead until nightfall . . .

'There they are!' a shout came from behind them. Immediately, Flax
whistled, crouched low on Cam's neck and urging him on, pushing him
to a canter and then a hand gallop along the narrow trail. Ash was
taken by surprise when Mud responded enthusiastically to the whistle,
following Cam along the trail. All he could do was cling on as the horses took the winding path as fast as they dared. His hood fell back in
the rush.

'Get them!' the shout came behind them. 'That black-haired bastard killed my friend!'

Ash recognised Horst's voice. Horst. Not some nameless pursuer,
but a real enemy. But why was he still here? He realised with a shock
that it had been only a couple of days since he had killed the war-lord's
man. Horst must have stayed for the quickening, which would come –
oh, gods, was it tomorrow or today? Sully's ghost would rise, looking
for acknowledgment and reparation from Ash, his killer. It was his
duty to be there, to set his spirit at rest.

He couldn't. He had other duties, more important; he had to forget
the image of Sully returning from beyond death to find his killer gone

and his friend – his friend more intent on revenge than on freeing him for rebirth. Ash put his head down on Mud's neck and trusted to the horses and to Flax, because it was all he could do.

The shadows were closing in . . . if they could keep ahead until nightfall, and lose them in the dark . . . it was a forlorn hope. Ash could hear the sounds of pursuit getting closer. They were nearing the cliff face. There might be caves, but surely going into a cave would be stupid? There would be no way out.

The trail branched and Flax unhesitatingly took the left-hand fork. Around two bends, low branches whipping their faces, and then they had reached a clearing before the cliff, broken here by huge boulders. There *were* clefts in the rock, not caves so much as fissures, but they were narrow and no doubt had dead ends which would trap them. But if they could hide in one until the others passed . . .

The party behind had taken the wrong fork, but it wouldn't be long before they realised their mistake. Flax jumped off Cam and came to take Mud's reins so Ash could jump down, too.

'What now?' Flax asked. Off the horse, it seemed that authority had passed back to Ash.

'Hide,' he said simply. They led the horses to one of the furthest fissures in the cliff face.

'They've got to be here somewhere,' Horst's voice came. 'I want them both, but don't kill the black-haired bastard. He's for me.'

'You're not the law in Golden Valley.' Ash recognised the voice of the second brother, the reasonable one. 'We have no warlords here, and no warlords' men, remember?'

There were rumbles of assent from other men – at least six or seven, Ash estimated.

'Then I'll take him back to my lord Thegan and he can decide his punishment. Your laws allow for that, don't they?'

'Aye,' the second brother said. 'That's allowed.'

Flax and Ash threaded their way through the fissure as fast as they could and found it led, not to a cave, but to another small clearing. Before them was a slope leading up to the top of the bluff. The going was rocky and perilous for the horses, full of sharp rocks and boulders, with no level ground at all. But they could manage it, if they had to.

At the top . . . wind spirits. Doronit had controlled them, with Ash's help, but he had only been helping. Just as with Safred, lending his strength to her will. He had never done anything like that by himself.

He had a queasy suspicion that his own will wasn't strong enough, that the spirits would simply laugh at him if he tried to control them. Laugh and reach those long, clawed hands for his eyes . . . He shuddered. He couldn't do it. Better to face the trial and be hanged.

'They must be here somewhere!' Horst's voice came from beyond the fissure, startlingly loud. 'I'll have both of them dragged before my lord and they'll pay.'

Both. Ash looked at Flax, who was pinching the noses of both horses to prevent them from whickering. He had promised Zel he would look after him. Dung and pissmire.

'Here they are,' the second brother said with a note of relief in his voice. Flax and Ash strained to hear and both they and the horses jumped when the hounds began to bay, the excited note of a fresh scent.

There was only one way to go. Up the slope, to wilderness. They scrambled as fast as they could on the rough surface, trying to find a way to go sideways, any way but straight up. Behind them, voices were arguing.

'I'm not losing my best pack for you!' the first brother's voice sounded. More shouting followed.

Any further and they would be beyond the screen of the trees, open to view – unless they threaded through the maze of rocks which led up to the bluff. The dogs were still sounding. Ash could hear them panting with eagerness – a sound from nightmares. He had once seen a man brought down by a warlord's dogs. Not even a Traveller – one of the lord's own farmers who had tried to cheat on his taxes. He had been begging for death by the time the warlord reached him.

Ash touched Flax on the shoulder and pointed upwards. Flax paled and shook his head vigorously. Ash moved very close, until his lips were by Flax's ear. 'I can control the spirits,' he said.

Flax drew back in astonishment, staring at him. Ash shrugged, trying to look as though this was something he did every day. He saw the moment when hero-worship kicked in, when hope overcame fear in Flax's eyes, and it made him feel sick.

They started up the slope as quietly as they could in the fading light, Flax leading both horses as trustingly as a child, sure that if Ash said he could do it, he could.

But Ash wasn't sure at all.

BRAMBLE

THUMP. THUMP. REGULAR, deep, but not like a drum. More like . . . a fist on flesh. Yet not quite . . .

Bramble's sight cleared and she felt herself back in Baluch's body, then wished she weren't. The sound wasn't a fist on flesh, but a thick wooden rod. On Acton's bare back and sides. Harald was wielding it, his face red and furious. Acton held on to one of the posts in the big hall, his head hanging and his body shaking with each blow. Blood dripped onto the floor from where a roughness in the rod had caught him. Bruises were already appearing under the skin.

A circle of people watched – men and women, but no children. Bramble could hear them playing outside, pretending to be invaders and defenders. The contrast made her shiver, but Baluch was barely conscious of the noise. He flinched with every blow. Asa stood next to Acton, her face like stone.

'You disobeyed my orders,' Harald said, finally standing back.

'He had good reason,' Baluch said. 'What we found –'

Harald wheeled on him. 'Keep silence! The only reason I'm not belting you the same is that you were bound to follow his orders, as he was bound to follow mine.'

Acton was breathing heavily. He used the post for support and pulled himself up to stand straight.

'We found –'

'I don't care what you found!' Herald shouted, breathing as heavily as Acton. He glared at his grandson. 'I should have known you had treachery in your blood. Your father had to show himself in you sooner or later. You have lost a fine young man, a man who would have been valuable to our people. For a boy's prank! An adventure! It makes me sick to look at you.'

He threw the rod on the floor and walked off. Asa picked it up and watched him walk out of the hall. Once he was through the door, she dropped the rod on a table and turned to Acton, putting an arm around him to support him. He pushed her gently away.

'I can walk.'

He made it to a table in four faltering steps and sat down on a bench. Ragni was at his side immediately, with a warm bowl of water and soft rags for cleaning his blood away, but the deep injuries she could do nothing about. A woman passed Asa a drinking horn smelling of mead and she held it to Acton's lips. The mead brought a little colour back to his cheeks.

He smiled ruefully. 'I didn't expect him to be back so soon.'

'That's why he's in a foul temper,' Asa said. 'The boats never sailed. First they had to fight their way through to the coast, past parties of raiders from the north, and then, when they got there, the bays were still iced over. In mid-summer. They couldn't get the boats out.'

'It's the King,' Baluch said. 'He brings winter with him.'

'Tell me,' Asa said. The others crowded around to hear, but before he could speak a man ran into the hall. Tall, with wiry hair the same colour as Sebbi's. Perhaps three or four years older. His face was pale, with tears running freely down his cheeks.

'You killed my brother!' he accused Acton.

Baluch intervened. 'No, Asgarn. Sebbi was chosen by the gods to die a man's death. A great death, which shall be told in song and story for all the generations of our people.'

Asgarn hesitated, and looked at Acton, who began to describe what they had found in the valley of the Ice King.

When Acton described Sebbi's death, Ragni said, 'His mother should know of this, that he had a hero's death,' and she hobbled out of the hall, looking as old as time itself.

After Acton had finished speaking, the hall was silent. Asgarn turned away, his shoulders hunched.

'He was only a boy,' he whispered, but the hall was so silent that his words echoed.

'He died a man,' Acton reassured him.

'For nothing! You say the ice will still keep coming.' He walked out of the hall with his fists clenched. They watched him go silently.

'The Ice King takes everything,' Baluch said. 'Those from whom he takes must go elsewhere.'

That brought a babble of talk, but one question kept recurring. Acton put it into words for them all.

'We can defend ourselves against the invaders, but if the sea lanes are blocked all year round, how can we trade? Without trade, we'll starve.'

Asa considered. 'There is a path over the mountains,' she said finally. 'People live there. Where there are people, there can be trade.' She looked into Acton's face and smiled wryly. 'I think it's time you met your uncle.'

Bramble was beginning to get a sense of what the gods were showing her. Not just Acton's life, but its turning points. The moments of destiny. She wondered again if she should try to change the events she witnessed, but again the gods rose in her with immense pressure. *What has happened must happen*, they insisted, and she surrendered to their surety with something like relief, as the waters rose gently and floated her away. So, she thought, we go to meet the uncle.

'Cast!' someone yelled, and she felt her body draw back its right arm and throw something. Then again. This time, she could feel the smooth shaft of a spear in her hand, and her eyes took in the light just in time to follow its flight. The spear soared high, in a perfect arc, and came to earth in a man's neck. Blood spurted.

Suddenly she was aware of the noise: men were yelling, screaming defiance at the approaching war party. Those who had cast their spears rattled their swords on their shields. The band of men was below them on a slope, and although they threw their own spears they didn't have the same heft as the one thrown by – Baluch, was it? No, there was no music in this head. It was someone else who danced on the rock's edge and shook his sword in the air. The war party was made up of red-headed warriors who reminded her of the men who had cut Sebbi to pieces.

She saw Acton and Baluch out of the corner of the man's eye. Acton was shouting and thumping his sword. Baluch was quiet, but he hefted his sword more comfortably in his hand and set his feet to give him the surest footing. Acton gave a whoop of exhilaration and the man turned to grin at him, his cheeks drawn back wide in enjoyment.

'That's it, lad!' he bellowed to Acton. 'Get your heart up!'

Acton grinned. 'It's a good day for a fight, Eddil!' he shouted back.

There was no doubt that he was genuinely having fun. Wait until the fighting really starts, Bramble thought. This lot won't retreat because of a few spears.

Nor did they. The war party, thirty strong, forged up the hill and came to grips with the defenders. Eddil yowled and swung his sword; not, as Bramble had expected, at the man's head, but at his legs. The blow was blocked and the shock of that ran up Eddil's arm and made his fingers numb. He held on and swung his sword again. His blood was running light in his veins and his breath came easily. They had been training, then, Bramble thought, trying to hold onto her own mind in a deafening flurry of blows and counterblows, any one of which could have killed. She was not prepared for the clamour of battle. Or the smell of sweat.

Although she could not hear Eddil's thoughts, she could sense his feelings, as she had with the girl on the mountainside. He was exalted, feeling intensely alive, as she had felt during a chase. She concentrated on the man Eddil was fighting, trying not to think of him as her own enemy. He was around forty, she estimated, thin, and his eyes were deep-set, as though he had gone without sleep for some time. Every sword swing tired him more, and Eddil pressed forwards harder, changing his grip so that as the man's sword drooped for a moment, he could use the sword like a dagger unexpectedly, piercing the man's side. The red-head gasped and sank as his knees buckled. Eddil pulled out the sword and ignored the fountain of blood that sprayed him. He leapt away to meet the next warrior, shouting, 'Harald! Harald!' Then something – sword, spear, a block of wood was what it felt like – came down on his head and he stumbled. As his sight darkened and the waters rose up to carry Bramble away, she heard again Acton's whoop of delight and then his laughter. The old songs are true, she thought, he really did laugh as he killed.

A larger body, and older, was her first thought. She was squinting in bright light, looking west into the sunset, hand coming up to shade her eyes. She knew that hand. She searched her memory for the name. Yes, she was sure it was Gris. So, she thought, now comes the first meeting with the uncle.

Gris was watching a curve in a path that came from over the western hills into the valley. The hills were so close that when, sure enough, horses appeared, it took them only a few minutes to reach him.

Asa was in the lead, followed by Acton with a string of four laden ponies. Bramble realised with a shock that Acton was some years older – perhaps seventeen or eighteen. This was clearly not their first meeting. Gris shouted, 'Welcome!' to them as soon as they appeared and called back to the steading, 'They're here!'

As Asa and Acton dismounted from the stocky little horses, Gris embraced them both in turn while his people rushed to take the horses to the stable. Acton delayed long enough to lift his saddlebag from his pony and then allowed Gris to put an arm around his shoulders and usher him into the hall.

The hall was smaller than Harald's and had no shields or spears as decoration. Instead, antlers and animal skins were nailed to the wall: boar's tusks, a bear's jaw, even an eagle's talons. Bramble did not like to see trophies of death flaunted. On the other hand, these were people who valued hunting above fighting, as she did. That thought made her pause for a moment, remembering moments when she had hunted to live or to feed her family, and so she did not hear the first few words of conversation. When her attention returned, Acton, Asa and Gris were sitting by the fire pit in the middle of the hall, sipping beer and talking about the weather. Bramble almost laughed. The weather! The gods had brought her here to listen to weather talk!

'Yes, it's cold for this time of year,' Gris said.

'Too cold,' Asa replied. 'The Ice king's talons reach further every year. We are hard pressed.'

'The people unlanded by the king are seeking new lands, and they don't care who they take them from. Old friends are become enemies,' Acton said. 'Even the chiefs at the Moot look askance at each other.'

'When your children are starving, you don't care who owns the bread, you just steal it,' Asa said.

'Mmm.' Gris drank, barely tasting the sharp beer. Bramble could not see into Gris's mind as she had Baluch's and it unsettled her. 'Does it come so fast?' he asked.

'So fast and so far,' Acton answered. 'In a few more winters he will reach us.'

Gris sat back in surprise. 'Surely it will not come so far south!'

Acton shrugged. 'Nothing has stopped him so far. Not summer, nor prayers nor . . . sacrifice.' His voice roughened a little. 'He comes, and we can't stop him.'

'It's just ice,' Gris said, determinedly practical.

'Perhaps. But what feeds the ice?' Acton asked. 'If the old stories are true, and the Ice Giants will come to devour the earth . . . it may be that we are in the last days. Or,' he paused, 'it may be that he cannot cross these mountains. They are much higher than the northern hills.'

His uncle was silent, turning the horn in his hands, avoiding their eyes.

'There was a day,' Asa said gently, 'when you named Acton your heir.'

Gris's head came back up as though he heard a warning shout. His heart beat faster.

'I thought, as you know, that I would never have a son. But since then,' he said, 'I have married and I have two sons, Tal and Garlock. They are my true heirs.'

Asa looked questioningly at him. 'It was thought,' she said carefully, 'that you would never marry.'

Gris smiled without humour. 'It's astonishing what you can do when people expect it of you.'

She raised her brows and nodded, then flicked her hand as though dismissing the subject. 'This valley is large,' she said. 'Would you have room for others here?'

Gris got up and began pacing around the fire, breathing a little hard through strong emotion.

'I am not a man who fears,' he said. 'Any more than my brother was. But I tell you: I fear this. You are the only ones to know the way over the mountain. Thus we stay protected from the Ice King's people. But if I took your people in, many would know. Sooner or later, someone would tell, and our protection would be gone.'

Asa nodded. 'That is a fair statement, and I honour it. But my people are being pressed from all sides, and we have no escape but this!'

Acton, curiously, said nothing. He just looked at the fire. Had he expected to be his uncle's heir?

Gris stopped pacing. 'I knew this was coming. From Acton's first visit, I knew this choice would be made. I have found another way.'

Acton rose slowly to face him, but Asa stayed seated, looking up calmly. 'Tell us.'

Gris licked his lips. 'There is another route through the mountains, through to the land beyond, which is as much larger than your country as your country is larger than this valley. We have raided there, from time to time. You remember, Asa, after you came here Hard-hand did not raid your people, and after you left I continued to respect your wishes.'

'Why raid anywhere?' Acton asked.

Gris frowned, then smiled, his mouth twisted. 'To keep our young men from killing each other, mostly. It's a small valley, and we needed thralls, goods. We have no access to the dragon's road, to trade with the Wind Cities. We had to have some way to build wealth.'

Acton was frowning, as though familiar with these arguments and not convinced by them. 'Thralls are slaves,' he said.

'Your grandfather keeps slaves,' Asa said impatiently.

'Yes,' Acton said. 'I know.'

Asa gestured him quiet. 'The way through . . .' she prompted.

'It's dangerous, even in summer,' Gris said. 'The pass is narrow. It's between two high peaks, Fang and Tooth, and they carry snow all year around. It's not unknown to have an avalanche there in mid-summer. But it leads through, and the entrance is outside this valley. Our people could be left in peace.'

'And once we were through?' Asa asked.

Gris shrugged. 'That's up to you. There is a lot of land unsettled, beyond the mountains. The people there may let you pass.'

Asa thought it over. 'We will need to send emissaries. A treaty . . .'

'The chieftains will need to approve it,' Acton cautioned. He seemed more unsure than Bramble had ever seen him. Was it the experience of battle that had sobered him? She doubted it. He was watching his mother closely. Perhaps it was something to do with Asa.

'Yes. Perhaps. But for our own people – we will do what we need to do to survive.'

'My grandfather won't like it.'

Asa laughed. 'That is certain. We must leave tomorrow,' she said with decision. 'The All Moot will still be in session if we ride quickly. We will put the plan to the chieftains.'

'You mean I will put the plan to the chieftain,' Acton said. He didn't sound enthusiastic. 'You are not allowed to speak.'

Asa frowned. 'There are laws which need to be re-examined,' she said. 'All should have the right to speak. Perhaps in the new land . . .'

'All?' Acton asked. 'Even slaves?'

'Don't be ridiculous,' Asa said. Gris laughed and she turned to him with mock severity.

'Don't you encourage him. He keeps making friends with the wrong people.'

Gris smiled. Bramble could feel his body relaxing as the difficult part of the conversation ended. This was just family talk. 'All boys do,' he said.

'Acton is not a boy any longer. He is a man, and should act like one,' Asa said, but she smiled as she said it and smoothed Acton's hair as though he were five summers old.

The waters this time were a river, sweeping her across country as well as time, moving her faster than she had gone before.

The smell was definitely male and definitely unwashed. It rose up around Bramble but didn't envelop her. As her sight cleared she seemed to see through a dozen pairs of eyes in turn; quick glimpses of the same scene from different positions, but without sound, as though she had gone deaf. Too many! she thought, fighting dizziness and nausea. Each pair of eyes saw the world differently. Colour was brighter in one, perhaps a younger pair of eyes. For another person, colour was less important but somehow the way people stood in particular groups had significance, and those eyes sorted the crowd that way. She paused there for a moment, as though the gods were testing whether this was the right observer, and in that moment saw a sea of men, filling a huge dip in the ground, one of the craters that the larger pieces of black rock had made when the gods sent it to earth. On one side of the crater a natural ledge held the men officiating. Acton was there, looking tall and strong.

The All Moot, Asa had said. They had Moot Halls where the ruling councils of the free towns met, like in Turvite and Carlion . . . her thoughts faltered at the memory that called up: Maryrose and Merrick showing her where his mother, the town clerk of Carlion, worked. In an office at the back of the Moot Hall. Maryrose had been so happy that day, two days before her wedding . . . The worst thing about living in someone else's body was that you could not weep when you needed to.

Bramble lost track of the switches from one pair of eyes to the next. Finally, she found herself looking out of the eyes of a man standing on the ledge. One of the chieftains, she presumed. An older man, then, but his body still felt strong and his eyes were sharp. He could see a feather stuck into the cap of a man in the very last group on the edge of the crater. A good archer, he would make, Bramble thought.

All this time, her hearing had been clouded, but now it sharpened and she could understand what was being said. The oldest man on the ledge, whose long beard was white streaked with grey, was speaking. He held a stick with eagle feathers bound to its top.

'Does the youngling Acton speak with the voice of his chieftain, Harald?' Though he was old, his voice rang out clearly across the Moot.

Harald was standing behind Acton. As the question was asked he stepped forwards, shouldering Acton aside. The old man handed him the stick.

'He does not!' Harald declared. A murmur ran through the Moot. Harald handed the stick back to the old man.

'Then Acton, son of Asa, cannot be heard.'

Bramble saw Acton's face harden. He wasn't surprised, and he had prepared for this.

'So, Oddi, you will let your people die rather than break a rule of precedence?' he said loudly.

The crowd and the men on the ledge burst into shouting, some saying, 'Let him speak!' and others calling shame on him for speaking without the Mootstaff. Bramble felt the heart of her chieftain speed up, but he kept silent.

The old man held up his hands for quiet and her chieftain looked up, tensing.

'It is true these are desperate times,' he said. 'But should we thus forsake the ways of our ancestors, we risk becoming men without honour, without ties, without land, as our enemies are.'

Bramble felt the chieftain clear his throat.

'Swef?' the old man enquired.

Swef stepped forward in boots of a distinctive red leather. She knew that leather – it was traded up from the Wind Cities and even in her time it was expensive. He took the staff. 'Acton. I know what you would say here, and I say this: the youngling Acton speaks with my voice, if he wishes.'

Silence fell over the Moot. Bramble realised that this was more than just a way around the rules. If she understood correctly, Swef was asking Acton to transfer his allegiance from his grandfather to him, in return for being allowed to speak.

Acton turned to Harald. 'Grandfather . . .' he said pleadingly. Harald stared away from him in silence, his arms folded. Acton swallowed hard, and then took a deep breath and reached for the Mootstaff. Swef handed it to him, and patted him on the arm as he did so. Acton nodded acknowledgment. He was paler than Bramble had seen him before.

'Because the future of my people – my grandfather's people – is at stake, I speak here with the voice of Swef.'

Bramble expected the crowd to react noisily, but they were completely silent, although some moved uneasily, putting their hands to their swords, or stroking their beards as if for comfort. Some of them had wounds bandaged; a few had an arm or an eye or an ear missing, the wounds still red and proud. Recent fighting, then. A lot of it.

'Brothers,' Acton said, 'we all know the dangers facing us. If danger was all that confronted us, we would laugh at it.' The men below nodded. 'If fighting were all that was required of us, we would fight. If dying were required of us, we would die. If killing were required of us, we would kill the enemy in their thousands!' They were nodding harder. 'We are warriors and we do not flee any man!'

They shouted agreement.

'But it is not men who confront us. It is the Ice King.'

He let that sink in. The crowd subsided, murmuring.

'I have seen the Ice King,' Acton said quietly, so that they had to be silent to hear him. 'I have seen the Ice King,' he said a little louder. 'I have seen the Ice King,' he shouted. 'And we cannot survive him!'

They were silent. Swef watched their faces – singling out some for special attention, Bramble realised. Key men. The ones whose opinions would sway others. Some were unconvinced, but most looked suitably grave. Bramble wondered how Acton knew what to say. She was reminded of the way Thegan had put on an act for his people at the Sendat fort, but that had been pure play-acting. No matter how rehearsed his words, Acton meant them. She wasn't even sure they were rehearsed. Perhaps he was speaking from the heart, remembering Sebbi and the cliffs of ice.

'He will come, and he will grind our halls into splinters and our fields he will crush and cover until there is no place to lay our heads nor even any place to burn our dead!' That was heartfelt, all right. Acton licked his lips, shifted his grip on the Mootstaff a little, and continued. 'To flee the Ice King is not cowardice, but courage. Courage to admit that he is greater than any of us. Courage to save our women and our children and our beasts from hunger and misery and want. Courage . . .' he paused, gauging the mood of the crowd. Swef seemed amused at the tone of the speech; Bramble felt him suppress a chuckle. 'Courage to leave the land of our fathers and find new lands to make our own.'

The crowd stirred at that and one man shouted out, 'The sea lanes are closed!'

'But the mountains are not,' Acton replied. 'There is a way through the mountains. A way of danger, a way for heroes. On the other side, with the good will of the people already there, we shall find a wide, empty land for us to settle. A good land, away from the fear of the Ice King. A land for adventure and trade and prosperity. If my brothers wish it so.'

The crowd clamoured, most in favour, it seemed to Bramble, but some objecting strongly.

Acton handed the stick back to the old man and, after hesitating, came to stand next to Swef. They exchanged glances. Swef murmured, '"With the good will of the people there"? That's a big if.'

Acton grinned at him, restored to his usual cheerfulness. 'First things first,' he whispered back. 'Let's get the Moot's permission and then go negotiate.'

Swef clapped him on the back. 'You're your mother's son,' he said, laughing as the waters rose up like a clear spring and floated Bramble away.

Not again! Bramble thought. The noise of battle was unmistakable. This time she was in Baluch's head, no doubt about it – each sword stroke was accompanied by martial music, horns and drums. His eyes were clouded by blood – he reached up to wipe it away and winced as the back of his hand caught on a tear in his scalp. From his right, an auburn-haired giant with plaits down to his waist screamed and brought down an axe – not a battleaxe, but the kind you used to chop wood. Baluch raised his shield, but it was clear the blow would shatter it and break the arm underneath, leaving him wide open for a killing blow.

Acton appeared out of nowhere and tripped the man neatly, so that he landed at Baluch's feet, face in the churned dirt. Baluch swallowed and brought his sword down on the man's neck. It was a huge blow. He was reluctant and spurred by his own reluctance and the shame it brought to greater strength. Blood spurted wildly and the legs and arms twitched while the head rolled away from the neck, showing the man's wild, dim eyes. Baluch spun away to block a spear thrust from another huge attacker. He and Acton stood back to back and fought together.

Around them, the melee swirled, blond heads and auburn heads intermingled, swords and shields swinging, spears flashing down and dripping as they came up again. The noise was tremendous, but Baluch didn't seem to hear. He was concentrated on the rhythm of sword stroke and shield parry. Acton pointed to the side. Harald was nearby, standing on a small rise, laying about him with vigour. Acton broke from their back-to-back position and moved towards Harald, Baluch guarding their progress from behind. But before they could reach the chieftain, a grinning berserker rose up behind him with spear in hand and thrust down hard into his back. Harald's arms went up in the air and he fell forwards.

Acton shouted and surged ahead, heaving aside ally and enemy alike until he reached his grandfather's side. He sank to his knees beside Harald's dead body. Baluch stood over them, fending off two attempts to spear Acton. The berserker returned and Baluch dropped his shield to make a huge two-handed blow straight down on his head. It split the auburn head, the left ear coming away with part of the skull, soft brain oozing out. Astonishingly, the man stood, swaying but still alive. Baluch put a foot on his chest and kicked him away, then swooped to pick up his own shield in time to take the next blow from a raider on his flank. Baluch's chest was tight and tears were running down his cheeks as he swung his sword. Bramble realised belatedly that they were not for Harald. Elric, Baluch's father, was lying beside his chieftain, a great wound in his chest, the blood already drying. Acton rolled both men into seemly positions, then rose and lifted his sword.

'To me!' he shouted. 'To me!'

The blond heads, one by one, turned and began to fight their way back towards the rise. Some fell on the way. When they were gathered, surrounded by a ring of swords and spears, Acton moved forwards. He pointed with his sword to an older man to the far right of the attackers.

'That is their chieftain,' he yelled to Baluch. 'We will feed him to the ravens!' Then he began to fight his way towards the man. His men fell in behind him, Baluch at one shoulder, Asgarn coming up to shield the other side.

'Kill them all!' Acton shouted, and his men howled back: 'Acton! Acton! Acton! Kill them all!'

Energy ran back into Baluch's limbs as the shout went up and he followed Acton with enthusiasm.

'Kill them all!' he shouted with the rest, the music in his head rising and rising until he could not think at all, just react: stab, swing, parry, block, swing again and rejoice as one of the attackers fell. No more reluctance, no more tears, just action and the satisfaction of killing those who deserved to die. Despite herself, Bramble was caught up in the storm of feeling and movement, in the music and the blood and the shouting. She felt Baluch's blood rise in a kind of exaltation.

Part of her, the part that had kicked the warlord's man out of instinct, out of a refusal to be conquered, understood that exaltation. Shared it. Kill them all, she thought. That's how it works. You have to try to kill them all, or die.

She was glad when the waters came like a thumping ocean wave, lifting her and tumbling her and scouring her mind clean of killing. So glad she wanted to cry, but she wasn't sure whether the tears were hers or from somewhere deep inside Baluch.

MARTINE

O N THE SECOND night of the vigil, Cael and Safred stayed up talking around the fire until late. Zel was sitting with Bramble for a
while. She and Martine had fallen into shifts. Cael was ruled out from
that duty because they had been successful at getting Bramble to drink,
which meant that occasionally she pissed and had to be cleaned up,
and they all knew she wouldn't want Cael involved with that. Or
Safred, though it was trickier to justify her exclusion. They let her sit
with Bramble every so often, in broad daylight, when one or the other
of them was near, so it wasn't so obvious, but they both knew Safred
realised what they were doing, and she didn't like it.

She retaliated by questioning them about their involvement with the
gods. She wanted to know everything about Martine's journey from
Turvite, every detail she could remember about the ghosts, what the
gods had said through Elva, and then everything about Elva and her
relationship with the gods. To Martine it seemed that Safred was both
reassured and piqued to learn that another woman had so close a tie to
them. She questioned Martine closely about how the gods possessed
Elva, how they spoke through her, what their voice was like when
they did.

Martine called a halt. If they didn't go to bed now, the others
wouldn't be asleep by midnight. 'When you meet her, you can ask her
yourself – or see for yourself. But I'm going to bed.'

'I just want to know –'

Martine lost patience. 'Safred, I know it bothers you that other
people have dealings with your gods, but they were our gods first. Lots
of us have special dealings with them. It's part of our lives. Every
stonecaster in the Domains hears the gods talk at some point. If you

try to know everything about every person who deals with the gods, you'll be dead of old age before you get halfway through.'

Safred went very still, a look in her eyes that balanced between hurt and revelation. She opened her mouth to ask another question, but Cael shook his head at her. He nodded to her tent. 'Bed, niece.'

She did what she was told.

Martine liked Cael, and right now she was thankful for his presence, but every now and then she looked at him and saw one of Acton's men: the big, fair-haired invaders who had dispossessed her people. She could imagine him laughing as he killed. The image made her voice sharper than she intended. 'Good night, Cael.'

He looked at her with surprise, but silently went to his bedroll, while she turned her back and walked over to Zel and Bramble. Bramble was crying, silently, tears rolling down her cheeks, her face set. It was a terrible sight, and Zel had hunched over so she didn't have to look at her, fighting her own tears.

Martine was struck again with the sense that what Bramble was undergoing was profoundly unnatural; that only grief would come of it. Saker, she thought, falcon, predator – you have hurt more people than you realise.

She stayed with Bramble while Zel went to the privy and then went herself, gathering dead pine needles for tinder as she walked back. Midnight wasn't far off, by the stars. Telling midnight by the stars at Spring Equinox was a trick every Traveller woman was taught by her mam. Martine wondered, not for the first time, what happened at the Autumn Equinox. The ritual then was reserved for older women, women who had gone through the change, the climacteric, and were past child-bearing age.

I'll find out soon enough, she thought wryly. Another ten, maybe fifteen years, and I'll be there. Excluded from the spring rituals, included in the autumn. Part of her found that depressing; part comforting. Somewhere to go to, somewhere where age had a purpose. Old women returned from the Autumn Equinox chuckling and grinning, but they didn't seek out men afterwards.

Martine and Zel walked out to the altar as they had done the night before, becoming a little more confident in finding their footing. Martine had no sense that the lake resented the ritual, but she did, again, have the feeling that it was watching. Tonight, it was Zel's turn to provide the flint and Martine's to hold the striking stone.

The small pile of birch fungus caught alight immediately, and the ritual went on as it had done the previous night, except that, as always on the second night, the kindling burned more slowly and Martine's arousal was greater, her need more intense. She surrendered to the fire more easily, closing her eyes and releasing her body, if not her whole mind, to feel whatever he wanted it to feel. Desired, that was what she felt. His great gift. No matter what she looked like, every Traveller woman knew, deep inside, that she was desirable, because he desired her. Often, the plainest women were the fire's most ardent followers.

As the fire died and she returned to herself, shivering, Martine wondered, as she often had, what it was they were doing. The ritual wasn't worship. The contact between fire and woman was too intimate for that. They didn't ever talk of the fire as a god, just as 'him' or 'he'. But – he gave and they took; they gave and he took. Was it simply a bargain, made and kept? Or was it something deeper? The old women said that it kept the Domains in balance. Woman to fire, man to water, they said in whispers. Sometimes they had whispered it to their stonecaster so that Martine had learnt things young women did not normally know, and the stones had said the same thing, in whispers to her, many times over the years.

There was healing in the ritual, too. Women who had been raped were placed closest to the fire, and he healed them, burned away any disgust or hatred of men or self-recrimination. Set them free to feel and love again. That was a great gift. The one time that Traveller women had tried to introduce a woman of Acton's blood to the fire, it had been out of compassion for her, because she had been raped by a raiding party from the next Domain, in the time when all the warlords raided each other.

The fire had burnt cleanly away and the altar was untouched. That was always a good sign – a sign that he was pleased with them. Martine flushed with gratification at the thought, then smiled at herself. Like a young girl with her first love. Well, the fire was everyone's first love. Some women's only love. Some never got over their first Spring Equinox. Never found satisfaction with a human male. Would rather have the intensity without the fulfilment than the flesh and blood encounter, which never quite matched up for them. Others went the opposite way; clung to flesh and blood and rejected the fire; stayed away from the ritual, especially those who secretly preferred women to men. Zel had said her mother had been like that – so obsessed with her husband that she had no interest in the ritual and only took Zel the one time, because it was her duty to introduce her to the fire. Martine's mother had steered the middle course that Martine tried for: to perform the ritual but not be consumed by it.

'The fire will never die,' they said in unison, and sighed.

Martine took Zel's hand and they went back to the camp, banked down the fire which was now leaping high, gave Bramble some water and laid down either side of her.

Zel sighed in the darkness. 'It's a shame he don't like us pleasuring our own selves after,' she said wistfully.

Martine laughed softly. 'He won't come tomorrow night if you do,' she warned, as her own mother had warned her.

'I know,' Zel sighed. 'Dung and pissmire. By the day after tomorrow, even Cael's going to start looking good to me!'

Bramble was shivering as though she, too, were feeling the effects of the Equinox, arousal without release. Martine reached out and patted her hand soothingly.

'Shh,' she said. 'It's all right. Shhh.'

Bramble quieted a little, and Martine let her hand fall away. She looked up into the star-blazing sky and wondered what they would do if they couldn't find a flint tomorrow. There was only one solution she could see, and it terrified her.

BRAMBLE

Her nose was twitching, like a rabbit's. The cold air hit as though a door had opened into hell. The body she was in was a man's. Don't think about it, she told herself, trying to ignore the sensation of testicles contracting as the cold surrounded them. She strained to see and suddenly was blinded by whiteness: snow lit by high sun, dazzling, painful. On one side cliffs sheered up to the bright blue sky, on the other, a high slope covered with snow threatened them. Snow thin on the ground, grey stone, a thin, rocky trail between high boulders. Any noise here would echo off the cliffs and grow as it echoed. Bramble wanted to shiver – fortunately, the man she was with was shivering anyway.

The man was riding a chestnut horse, last in a line of four of the stocky little horses she had seen before. Asa was in the lead, followed by Acton, with another man behind them. That man wore bright red boots. Bramble felt herself smile at the sight of them, as if she had glimpsed something homely and reassuring. Swef, she thought. All she could see was his back, which was broad. Younger than Harald, but with grey hair showing beneath his cap, red to match his boots. He sat his horse well enough, but without the ease that familiarity brought. The bridle and bit were muffled with rags, and the hooves of the horses in front were in rag boots. Swef looked apprehensively up at the snow-covered slopes.

Death Pass, Bramble thought. They were in Death Pass. She realised she was looking through Gris's eyes.

There was an end to the defile in sight just ahead. She had only a glimpse of the mountain falling away sharply, of green land below, of trees far beneath and then the waters swept in and seemed to knock her sideways.

A fire. Warmth. Flickering shadows. A deep, accusing voice.

'You ask for privileges in words you learnt from those of our people whom you stole to be your slaves!'

Gris raised his head to stare straight into the speaker's eyes. A younger man than Bramble expected, only about forty, and at last, at last, someone with dark hair! She hadn't realised how much the eternal blondness and redness was irritating her. The man stared back at Gris with something like hatred.

'True,' Gris said. 'We have stolen. We have enslaved. We have killed. That is true. Have you never raided, Hawk?'

The man looked aside, and then brushed the question away. His hand movements were odd: larger than Bramble was used to, and with the second finger touching the thumb. They were sitting by a proper hearth, not a fire pit, in a house which only seemed small because she had become accustomed to the large halls of Acton's home. The walls of the house were wattle and daub, but the chimney was made of flat field stones, intricately pieced together without mortar.

'We have had no time for raiding for some years. We must defend ourselves instead,' the man – she must not think of him as a Traveller – said.

'But what if that were to change?' Asa leaned forwards to speak persuasively. 'What if your people were returned to you? If you no longer had to worry about raids? If you had strong friends at your back?'

Hawk ignored her as though she were not there.

'We could make you strong,' she said, trying again. She exchanged a puzzled glance with Acton and gave a little shrug.

Acton raised his eyebrows and repeated, 'We could make you strong.'

'At what cost?' he countered immediately. In the pause that followed, he turned to Asa as though seeing her for the first time.

'The women are in the scullery,' he said, and pointed to an open door on the far side of the fireplace.

For a moment, the three other men froze. Swef bit his lip. Asa's face went blank but Bramble could almost hear the thoughts racing through her mind: her dignity was not important enough to risk this negotiation.

'My mother is a wise counsellor,' Acton began, but she hushed him.

'I will speak to the women,' she said. She rose and went in stately silence to the door. The dark-haired man smiled thinly in triumph.

Bramble was shocked. She had always assumed that women were less esteemed than men in the Domains because of the invasion, because Acton's people were flawed. She had never wondered how they had been treated in the old days.

'How strong can men be who take counsel from women?' Hawk asked scornfully.

Gris smiled. 'Easy enough to control weak women, cowed from birth. It takes a real man to control a woman who knows her own mind.'

'And you do?'

'My wife has a sharp mind and a sharp tongue, but she follows my lead.'

'As you would have me do. You wish me to follow your instructions like a woman.'

Bramble lost interest in the manoeuvring for position and dominance, in the promises of alliance and mutual support. What was the point of listening, she thought, when they didn't keep any of those promises? When they slaughtered everyone instead? She wondered what Asa was doing and saying in the kitchen. Probably promising the women that their stolen children, siblings and husbands would be returned to them. Bramble suspected that even in this culture, men listened to their women behind closed doors. Unlike the sleeping halls of Acton's people, there were lots of closed doors in houses like these.

Her attention was reclaimed when Swef sat up straight and said, 'So it is agreed?'

The man put up a delaying hand. 'It is agreed that I will discuss it with my advisers, and ask their counsel. If they agree, we may try next summer – a small settlement, to the north where the forest ends. If that is successful, more may be possible.' He spoke as though he were a chief and they were slaves, but Gris nodded in thanks.

Acton looked impatient, and annoyed by the man's pretensions. 'Hawk, who will decide if it is successful?' he asked.

Well done, lad, Bramble thought. That's the real question. Who's got the power?

'I will,' Hawk said, standing and looking down his nose at the three of them, even though he was shorter than they were. Swef let out a breath that was almost a snort. Gris simply nodded.

A girl came from the scullery with a platter of cheese and bread and apricots and put it down on a small stool next to Acton. She was pretty:

black-haired and dark-eyed, honey skin and red lips, slim and very slight compared to the blonde girls over the mountains. He smiled at her, that sideways smile that all the old stories mentioned, and she blushed and smiled back. Bramble could see why. That smile *was* attractive, the invitation to shared mischief, if you didn't know that this man would soon butcher all your relatives – perhaps even the girl herself.

This is dispiriting, Bramble thought, and if the water which came up then had been real she would not have had the energy to save herself.

Still in Gris's body – she was coming to recognise his scent, if not his mind – she surfaced to find him in a cave with Hawk and Acton and a woman. Bramble wondered where Swef was, whether this was another visit altogether. Jumping about in time was wearying. She longed for it to be over.

The woman was old, the oldest person Bramble had seen so far on this journey, and she wore animal skins roughly stitched together. Her white hair was felted together like a mess of snakes and her skin was dirty. She sat on a bear skin in front of a small fire, toying with a set of stones. The air should have been smokier here than it was.

Acton seemed to share the thought, because he looked up to the shadows above, and Gris followed his glance. The smoke wound its way out of a vent at the top of the cave. The woman caught Acton looking and gave a toothless grin.

'Clever one, aren't you?' she asked, casting stones casually across the skin. Without looking at them, she gathered them in.

'I don't understand you,' Acton said slowly, still finding his way in a foreign tongue. 'What do you want?'

'Sit down,' the woman said, but it wasn't a reply. She was looking at Gris hard and leant forward, as he sat on the other side of the bear skin, peering into his eyes. Her breath was rank, like dog breath.

'And you, kinslayer, you've got a passenger. Hello, girl.'

If she'd been in her body, Bramble would have jumped at the words. The woman was clearly looking straight at her, *seeing* her in Gris's eyes. Gris had tensed at her words, but more at the word 'kinslayer' than the greeting.

'Dotta!' Hawk reproved her. 'This is important.'

'You think this is not?' Dotta replied, but she leaned back and spat into her left hand. Hawk copied her and they clasped, palm to palm. Hawk prepared himself, as though he had thought the question out carefully.

'What will be the results of allowing the strangers to settle in our territory?'

Dotta drew out the five stones – so little of this ritual has changed, Bramble thought, I wonder why? The stones were mountain stones, grey and black and silverfish. They fell face up.

'Death. Betrayal. Chaos. Ruin. Destiny.' Dotta poked at each stone in turn like a baker testing if dough has risen enough, then gathered them in. She didn't look at the men.

'Hah!' Hawk broke his hand free and glared at Gris. 'So.'

'Wait!' Acton said. 'I have a question.'

Dotta didn't speak; she simply spat in her hand again and held it out to Acton. Reluctantly, he spat in his own palm and clasped hers. They don't have stonecasting, Bramble realised. I never thought before, but no one consulted the casters about the Ice King. The stonecasting is part of the Domains, not the Ice King's land . . . she wasn't sure what that meant, but it seemed important, somehow.

Acton's gold hair shone in the firelight. He bowed his head for a moment as though praying, then asked carefully, in a halting accent, 'What will be the results of *not* allowing us to settle in your territory?'

Dotta laughed and cast the stones.

'Death. Betrayal. Chaos. Ruin. Destiny,' she chanted as they fell. They stared at her in astonishment, but she was right. The same stones, in the same order. Dotta hawked and spat in the fire and laughed at their expressions. 'Did you think the Destiny stone meant nothing?'

'If we don't let them come . . .'

'They will come anyway,' she said. 'If not these men, then others. I have advice for you, Hawk, which you will not take. Run! Take your women and your children and your animals and your chattels and run a long, long way from here. The world is wide, but the Ice King's country is small and getting smaller. Run, little one! Or you will not see two more summers.'

Hawk sat very still. 'Is that prophecy?'

'It's common sense, which is worth more!' she retorted, reminding Bramble of Martine in Oakmere.

He relaxed a little. 'Then there is still room to prevent the worst.'

He turned to Gris. 'If we let your people in, you can support us against the others. The stones say Death and Ruin, but not *whose* death. Let us make it the deaths of others!'

Dotta made a disgusted noise and rose with audibly creaking bones. 'You,' she said to Gris. 'Come.'

She picked up a piece of bone with a plug on one end. It hung by a cord from her fingers. With the hem of her skirt guarding her other hand, she plucked an ember from the fire and dropped it in the bone, and put in tinder which she had had lying ready. Then she took a step back and began to swing the bone around and around her head, like a slingshot. Gris, Acton and Hawk scrambled up and out of the way. Dotta chuckled.

'The old ways still work,' she said. The tinder burst into flame like a torch. 'My sisters are dead,' she added, 'but I still keep the flame. My sister's daughters have taken it now, far away, where it will be safe. For a time, a long time.'

The men were silent.

'Come,' she said again to Gris, swinging the bone lightly from side to side, so that the tinder burnt just enough to give off light.

He followed her deeper into the cave, to a passageway. She turned and put her hand on his sleeve, looking into his eyes intently. Her smell was overwhelming, so close.

'Girl,' she said. 'Remember this. You will have need of it later.'

Bramble shivered and wondered if it were her own body or Gris's that trembled. There was no doubt that Dotta was seeing her, talking to her as though Gris weren't there.

She led him through a labyrinth of passageways, telling Bramble each turning. 'Three down and then left. Two down and right. Four down, past this outcrop and sharp right. Down on your knees, now, for a while . . .'

The path went on for some time, Bramble trying frantically to memorise all the turnings and twistings. At last they came to a larger space and Dotta stopped. She whirled the bone on its cord in a wide circle above her head, illuminating the walls and ceiling of a large cave. There, floating on the walls above them, vivid with ochre – red and brown and charcoal black – were paintings. Animals. Aurochs, the wild cows that still could be found in these mountains, even in Bramble's day. Hares, their long ears absurdly pricked. Elk raising noble antlers to the sky. Deer running and leaping in a herd. Running from a pack of men with spears. Tiny black figures, but unmistakable. Other figures, too, smaller, rounder, darker altogether. Bramble had no idea what they were.

'Why have you brought me here?' Gris asked with a croaking voice. He cleared his throat. 'What do you want?'

Dotta moved closer to Gris and looked into his eyes. 'You'll need this place, girl, when you make your search. This is a place where calling is done. When you need the earth spirits, come here and call them.'

'What are you talking about, woman?' Gris said, his mind feeling deeply unsettled. But Bramble was tense with frustration. *How?* She wanted to shout.

Dotta smiled, the toothless mouth gleaming wet in the flickering light. 'How?' she echoed. 'The way the hunters drew the prey to them. How else?'

She touched the wall lightly where the dark, rounded shapes were. Shadows flowed across them as the bone swung back and forward, making them seem to move, seem to writhe and deform. 'The prey must be called with love, though, or it does not come. Remember that.'

Bramble stared at the drawings, trying to remember the sequence of passages and turns that had brought them here.

'You can go now,' Dotta said casually, and as if at her command the waters rose and carried Bramble away.

DOTTA'S STORY

MY AUNTY LIG was one of three sisters, as her mother had been, and her mother before her. She was the middle child. Brond was the eldest and Gledda the youngest, and they lived together. The way I was told it, Brond was Mim's mother, both of them black-haired charmers, and she was carrying a second girl. Gledda was sure that the father was the travelling skald who'd been around the season before.

'Well, we'll never know,' Lig said philosophically, 'for sure as ash follows flame, Brond'll never tell us, and there'll be no telling from looking at the baby.'

She knew the new baby would have red hair, like Lig. And the third girl, which was me, whom Brond would bear in a couple more years, would be chestnut-haired, like Gledda, flame there, but buried deep. It was always so in our family: three girls, the first black-haired, like charcoal, the second with hair as red as flame, the third with hair like banked embers. But only one of them would bear children, and then there would be three daughters, and three daughters only.

Our lives had been so for as long as memory, since the first Mim had made her bargain with the Fire God and brought down a piece of the fire mountain to warm the hearth of her people. The Byman girls, our family were called, which means burning, and alone of all the women of our people, we didn't attend the ritual at Spring Equinox, because the wildfire was with us all year round.

The Byman girls didn't have much need for men, except to get their daughters. We did for ourselves, as crafters of one kind or another, but mostly potters. Over the generations our old stone house had filled with the results of our work and it was like walking into a treasure chamber, with old wall-hangings and shining platters on the wall, with glazeware in every colour gleaming: pale green and midnight blue, and the special deep red glaze that people from as far away as Turvite came to buy. That red glaze made looking into a bowl like looking into the depths of the earth, and there were some who said that the recipe for it had been given to the first Mim, from the Fire God himself. But when I asked one of my aunts, all she would do was smile and say, 'I learnt it from my mother, and where she learnt it, only she knows.' Which was no help at all because their mother and their aunts were dead, since the winter after young Mim was born.

That was the way it always happened, too.

Lig told me she had always hoped that she would be the one to have the children. When she was little, she planned what she would call them. Bryne, perhaps, or Ban, for the bone the first Mim had carried down the mountainside, full of fire. Or even, daring thought, Rosa, the name of her friend from the village. She played with dolls, while Brond and Gledda were only interested in messing around with clay. Even her mother thought she would be the one to carry on the line.

'Look at her,' she would say to her sisters, watching Lig croon a dolly to sleep, 'she's made for it.'

'Well, I hope so,' the girls' Aunt Bryne had answered once, thinking Lig couldn't hear, 'for she's not half the potter the others are.'

Lig knew it was true. Brond and Gledda were potters born, crafting reasonable bowls before they could sew. So as she grew up she took on most of the cooking and the cleaning, and left them free to perfect their craft, sure that she would have the most important role of all, to mother the next batch of daughters.

But by the time she was old enough to dance the Springtree and run off to the woods afterwards with a sweet young man, Brond was already pregnant with Mim. That first Springtree morning had put a sharp taste in her mouth, the taste of uselessness. For if Brond was bearing, then she and Gledda were barren. That was the way of it. Poor Ham the farrier hadn't known what to do when she'd rolled away from him, after, and cried into the new grass. She'd tried to reassure him, but to the day of her death when he looked at her a cloud went over his face, as it will over the face of a man who remembers failure. He married Rosa and had six children who followed him around like puppies. Lig had always known he'd make a good father. She didn't go to their house much, though, and her old friendship with Rosa withered away.

Brond had been glad enough to let her look after Mim, especially during the bad time, when they were dealing with the shock of their mother's death, and then their aunts'. Even though they knew it was coming, it was still a shock. No one had told them what to expect until after Mim was born.

'You mustn't tell her or the other girls, when they come,' Aunt Bryne had said sternly, coughing her life away with fever. 'For then they'd never try for a child until you were all dead, and it might be too late. Just let them choose their own time, and be thankful.'

'Aye,' their mam said. 'We've made a good bargain with the Fire God. He gives us health and prosperity, he protects us from ill, and he gives us a quick death when the time comes. But he likes his servants to be young, and vigorous, like him. Small blame to him.'

'Our line will never die,' Aunt Aesca breathed. 'Remember that. Never so long as the fire burns.'

That was small comfort to Lig or to the others, as they watched the three of them, their three beloveds, waste away and die. Afterwards, though, they clung to it as a solace. At least there was a reason for the deaths. Most people, Brond pointed out, die for no reason at all. Surely that would be harder to cope with.

Lig wondered.

Watching Brond feed Mim had been like a pain, like an ache in her own breast, but it was bound up with the general pain of grief and misery they all lived in at the time. Since then she had grown to love Mim as her own.

But she didn't think she could bear to see Brond have another daughter, and this one a girl with flame hair, like hers.

'She should be mine,' Lig muttered to her pillow. 'We should have one each. That would be fair.'

As Brond rounded out and slowed down, sitting more by the fire in the kitchen than by the potter's wheel in the workshop, Lig found it hard to be in the same room with her. She spent more time in the garden. She raised most of their food anyway: vegetables and herbs, fruits, chickens and ducks and eggs. There were two gardens: a walled garden next to the kitchen, and an orchard which ran from the other side of the house down to the river.

In the walled garden she grew vegetables and herbs and kept two espaliered fruit trees, apricot and cherry. Her aunt Aesca had tended the garden while she was alive, and she had believed that it was no use growing anything you couldn't eat or use for medicine. There were no flowers, except the few plants she let grow to seed for next years' planting. Nothing there just for the beauty of it.

'A rose,' Lig thought one day, on her knees by the carrots. 'A white rose. That's what I'd like. A white rose.'

It was only a small tradition she was breaking, but it felt satisfying all the same. She traded a blue bowl for a cutting of a white rose from Vine the thatcher's garden, and planted it and some cornflower seeds, for good measure.

She tended that baby rose all through spring and all through summer, mulching and watering it, soaping off the aphids and using dark brown ale on the thrips. She left the kitchen to Brond, before and after the baby's birth. They called her Blaise and she was as red-headed as Lig.

Lig couldn't help but love her, but this time she left the tending of her to Brond, along with tending the fire.

The fire didn't like it.

That was what they told me, when I was old enough to hear the story, when my chestnut hair was down past my shoulders and I could climb Aunty Gledda's legs like climbing up a tree, her strong hands helping me. They said that Lig had made a mistake, thinking that the Fire God only cared about the ones he'd blessed with children, when he cared more, maybe, about the other two, the ones he had all to himself.

Lig decided, they said, that if she couldn't leave a child in the world, she'd leave a rose. A perfect white rose, more beautiful than any anyone had ever seen. So she begged cuttings from anyone who had a rosebush, and she went out searching the hillsides for wild roses, and she moved the carrots and the spinach and the onions out to the edge of the orchard, and took over the walled garden for her roses.

Some had small, tender buds. Others were wide, blowsy things with few petals but a rich, heady scent. I can just remember the smell, dizzying in the walled summer garden. Years it took her, to match and cross the blooms.

With each year of neglect for the vegetable garden, the fire grew angrier.

Not that it wasn't tended. No, all of them tended it. Brond and Gledda, both, and Mim, too, when she was old enough. And then Blaise. Even me. And Lig, when she felt like it, when she was passing.

But she didn't sit staring into the flames anymore, and she didn't sing softly to it as she went about the cooking and the cleaning, for she was thinking about her roses. She smelt of rose, now, not of charcoal and warm wool. Even in winter. She made rose-petal jam, rose-leaf pillows and rosehip tea. After much trial and error, she learnt to make an unguent of roses, and the merchants who came to buy glazeware began to buy her vials of perfume and unguent as well.

It soothed an old hurt, I suspect, to be able to bring silver into the house as well as food from her garden.

The fire smouldered.

Then came the year when Lig achieved her goal. The perfect white rose. She ran into the house one spring morning and dragged us all out to the garden. My feet were cold in the dew, I remember, and I couldn't understand why Aunty Lig was so excited about a tiny rosebush, no bigger than I was, with only one rose on it.

We went into breakfast, Lig floating.

'If I never do anything else in my life,' she said. 'I've done this. The perfect rose.'

The fire blazed up in a roar.

I remember it. The terror of it, the sound, the fierce heat. I remember Mam Brond grabbing me and running, calling for Blaise and Mim, screaming to Lig to run, run, *run*!

For Lig was standing there, staring at the fire as if bespelled. As if in love.

'For me?' she said. 'You've come just for me?'

I looked back from the door and I saw him. I saw him reach out for her, and I saw her smile and walk straight into his arms.

He consumed the house and everything in it. Only the stone walls were left. But he left the orchard and the pottery alone.

We huddled in the street, watching, and Mam Brond and Aunt Gledda stopped anyone going too close or trying to put it out. The heat drove us back fifty paces. The thatch flamed so bright we couldn't look at it. Then it was gone. Just gone in a moment, as if it had never been.

We spent the night at Vine's, sitting close together, not talking. Blaise cried, they say, and I just sucked my thumb and clung to Mam. In the morning we went back.

The main room was still uncomfortably warm. There was nothing left, not even the shapes of things. Everything was consumed except the glazeware, which was all cracked and broken, crazed and dull, but there. The floor was slate, and it had cracked as well, but it was so well packed down on the earth below it that we could walk on it safely. The ashes crunched beneath our feet. Gledda cried as she walked.

The crock where the silver was kept had cracked open and the silver had melted into a sharp-edged puddle.

The kitchen was just a shell. Here, even the glazeware hadn't survived. All that remained was the chimney and the hearth. There were no bones, no sign of Lig at all. In the hearth, burning cheerfully as though this were any ordinary morning, was the fire.

Gledda went out straight away to get it some kindling. Mam went into the garden.

He had swept through the garden so fast that he just sucked the moisture out of everything and left it charcoal. Each rosebush was a ghostly black image of itself. On Lig's special bush, her perfect bud was still there, every petal intact, black and crisp and dead as Lig itself.

'It was a warning,' said Mam Brond.

'It was a punishment,' said Gledda, tending the fire frantically.

'It was a bloody temper tantrum,' Mim said, years later, but only outside, in the market, away from the fire.

Blaise, whose daughters grew up to tend the Fire God in their turn, said, 'It was love abandoned.'

But I saw it, over Mam's shoulder, and it was murder and love fulfilled, both at once. I saw it, and I wondered, all through the years of my girlhood: Does he love all of us, or only Lig? Was it simple jealousy of her time and care, or a deeper jealousy of living things?

After Blaise had her first daughter, and I knew there would be no children for me, I wondered: Would he come for me if *I* planted a rose?

I knew the answer, knew it certain in my bones, and that was how I found I had the Sight, and I had to combine his service with service to newer gods, and they extended my life after my sister's daughter bore her first girl. But still, even as I cast the stones and listened to them whisper the black rock gods' answers, still and always I tended the fire.

ASH

HARD COUNTRY BY daylight was a nightmare in the dark, and soon they were leading the horses as much by feel as by their sight, the strengthening starlight interrupted by cloud and trees and towering rocks. Irrationally, Ash felt safer on the ground, although he would be far safer on Mud if the dogs ever caught up to them. He had to hope that the first brother wouldn't risk his hounds in the wilderness, but if he did, they could be caught between two sets of claws and teeth. He distracted himself from that thought by trying to remember the sequence of notes Doronit had whistled to send the wind wraiths away. He had stood on the cliffs above Turvite with her and she had whistled two tunes: one to control them, so they could parley, and one to send them away. He had tried to forget that night . . .

As they made their way upwards, the slope grew steeper, the trees fewer, and the rocks slid beneath them. The horses didn't like it when the trail shifted under their hooves, especially Cam. She shied and slid again, pulling on the reins so often that Flax had to swap over with Ash to give his arms a rest.

The last stretch was the steepest, the horses scrabbling for purchase, Flax and Ash on hands and knees. At the top they paused for a moment, and Ash was sure he could hear the scrabbling sounds continue. An echo? Or . . . Surely the men wouldn't follow them up here? They'd be insane to do so.

The top of the bluff was a plateau, dangerous even in daylight, and crowned with whirling winds which ripped between boulders and down crevices moaning unendingly. The horses didn't like it at all. A little way forwards, Mud stuck his hooves in the thin soil and refused to go any further.

'We have to find shelter until daylight,' Ash shouted above the wind. There was a sudden silence. The wind just stopped, as though it had heard him.

'That's not good,' Flax said.

Wind wraiths, Ash thought in terror, just before they came. He and Flax were outside the old compact between the wind wraiths and humans: they could not take humans unless the humans were delivered to them by an act of treachery. The agreement was so old that some believed it had been arranged by the gods themselves, long, long before Acton's forces had come over the mountains. But it had force only in set-tled lands. He and Flax were in the wilderness, and they were fair game.

The thin pale wraiths swerved in from all directions, around large boulders and small, screaming and moaning, sounding like all the storms, all the evil, in the world. Close enough, Ash thought, as he tried frantically to remember the sequence of notes that Doronit had used to send them away.

Like all the air spirits, wind wraiths liked to play with their prey. They streamed past, thin claws flicking out at the last moment to scratch a cheek, a hand, to cut through a shirt. Although they ignored the horses, Cam and Mud had their hooves firmly planted, shaking with frozen terror. The wind wraiths licked their claws and rounded back again, six of them, swirling like a cloud with needles hidden in its centre. Ash couldn't remember the notes that would send them away. In desperation, he worked his dry mouth to make saliva and began to whistle. Five notes, notes that had been burned into his brain in the dark wind above Turvite. Five notes which controlled them.

They shrieked with displeasure, but their wild flight slowed and they came to hover in front of Ash. Flax looked from side to side, as though he couldn't quite see them, just hear them.

'Who calls us?'

Flax, getting the idea, was picking up the tune and whistling too. Ash waited until he was perfect in rhythm, perfectly in pitch, and then stopped, and spoke.

'We do.'

The leading wraith spat on the ground and snarled at Ash, arms stretched towards his face, claws curling. He forced himself to remain still. '*Name*, ignorance.'

'Ash.' Flax flicked him a look, as though to say 'What about me?' but Ash didn't know what the consequences would be of giving your name to a wind wraith, and he didn't want Flax to suffer if the results were bad.

'What would you have us do, *Ash*, little tree? Remember, trees can be uprooted if the wind is strong enough.' It laughed.

'Leave us alone.'

Flax gestured strongly to the horses.

'Leave us and our horses alone,' Ash amended. 'Let us pass safely through this place.'

'What do you offer in exchange?' the wraith hissed. It looked consideringly at Flax.

Ash thought fast. He was certainly not going to make the kind of bargain that Doronit had. She had traded lives for information, had told them where to find whole ships for killing so she could collect the insurance silver. He would not trade Flax's life for his. But he had to give them something . . .

Behind them, stones shifted and scraped each other. The wind wraiths whirled up and shrieked and Ash risked a glance behind them. He began to whistle again, in case this was a trick to distract them. No trick. Behind them was a man, wrapping one arm around his head to protect his face from the wind wraiths' claws and swiping the air with his sword uselessly. The man was hard to see in the starlight, but Ash had no doubt about who it was. He made sure Flax was still keeping time, keeping pitch, and then he stopped whistling.

'Horst!' he called. 'Come this way.'

Horst stumbled towards them, the wind wraiths following and slicing at him viciously. They plucked away the sword in his hand and let it drop.

'You have brought us a sacrifice, friend!' the leading wraith said with satisfaction. 'It is a good bargain!'

The wraith reached long claws towards Horst's face. He stepped back, screaming, 'No!'

'No!' Ash shouted at the same moment, and batted the wraith's hands away.

The wraiths shrieked and spurted upwards again, coming down a little further away. Ash had a moment to think. *Should* he sacrifice Horst?

He glanced at Flax and saw that he was just plain terrified – that he'd accept any bargain to get them out safely. Ash saw himself on the cliffs above Turvite, whistling frantically to keep himself and Doronit safe. If someone had said to him then, 'Sacrifice someone who wants you dead and you'll be safe,' what would he have answered?

Tactically, he knew what he should do. Probably no one, not even Martine, would blame him. But he had made this decision when he hadn't killed the carter, and besides that, he couldn't, he just *couldn't*, hand another person over to the wraiths.

'No,' he said. 'This is not a sacrifice. The bargain includes his safety.'

Horst looked at him in astonishment.

'What do you offer, then,' the wraith hissed, 'that is worth three lives?'

Ash cast around frantically for something, anything, he could offer them. 'Information,' he said at last.

'What?'

Ash swallowed. He just hoped this news would be astonishing enough. 'The barrier between life and death has been breached. Ghosts walk the land, killing the living.'

'Sooooo.' The wraith shot up into the sky like a fountain of white and returned to hover again in front of him. 'Broken by a *human*?'

Ash nodded.

'Where?'

'South,' Ash said. 'In Carlion.'

'Come, then, brothers,' it shrieked. 'Come to feast.'

Laughing, cackling, screaming, the wraiths sped into the sky and headed south, a cloud travelling as no cloud could or ever should, against the wind.

Horst sank to the ground, shivering, blood running down his face and arms from hundreds of tiny wounds. The wraiths had done much more damage to him, thinking he was theirs.

Ash and Flax remained stock still for a long moment, until they were sure the wraiths weren't coming back, and then checked the horses, patting their sweating flanks and murmuring comfort, taking reassurance from their warmth and solid flesh, trying to keep an eye on Horst at the same time.

'What have you done?' Flax asked.

Ash wondered that himself. It hadn't occurred to him that the wraiths would react like that – he had just hoped that the information would be enough to make a bargain. He licked his lips nervously. He knew he was going to get into trouble over this, but he didn't know from whom.

'I . . . I don't know. But at least we're alive. Let's get going before they come back.'

That got through to Horst. He clambered to his feet and faced Ash. 'You could have fed me to them. You'd have been safe, then.'

Ash shrugged. What could he say? In the darkness Horst's face was hard to see, but his voice was full of emotion: confusion, gratitude, anger. Ash would feel like that, too, if an enemy had saved him.

'I can't let you go,' Horst said reluctantly. 'It's my duty to my lord to take you back. Or kill you.'

Ash felt very tired. 'Kill me if you want, but you're still in Golden Valley and that makes it murder, not warlord's justice.'

Horst hestitated. Ash wished he could see better, but the starlight was faint and interrupted by high clouds.

'I have to take you back,' Horst said eventually.

'You can't,' Ash said. 'There are two of us, and we're both armed. We have horses, you don't. You're wounded. There's no chance you could take us both and drag us down the side of this shagging mountain without one of us clouting you on the head with a rock. And your lord should know the news we gave to the wraiths. There is an enchanter raising ghosts and giving them body. Your lord should be told.'

The next pause seemed very long as Horst considered. Flax moved quietly around the side of the horses, trying, Ash could see, to get behind Horst in case it came to a fight. But then the wind wuthered through a gap in the rocks, sounding just like a wind wraith, and they all flinched. Horst let out a long sigh.

'You'll still be a wanted man,' he said. 'I can't let you off Sully's murder.'

Ash nodded. 'Fair enough,' he said.

Horst turned back the way he had come, then paused. Speaking with difficulty, he said, 'Thanks.' Then he started walking, head down.

Flax came up beside Ash and clapped him on the shoulder. 'Let's get out of here,' he said.

It was easier said than done. The moon was on its downward slide and its light was interrupted by clouds building from the south. Ash and Flax took it in turns to go in front of the one leading the horses, poking at the ground with a stick to make sure it was solid, to make sure they wouldn't tumble headlong into a crevasse or have one of the horses break a leg in a pothole. All the time the wind was building, sounding more and more like the wind wraiths returning, until they were soaked with sweat from the tension and the concentration. When the moon was about to set, Ash decided they had to find somewhere to spend the rest of the night.

They found a nest of large boulders which had a sheltered spot in the centre and a small overhang where they could sit, glad to have their backs against something solid, glad to be out of the wind, but not willing to sleep. Just in case. The horses, however, settled down as soon as they came within the circle of rocks, and Ash decided to take that as a sign they were safe. As they unsaddled and groomed the horses, the dusty scent of their hides and the routine way Mud shifted to let Ash move from one side to the other created a sense of normalcy that settled him, too.

They drank in silence while the horses found rainwater in hollows and lipped at the coarse grass. Ash wondered where the wind wraiths were, what they were doing. But there was nothing he could do about it. He remembered Doronit saying, 'Concentrate on things you can do something about.' She had been right. He had to concentrate on getting Flax and himself safely to the Deep. At least this trail should cut their travel time down considerably. Once they were off the plateau, they should be only a couple of days' ride to Gabriston. And then, the Deep.

'What made you think of the lie, back there?' he asked, after a long silence.

'What lie?'

'You being a rich kid of the new blood.'

Flax laughed. 'It *was* a good notion, wasn't it? I can go as one of them, just like my da. Comes in handy, sometimes.'

Ash could imagine his mother's reaction to that. She despised Travellers who impersonated Acton's people. She could always pick them, and Ash had heard her snap her knowledge out of the side of her mouth as they passed someone pretending. She wouldn't approve of this charade. His mouth firmed. Well, it wasn't her life at risk, was it? She had given up all right to tell him what to do when she had handed him over to Doronit. Time for him to make his own decisions.

'I think we should keep up the act,' he said.

'Sure and certain,' Flax said comfortably. 'I might even get you to shine my boots!'

Ash laughed unwillingly. He had never been closer to liking Flax.

'Safeguarders are skilled professionals, I'll have you know,' he said with mock sternness. 'We don't shine boots.'

'Shame.' Grinning, Flax settled down with his head on Cam's saddle. 'You can take first watch.'

Liking him didn't last long, Ash thought. Spoilt brat. But there was something comforting about Flax's insouciance, about his resilience after the terrors of the night. Ash loosened his knife, just in case, and watched as the moon set and the dark crowded in.

In daylight the plateau was still remarkable, windshaped rocks taking on the appearance of hunched figures, of curving waves, of flames reaching to the sky. There was rainwater in rock hollows to drink, but nothing to eat, and Ash's stomach growled constantly once the sun was high.

Then they reached the edge of the bluff, and could see Far North Domain spread out below them. Wheat fields shining golden in the sun. As they took their first steps off the plateau, Ash felt sharp relief flood him. They were out of the wilderness now, and safe from the wraiths. Flax grinned at him, mirroring his relief.

The way down was treacherous, the ground covered with scree that shifted under their feet and the horses' hooves. They slithered down as much as walked, leading Cam and Mud, who picked their way delicately, lifting their hooves high and looking hard done by.

Reaching the valley floor was almost an anti-climax. They found a small waterfall trickling over the rocks and flung themselves down to rest while the horses drank. Ash's legs were so rubbery, he almost looked forward to getting back on Mud.

They had descended into a wide valley, with the first shoots showing in the ploughed fields. This was grain country, the Far North Domain; not an area Ash had been in much, but he knew it well enough to know that the valley held the Snake River – called so because of its curving, curling path that snaked around the flat valley bottom so much that there were places where it almost met itself. Villages were found in the centre of the curves, protected on three sides by water, but vulnerable to flooding, so their houses were built high on stone pilings, with chicken roosts and rabbit hutches underneath, and stone-built silos were connected with the houses by causeways an arm's length off the ground.

As Ash and Flax rode along the rutted track that passed for the main road, they passed farm after farm where wild-eyed cats spat at them from barn doorways, and terriers yapped at their heels, while freckle-faced children peered at them from around corners.

'They're not called cats and dogs around here,' Ash said to Flax as Cam kicked out at a snapping brindled mutt. 'They're called mousers and ratters. Their job is to keep the pests from the grain.'

'Do I look like a rat?' Flax demanded. Then he laughed. 'Don't answer that!'

The farmers and their wives were out in the fields planting the second spring sowing, hoeing vegetable rows, tending the few new calves and lambs. There was not much pasture, here, where most land was given over to wheat and oats and maize.

The black stone altars were few and far between, but they found one in a grove of trees in a river bend and each sacrificed a lock of hair for their salvation on the plateau. Ash prayed for Sully, the man he had killed, who would have quickened yesterday. He hoped that Sully's ghost would find rest even though his killer had not offered reparation.

Sully's quickening set him wondering, as he had often wondered, about the dark after death, and the gate to rebirth. His father had told him that those who earned it were reborn. Rebirth was bought with courage and compassion and perseverance, tolerance and joy and generosity. There was a song . . . Ash stopped himself thinking about the song because any thought of his father teaching him – and *not* teaching him – made his gut clench. Rebirth – think about rebirth. The gods said it was true, but they refused to tell how, or when, any person would be reborn, or anything about someone's last life. Live the body in the body, Elva had told him they said, one morning when they'd been washing dishes together in the kitchen in Hidden Valley. No one knew for sure if the rebirths were endless, or if somehow, sometime, you stopped. Some people said that if you were good enough, wise enough, kind enough, you eventually became a local god. Elva had asked about that, she had said, and the gods just laughed, which could have meant anything.

They stopped in a village to buy supplies, and Ash stood scowling while Flax bargained amiably with the market stall owner. No doubt, he got a better price than Ash would have, and the man threw in a joke for good measure, about staying clear of the black dog, the spirit that led you astray.

Flax laughed and lifted a hand in farewell. Ash realised that the resentment he felt was not just because fairer-haired people were treated so differently. He also resented Flax's ease with people, his self-assurance, his conviction that everyone would like him, because everyone always had.

He pushed the emotion down. Why should he envy Flax? After all, from what he could gather, Flax's parents had sent him out on the Road when he was only twelve. At least *his* parents had waited until he was old enough to look after himself. Of course, Flax had Zel . . . Yes, he thought, he was definitely better off than Flax, and smiled to himself. Poor Zel, worrying about her little chick, gone off exploring the world.

The people of Far North had mined their fields for stones and built their houses, their silos, and weirs across their slow-flowing rivers to make races for the water-mills which ground their grain. There was no need for ferries, or bridges, or fords. The horses crossed with no more than wet ankles, and Ash and Flax didn't have to pay tolls.

'I like this country!' Flax said, popping a strawberry into his mouth. The horses liked it too, and cantered happily on the grass by the side of the track, so that they made good time.

Ash's purse was empty.

They had to get some silver. Copper even, would do. 'Guess it's up to me, then,' Flax said cheerfully.

'I thought Zel told you to stay out of taverns?' Ash said. He raised his eyebrows to imply that Flax couldn't do anything that Zel forbade.

Flax made a face back at him, looking very young. 'I don't have to go to a tavern to make silver,' he said.

They had a choice of ways not long after. Either would lead them eventually to Gabriston, although the road that went by Cold Hill, the next town, was longer. At the crossroads, Ash knew they ought to take the shorter way, but the other road called to him strongly, with something like Sight but not exactly the same. The sensation worried him, but in the end he decided on the longer way, reasoning that they were being led by the gods, and shouldn't ignore Sight or anything like it if they hoped to get through the journey unscathed.

In Cold Hill, which was barely larger than a village, they tied their horses next to a horse trough on the green, unsaddled them and gave them nosebags. Flax made his way to the side of the green closest to the inn. They had ridden all day, and it was evening, the night approaching in the slow, incremental way it did in the north, the sky lavender and lilac, the evening air scented with a stand of lilies growing in the inn's front garden. There were tables set out there, and most of the inn's patrons had chosen to bring their tankards out to sit in the mild air.

Flax stopped opposite the inn, put down a large square of umber cloth, and began to sing. He just stood there, unselfconscious, relaxed, and let the warm notes rise gently over the drinkers' heads.

He sang a popular, sentimental song, to get their attention. Ash had seen it done often enough. Get them listening, without realising it, and then bring out some louder or more startling song. He sighed. I should do my bit, he thought. There was a bench not far away, set no doubt for the use of older people when the green was busy as a market square. He knelt down beside it and began a gentle drumming on it with the flat of his hands, underscoring the rhythm of the song. Flax cast him a startled glance and then grinned.

> *In the cool wilds of twilight, my lover comes to me,*
> *Gold in the sunset, her hair like summer corn*
> *Deep in the Forest, snug beneath a tree*
> *My love and I lie warm until the morn . . .*

They were listening. How could they not? Ash thought. He had half-wished that Flax would be bad, would have no strength to his voice to buttress the sweetness Ash had already heard while they were riding. But no, his voice rose strong and clear and wholly beautiful, and he sang without strain, without effort, letting the notes go fully, opening himself to the song so that it was like the song sang him instead of the other way around. He had been well taught, somewhere, somehow. Ash felt the labour with which he was drumming and flushed. It was a simple rhythm and in his head it was clear and easy, but once he tried to reproduce it his hands faltered.

He concentrated. He could do this; he *had* done it, night after night, well enough so that the drinkers never noticed that he wasn't a real musician. But what did they know? If he made a mistake, Flax would certainly notice, and he couldn't stand that.

He made it to the end of the song without an error and relaxed a little, rubbing his reddening hands and wishing he had a drum. A few of the drinkers nodded to him and kept drinking, without so much as looking like throwing a coin. Ash didn't worry. This was the way it worked.

Flax looked at him and mouthed: 'Death Pass?' Ash nodded. The ballard about Acton was a well-known and much-loved one and it had a strong beat. You couldn't do it without a drummer; there were sections where only the rhythm moved forward. He flexed his fingers and used his full palm to make the starting drumbeats as loud as he could. The drinkers stopped and looked, and Flax launched into the chorus straight away. A good decision. They grinned and listened, and a couple, who'd clearly had the most to drink, even sang along.

> Bright flowed the blood of the dark-haired foe
> Red flowed the swords of the conquering ones
> Mighty the battles, mighty the deeds
> Of Acton's companions, the valiant men.

Ash wondered about Bramble. He kept his mind on the drumming, but the lower level of thought had to be busy with something, and he didn't want to think about Flax, about how perfectly he sang, about how he was exactly the son Ash's parents had hoped for. So he thought about Bramble instead, and wondered what was happening to her. They came to the first section where he had to drum alone and he cast everything out of his thoughts except the rhythm, determined not to disgrace himself in front of Flax. Flax came back in exactly on the beat, as precise as Swallow, and Ash increased the pace, as he was supposed to. It felt as bad as drumming for his parents. Worse, because he had been in constant practice then. He hadn't played this song for more than three years. But the music was clear in his head. If nothing else, he knew the songs. Except the ones his father hadn't taught him.

That thought made his hands falter, although he corrected himself immediately. Flax didn't appear to notice, but Ash was sure he would have. His face burned red. But the drinkers hadn't noticed. They were banging their tankards in time with his drumming, so that he could ease off a little to protect his hands. When Flax sang the first words of the chorus again, the drinkers joined in enthusiastically. They sang the last chorus three times and this time, when the song ended, coins came flying through the air to them.

Then the innkeeper came out with a small beer each and invited them to move to the inn garden.

'I guess that's not exactly *in* a tavern, is it?' Flax said, grinning.

Ash moved to a table, which was better for his back and gave more resonance, but still hurt his hands. Flax stood beside him, and they performed another half-dozen songs; war songs and love songs and, at the end, when the innkeeper nodded to them to finish up, a cradle song that everyone present had always known.

> *Close your eyes, close your eyes,*
> *My own little sweetheart*
> *You are tired, little boy*
> *So sleep now, my joy . . .*

Grown men wept the easy tears of the drunk as they remembered dead mothers, and young women grew sentimental, thinking of the children they would have some day. The soft notes rose clear and gentle into the dark sky, floating away to join the stars. This song needed no drumming. Flax sang alone, using the high part of his register so that it might well have been a woman singing. Ash felt almost as if he could hear an accompaniment, some impossible instrument which could play high and low at the same time, resonating behind and before each note. He wasn't sure if the music was in his own mind or some quality of echo from the inn walls. While it was beautiful, the last, soft song hardly ever produced coins. Still, it sometimes produced other things, like a girl to spend the night with or a place in the inn stable.

As he finished, Flax remained standing there, waiting. Ash realised, with a flash of humour, that he was waiting for Zel to come over and organise him. Instead, it was the innkeeper, bringing them ale.

'Bring your animals round to the stable,' she said, kindly enough, as she handed the mugs to Ash. 'But no light in there.'

'Thank you, keeper,' Ash said. He resisted the temptation to tell Flax what to do. He wasn't Flax's big brother, and the boy was old enough to work out for himself what should be done next.

But with the singing finished, Flax seemed a little dazed, so in the end Ash chivvied him over to the horses and got them, their gear and Flax around to the stable and settled in. They sat with their backs to the stable wall and slowly drank their ale. There was enough light coming from the inn's windows for them to see each other and the horses. Cam and Mud shifted from hoof to hoof and whoofed their breath out a couple of times, half-talking to each other and half-reassuring themselves that this strange stable was *their* stable, at least for tonight.

It had to be said, although he'd rather have cut out his tongue. 'You sing well.'

'Thanks,' Flax said.

Ash wanted to hit him. It was all so *easy* for him. He just stood there and sang, and everyone around him managed life so that he could. 'Who taught you?'

'Mam, to start with, while I were a youngling. Then Zel organised it. Any time we met up with other singers on the Road, she'd bargain for me to have some lessons. Mostly people was free with their time. Travellers, that is. We never asked blondies.'

'Have you ever Travelled with anyone else?'

Flax laughed shortly. 'Not Zel. Keeps herself to herself. I don't mind. We do all right.'

Ash imagined Zel and his mother coming up against each other, and shivered. There'd either be coldness like the chill of hell, or they'd take one look at each other, recognise a like spirit, and be unbreakable allies. Either way, the men in their families would fall in with their wishes, as they always had. Except, of course, for the matter of the Deep. Swallow had never quite approved. She didn't like having to stay alone with the wives of the other musicians, camping out or taking over a cottage for the days the men were away. Ash never asked what went on during those days, and she had not volunteered the information, but he had gathered from some of the other women that a lot of praying went on, and a lot of partying, and his mother was not fond of either. But she always met them with a heavy purse, because the parties included dice, and she had Death's own luck with the bones.

Ash thought of Swallow's face: thin, intense, beautiful. Bramble was beautiful, too, but although her colouring was Traveller, her bone structure and build were more like Acton's people. Her face was broader across the high cheekbones and her chin was less pointed. She looked more robust. His mother looked like a wind would blow her away, which was so misleading as to be funny. No one was tougher or healthier. He had inherited that from her, at least. He was never sick. The longer he sat in the dark, the harder it was to keep his thoughts from the sharp realisation that he would have to take Flax to meet Swallow, afterwards. That he would have to hand him over to her and watch her listen to him sing. The meeting with his father would be bad enough. With Swallow, who lived singing so much that the rest of the world was a shadow to her, it would be a knife in his guts.

Well, he had learned about knives, and how to avoid them, and how to take them if he had to, for the benefit of others. That was what a safeguarder did.

Obscurely comforted by the thought, he got up to lay out his blankets, but was interrupted by a sound from outside. He drew his knife and put his back to the door, motioning to Flax to stay back. Flax just stared, his eyes wide.

The door creaked open slowly. Ash tensed, ready for anything. There was a noise outside that he had never heard before. Like someone – a whole group of people – humming. Singing. Very high, very deep, some sweet and some harsh. Not quite on the same note. The noise set his teeth on edge and yet he wanted to hear more of it. Was this how the people of Cold Hill came to kill Travellers? Singing?

'Hello? Is anyone there?'

It was a man's voice, unsure of itself. He was standing in the light from the doorway. Ash peered through the gap between door and hinge and examined him carefully. A Traveller. Ash relaxed and slipped the knife back into his boot.

'We're here.'

The man pushed the door fully open and peered into the dark. 'I can't see you.'

Ash stepped forward, making sure that he was balanced and ready to fight in case this was a trick.

'Oh, there you are,' the man said, sounding relieved. 'I have something for you.' He held out a pouch. A stonecaster's pouch.

'They've been calling for a week now,' he said.

Ash swallowed. He could hear the same descant that he had heard while Flax was singing the lullaby, and it was coming from the pouch. He could *hear* the stones. Just as Martine had said.

'For me?' he said.

The man nodded. 'I thought it mighta been for the singer, but no, it were you, drummer.' He gestured with the pouch. 'Go on. Take them.'

There was something in his voice, a deep desire to be rid of the pouch, that made Flax reach out and put a hand on Ash's arm.

'Don't take them. It's a trick,' he said.

'No trick!' the man said. 'I'm not out to cause anyone harm. My name's Auroch – I'm a chimney-maker, well known in these parts. And I'm a stonemaker, which aren't so well known, if you take my meaning.'

They did. Stonemakers were few and far between and only stonecasters really knew who they were. Flax relaxed a little, but he still held Ash back. Ash wanted to throw him off and grab the stones, but he knew Flax was being sensible, so he stayed still. But his eyes never left the pouch of stones.

'Why are you so keen to give my friend the pouch?' Flax asked suspiciously.

'To get rid of it,' Auroch said honestly. 'It's an unchancy set, this one.' His voice dropped to a whisper. 'It's got a new stone in it.'

They stood in silence. Ash breathed heavily, remembering a song his mother had only sung once, about the stones.

> *Cast a new stone, cast a new stone*
> *And change the woven power of the world*

So. This was why the other stones were wrong for him, yet Martine's casting insisted he was a stonecaster. These had been waiting for him. A new set. A new stone.

He reached out his hand for the pouch, and Auroch dropped it into his palm, and then turned and hurried off into the darkness.

A crescendo of song enveloped Ash, the stones singing high and low, sweet and harsh, loud and soft, each with its own note, all of them blending into something extraordinary. There was a central note, he could hear it, could hear how all the others twined around it.

Something no stonecaster had ever heard before.

AUROCH'S STORY

INEVER WANTED IT. When I were a nipper and my mam told me the stories about stonemakers who were chosen to find a new stone, I thought, I hope that don't happen to me. A new stone coming into the pouch means the world's going to change, because the stones and the world reflect each other, although which is the reflection I've never figured. I wondered, sometimes, how stonecasters could walk around so easy with the world hanging at their waist.

Changing the world seemed too big a thing for me. Too scary. So. I were right there. Maybe it picked me because I didn't want it. That's likely. That's how the gods work. Or maybe I was just the only one nearby. There's only three of us stonemakers living, after all. It runs in families, like with my mam and me, and somehow it only goes to one or two in a generation.

Stonemaking's not all I do. Stones can't be bought or sold, only given. Just as well. A good stonemaker might make twenty sets, their whole life, and Travellers aren't the richest customers, so you'd never make a living.

I'm a chimney-maker by trade. You might think that any builder can make a chimney, but once you get more than one fireplace on the flue it's an expert job, and the best builders know it, and bring me in for that part of the job.

Turvite's got so big we are half Settled now, me and Cricket and Grass, our daughter. Winters here, summers on the Road. It's in the summer that I find the stones. Up north, mostly, because the northerners like chimneys made of river stones, and I go collecting. River stones are good for about half the casting stones. They carry the changing elements: Birth, Death, Chaos, Travel, Growth. They whistle and sing and hum to me as I handle the larger chimney stones, and I slip them into my pocket as gently as a bird lays moss in her nest.

The rest I find as I go. The harsh stones call strongly: Murder, Betrayal, Anger. A good Jealousy stone is the loudest of all. The last one I found fairly shouted at me from the side of a track way up near Mitchen, a flint in a field of chalk.

I don't like finding the harsh stones. The cry they make in my mind is as nasty as their meaning, and I get a headache for days afterwards.

Now the puzzling thing about stones is that they don't all like each other. Each new stone has to pick its set, and some of them are very choosy. I had three sets building at the time this happened. Two almost done, waiting for a couple of stones. One of those needed only the blank stone. Another one just started, with only three in it; the ones that always come first when a set starts: Birth, Death, Rebirth. The blank stone is always last, and that tells you the set is complete, even if it doesn't have every single stone you know exists. That's because some stonecasters can also hear their own stones before they are in the pouch. They pick them up as children and use them for luck, although they don't understand why at that age. If you make a set with a stone missing, sure enough you'll find the person the pouch goes to has the missing stone in their pocket. Then all you have to do is mark one side of it for them and tell them which stone it is, though once it gets with the others in the pouch it usually starts to talk to the caster.

It might take ten years to make a set, normally. As it happened, one set that were nearly complete had taken me almost all my life. I'd found the first stone when I were only a babe, my mam said, playing by the side of a stream where she was searching for lily roots. I grubbed in the river sand with my fat baby hands, she said, laughing, and then tried to eat what I found. I would have choked on Birth, she said, if she hadn't heard the stone call out and grabbed it out of my hands.

So that were my first stone ever, and it is beautiful: flat and oval, smooth white quartz without a seam in it. Rare, and singing of beginnings whenever I went near it. I loved that stone, and thought I'd have it always.

Then, when I were eight or so, and my first set was starting to weigh heavy in the pouch, I were with my mam when she went to see a stonecaster who'd taken on a new apprentice. Mam was checking to see if the set she'd completed the winter before would suit this young one.

Someone from the outside wouldn't have seen much. We sat down, the old stonecaster served us some tea, he chatted with Mam about nothing much: the weather, the warlord's latest execution, the price of barley. The apprentice, a plain young woman who seemed grown up to me then but who was surely only sixteen or so, sat and looked hard at Mam's pouch on the table. I could hear the stones talking in their darkness, as they always did, out of tune and jangling, each of them trying their best to be heard, although some, like Justice, speak in a whisper, and some shout.

The apprentice heard them too, I were sure from the look on her face. Her hand crept closer and closer to the bag. Then the strange thing happened, which changed my life. As her hand approached, the stones began to change their noise. The closer she came, the more they seemed to sing together, the harsh stones providing the rhythm of the song, the gentle ones the melody. When she actually touched the pouch, they came into full harmony, all singing the same song, although the harsh was still harsh and the soft was still soft. Mam nodded at her kindly.

'I reckon they're yours, right enough,' she said with satisfaction. The apprentice beamed at her, looking suddenly beautiful. That moment, I realised that all my work'd be for other people. That my lovely Birth stone would go to someone else; that no matter how many sets I made, none of them would sing for me the way that pouch had sung for her. That I could not bring the stones into tune.

On the way home, Mam were cock-a-hoop.

'No doubt about that,' she said. 'It's nice when it's so clear cut. Sometimes the stones stay a little out of tune, and it's hard to know whether that means they need another caster, or just that the young one hasn't grown into themselves yet.'

I said nothing, and she looked at me.

'What's the matter?'

'Nothing,' I said, but she knew me too well to take that. She cuffed me lightly on the back of the head.

'What?' she demanded.

'We never get to keep them,' I said. 'They never sing like that for us.'

'They change their song when we make a set complete,' she said.

'Not like that. Not *singing together*.'

She were quiet for a bit, then sighed. 'No. That's so,' she admitted. 'But think of it like this: a builder builds a house for a new couple. Does he expect to live in it? A brewer makes a cask of ale for the warlord. Does she expect to drink it? Or even closer, a flute-maker makes a flute: does he expect to perform with it?' She shook her head. 'We're makers, Auroch, and that's the fate of makers: to give what we make to others.'

I hung my head. 'Flutes aren't alive. They don't sing differently for maker and flautist.'

'No?' Mam laughed. 'That's not what my friend Rowan says. He reckons his flute don't sound the same for anyone else.'

I hunched my shoulders at her and she tousled my hair. 'It's the way of things, lad,' she said sympathetically. 'No stonemaker has ever been a stonecaster. They are different talents. Remember, without us, there'd be no stonecasting. Think of that.'

I did think about it, on and off, about a world where the future were blank and dark, where fears could not be examined and lessened, where hopes could grow unchecked by reality. I imagined a world with no sense of what were to come, and I shivered and thought my mother were right. We was important. But I didn't realise then that the future can change; I didn't know that I would change it.

So that day, that fine spring day, I were working on a chimney in a village called Cold Hill. I were building with bricks, not stone, but that was the owner's problem; bricks are easier to lay, but not so good at holding heat. It were going to be a big, two-storey house with four fire-places and two chimneys, and the owner were trying to talk me into putting another little fireplace up in the attic, which woulda ruined the draw of the flue and made the lower hearths smoky in bad weather. But would she listen? No. She were arguing without taking breath so I stopped attending to her, and then I heard it calling.

A song, a call, a cry I'd never heard before from any stone, out of the pouch or in it. I'm not a word-maker, I can't describe it. It was like the hum of a distant beehive, or the constant sound of the surf from a long way off. Not loud, but soothing, somehow. I must have looked strange, because the owner said, 'Well, if that's your attitude, I can always get another builder!'

'Go ahead,' I said. I walked away from the chimney and the house, down to the stream at the end of the garden, where the call were coming from. As I got closer it became more like a song: all on a single note, like a singer trying to impress the audience with the size of his lungs. But that note had tones in it that I couldn't quite hear. They buzzed at the back of my head, they made lights dance in front of my eyes. The stone were easy to find, although it were buried a foot deep. I just reached down and pushed through the soft cool mud and took it up in my hand. It weren't big, half the size of most stones, but it felt good in my hand, and as I touched it the note changed, deepened, quickened somehow, as though the stone itself were excited.

I washed it off. Jet black, it were, black as pitch. Blacker. That's rarer than you think, a completely black stone. It were perfectly round, and perfectly flat on both sides, like a coin. But the strange thing was that it weren't any of the stones I knew. That song, that feel, didn't belong to any of the stones in any pouch anywhere in the Domains. As I realised that, I felt cold all over, and began to shake. But it might be a stone that were common in other countries. The Wind Cities had stones we did not, and I knew the names of them all.

'What are you?' I whispered, and the stone sang back. Evenness, it said. Balance on the scales.

I'd never heard of that stone, and I felt sick. To bring a new stone into the world was to change the world itself . . . it were still too big for me. I didn't know what to do. I wished that my mam were still alive.

I left the stream and the complaining house owner and walked back to the cottage where we was staying, renting a room from a Settled Traveller. As I went through the cottage gate I heard a song from a little further down the road. A song I knew. The blank stone. It were just lying there in the middle of the track, plain and simple, as though it had been waiting for me to notice it. Grey, with silver streaks. Nothing special. I'd seen blank stones like this one a dozen times. It meant the set was complete.

I sat at my work table and looked at the stone, then took out the flint I used to make a mark on one side of each stone in the pouch, except the blank stone. Some stones tell you which side to make the mark on. Others don't care. But as I brought the flint closer to the black stone, it shrilled a warning. No mark, it sang. We are the same, both sides. That is the point.

My stomach churned. I went to my chest and got out the pouch, the set that just needed a blank stone – the set that I had been making my whole life. I put the blank stone in the pouch but kept the other tight in my fist. When a set is made complete, the cries of the stones change. Just a little. But not this time. The blank stone made no difference. I loosed my hold on the other stone and put it in the pouch.

The stones began to sing. Just like they had for the apprentice, just like they had for other stonecasters I had given pouches to.

They sang for me.

I shoulda been happy. At last, they was singing. But I were afraid, and a moment later I knew that though the set were singing, it weren't singing for me. They was calling their stonecaster. Calling like the goatherds in the Western Mountains yodel the flock home. The calls became notes, deep and high. Under them all I could hear the new note, the call of the black stone. The sound of the world changing.

LEOF

THE MEN CAME marching through the next afternoon, after what had clearly been a short night's rest. They looked ragged with exhaustion, even the officers on their mounts. Thegan kept them marching, allowing family and friends to walk alongside and hand over extra food or comforts, snatch a kiss or two, as long as they didn't slow the pace.

'Who knows what difference an hour may make?' he said to Leof, who came to ride alongside him through the town.

'We have thirty-seven axes of various kinds ready, my lord,' Leof reported. 'I have loaded them into a cart so that the men will not tire from carrying them. Also, a quantity of boar spear.' That thought had come to him late the night before and he had rousted out every huntsman in Sendat to find the spears. Boar spears had a crosspiece about halfway up, intended to stop a boar simply running up the length of the spear to gore the spearsman, which they were prone to do. Too stubborn to know when they were dead, boars. Like the ghosts.

Thegan nodded approval. 'You have done a great deal in a very short time.'

'Otter came through here trying to find you, my lord. The Lady Sorn ordered the axes made ready.'

Thegan raised an eyebrow, amused. 'She is very martial of a sudden!'

'She acts to protect you and your men,' Leof said.

Thegan nodded. 'She's a warlord's daughter, after all. I suppose she's learnt something of warfare, living in a fort all her life.' He dismissed the thought and turned to other matters. 'The fort –'

'Aye.' Leof nodded. 'The fortifications won't stop the ghosts. They'll need to be rebuilt, and more axes, more boar spears made. The call has gone out to the oath men this morning.'

'Good. I'll leave you Alston for their training; he's reliable. Tell him the truth. And the men will need reprovisioning. We don't know what we will find in Carlion.'

'At least ghosts don't eat much,' Leof said dryly. 'They won't strip the land bare as a living enemy might.'

'Who knows what these ghosts will do. If they have flesh, perhaps they eat.' Thegan paused, choosing his words carefully. 'I know you would rather be with me in battle, but I need someone I can trust here. Supply lines, provisioning, they are the heart of warfare, no matter what the songs say. Men will not fight for glory on an empty stomach, with empty hands.' They had reached the end of town, and Thegan gestured to the townsfolk to fall back and let the men proceed.

'I will do the best I can, my lord,' Leof said formally, and saluted. Thegan returned the salute gravely, hand over heart, and then smiled.

'Keep my fort safe, boy,' he said, spurring the chestnut gelding he rode to a canter, taking the lead, his banner rider following close behind so that the gold and brown banner floated out behind him – sword and spear crossed, glittering in the sunlight. The Lady Sorn had sewn that banner, Leof remembered, all of last winter.

He returned to the fort and only on the way up the hill realised that Thegan had left no word for his lady, hadn't even thought about visiting her, however briefly. When he came into the hall, hesitantly, she was waiting for him again in the shaft of sunlight. She saw his face, and smiled reassuringly.

'My lord does *not* send to say that he thinks of me?' she said, laughter in her voice. 'I did not expect that he would, my lord. When a warlord goes to war, he thinks of nothing else.'

He smiled back, relieved to find her so reasonable. Other women, he reflected, might well have taken offence. His mother, for one, would have had his father's ears pinned to the black rock altar if he'd slighted her so. Thank the gods Sorn was different. Later, though, he wondered why a great lady expected so little attention to be paid to her.

The oath men – farmers, labourers, tax bondsmen – came straggling in reluctantly the next day. Alston, the sergeant Thegan had detached for training duty, was younger than most sergeants and less annoyed than most would have been to miss the fighting, due to him being body and soul in love with the Lady Sorn's maid, Faina. Being around her made him cheerful and energetic, both qualities that were needed in turning the raggle-taggle mass of men into a fighting force. A force that could hew off arms and legs.

Alston was one of those sensible, stalwart men that every officer dreamt of having as a sergeant. He was tall and had light brown hair, a physique big enough to impress young recruits and a hand hard enough to impress the old campaigners. He brooked no nonsense, but he wasn't cruel and he didn't seek out power. He just did his job.

Fortunately, none of the oath men had given service before, so they didn't question the training methods Leof and Alston had devised, which were certainly not standard. They taught the men to work in pairs – one to engage the enemy and keep him at a distance, the other to come in from the side and hack off the arm. It occurred to Leof that outnumbering the enemy wasn't a bad approach to normal opponents, either. That cheered him somewhat, although he worried a lot about what would happen if the ghosts outnumbered them.

More and more, Leof blessed his experience in fortification and long defensive campaigns in the Cliff Domain. The Centralites had no real idea what war could be like. Moreover, since the rumours about why the men had marched to Carlion were even more unlikely than the truth, no one took the preparations all that seriously, no matter how hard Leof drove them. They were the strongest Domain of the Eleven; they had Lord Thegan leading them; why should they worry about attack? Only a fool would attack Sendat.

That was the general belief, and it made getting masons and carpenters to work all the hours of daylight difficult. They grumbled, they moaned, and they frequently slipped away to do some 'little job' in the town. The blacksmiths were even worse. In the end, Leof decided that he had to confide something – not everything – to Affo and the head mason, Gris.

He took them and Alston into the tack room of the stables, where he had some strong brown ale ready, and served them himself. That alone put them on the alert. He chuckled as he saw their faces.

'No, no, lads, I'm not going to ask you to work through the night, don't worry.' They smiled back and relaxed a little, but remained wary. 'But I do need your help,' he continued, growing serious. 'I can't tell you everything . . . my lord has given strict instructions. But I can tell you that we were attacked by the Lake.'

They nodded. Old news. The list of the dead had gone around; the families had been personally informed by the Lady Sorn, who had been generous – astonishingly generous – for those left without support.

'What you do not know,' Leof paused, milking the moment for all the suspense he could. They leant forwards. 'What you do not know, is that my lord believes it was *not* the Lake who attacked us.'

They sat up at that, the two of them. He had their full attention now.

'My lord has found out that there is an enchanter working against the people of the Domains. That is what we prepare against.'

'Swith the Strong!' Gris exclaimed. 'He's good enough to control the Lake?'

'So it seems,' Leof said, hoping the gods would forgive the lie, not sure if it were a lie. 'This information is secret,' he cautioned. 'Only those in this room know it. If it comes to be talked about abroad, I will know who to blame, and I will dispense my lord's justice swiftly.'

Affo and Gris nodded in unison, like twins, and he fought down a smile. One day his sense of humour would get him into trouble. His mother had always said so.

'You see why I need you to push your men. We don't know when this enchanter may strike again.'

'He's attacked Carlion?' Affo asked. 'That's where the troops have gone, isn't it?'

Leof assumed an air of great solemnity. 'I can tell you no more,' he said, 'without betraying my lord.' That was the simple truth. 'Will you help us?'

They nodded again, and this time he let himself smile, a friendly smile that had them smiling back.

'Good. Drink up, then, and back to work.'

He and Alston watched them go, talking animatedly to each other.

'They'll tell their wives,' Alston said gloomily, 'and then it'll be all over town.'

'Have you told Faina?' Leof asked.

Alston blushed and shook his head. 'She'd never ask,' he said simply. 'She belongs to the gods, that one, and can't do a dishonourable thing.'

Leof clapped him on the back and sent him back to the muster yard, where the last batch of oath men were labouring to swing the weighted poles they practised with. Affo's men were working to make spears and axes for them in time. But in time for what? Leof wondered. They were expecting word from Carlion any moment; the messenger horses were fast and surely there had been time by now to get a message back?

He went into supper as the sun dipped below the western hills, and found Lady Sorn and the two junior officers Thegan had left at the fort already eating at the glass table. It was called that because those who sat there had their wine served to them in clear glass goblets instead of pottery ones, and it was a pretty sight, the flames of the candles reflecting in the curved glass. He had always enjoyed it at Cliff Domain, watching Thegan and his father and the other lords draining their glasses so that the fire winked from the bases like stars. Now he was nominal lord here. He felt a poor substitute for his father, and wondered what Cliff Domain was doing to prepare. Thegan would have sent word there and to the other warlords.

Sorn and the officers rose and bowed as he approached. He bowed back, apologising as he did so. 'I seem to be always tardy these days, my lady,' he said. Sorn smiled and sat again, gesturing for her maid, Faina, to serve him. He watched Faina curiously. Not all that pretty, but with big blue eyes that looked on the world as cleanly as a child, yet with a woman's intelligence. He could see why Alston, a man of clear thoughts and absolute loyalty, would be attracted. But then, he thought ruefully, I can always see why a woman is attractive. He wondered how long it had been since he had lain with anyone. It felt like months since that waitress in Connay, when he went there for the chases, but surely it couldn't be that long? After Bramble, he had pursued women obsessively for almost a year, trying to prove that she had been nothing special, and when that hadn't worked he'd let the women pursue him, when they chose, which was often enough to keep him satisfied. But it had been a while.

He smiled his thanks at Faina for the roast kid and vegetables she served, then poured more wine for the Lady Sorn.

'How goes it, Lord Leof?' she asked, the question she asked every evening.

He outlined the day's work and she listened and nodded and gave compliments, as she always did. He was never sure how much she understood of the technical aspects of what he told her, but he suspected it was more than she showed. He suspected that Sorn always knew and felt much more than she showed.

He was deep in an outline of the need to requisition more stone from the blue stone quarry in Springhill, a nearby town, when there was a disturbance at the door and Hodge entered the hall. Sorn and Leof both rose and moved to meet him.

He was dusty from the road and tired, but he bowed formally to them both and then looked from one to the other, not sure to whom he should report.

'If your news is private, sergeant, the Lord Leof can take you to my setting room.'

Leof nodded, but motioned her to join them. 'My lord said to keep you informed,' he told her, and saw her flush, delicately, as though she had not expected that. Fortune came prancing up to Sorn as they went into the setting room, but Sorn shushed him and he went back to his accustomed place by the fire, head up, watching the flames and Sorn alternately.

As soon as the door closed, Hodge came to the point. 'The ghosts were gone when we arrived, but the town was a shambles. They'd killed, we think, about half of the townsfolk. We're not sure, because some of them jumped off the cliffs to get away and we couldn't get all the bodies back, and others simply ran and haven't returned. I don't blame them.'

'My lord is occupying the town?' Sorn asked.

Hodge nodded. 'The town clerk and most of the council are dead. The townsfolk are terrified that the ghosts will come back. They welcomed us with open arms. The lads are living high – there's plenty of room for them.' He spoke grimly, and Leof caught a sense of what the town had been like when he had arrived.

'Lord Thegan is organising what's left of the townsfolk to fortify the town; taking stone from the empty buildings to make walls and so forth.'

Leof nodded. 'What does he need from us?'

Hodge handed over a list. 'Supplies; armour; weapons, mostly. And to recruit some stonemasons from other towns to go to Carlion to help fortify it. But he says on no account deplete the workers from Sendat.'

'Anything else?' Leof asked, studying the list. Hodge hesitated. 'For your ears only, my lord.' He looked at Sorn. 'And I suppose yours, too, my lady . . . we found, out beyond the town, a great burial uncovered. Bones everywhere. Old bones. Very, very old.'

Sorn went quiet, and then began pacing around the room, as though she could not contain her anger. 'He is using the bones to raise the ghosts,' she said. 'The bones of the slain. Angry bones. Oh, this is a great blasphemy against the gods!'

Leof had never seen her show such emotion.

'Then let us hope they will aid us,' he said seriously.

Sorn nodded. 'I will pray for it,' she said simply, then turned to Hodge.

'Sergeant, come and I will arrange food and rest for you.'

Hodge smiled. 'Thank you, my lady, but I have a home of my own to go to in the town. With my lord's permission?'

Leof motioned for him to go. 'But be back here early. Does my lord want you back?'

Hodge shook his head. 'I'm to help Alston train the oath men. We know more about how these ghosts fight, now.' He paused, as though wondering if he should launch into a description now.

'In the morning,' Sorn said, with mock severity. 'Go to your home now.'

'Thank you, my lady,' Hodge said and left with more energy than he had when he arrived.

Sorn and Leof looked at each other. He wondered if Sorn had understood the implications of what Hodge had said.

'So,' she said carefully, 'my lord is now the warlord of a free town, with a nice, deep harbour.'

He drew in a deep breath. She understood, that was certain. 'Aye,' he said. 'Without a single protest.'

Their eyes met and they nodded, very slightly, aware of Thegan's ambitions and, surprising to learn of each other, uncomfortable with them.

'I wonder,' Sorn said, 'if anyone has asked the local gods of Carlion what they think should be done?'

'Thegan doesn't consult the gods,' Leof said without thinking. But it was true. Thegan never prayed at the altar except on festival days, in front of everyone.

'I know,' Sorn said. That was all. But Leof suddenly saw a deep fissure between Sorn and Thegan, this matter of belief. She was devout, as everyone in Sendat knew, and he ... Leof wasn't sure Thegan even believed in the gods, although how someone could not was beyond Leof's understanding. But it was obvious in Thegan's attitude to the Lake – as though he could not bear *anything* to be more powerful than he was.

Pity this enchanter, Leof thought, if Thegan gets hold of him. If he can't bear the gods to be powerful, he will do more than destroy a man who had such power.

Sorn stood, her earlier energy contained again. 'Your meal is unfinished, and you should announce that all our people are safe and have come to the aid of Carlion after an attack by an unknown aggressor.'

'Yes,' he said, nodding. 'That is exactly what I should do.'

She flushed, as though caught out in something dishonourable. 'My lord, I did not mean to instruct you –'

He laughed. His reaction startled her, but she smiled tentatively back. Fortune sprang gladly up from the hearthrug, ready for a game. He sidled up to Leof and Leof pulled gently on his ears, grinning at Sorn.

'My lady, I find myself in unknown country without a map, and I am grateful for any instruction.'

She smiled more widely at that, a true smile with a hint of humour in it. 'We are all walking unknown paths, my lord, and some of them are very rough.'

'Well, we'll just have to help each other not to fall smack on our behinds,' he said cheerfully, offering her his arm to go back into the hall.

She began to laugh. It was the first time he had heard her laugh, and it was a very pleasant sound. He had missed the sound of women's laughter. They walked back into the hall together still laughing, Fortune dancing behind them, and he saw that it was the best thing they could have done, because the tension in the room reduced immediately and was banished altogether by Leof's announcement. Banished by gossip and speculation about the 'unknown aggressor'.

Speculate all you like, Leof thought. None of us can tell you who he is. He handed Sorn into her chair and sat back down to a fresh plate of kid, conjured from somewhere at Sorn's signal. He ate it gratefully, and smiled at her as he swallowed. A woman who fed you was worth just as much as a woman who bed you, he thought. Sorn smiled calmly at him, the lady in her hall back in full force. What a warlord she'd make! Leof thought idly, then laughed at himself. Calm, serene ladylike Sorn! He was more tired than he'd realised. At least tonight he could sleep without wondering what was happening in Carlion.

BRAMBLE

'YOU CAN GO now,' Dotta had said, as though she were a warlord's wife dismissing a servant. Bramble found it amusing rather than annoying, but knew she was using the laughter as a distraction to hide her uncertainty. What did it mean, that Dotta had seen her? Was she *really* present, then, truly experiencing these times and events? Half of her had thought it was like a story being played out in front of her, a message from the gods put into her mind. Part of her had thought she was, in truth, back at Oakmere, and these were just illusions – true illusions, perhaps, faithful to history, but still just a glamour the gods had cast.

If she was really here . . . Could she change things?

She'd thought it before, but not seriously. The gods had showed their disapproval even of the thought. But as the waters floated her away, the thought came back stronger than ever. If it were possible to change things, to communicate with Baluch, say, or Gris . . . If she could shift events so that the peoples of the Domains didn't die . . . The best way would be to make an avalanche in Death Pass as Acton and his men were coming through that first spring morning.

Change history. Kill Acton and Baluch and the rest, the invaders.

She remembered Dotta saying, 'Did you think the Destiny stone meant nothing?'

She remembered Acton saying, 'I have seen the Ice King and we cannot survive him!'

She remembered Sebbi's blood, sprayed across the ice.

If she changed history, Acton's people would die.

Her people. Her ancestors.

She understood, bitterly, why Safred had needed someone of mixed blood for this task. Someone with divided loyalties, who could not, in the end, be on anyone's side.

If she did not change history, her people would die. If she did, her people would die. There was no good outcome. She was under no illusion that she could change things enough so that the invasion would be peacefully negotiated. Even if she could take over Acton's mind, that wouldn't happen. There were too many men too used to fighting to let it happen. Men who *liked* fighting, who enjoyed the intensity, the vividness of life on the edge of death, as she had liked the intensity of chasing.

If she let the invasion go ahead, she was as guilty as Acton.

She let that thought settle into her as the waters buoyed her up and landed her on another shore.

At least it was warmer, but the yoke she carried on her back was so heavy that when her sight cleared all she could see was the earth in front of her. Stony earth, the kind you got near mountains, full of sharp stones and hidden rocks. She was pulling. Gods, she was pulling a plough! No wonder it was shagging hard work. Hadn't these people learned how to use oxen for this? Or horses, even? They had horses!

'Get moving, thrall!' a voice shouted. 'We need to get the seed in before the rains come!'

A thrall. Not quite a slave, not in the way the Wind Cities kept slaves. They weren't locked up at night or sold off. They were perhaps more like bond-servants. At least, some of the old stories Bramble had heard said so. But there were no thralls in the Domains. She wasn't sure why. The stories said Acton had forbidden it . . . that only free men could cross the mountains. No doubt she'd find out the truth of it, sooner or later . . .

The thrall paused and wiped sweat from his face – definitely *his*; a woman couldn't have pulled this plough through the stony ground. Not far away, Acton and a group of young men were building a house from wood and stone. An older man, the stone-layer, probably, was directing them, choosing the stones for each course, making sure they fitted together and sloped gradually inwards from the wide base. There was no mortar. At intervals, strong posts were held up by younger boys until the stones reached high enough to support them. The posts, Bramble thought, would form the basis for the wattle sections that were being woven by a group of women sitting under a tree. Asa was there, and the mother of the girl Friede who had been lost in the storm.

There the girl herself was, a woman now, limping along with her crutch, carrying a bundle of wattle withies on the other shoulder. She was laughing at something her mother had said, and her face was alight. Not beautiful, but strong and happy, despite the ever-present crutch. She dumped her bundle of withies at Asa's feet and rolled her shoulders as if they had been heavy. Her mother said something, with a face full of concern, but Friede brushed it off and swung around to collect another bundle from a group of young girls who were stripping the willow branches of their leaves. It was typical of Friede, Bramble thought, that she didn't simply sit down and strip leaves with the others. Typical of her to take the harder task; the more active. She wished for a moment that she could see this world through Friede's eyes instead of the thrall's. She suspected she would feel right at home in that mind.

The sun was at mid-morning and Bramble realised that it was coming not from the mountains but from the plains beyond. They were in the Domains, building a new settlement. She was puzzled. Had the battle of Death Pass already happened? Was the invasion over? She thought it would be just like the gods, to let her agonise over whether to stop the invasion and then to move her straight past it. A weight of responsibility lifted from her shoulders.

Now all she had to do was watch Acton until he died, and see where his bones lay. No decisions, no need to understand. The invasion was over and a thousand years past and no business of hers. She felt light, and free, even under the heavy yoke. It was not her burden, after all.

The thrall reached the end of the furrow and stopped to rest, looking down the valley to where a rough track emerged from a stand of larch and spruce. The grass either side of the track was spring green, but there was snow on the hillsides not far up and the air nipped cold at the thrall's lungs. He had a quick, lively mind, if the rhythm and speed of his glance could be read right. He took the opportunity to observe all he could: the house-building, the women (lingering on one girl in particular, a young blonde who giggled to Friede about something), the track again. There were riders coming out of the trees and the thrall raised a shout. Warning or welcome? Bramble wondered.

The men stopped working on the building and dusted off their hands, moving to greet the newcomers. Hawk was in the lead on a chestnut, a longer-legged version of the shaggy hill ponies from the other side of the mountain. One of the Wind Cities' desert horses cross-bred with the mountain horses?

As he dismounted and threw his reins to one of his followers, Hawk pointed at the thrall and laughed. 'Have you tamed no working beasts, then, in your Ice King's country?'

Although she had thought exactly the same thing, Hawk's mocking tone annoyed Bramble. Who was he to criticise?

Acton came forward, smiling. 'Our ox broke his leg on the mountain path, and fell,' he said. 'The wolves will eat well for while. We make do.'

'Hmm.' Hawk pretended to consider, sending quick glances towards the women who had stopped work to listen. Asa had apparently accepted Hawk's contempt towards women, for she made no move to join the men. Hawk's glance lingered on the blonde girl and Friede. The thrall saw it, and his heart sped up, his hands clenched.

'So,' Hawk said. 'Perhaps we can lend you one of our beasts until you can bring another over the mountains.'

Cooperating? Hawk letting Acton build a settlement near his land? No! This wasn't what had happened! Could she have changed history without even knowing it? Could the past have shifted so much just because she had observed it? Or had Dotta changed things somehow?

'That would be most kind.' Swef's voice came from behind the thrall and he and the others turned around in surprise. Swef moved easily down the hillside, carrying a huge pile of withies across his shoulders. For this gathering chore, he had swapped his good red leather boots for the plain sheepskin ones everyone else wore. 'If we do not get the seeds in, it will be a hard winter and a harder spring.'

Hawk nodded. Swef dumped the withies at the feet of the blonde girl. She giggled. Gods give me patience! Bramble thought. What *is* it about pretty girls and giggles? But she knew very well what it was. Every man there was aware of the blonde. Except Acton, who was ignoring her, inspecting the next set of stones for the wall. Now that was strange. She didn't want her opinion of him to improve, but she had to admire his lack of interest in the giggler.

Asa rose and took several of the girls behind the building to where a line of carts with blankets stretched between them served as storage as well as sleeping tents. She came back with drinking horns and sent the girls around with them. Even Friede took a horn to a young man working a little way away, using a hatchet to lop branches and bark from more of the thick supporting posts. It was Baluch. He had grown and filled out, like Acton, so that he looked more like a young man than a boy. Acton was handsome in a lithe, muscular way, and he moved like a hunting animal, but Baluch had a grace of movement which said to Bramble that he was working in time to some internal music. Friede lingered as he drank and took back the horn with a few words. Baluch laughed. Friede was attractive in a way completely different from the giggling blonde, and Baluch clearly knew it. Their eyes were warm on each other.

The thrall's gaze returned to Hawk and Swef, who were looking over the new building. Acton was a little way off, staring back towards Baluch. Or towards Friede? Bramble wondered, but doubted it. Unlikely that a warrior like Acton would want a girl on a crutch.

'Acton!' Swef called. 'Show our guest your work!'

Acton went over to them readily enough to point out the elements of the building. The thrall lost interest and began to settle the yoke back onto his shoulders. He still watched the chieftains. Delaying the moment of hard work a little longer, Bramble guessed.

'Only one building?' Hawk asked, that superior tone in his voice.

'The hall comes first. After that, the women's quarters and the out-buildings.'

'You don't have separate houses?' Again the barely suppressed scorn. Acton smiled, a smile the thrall recognised as dangerous, because he gripped the yoke harder as though he held a weapon, ready to defend if necessary.

'We do best when we live and work together,' Swef said smoothly. 'You can see,' he pointed to the carts lined up behind the building, 'we need a good large storage area before anything else.'

'Yes,' Hawk said. 'I can see that.'

Swef laid a hand familiarly on his shoulder, guiding him away from the building towards where the thrall was working. He smiled a companionable smile, but the thrall still kept hold of his yoke. 'We're planning to put our sheep fold over here.'

The waters came as a surprise. But what happened? Bramble thought as they tumbled her helplessly, as though she were a leaf in a mountain stream. What had happened to change history? Cooperation. Peace. A gradual settlement, not sudden invasion. Bramble swelled with gratitude and happiness. No matter how it had happened, there it was.

There was only one thing which worried her now. If the past had changed so that the invasion was peaceful, why was she still here? Perhaps, in the Domains created by this new past, she didn't exist? Or was she condemned to live out Acton's life no matter what happened in it? The thought puzzled her, but it could not cut deeply into the great sense of relief and joy she felt.

Her bones ached. Every bone, each of them with its own special pain.

'I'm too old,' her voice was saying, creaking a little. 'I'm too old to go stravaging across mountains like a goat.'

'Never too old, Ragni,' Acton's voice came back, warm and teasing. 'You're just a lass! Never fear, I'll carry you across myself and give you a good cuddling on the way!'

Ragni laughed and coughed as she laughed. She was sick, clearly. Every cough hurt her chest like it was being torn open. Phlegm filled her throat and she turned to spit politely in the fire. It was the fire in Harald's hall. They were back over the mountains at Harald's steading and it was cold, cold, colder than hell. Much colder than it had been the night Acton and Baluch had gone looking for Friede. Was that the Ice King's doing?

'You save your cuddles for them as wants them!' Ragni scolded Acton tenderly. 'There's plenty as does, I hear!'

Acton shrugged. He was sitting with his back to the fire, resting against the raised stones of the hearth. His hair was lit up and his face was in shadow, but Ragni saw something, Bramble couldn't tell what, and leant forwards.

'What is it, lad?'

'Oh, the only girl I want doesn't want me, of course,' he said, brushing off her concern as a joke. 'Isn't that always the way of it?'

Ragni clucked her tongue. 'She's a fool, then,' she said roundly. 'Her loss, lad, her loss.'

'Mmm . . .' he said.

'It's not that silly chit Edwa, is it?' Ragni said sharply. 'She's got all the boys after her but she's not worth a piece of rag, not in her bones. She'd make a bad wife, boy, a bad, wilful wife.'

Acton chuckled. 'No, no, I'm not such a fool as that. I can't stand the giggles!'

Ragni nodded with satisfaction. 'Well, then. Who?'

Acton shook his head, his face unreadable. 'Fewer words, less regret,' he said. It was a very old saying. Bramble had always thought it was a Traveller proverb.

'Huh . . .' Ragni said, unconvinced. 'Well, it's good to have you back from Swef's new steading, lad. It was the worst day's work Harald ever did, when he let you go. Asgarn has done as he should, letting you come back, even if it's only for a visit.'

'Asgarn's a good chieftain,' Acton said. 'He's looking after things well, and he'll lead you well when the time comes to make the trip across to the new settlement.'

Ragni sniffed and spat again, looking across the fire to where a table of men sat, talking. Asgarn was one of them, Bramble saw, and the others were some of the chieftains who had stood on the ledge at the All Moot.

'You should be over there,' Ragni said stubbornly.

'Oh, I'm no good at figuring how many barrels can fit into so many carts, Ragni,' Acton said comfortably. 'They can have their planning, and welcome to it. We'll need good plans, to get everyone who wants to come over the mountains and into good, solid halls by next winter.'

'It's not going to work.'

'Not in one year,' Acton agreed. 'It'll have to happen in stages, as the steadings closest to the mountains move over first, and let the ones further out, the ones who are being hard-pressed by the Ice King's men, shift in as they leave.'

'Thought you were no good at planning?' Ragni said. He laughed.

The fire spat and hissed as a cow pat broke apart and burnt, smouldering. 'That's the scent of home,' Acton said. 'Over the mountains they burn wood all the time, can you believe it?'

Ragni sniffed. 'I miss your mother,' she said.

Acton patted her on the knee – a comforting touch, warm and gentle. 'So do I,' he agreed.

He looked up as the door opened to show a winter evening, light snow falling steadily, transformed for a moment into small flames by the light of the fire.

'Here's Baluch,' Ragni said with pleasure. 'Give us a tune, boy.'

Baluch came in unwinding a hat-scarf from around his face. He pulled off his gloves and coat and sat down gladly by the fire, fishing a pipe out of his pocket. 'It's building up to be a wild night,' he said cheerfully. 'I wonder how they're doing, over the other side of the mountain? I'll wager it's not as cold as here.'

Acton grinned at him. 'And there's no Asgarn to make you go out in the cold to tend the sheep,' he teased.

'You'd be just as bad, over the mountains,' Baluch retorted.

'Oh, I'm not chieftain there, Bal, any more than I am here. I'm just another pair of hands.'

'You're Swef's heir,' Ragni interjected with energy. 'Don't you let him forget it!'

Acton laughed. 'Wili is Swef's heir, Ragni.'

'A girl! Well, there's a way to solve that. It'd be a good marriage for you both, and your place as chieftain would be safe.'

Acton waved that idea away. 'Tell you the truth, Ragni, I don't care if I'm never chieftain, there or anywhere.'

The old woman made the sign averting evil. 'Don't let the gods hear you say that, lad!'

Both the young men laughed, as Ragni shook her head at them, clucking her tongue.

'Tch! You should be ashamed, laughing at an old woman!' But her tone was indulgent.

Bramble wondered again if she were just going to live through Acton's life now, day by day, bit by bit, until he died and the spell came undone. Then where would she find herself? Back at Obsidian Lake, or in the darkness beyond death, waiting to be reborn? Part of her didn't really care. Then, as if in response to her thought, Baluch stopped laughing and stood up.

His face was white, his eyes stretched wide as if trying to see beyond the walls of the hall. He dropped the pipe and it fell into the fire, but he didn't notice. Acton tried to flick it out with a stick, but the pipe flared up in a sudden brightness. The flame lit Baluch's face from below, turning it into a death's head, a skull mask over the man beneath.

No, Bramble thought, recognising the gods' touch even at a distance, feeling them pour into Baluch and open his mind. *No. It was going so well . . .*

Baluch screamed. His mouth opened wider than seemed possible and the scream came out wild and tortured, without thought or control. It was the kind of scream a woman makes in childbirth, when the pain has pushed her beyond being human, back into the animal life. But worse, because underneath was grief and horror.

Everyone in the hall came to their feet. Acton stood close to Baluch, a hand reaching out but pausing, waiting. Asgarn and the chieftains ran from the other side of the fire and stopped as he screamed again, and then gulped air and started to speak, his eyes wide but his own again, Baluch's eyes.

'Stop! Stop!'

'Is it a fit?' one of the chieftains asked.

Acton shook his head. 'No. No. Sometimes, the gods speak to him.'

'He's not a chieftain,' Asgarn said.

'Even so, Ragni knows.'

The old woman nodded. 'Harald would never accept it, but we all knew. The gods speak to him.'

Acton laid his hand delicately on Baluch's shoulder. Baluch was trembling.

'What has happened?' Acton asked gently.

Baluch's shaking increased until only Acton's support kept him from falling.

'They are killing them.'

'Who?' Asgarn said. He moved closer, taking command, and Acton fell silent but put his arm around Baluch, physically holding him up.

'Hawk. Hawk and his men . . .' Baluch's eyes snapped shut as though he couldn't bear to look at something. 'No!' he howled. 'Friede!' He struggled against Acton's hold as if he could walk through the fire to save her. Acton's face paled but he hung on tighter.

'Hawk has attacked?' Asgarn asked.

'Attacked,' Baluch moaned. 'Killed. Friede. All the men. Taken. Edwa! Asa . . .' He drew out Asa's name on a long breath and then fell silent.

The hall was deathly quiet. Baluch's head dropped and Bramble could feel the gods leave him. If she had been in her own body she would have been shaking and crying with anger. How could she have thought it would happen easily? Why had she let herself hope? Cooperation! Hah! You couldn't expect cooperation from warriors, she didn't care what colour hair they had. All they wanted to do was kill. Her heart had shrivelled inside her and sat in her chest like a sharp rock. Or was that Ragni's pain?

Baluch raised his head and turned it with an effort, looking into Acton's eyes. 'Asa. Your mother fought. She killed one as he, as he tried to . . .' Baluch shook his head. 'Another struck her down.'

'She has killed a rapist before,' Acton said, his voice flat. 'My father will no doubt welcome him to the coldest pit of hell.'

'Friede . . .' Baluch sighed.

'Tell us of Friede,' Acton said, suddenly urgent.

Baluch hid his face in his hands and wept. 'She fought also. Swef tried to protect her. It took three of them to kill him. Then they killed her. It was –' His voice hiccupped. 'It was quick, at least.'

Acton turned away. Ragni watched him, her heart twisting in her. The one girl, Bramble thought, who wasn't interested in him . . . She didn't want to feel sympathy for any of them, but how could she help it?

'Edwa?' Asgarn said. 'You said her name . . . ?'

Baluch wiped his tears away and looked around the group of chieftains. 'They have taken the younger girls. To use later. To be slaves. Killed the men, stole everything, burnt the hall. They . . .' he faltered, 'they killed the older women, too, after they . . . used them. Who kills women who don't fight? More than a raid. It was more than a raid. They wanted to wipe us out.'

'She's still alive?' Asgarn was intent.

'Edwa. Wili. A few others. The prettiest ones.' His voice was thick with scorn and hatred.

As if Baluch's words were a signal, talk broke out in the hall. Shouts, cries, sobs. Acton turned back to the group of chieftains. Baluch sank down and laid his head in Ragni's lap. She stroked his hair unsteadily.

'I claim revenge,' Acton said. 'My mother. My chieftain. My friends.' He turned to Asgarn. 'I know you are chieftain here now, and that I do not dispute. But we must return death for death to these animals, these lying, scheming traitors, and I will do it.'

His voice was without emotion. His anger, his grief, had pushed him past feeling. All that was left was the desire to kill, and it shone clearly in his eyes and showed in the set of his shoulders and the tightness of his fists. At last, Bramble thought, with a kind of relief. Here he is: Acton the killer. He's so young. What, eighteen? Nineteen? Young.

She wanted to fall backwards into hate for him, back into the scorn and anger she had always felt towards Acton the invader. There he was, wanting to kill, wanting to wipe out. But she remembered how she had felt, after she'd learnt of Maryrose's death. Just like this. Exactly. Her face had been set in the same dead calm. Wanting to kill, wanting to wipe out. If Saker had been there, she would have done it. If Saker appeared before her when she awoke at Obsidian Lake, she would do it then. Gladly. Fiercely. Without regret. Just like Acton. She pushed the thought away from her. Killing one man, the murderer of your loved ones, that she could understand. But Acton had killed a whole nation.

The chieftains exchanged glances, nodding to each other. There was something there, Bramble thought, something they're not saying, not out loud. But there was an element of calculation in their assessment of Acton. Something . . . political.

'Kill them all,' Asgarn said softly. 'We will kill them all and take everything they have and laugh while we do it. Yes. You have the right, Acton. You will be the hand of the gods on these butchers.'

The other chieftains murmured agreement. Acton nodded and stood straighter. Ragni put a hand to her heart and then to her mouth, as though she wanted to stop her own words. She began to sob quietly, and Baluch raised his head in her lap to comfort her, patting her shoulder, rising to put an arm around her, rocking her.

The old man from the Moot, the one who had controlled the staff, laid a hand on Acton's shoulder. 'For this battle, you shall be the lord of war, Acton. We so appoint you and bind ourselves to support you.'

Silence fell. Through Ragni's tears, Bramble could read the faces of the chieftains. The old man had gone further than they had intended. That was a mistake, old man, she thought bitterly. A bad, bad mistake.

MARTINE

AFTER LUNCH, ZEL and Martine buried the food scraps under a tree not too far into the Forest, in case they attracted bear or wolverine.

'We don't have a new flint,' Zel said as she filled in the hole. 'I looked all morning, but there are none around here at all.'

'I know. I looked too, yesterday.'

'What are we going to do?'

Zel looked worried, as she should be. Martine thought about the warnings she had received so many times as a youngster: the ritual was three nights, and all three must be completed, or disaster would occur during the following year. There were always lots of instances cited, too: forest fires, houses burnt down, even people themselves suddenly bursting into flame. At a time like now, with the future in balance, they couldn't afford to anger him.

Martine had thought about the problem, but she was still unsure of her answer. 'One of my casting stones is a flint,' she said.

Zel stopped shovelling and stared at her. 'Use a casting stone?' she queried. 'Can you do that?'

Martine shrugged. 'I don't know. I've never heard of anyone doing it, but it was a flint before it was a casting stone.'

Zel thought about it. 'Which stone is it?'

'The blank stone.'

'Dung and pissmire, Martine, are you crazy?' Her voice rose in panic. 'That's the Chaos stone! Anything could happen!'

'The blank stone represents possibilities.'

'Bad ones as well as good ones,' Zel said.

'It's all we've got – unless you want to chip off a piece of the lake obsidian and use that.'

A shudder went through them both.

'No,' Zel said, breathless with horror at the thought. 'No.'

'Well, then. We can't leave the ritual unfinished. It would set him loose on us and those with us.'

Zel was silent for a moment, her face unreadable, then said, 'Ask 'em. Ask the stones if you should use it.'

Martine crouched on the grass, spat on her hand and held it out to Zel. She couldn't ask herself. A fool's pursuit, when a caster threw for herself, but if Zel asked it might work.

Zel clasped her hand and whispered, 'Should we use the blank stone as our new flint?'

Martine's fingers in the pouch drew five stones without hesitation. That alone told her it was a real casting, strong and true. She cast the stones. The blank stone, first. Then Mystery, Night, Rejoicing and Sorrow.

'Shagging hells!' Zel said.

Martine smiled grimly. 'Well? Will you risk it?'

'Are they talking to you?'

She shook her head. 'But it's a true casting. As true as you'll get. We'll have both rejoicing and sorrow, and anything could happen.'

Zel straightened up in a smooth movement that made Martine envy her youth. She stood for a moment, staring out at the altar.

'If it gets bad, we can jump in the mere,' Zel said.

'It'd have to be pretty bad before I'd jump in there.'

They stood in silence. The breeze had died. The mere reflected the sky perfectly, so that it seemed to hold all the heavens. Only the altar was dull, a black stain on the blue.

'The altar should not be dark on this night,' Martine said, suddenly sure. 'We will use the tools we have.'

Zel nodded. 'If you say so.'

Zel held the casting stone and Martine hit it cleanly with the striking stone, hard and fast as it should be done, so that bright sparks leapt out onto the tinder. Zel blew softly to make the sparks catch, and Martine said, 'Take our breath to speed your growth.'

As the tinder caught and small flames started to lick upwards, she felt him come. But there was no gradually building arousal, no heat in her loins, no sense of being desired. There was just fire, shooting upwards.

She hurriedly moved back, dragging Zel with her.

A lifetime of living with the gods hadn't prepared her for this. The fire roared up, higher and higher, far beyond the capacity of the fuel they had given it. The heat was intense; they fell back further, to the edge of the island. Martine hesitated: should they turn and run, or would that make it worse?

Then the choice was taken from them.

Obsidian Lake responded. Around them, in a perfect circle, the waters of the mere rose like a rampart, shielding the Forest from the fire, cutting off their escape. The waters began to move, to spin skywards, becoming a whirlpool with standing sides, rising higher and higher until they were stranded between fire and water, both roaring, both rearing, enemies confronting each other, implacable.

Zel stood immovable, eyes wide and fixed on the fire.

Martine looked where Zel looked, and saw him.

She had thought she was old enough to be invulnerable to the lure of the wild boys, the bad boys with full mouths and piercing eyes. She had thought she was too old for the promise of unbridled sex, unconstrained, unashamed – that she would never give anyone complete surrender, not even him.

But if he had looked at her as he was looking at Zel, she would have thrown herself into the fire without a second's thought.

Zel took a step forwards. He reached out a hand. He was everything puberty promised but never delivered: intensity, ecstasy, freedom.

Zel took another step, her gaze never leaving his.

Martine was torn. Should she stop Zel? Did she have the right? Was it her choice, or Zel's? Or his? In desperation, she found her voice.

'We are daughters of the fire,' she said to him. 'Will you destroy your daughter?'

He turned his head and stared at her. Then he smiled and she saw death through his eyes, as a glorious transfiguration into flame.

She was transfixed, longing herself for that exaltation. The heat from the past two nights had come back as soon as he looked at her, wilder, stronger, more insistent. The aching need for him felt as though it would split her in two. She took a step towards him. But he didn't want her. He looked back to Zel. The young one.

Too late. When he looked back Zel was no longer staring at him, but at the ground.

'Hazel?' the fire said, in a voice of rushing wind and crackling power and deep, deep longing. Martine was filled with envy, wanting him, oh, wanting him to look at her like that, to say her name.

But Zel's mouth was set like stone. 'I have to look after Flax,' she said.

It was enough. He would never plead, never beg. He invited. Or he took. Martine grabbed Zel and began to pull her back, away, towards the wall of water. Better drowned than burnt, as he would burn them now. The heat escalated suddenly, harsh on their skin where it had been loving. He reached for them and the flames began to spread outwards from the altar.

As though Zel's rejection of him had given the waters strength, they began to grow higher, curving over at the top so that the altar was almost enclosed in a dome of waves, an impossible inverted whirlpool. The air was sucked upwards through the small opening at the top, and Martine staggered as the wind whipped around them, blinded them, caught their breath away, dragged them towards him. Waves from above crashed onto the island, plumes of water splashing down on the base of the altar, drenching them. Every drop stung like acid but the fire was so strong that their clothes dried again almost instantly.

Martine forced herself to turn around, fighting the pull of the wind towards the centre, the heat scorching on her back. She and Zel clung to each other, crouching at the very edge of the water, Zel's head in Martine's arm, hiding her eyes against him as though she didn't trust her own resolution. She was trembling violently.

The flames were struggling, now. He could live without fuel, but not without air. Surely he would not let himself be extinguished? Martine looked back at him.

As if in response to her thought, he stared straight at Martine and then the fire rose in a single great column, pure flame, no sign of him left, and pierced through the narrow opening between the waves. Steam hissed. The water faltered and the spin slowed, droplets falling and spitting on the altar. The column of fire left the altar, shooting straight up through the waves, rising impossibly fast towards the night sky until it became another star, and was gone from sight.

For a moment the waves loomed over them and Martine wondered if the mere needed some acknowledgment, some recompense for the trouble they had caused. But she was not minded to apologise to water.

'We are daughters of the fire,' she said clearly. 'What was done was done with respect and reverence.'

The water slowed its spin, sinking gradually back towards the surface of the mere. Zel and Martine stayed where they were, not too near the altar which still gave off a startling heat, as the waters became calm again.

Before she moved, Martine forced herself to wait for one moment more, though every instinct was shouting at her to run. She took Zel's hand and squeezed it.

'The fire . . .' she prompted, waiting for Zel to catch up with her. Zel's eyes went wide but she cleared her throat with some difficulty.

'The fire,' she said, and they completed it together, as it had to be said, 'will never die.'

Martine felt a slight easing in the tightness around her heart, as though the fire had heard them and acknowledged their fealty. The water paused in its movement, as though stopped in time. Martine went cold. Had they offended the mere? But the ritual had to be safely ended, or the fire could return whenever he wanted. That was part of the bargain. Perhaps the mere knew that, because after a heart-shattering pause it allowed the waters to continue settling.

When the water was once again clear and flat, reflecting the sky, they went back, holding hands, shaking, expecting Safred and Cael to meet them full of questions and exclamations.

But the camp was quiet, Cael and Safred still asleep. Martine and Zel sat well away from the campfire, shoulder to shoulder, still shaking.

'The ground was dry,' Zel said finally, as though grabbing onto something real.

'What?' Martine said. Her mind felt overloaded, like a mill race with too much water going through it. She couldn't concentrate on anything except her memory of him.

'On the island, the ground was dry. As though the waves hadn't been there at all. *We're* dry. My skin – the water felt like it burned . . . but there are no marks.' She paused, indicating Cael in his blanket and Safred's tent. 'They didn't hear anything. Did it – was it real?'

Her tone was wistful. That jolted Martine into paying attention.

'If you mean, would you have burnt to a crisp if you'd walked into the fire, yes, you would have,' she said tartly.

Zel bit her lip, tears rising in her eyes. 'He'll never forgive me,' she said.

'No. He never forgives.'

'I'll never be able to do the ritual again.'

Martine nodded, thinking it through. 'You'd be too much of a risk to the others with you.'

Zel looked down at the ground, her head hanging. 'But we saw him,' she whispered.

Martine felt the triumph, the astonishment, and finally the exaltation he had promised them. She smiled slowly. 'Yes. We saw him. Remember,' she touched Zel's shoulder, 'it was you he wanted.'

Zel turned curious eyes to her. 'You didn't mind?'

How to answer that honestly? Martine felt again the agony of realising it was Zel he was staring at. The envy. The despair. The longing.

'I minded,' she said. 'But now that he's gone, I know he was right. Of the two of us, it should have been you. I have not enough passion left for him.'

She believed the words as she spoke them, but as soon as they had left her mouth she knew them to be a lie. Every breath taken in the memory of him told her that she was as made of passion as he was. She had forgotten it, but now her body remembered, and she and Zel wept in each other's arms because they were alive, and without him.

ASH

ASH SAT IN the dark stable for more than an hour, sliding the stones through his fingers, listening as they whispered their names: Love, Chaos, Murder, Revenge, Child, Woman, Death, Evenness . . .

Each stone was different, and each fitted his fingers and his mind as if crafted especially for him. He knew that a stonecaster's stones and his soul became entwined, and he could feel it happening, slowly, feeling the stones become *his*; only his. The process was both terrifying and exhilarating; scary and deeply comforting. There was nothing else that was *his*. He began to understand why stonecasters all seemed to have an unshakeable air of calm around them. The centre of their lives was not touched by time or circumstance; their souls were as safe as stone.

Unlike Flax's singing, the stones didn't cut across his own mental music; rather, they seemed to harmonise with it, giving it more depth and colour. He longed to use them. Flax was sitting beside him, nursing the last of his ale. He had the gift of happily doing nothing, which Ash had never mastered.

'I think I should practise before I try a paying customer,' Ash said, as nonchalantly as he could. 'Do you want me to read for you?'

Flax smiled with pleasure. 'Oh, yes.' He wriggled around until he was facing Ash and then spat in his left hand and held it out expectantly.

Ash put the pouch on the ground in front of him, spread out his own napkin, and spat in his own palm. They clasped hands.

'Ask your question,' he said.

'Um . . . will Zel ever get married?'

Ash didn't let his surprise show, because that was also part of being a stonecaster, keeping your face blank. But he was suddenly curious about Flax; about whether he wanted the answer to be yes, or no. Was he so dependent on Zel that he couldn't bear the thought of her leaving? Or was he chafing under his big sister's competent management?

The stones in the bag were both strange and familiar to his fingers. It was a different feeling from just touching them, as he had earlier. Some seemed to slide past his fingertips as though waxed, others clung to his hand. It was easy, the work of only a moment, to gather the five that wanted to be drawn out. Ash breathed deeply to control his astonishment. He had always thought it was just chance – well, chance controlled by the gods – which stones were chosen. He'd had no idea that the stones chose themselves. The choice was so *clear*. It was so easy to tell which ones to grasp and which to let go. He felt euphoria building in him. This was something he could do, after all, something respected far more than safeguarding, something that – something that could take him back on the Road. With his parents, if they wanted.

A whole bright future rolled out in his mind in the moments that his hand drew the five stones out of the bag and cast them on the napkin of undyed linen. The stones stood out clearly against the pale fabric, but Ash didn't need the fading light to know which stones lay there. It was easy.

Then, as the stones spoke to him, it stopped being easy. He touched them, one by one, as he had seen Martine do, and they reached up into his mind and spoke, in sounds and music and images and smells. The smell of blood. The flight of an arrow. The sound of the sea.

'Time,' he said with difficulty, and was appalled at the sound. The words came out harsh, grating, the unmistakable voice of the dead.

Flax recoiled, paling, and let go of Ash's hand. Then, slowly, he took it again, ignoring the fact that Ash was shaking.

'That's the voice of the Well of Secrets,' he said slowly. 'That's how she heals. With that voice.'

Ash looked down at their hands, not sure what to say. Not wanting to admit to speaking with the voice of the dead. He shrugged, trying to imply that it was a surprise to him, too. But Flax had seen that already.

'You weren't trying to use that voice?' he asked warily.

Ash shook his head, afraid to speak. Afraid, oh gods, that his normal voice had gone completely.

'Has it happened before?'

'Only when I sing.' The admission burst out before he could stop it, and it was his own voice, although a little higher than normal because he was frightened. But it was his voice. Turning back to the stones lying on the napkin was one of the hardest things he had ever done. He took a very deep breath, and touched one.

'Parting,' he said, in the voice of the dead, and as he spoke the images, like memories, washed over him, full of treachery and blood. 'Woman. Change. The blank stone.'

He sat breathing heavily, glad it was over, not meeting Flax's eyes. But Flax was a Traveller born and bred, and the Sight, whatever form it took, was a part of his world. He accepted Ash's voice without further comment and looked at the blank stone consideringly.

'So. That means anything can happen, yes?'

Ash paused. The blank stone *did* mean that, but the stones were telling him something else; death, they said, murder. Yet those stones were not on the napkin. So what should he say to Flax? How much should he say? It might not be Zel's death, he told himself, although he was sure it was. But if the death stone wasn't there . . . perhaps Flax wasn't meant to know . . . Ash could have screamed from frustration. This was supposed to be a practice run, not an impossible choice! Then he remembered Martine's voice, 'Answer the question. Don't make my mistake . . . don't give them more than they ask for.'

'I don't . . .' Thank the gods, it was his own voice again. Perhaps the other voice only came when he was touching the stones, or naming them. 'I don't see a wedding,' he said and tried not to laugh hysterically at the understatement. 'But there is a parting of the ways.' A big parting, but perhaps not the final one. Perhaps that was what the blank stone meant.

Flax scratched his chin, a curiously old movement. 'Time,' he said.

'Yes,' Ash replied, sure of that. 'Months, at least.'

Flax let go of his hand. 'Months,' he said, in a tone which meant that months might as well have been years. 'I thought . . . there was a cobbler who wanted to marry her a while back. I just wondered . . . but I guess not, huh?'

Ash shrugged and swept the stones up into the pouch. They were once again just pieces of rock with carvings on them. That was all. The surge of feeling, of sight and smell and what had seemed like memory, was gone. He felt empty and tired.

'You know, I don't think your average stonecaster talks like that,' Flax said. 'Might cause a bit of a stir.'

He was right. No one would want to consult a stonecaster who grated an answer like stone on stone. Like Death herself. They certainly didn't want to attract attention while they were on their way to the Deep.

'Dung and pissmire!' Ash cursed. All his bright plans crashed around him. Even this talent was useless to him. 'Go to sleep!' he snarled at Flax, as though it were all his fault. Flax grinned and rolled himself into his blanket as though nothing were wrong.

The next day, they were more circumspect on the Road, because they were closer to Gabriston. Although Flax complained, they camped that night instead of going to one of the village inns.

'We don't need more silver. Best not to draw attention,' Ash said. 'That's the way of it, going to the Deep. Don't draw attention.'

Or someone, sometime, would notice the trickle of Traveller men heading through Gabriston into the wilds, and ask questions. That would mean death, for someone – the questioner or the questioned. So the demons said.

They bought small amounts of food in each village they passed the day after, until their saddlebags were swollen, so they could skirt Gabriston and go on to the wilds without being noticed.

They were out of grain country now and into North Domain's vineyards, famous from cliff to cove for their fine vintages. Flax eyed the inns with some wistfulness, but Ash was firm.

'On the way out, maybe. Maybe, if all goes well. But no sane man goes to the Deep with drink in him.'

The vines were planted on hillsides, so steep that in some places they were terraced to make more flat ground. The hills grew rougher, and the vines less abundant as they approached the wilds. Finally, they found their way to a bluff which overlooked the wilds: a network of canyons and chasms, stream-cut gorges and dead ends, all formed of the red sandstone that was quarried further downstream and sent all over the Domains. In Turvite, in rich merchants' houses, Ash had seen intricately carved mantelpieces and balustrades in the fine stone, streaked golden and blood red in intertwining layers. The sandstone was very beautiful, but the sight of it had always made him nervous – it reminded him of the Deep, and the Spring Equinox.

The canyons of the wilds had been worn away by water over thousands of years, many more thousands than Acton's people had been in the Domains. Every spring, his father had said, the singers and the poets had made their way here. Spring was the time for music and stories, he said, when things began to flow again. Summer was the time for those in the living trades: horse trainers and animal healers and drovers. Autumn for the dead trades: tinkers and painters and drystone wallers. Winter for the wood trades: carvers and carpenters and turners, chair-makers and basketweavers. Every craft had its time, its gods-chosen time, for the Deep. Except, Ash thought now, looking down at the stream below the bluff as it leapt and danced over the red rocks, except safeguarders. Perhaps he belonged with the shepherds. He laughed, shortly, and nudged Mud with his heels. The sun was setting. It was time for the Deep.

SAKER

SAKER HAD DECIDED to get well away from Carlion before he searched for more bones. Yet no matter where he went, people were afraid. They gathered in inns, talking agitatedly, calling each other over to confirm some part of the story, worrying, fretting. Or else they shut themselves up in their houses.

Whenever he passed a black rock altar there were people making sacrifices to the gods, praying hard. Useless, he wanted to tell them. The gods have sent me. Once, there was a Traveller family at the altar, and he wanted to stop and say, 'You don't need to worry. If you stay out of the way, you won't be hurt.' But of course he couldn't, without revealing himself.

In each village he passed, men and women were out nailing shutters firmly to the windows, or installing bars for the doors. Carpenters had notices pinned to their workshop doors: Too busy!

Smiths were making weapons instead of horseshoes. The local officers, who held large sections of the land in the warlord's name, had sent their sergeants out to collect their oath men, and hauled them away, complaining, from barricading their cottages.

All the activity should have made him feel triumphant. He had done this. *He*, Saker, had scared all these people. Part of him wished his father could be here to witness it. But . . . he didn't want it to be like this. The anxiety – oddly, he'd never imagined his actions leading to worry. Terror, yes. Terror in the night, death cleanly delivered a moment afterwards, he had been expecting that. The killing was necessary, to retrieve the land from its usurpers. But worry, even this extraordinary worry, he hadn't expected that, and it felt wrong.

He knew what his father would say: you just didn't think it

through, boy! He'd said it often to Saker in his childhood, when Saker rushed impetuously into some scheme. Like the time he'd wanted to raise snails to eat, as he'd heard the Wind Cities people did, and the box overturned. The snails got into the vegetable garden and ate all his father's plants. He winced at the memory of that beating, and of his father's voice saying, 'You just didn't think it through, did you, boy? Well, think this through!' Down came the cane.

When he stopped for the night at an inn where he had been once before in his wanderings, he was besieged for castings. But he shook his head.

'Even the gods do not know the outcome,' he said portentously. The innkeeper's wife burst into tears and his son paled, but the man himself sniffed.

'Good. You remember that, boy. Our fate is in our own hands.'

Saker disliked him intensely in that moment, and it was only later that he realised the man reminded him of his father. But he didn't think about that. By that time he was occupied in finding bones.

LEOF

THE NEXT FEW days were a whirl of messages and reports. Leof sent recruiting parties to towns in the Domain furthest from Carlion. There was no use trying to get masons in closer towns to go to Carlion; refugees from the slaughter had already spread the story of the ghosts and the nearest towns were busy fortifying themselves.

The stories reached Sendat. Hodge came to Leof in the officers' workroom, where he was sorting through reports from two recruiting parties who had managed to scrape up some apprentice masons eager for adventure and a couple of older men who didn't work much these days but were prepared to take a trip to the coast at the warlord's expense. There was no door to the officers' workroom – it was an annexe between the room where Thegan held his meetings and Thegan's workroom. Hodge stood a little uncomfortably in the doorway and cleared his throat.

'Yes?' Leof said, looking up. 'Oh, it's you, Hodge. What's the problem?'

'We've got some people from Carlion come to town, my lord. Paying for their drinks at the inn with stories.'

Leof put down the papers he had been reading. 'Well, it had to come some time. Call a muster and send to the town to say I'll address everyone in the square an hour before sunset.'

Hodge nodded and left. A moment later Leof heard the bell that called the men to muster. He went out of the barracks building and stood in front of the hall. Should he tell Sorn? Hodge was waiting by the muster point.

'Sergeant, go and tell the Lady Sorn that she and her ladies and the rest of the household are invited to this muster. And get me a halberd.'

Sorn had been waiting for this moment, it was clear. The maids had probably brought back the news from the town as well – maybe that was how Hodge had found out. She swept out of the hall with her ladies and maids in tow, Fortune hiding in her skirts, and behind them came the cooks and the kitchen boys and the fire tender; and from around the side of the hall came the gardeners and the dairymaid and the woodman and the lads who looked after the chickens and the ducks and the pigs. The brewer came out from her oast-house, the cheese-maker from her loft, the carpenter from his workshop. Leof hadn't reflected before on how big and complex the staff was that Sorn managed.

They waited to the side of the assembled troops. Knowing that it was bound to come, Leof had worried over what to say in this moment. But it was a lovely day, spring edging into summer, and all their own people were safe for the moment. His natural optimism asserted itself so that he smiled at the assembly with real reassurance.

'You've all heard the stories,' he said simply. 'Evil bloodsucking ghosts rising from the dead to slaughter us, yes?' Men in the ranks nodded, a little shamefacedly, expecting to be told none of it was true, that they were fools for listening to fireside tales. They shuffled their feet, a soft susurration in the dust.

'As far as we know, they don't suck blood.' As they realised what he meant, they stood still and silence fell. 'There are ghosts, raised by an enchanter. They do have bodily strength. They cannot be killed again.'

Murmurs rose from both the men and from Sorn's household. One girl was giggling wildly, another gasping with fright and looking around as though expecting the ghosts to jump on them immediately.

'But . . .' Leof shouted, and they quieted. 'But, the spell is of limited time. In Carlion, they faded as the sun came up. They have no more strength than they had when they were alive. Although they cannot be killed, they can be stopped. They cannot enter a barred door or a shuttered window, any more than a man can.' He held out his hand and Hodge put the halberd into it. He brought it round in a wide, hissing swipe and smacked the pole into his other hand. All eyes followed its sweep. 'If you cut off their arms, they will do no more damage.'

A few men in the ranks began to smile. Leof nodded to them.

'Yes. That is why we have been practising with battleaxes and halberds these last days. That is why you will all learn to use boar spear, because if you impale one of these ghosts on one, he will be easy prey for the man with the battleaxe. Do you understand?'

'Aye, my lord,' a few enthusiastic ones shouted.

'Do *all* of you understand?' Leof called.

'*Aye*, my lord,' they shouted back.

He nodded to them and smiled again. 'They are an unusual enemy, my friends. But they are *not* unstoppable. So far they have taken on unarmed townsfolk, who have never before even *seen* an enemy. I think they will get a surprise when they come up against *us*.'

He tossed the halberd in the air so that it gleamed in the sun and caught it again with a flourish and they cheered. Then he turned to the household and bowed to Sorn. 'My lady, you and your people should be in no fear. Sendat is well protected and well armed against this enemy. You are in no danger.'

She smiled at the halberd in his hand with real humour. 'So I see, my lord.'

The cook laughed at that and, when Sorn smiled in response, the others laughed, too. Sorn and Leof bowed to each other and she went back in to the hall, calm as ever. Leof watched her go with a half-smile on his face. She made everything so easy.

Hodge dismissed the men and Leof went down to the town to make the same speech, with a few small variations, to the townsfolk. To them he emphasised the fact that barred doors and good shutters would keep out the ghosts, and that the fort was being rebuilt so that, in an emergency, it would safely hold all the people from the town.

'Not that we'll need that,' he said cheerily. 'My men are training now to make sure that, *if* these ghosts turn up anywhere near here, they'll have their arms and legs cut off and be squirming on the grass like fat white worms before they know what's hit them!'

They laughed a little, but were not so easily reassured as the soldiers had been. Leof sobered.

'Remember, my friends, these ghosts have not been seen again since Carlion. It may be that this was a spell which could only be used there.'

'What about Spritford?' someone at the back yelled.

'You, come forward,' Leof said. He thought quickly as the older woman struggled towards the bench on which he stood. If there had been another incident, it would be best if news didn't get out about it now. He leapt down from the bench and waited for her to reach him.

The woman was middle-aged and truculent, in no mind to take orders from a young man, even a warlord's officer.

'Spritford?' Leof said quietly. 'When was that?'

'Last autumn,' she said. 'My sister's man was killed there, and she came to live with me.'

'So,' he said, raising his voice, 'nothing has happened since Carlion?'

She shook her head, and the people around her relaxed.

'Wait here for a moment,' he said to the woman and climbed back on the bench. 'My friends, you know the truth now. Go home and prepare, as we have been preparing for you. Remember that your warlord ordered you to secure your homes many months ago, so that no matter what enemy faced us, you would be safe. Remember that he lent you his own carpenters and smiths to help fortify your homes.'

'That's true,' he heard someone mutter. 'We're in good shape.'

'Go home and give thanks to the gods for our safety and pray to them for the warlord's wellbeing.'

They drifted away, some to their houses but more to the road that led outside town to the black rock altar near the stream. The woman waited stolidly.

'Can you bring your sister to the fort?' Leof asked. She nodded and turned away.

Leof wondered if he should go with her and see the woman straight away; but he wanted Sorn to be part of this meeting. She will be better at talking to women, he told himself. Particularly a grieving widow.

He went back to the fort and found Sorn in the kitchens, discussing the evening meal with the cook. She looked up and smiled as he came in.

'Roast kid for supper, my lord?' she asked.

'Always good,' Leof said half-heartedly, his mind on Spritford and ghosts.

She mistook his lack of enthusiasm. 'Something different tomorrow perhaps, then, Ael. An ash-baked dish, perhaps. Lamb with onions and wild greens and parsnips in some stock with lemon and rosemary, I think.'

The cook shrugged, resigned. 'Too late to start that tonight, my lady.'

'Which is why I said "tomorrow",' Sorn said gently. The cook flushed and shifted his feet. 'Tonight you will take the roast kid and fry it with brown ale and onions and thyme and some of the olives from the Wind

Cities. You will cook the carrots with honey and serve a bitter salad of dandelion greens and wilted spinach in lemon juice, to aid digestion. There will also be dessert.'

'Yes, my lady. What kind of dessert?'

It amused Leof to see how thoroughly Sorn had cowed the cook, who was a big man and known to be free with his fists after he'd had a few drinks. Sorn smiled graciously at him and turned to Leof.

'My lord? Do you have a favourite dessert?'

'Strawberries?' Leof suggested.

'Griddle cakes served with strawberries and the first skimming of cream,' Sorn instructed.

'Yes, my lady,' the cook said, looking at his feet.

Leof's lips twitched and a dimple showed briefly in Sorn's cheek but was banished immediately. She patted the cook on the arm.

'The bacon and barley soup was excellent this noon, Ael,' she said.

The cook looked up, met her smile and smiled back. 'Thank you, my lady,' he said.

Fortune was waiting resignedly outside the kitchen door, and jumped up, barking softly, as Sorn appeared. Leof clicked his fingers and the dog danced up to him and licked his thumb. Sorn smiled. They strolled back to the hall together.

'You have a big household,' he commented.

'It was enlarged considerably when I was married,' she said. 'My father did not care for home comforts in the same way that my lord Thegan does.'

Leof had never thought of Thegan as caring about comfort in any way.

Sorn caught his expression and smiled, a little grimly. 'My lord appreciates good food and good service,' she said. 'Such things do not happen by chance.'

Leof nodded. 'Anything of excellence is the product of hard work,' he agreed. He led Sorn over to her customary chair and seated her with the appropriate bow. Fortune gave a sigh as he realised they were not going for a walk, and sat down. 'Your household is exemplary and I am interested in how you organise it. Unfortunately, there is another matter to deal with at this time. A woman in the town reported an earlier uprising of ghosts in a town called Spritford.'

'That is in the Western Mountains Domain, near the Sharp River,' Sorn said.

Leof was surprised that she knew the Domains so well, and it showed in his face. She smiled wryly.

'I was courted by quite a few warlords and their sons and for a while studied the other Domains with a great deal of interest.'

He laughed. 'No doubt you did!'

She smiled back and laughed a little herself, her green eyes shining, then sobered quickly. 'Spritford,' she said. He sobered, too, indicating the door where the woman from the town had appeared, arm-in-arm with a slighter, shorter woman with strikingly similar features.

Sorn rose immediately and went to greet them. They bowed low, but she raised them up by the arms and led them to seats. Fortune hid behind Sorn's chair from the strangers.

'Come,' she invited them. 'Tell us about these ghosts.'

The shorter woman, Ulma, was as stern-faced as her sister, and stoic. Not the wailing widow Leof had expected, but the grief was real enough. She told the story: ghosts appearing out of nowhere, solid, armed, angry. Seven dead in Spritford, she said, including her husband, struck down by a small man wielding a scythe, in the full light of the sun. That was unwelcome news; more welcome was the fact that they had faded at sunset.

'So I came here,' she said finally, 'thinking to find safety, but it seems maybe there's no safety anywhere.'

Sorn nodded sympathetically, asked a few tactful questions about finances and ways she could help, and eased the women out the door having charmed them thoroughly. No, Leof corrected himself, watching as Sorn bid them farewell at the door, they're not charmed. That's respect in their faces, and not simply because she's the Lady. They are strong women and they recognise strength when they see it in others.

That was a striking thought, because strength was not a quality he had associated with Sorn. His own mother was strong, but in a very different way – decisive, outspoken, like many of the women in Cliff Domain, where the men were away fighting so often that the women had had to learn how to do without them. Sorn was another vintage entirely.

'That news is not good,' she said seriously, coming back to where he stood, resting her hands on the back of her tall chair. 'Fighting in broad sun. They are not restricted to the night, it seems.'

'But they faded at sunset,' he replied. 'Perhaps they may have a night or a day, but not both?'

'It has been months since Spritford. Perhaps there have been other quickenings that we have not heard of?'

Leof shrugged. They just didn't know enough. 'I'll send news of this to my lord,' he said. 'Do you have any message for him? I would be happy to include a letter in the package . . .'

Sorn considered, then shook her head. 'My lord is involved in men's business. The only news I have is about women's work, and would not interest him.' She said it simply, without resentment, but her reply sent a pang through Leof. It spoke of loneliness. She had no real friends among her ladies, he realised. Her maid, Faina, was devoted, but hardly a friend. There was no nearby officer's estate with its complement of wives and daughters who might provide companionship – only Fortune.

Difficult for her, he thought. Well, perhaps he could provide some friendly company while her lord was away. Impulsively, he reached out and touched the back of her hand.

'Anything about you must interest him,' he said. Too late, he heard the note of sincerity in his voice. In that moment Leof felt the softness of her skin. Warmth and silk moving swiftly under his fingers. He felt a flood tide of desire sweep through him, overwhelm him as surely as the Lake had done. He was just as helpless as he had been then, tossed on a wave too big for him.

Sorn flushed and pulled her hand away. She half-turned, as though to leave, then stopped herself.

Leof spoke quickly. He couldn't bear to see her force herself to look at him. 'I will send your regards in my letter, my lady.'

Then he turned and left the hall, breaking etiquette by not waiting for her dismissal; not daring to wait for it.

ASH

COMING TO THE Deep set Ash's hair prickling on the back of his neck.

From the bluff outside Gabriston, they could see the wilds that lay to the north of the Hidden River. On the other side of the water was a simple cliff, but on this side the soft sandstone had been eroded by countless streams into a nightmare maze of canyons and crevasses, impossible to map. In the middle of the maze was the Deep, a series of caves and canyons which led to the heart of the demons' mysteries. Each man who came to the deep found something different there, but each man also found the same thing: the truth about himself. Which was why Ash's heart was pounding.

They paused at the beginning, at the bottom of the bluff, where the canyons started and the sound of the river swelled into a chorus that filled his head. He must make Flax swear the oath. He remembered the words easily enough. He spat in his hand and offered it to Flax, who copied him and grasped firmly.

'This is the oath we ask of you: will you give it? To be silent to death of what you see, of what you hear, of what you do?'

Flax had picked up on his mood and was uncharacteristically solemn. 'I swear,' he said.

'Do you swear upon pain of shunning, never to speak of this place outside of this place?'

'I swear.'

'Do you swear upon pain of death never to guide another to this place who has not the blood right?'

Flax swallowed. 'I swear.'

'Do you swear upon pain beyond death, the pain of never being reborn, to keep the secrets of this place with your honour, with your strength, with your life?'

This time, Flax had to work his mouth for enough spit to form the words. 'I swear.'

There was sweat on Flax's forehead. Ash was glad to see it.

He let go of the boy's hand.

Ash led Flax down one narrow defile after another, the fern-covered walls of red sandstone rising higher as they went, until they moved in a green gloom. Water seeping through the stone made it glisten in the shadows, as though the hills were bleeding. Ash always felt that he should have smelt blood here, and death, instead of the clear scent of water, the must of leaf mould, and the occasional waft of early jasmine. His nose told him it was safe, but his ears strained past the endless trickle of water and the wind moaning through the rocks, waiting to hear the demons.

He checked on Flax regularly, knowing the lad was nervous and knowing he should be. The Deep was dangerous, and not just because of the demons. Vipers, spiders, scorpions lurked beneath every rock, every leaf. Poison tainted the beauty; he was reminded of Doronit.

The outsiders, Acton's people, thought the stones were a maze, difficult to find the way through because of their complexity. But that was just the wilds, the outside skin of the Deep, where the River allowed the fair-haired ones to penetrate. Further in, the truth was stranger. Ash had been here six years running with his father, the years between his voice breaking and his apprenticeship to Doronit, and it had never been the same twice. No one could penetrate the Deep unless the River willed it. Rock walls shifted; streams bubbled up where there had been solid rock the day before; bogs appeared that could suck a man down in three heartbeats, too quick even for a scream. Ash had seen that, once, when he was fourteen.

'Turn away,' his father had said. 'He came here with treachery; the River claimed him.'

Ash found a clearing, a place with good water and grass, where they could leave the horses. They watered and groomed them and hung nosebags from the cliff wall as temporary mangers. By that time it was dark.

'Do we light a fire?' Flax asked hopefully.

Ash shook his head. 'Follow me. Your eyes will adjust.'

This was his favourite time in the Deep, just after sunset when the enchantment started. At least it had seemed enchantment, the first time, and every time afterwards, too, even when he understood how it happened. As they walked further into the difficult passageways of stone, the walls began to acquire stars. Small, green, they glowed so faintly that it seemed like a trick of the eyes. Then, as the darkness gathered and his eyes adjusted, they became brighter, casual constellations scattered across the rock walls, clumped together in shining clusters, lighting their way.

Ash looked back at Flax, and was satisfied by the wonder on his face.

'What are they?' Flax asked.

Ash contemplated telling him the truth: little glowing insects. Glow worms. But he'd always hated that name. It diminished the beauty.

'The stars of the Deep,' he said. 'Come on.'

They turned a corner and found themselves in a larger defile, with a stream pelting down the middle, splashing and leaping, throwing small pebbles and grit into the air. The edges of the defile were covered with fallen rocks and the way out was blocked by them, except for the stream, which launched itself from a small gap between the rock walls into the darkness. If they tried to wade through the stream and edge through the gap, they would be thrown helpless as dolls against the sharp rocks, or over the edge, to where they could hear the water plummet down to smash on rocks far below.

'Careful,' Ash said. 'From here, the demons watch.'

He stood up straight and said clearly, 'I am Ash, son of Rowan. I am known to this place. My blood is known. I give it again, that this place may know me afresh.'

He took his belt knife and moved to the stream, then pricked his finger and let three drops of blood fall into the water. The stream quietened immediately. The water still flowed fast, but it no longer leapt and challenged.

Ash beckoned Flax towards him. As he approached, the stream again became wild, leaping high in menace. Ash took Flax's hand and held it over the stream.

'This is Flax, son of Gorham, come to meet his blood in the Deep.' He pricked Flax's finger and let the blood drop into the water. It calmed immediately.

'Come on,' Ash said. 'Now.'

Quickly he led Flax into the stream, stumbling a little on the rocky bottom, but striding as fast as he dared through the gap in the rocks. The stream pushed against his boots, but it didn't thrust him hard enough to make him fall; it didn't suddenly spring up when they were halfway through. He had seen that happen, too, to a scrawny friend of his father's, a storyteller. The man's body was never found.

'The River protects itself, and us,' his father had said, as though trying to convince himself. But no one had said what the River was protecting itself from that day.

They had to turn at the very edge of the waterfall and sidle along a ledge. The ledge was narrow and there were rocks underfoot. It led along a sheer cliff wall to another gap in the rocks, and another canyon beyond. They stepped carefully through the gap and made their way down the canyon, and from there onto another high ledge. Ash could hear Flax breathing hard. He remembered the first time he had done this, or something like it, because it was never the same twice. The physical danger hadn't been as bad as the threat of the unknown, the demons waiting out in the darkness.

As though the thought had called them – and maybe it had – they heard the demons howling. The sound wasn't exactly like the howling of wolves, but it wasn't human. Flax stumbled as the first long wail reached them and Ash put out a hand to push him safely against the cliff face. They stopped for a moment, listening to the grief and hunger in the demon howl. Both of them were shivering.

Beyond this canyon was another one, and then another one after that. They twisted and turned and Ash knew it was useless to try to remember them, but he tried anyway. His safeguarder training was no use here, but he had been trained so long that he couldn't just abandon it.

Finally, they came into a large space ringed with cliff walls that were broken by caves and cracks. Inside one of the caves, a fire blazed just out of sight. Shadows flickered on the cave walls and out onto the beaten earth floor of the clearing. The sudden gold and orange of its light was almost too much for their dark-adjusted eyes.

Flax gasped. From behind rocks, from fissures and caves, figures emerged from the darkness. Naked, male, thin and solid, and tall and short, all with dark hair across their arms and bodies. The bodies seemed to be striped with blood. But it was their faces which had scared him, Ash knew. He remembered the first time he had been confronted by those snarling snouts, the sharp teeth, the animal eyes. Each man had the head of an animal: badger or otter or fox or deer, varied but all wild animals. There were no cows or pigs or sheep. A wildcat, but no cats; a wolf, but no dogs.

He knew what Flax was thinking: masks, surely they were masks? But they were not. Of course not. What would be the point of pretending? Dressing up in silly clothes, painting their bodies – that would not be work for men.

The demons closed towards them, slowly, and in their hands were stones; flint, sharp as knives. Flax's breathing was faster and shallower. He was getting ready to run. Ash put a hand on his arm, to calm him.

'We are members of the blood,' he called to the demons. 'I am Ash, son of Rowan, whose blood has calmed the waters.' He nudged Flax. Flax had to clear his throat before he could talk.

'I am Flax, son of Gorham . . . whose blood has calmed the waters.'

The hands holding the stones lowered to the men's sides. One of them, a badger, came forward to place his hands on Ash's shoulders. Ash looked deep into the dark eyes which glinted orange in the firelight and breathed in the sharp badger scent. He felt a swirl of emotions: anger, happiness, resentment, love.

'Fire and water, Father,' he said.

BRAMBLE

THERE WAS A marching song playing at a dirge pace in her head – in Baluch's head. Bramble felt relief at being back with Baluch, despite the severe cold. Vision came back with a rush of white, dazzling. Snow, everywhere. Rough ground underfoot, invisible under the snow. Cliffs on one side, a high, rocky white slope on the other. Oh gods, Bramble thought. We're in Death Pass again! On the slope lay tons of snow which would crash down to bury them all at the slightest sound. Even though Bramble knew that the raiders – the invaders – had made it through unscathed, the sight of that burden of snow made her nervous, threatening with the same kind of impartial animosity as the Ice King. The silence was intense; the men pushed through the snow so slowly that even Baluch's sharp ears could only just catch a faint susurration at each step.

Acton was in front of Baluch, his gold head shrouded in hat and scarf, his shield slung over his shoulder, but his back unmistakable as he waded slowly through the breast-high snow. For a moment, hysteria flickered in Bramble. How had she become so shagging familiar with Acton's back? But she was, or Baluch was, or both. Baluch could see the profile of the man next to Acton – it was Asgarn, which vaguely surprised Bramble. Asgarn hadn't seemed the type to volunteer for something as chancy as this. Perhaps, she thought, the lord of war picked his men. Part of Bramble found that amusing; that Asgarn might have been caught in his own snare, and then she wondered why she assumed Asgarn had been laying traps, why she just plain didn't like him.

Acton and Asgarn led, just as in all the ballads, the two thickset men ploughing gradually, silently, towards the gap between cliff and slope, towards the triangle of ridiculously blue sky. Bramble had always imagined this day as being cloudy and grey, but it was a beautiful day, crisp and sunny.

The man next to Baluch stumbled and flung out a hand. Baluch grabbed it and hauled him back up. The man's gasp sounded overly loud and the entire band paused, terrified, in mid-step. A thin trickle of snow slid off a rock on the lower slope. They froze in place, waiting. Baluch was praying, Bramble realised, opening himself to the gods, but the gods refused to come. There was only a long moment of fear before the trickle of snow stopped.

They began moving again, slower than before despite the cold. Baluch's hands and feet were numb but his cheeks burnt and his mouth ached every time he drew a breath. For a while it seemed that the end of the pass was as far away as ever, that they would trudge through burning cold forever. But gradually, inevitably, the triangle of blue grew larger. Then the snow was not breast-high, but waist-high. Then thigh-high. Knee-high. Then the triangle of blue stretched to cover the whole sky, and they were out of the pass, standing on a lip of ground looking down into the valley, slapping each other on the back in congratulation, but silent still.

Silent, because below them in the morning light lay Hawk's steading. Smoke rose from its chimneys, but no one was about yet. There were no guards. The steading was undefended in early spring, because Death Pass was its defence. Silently, Acton drew his sword and settled his shield onto his left arm. The others did the same. Acton nodded to them, all fifty of them, and slapped Baluch on the arm. For a moment his face was serious, then he grinned at them, the joy of battle alight on his face. Baluch smiled involuntarily and hefted his sword. Bramble could feel the tension in him but also the excitement and, with it this time, a sense of grim purpose. Acton saw it in his face and nodded, a darker expression in his eyes.

'Let us take our revenge,' he said so quietly that the others had to strain to hear. 'Make them regret their treachery.'

'Yes,' Asgarn said. 'Kill them all.'

Baluch raised his sword high in acknowledgment, and the others copied him. The sun shimmered off their blades and blinded Baluch; and for a moment it became morning sunlight on water and the water rose to blind Bramble in its turn.

~~~~~

Blood in her mouth. Blood trickling down from her lip onto her chin. Her back was against a wall, and her legs were unsteady. The woman – yes, this was definitely a woman, a young woman clutching a blanket to her naked chest – lifted a hand to wipe away the blood. The movement brought back sight, and Bramble wished it hadn't. They were inside, in a small wooden room with a shuttered window and a bed. It smelled of woodsmoke and sex and fear.

The girl who had giggled, Edwa, lay on the bed, trying to pull her shift down around her buttocks. She was bleeding, too, the blood oozing down her inner thighs. There were bruises on her legs and arms. Her long hair was loose and snarled.

'Please . . .' Edwa said, raising her face in supplication to the man who stood in front of her, his left arm raised high as though about to strike her. Hawk. Edwa's face was dark with bruises all down one side. Hawk lowered his arm and began to undo his trouser drawstring.

'Come to your senses, have you?' he snarled.

Bramble could feel the woman whose eyes she saw through move her lips, her tongue, wanting to say something, to protest. But she had clearly learnt that protesting brought nothing but blows. She dug her fingers into her own palms in an effort to keep quiet.

Bramble desperately wanted to be somewhere else, to *not see*. She was shocked to the core. Hawk was black-haired. Black-eyed. Like her. She had *known* that he and his men were using the girls, but to *see* it. To see a Traveller, as he looked to her, abuse a gold-haired girl . . . It went against all her prejudices, all that she wanted to be true.

Come on, Acton, she thought, where are you? Get in here and save them. Then she realised that she was urging on the invasion. She didn't know which made her sicker, the impending rape or her own thoughts.

The noise started outside: yells, the crash of swords and shields, screams. Hawk spun around at the sounds, his back to both women. He fumbled to pull up his trousers.

The woman dropped the blanket to the floor and jumped on his back as he bent over. She grabbed his belt knife at the same time. He straightened explosively, trying to throw her off. She locked her arms around his neck and strained to pull his head back, but he was too strong.

'Edwa!' she yelled, 'take the knife.'

Hawk was trying to drag the woman off his back, but she was holding on with all her strength. Edwa put out both hands for the knife. The man whirled and the knife slashed across the back of her hand, drawing blood. She ignored the wound and his clubbing hands and grabbed the knife, holding it confidently, as though she had been longing for this moment. With both hands now free, the woman dragged back his head. As soon as his throat was bared, Edwa raised the knife and plunged it deeply into his neck. Blood spurted out, *poured* out all over her. Hawk fell to the floor with a wet gasp, dead already. Bramble was ashamed of how satisfied she felt as he collapsed.

The other woman ran to the door and shut it, then began looking around for something to barricade it with. Her red-gold braid lay over her wrist, matted and untidy. Bramble was abruptly aware of her smell. It had been a long time since anyone had let these girls wash.

'Help me move the bed against the door, Edwa,' the woman ordered, but Edwa just stood, looking at the knife and the body.

The woman took her by the shoulder and shook her. 'Don't you understand? They've come for us! I knew Acton wouldn't leave us here! All we have to do is keep Hawk's men out until after it's over and we'll be safe.'

Edwa focused on her face, her blue eyes becoming less clouded. 'They're here?' she whispered. The woman nodded. She began to dress herself hurriedly, dragging on shift and dress and snatching up a man's leather belt to girdle herself. She shook Edwa again, and this time Edwa moved, but not to help. She went down on one knee and got Hawk's other knife out of his boot. It was much longer, a dagger for fighting rather than the eating knife they had used to kill him.

The woman nodded. 'Good. We might need that.' She went to the other side of the bed and began to push it towards the door. 'Come and *help*, Edwa! We can't let Hawk's men use us as hostages!'

Edwa was staring at the two knives, one in each hand. She put the smaller one against her wrist and drew it down slowly. Blood welled.

Bramble expected the woman by the bed to jump up and grab the knife, but she stayed very still. 'Edwa?' she said gently.

'They mustn't see, Wili. They mustn't see me,' Edwa whispered, finding a new place to cut and pushing the knife in.

Wili straightened up from the bed and turned to look fully at Edwa. The blonde girl was painted in blood. Her hair was as dark as a

Traveller's now, and her face was smeared and purple with bruises. Bramble could feel Wili's heart beating in deep, heavy thumps. Her sight blurred as the girl's eyes filled with tears.

'That won't kill you, Edwa,' she said with a break in her voice. 'It'll just make you more bloody.'

Edwa looked up at Wili. Her eyes were dry and bleak. She nodded slowly, as though Wili had told her something hard to understand, but important. She dropped the belt knife and, bringing her other hand up in the same movement, thrust the long dagger in under her breastbone. Then she crumpled to the floor.

Wili sat down on the bed, as though it didn't matter anymore if Hawk's men found her. She stared at her hands. The nails were bitten down to the quick. Bramble could feel the knot of grief between her breastbone and her throat, and feel something else as well, a kind of heaviness that made movement impossible, even the movement that would be needed to cry.

The door slammed back and Acton sprang into the room, his sword and shield ready, blood and sweat running down his cheeks. He saw Wili first, and shuddered to a halt, visibly changing from berserker to concerned friend.

'Wili! Are you all right?' He closed the door behind him.

Wili's eyes overflowed and she started to cry. Not the choking sobs of grief, Bramble thought. That would come later. These were the tears of relief. She brushed them away almost angrily and stood up.

'*I'll* survive,' she said, and looked at Edwa.

Acton knelt beside Edwa's body. He put down his shield but not his sword and reached his shield hand to touch the knife hilt that stood out from her shift. It had an antler handle, Bramble saw, left rough for a better grip. Edwa's hold had loosened and her hands had fallen away to lie empty and soft on the wooden floor. Acton closed the dull blue eyes and looked up at Wili.

'She didn't want you to see her – anyone to see her, after what had happened.' Wili's voice was astonishingly calm, the tears gone.

'You didn't stop her.' His tone wasn't accusing, not even wondering. He just said it.

'Her choice,' Wili said. 'I understood why.'

Acton nodded slowly and stood up. He picked up his shield and gripped his sword more firmly. Bramble saw the fury build in him again and, like Wili, she understood it.

'Close the door behind me,' he said. 'I'll be back for you.'

Wili nodded. He faced the doorway and then hesitated, turned back, as if he were impelled to ask.

'Friede?'

Wili shook her head. 'She died in the attack. Took three of them with her, too, because they weren't expecting a cripple to fight.' Her voice was bitter. 'I should have fought harder. Maybe they would have killed me as well.'

Acton raised his hand in denial, the sword pointing up. His eyes were dark with fury and determination. 'You are the treasure we have saved from this wreck,' he said. Bramble felt the warmth spread out from Wili's gut at his words, as though she had been waiting for a judgment, a death sentence, and had instead received a reprieve.

Acton went out the door in a rush, back into the shouting and screaming and hard, thudding noise. 'Kill them all!' he shouted as he went, sword ready.

Wili began to cry again, sinking down to the floor and letting her head droop. The tears washed Bramble away gently, like a soft slide into sleep.

All she could feel was her heart, beating too fast, as though it was going to spasm. She couldn't catch her breath. It took all her strength, but she pulled back from the mind she was in, from the body's distress. She could see little except some cracks of light. A small room. Maybe a storeroom. Her hands were bound with cloth. The air was cold; her breath was the warmest thing here. *His* breath; it was a man, again, but she couldn't tell whom. His mind had a faintly familiar taste to it, but he was so frightened that all personality had been stamped out.

A door in the wall opposite crashed back and a red-headed man appeared. He was followed by a stocky blond with big shoulders. Together, they hoisted the man under the armpits and dragged him out the door, then threw him down onto the cold ground of a yard behind a big building. Hawk's house? Bramble wondered.

Acton and Baluch were standing there, their clothes smirched with blood, their eyes red with exhaustion. Acton was cleaning his sword with a snatch of cloth, paying great attention to the detail around the hilt. Baluch looked at him in concern, and then cast a quick glance at a corner of the yard. The man she inhabited looked too, and shuddered.

A woman's body lay sprawled against the wall of an animal shed. Bramble could hear pigs inside squealing for food, that terrible squeal that sounded like they were having their throats cut.

Acton was very definitely not looking at the body of the woman. The red-head and the blond came back to the yard and dragged the corpse away, and only then did Acton look up, in time to see Asgarn pass the two and come on without a glance. Acton sheathed his sword as though he were glad to put it away.

Asgarn was in high spirits. He was just as bloody as the others, and just as tired, but he was smiling in satisfaction.

'That's a good day's work,' he said. He clapped a hand on Baluch's shoulder. 'Maybe you'll make a song of it, eh? The Saga of Hawk's Hall.'

Baluch shook his head. 'The Saga of Death Pass, maybe.' Bramble wanted to smile. He'd clearly been thinking about it already, probably while they were making the trek through the pass.

'There's no one left?' Acton said.

'Except this one.' Asgarn casually kicked the man on the ground. 'When you say, "Kill them all" that's what we do.' Acton winced. 'You did *want* them all dead, didn't you?'

'The men,' Acton said. 'I wanted the warriors killed.'

'Ah . . .' Asgarn shrugged. 'Well, next time you'd better tell us that first, lord of war.' He turned away and kicked the man again, hard, on the shoulder. 'So, what do we do with him, then? You want me to finish him off?'

'No!' Acton said. He looked at the man more closely, and was surprised. 'You're one of ours, aren't you? One of Swef's thralls? Uen, isn't that your name?'

Baluch looked at Uen in surprise. Uen was looking up in hope. Bramble could feel the welling up of pleading; he was trying not to beg. She recognised his mind now. The thrall who had been ploughing the day Hawk came to visit Swef's steading.

'One of *ours*?' Baluch said. His voice was dark. Shaking. With compassion, or something else?

Acton reached down to help Uen up, but Baluch put out a hand and stopped him.

'If he's one of ours,' he said, his voice flat, his hand on his sword hilt, 'why was he the one who killed Friede?'

Acton froze and pulled his hand back. Put it on his sword hilt.

Uen's heart had started to thump and leap wildly with panic, and memories flooded his mind. Bramble caught at them with determination. She had liked Friede. She wanted to know the truth.

Uen's memory was one of noise and shouting and rushing; rushing through Swef's big, new-smelling hall, its walls barely smoothed. The rushes on the floor made him stumble, he was running so fast and, unlike the men around him, who were just hacking at anyone they met, he was searching for someone. Friede. He was frantic, looking for her, running and dodging because he had no time to fight, he had to find her first, before any of Hawk's men. But he was too late.

She was in the kitchen. She had wedged herself in a corner and was using a stool as a shield and her crutch as a weapon. So many years of hobbling had made her arms strong. There was a man on the ground in front of her, his skull stove in. She was keeping the other two off, but only barely. One man's sword cut into the stool and as he wrenched it back the stool came with it, dragged out of her hand.

'Stop!' Uen said, and leapt towards them, pulling on the men's shoulders with wild hands. 'Stop! This one is mine.'

They turned in exasperation. 'What?'

'My lord Hawk gave her to me. She's mine!'

They sneered at him, dark eyes scornful. 'Oh, it's the traitor. Hah! Take her, then, oath-breaker.' Their backs were towards Friede and she took the opportunity to hit twice more, hard, with full control. They dropped like felled bullocks and Friede and Uen were left staring at each other.

'Traitor?' she said with venom.

'They were going to attack anyway,' Uen said, desperate. 'This way I got to save you.'

She raised her crutch and hit at him, but he pushed it sideways.

'Oath-breaker!' she shouted.

'I never took an oath! I'm a thrall, remember!'

She paused, considering, her green eyes cold. 'That's true. Good. You'll go to the cold hells, then, not to Swith's Hall.' She raised her crutch again deliberately.

'I love you,' he said.

'I spit on you,' she said, and brought the crutch down.

A scream rose in Uen's throat and he brought his sword around in a great flat circle. He had no skill, but he was very strong from years of physical work. The stroke almost cut her in half. Then he fell on his knees and gathered her into his arms and wept.

L

Now, in the courtyard, he wept again, the tears a mingling of grief and fear. He held out supplicating hands to Acton. His bladder loosened and urine gushed down his legs, but he barely felt it.

Acton drew his sword in one movement and swung it, much as Uen had swung. As the sword bit into Uen's neck the water rose, but it was blood this time and it was warm, sickeningly warm, so that Bramble wanted to vomit at the touch and at the memory of the cold fury on Acton's face and the thwarted desire on Baluch's. He had wanted to kill Uen himself, but he had waited too long to act. As the blood swamped her she heard Asgarn laughing.

'That's it! Kill 'em all,' he said.

UEN'S STORY

I'D DO IT again. Even having to kill her, I'd do it again.

It was sweet to see them go down under the dark-hairs' swords. They weren't expecting anything, and they died like flies. Hah!

By all the gods that are, I am not an oath-breaker. What were Swef's people to me? Gaolers. I am, I *was*, a thrall. If the only freedom I could have was death, then I took it with both hands.

Better than thralling. Better than carrying muck and being used as an *ox*, as though I was no better. Better than being yelled at and struck at when I was too slow and never thanked, no matter how hard I tried.

Except by Friede. Oh, and that friend of hers, Wili. But it was Friede who set the example. She was so kind, always.

I didn't expect her to hate me.

But I'd still do it again.

Because Swef was very loud, talking about the new land, the fresh land, the big land that had room for all. But it was too late for my people, wasn't it? Too late for the ones the Ice King had already conquered, who had to go cap in hand to the southerners to beg for living room. My father went. We were a small valley. There weren't enough of us to fight for new land. We kept to ourselves, we did, and that had worked well enough in the bountiful days, but when the King clawed our land away from us we had no allies to turn to.

So my father, who was chieftain, and his brother, who would have been lord of war if we'd fought, went to the Moot and asked for land. But none would give it. And then they asked for honourable service, as oath men to a chieftain. But none would give it. So rather than have their families starve, they agreed to thraldom, until they had worked back their price, which was the price of feeding them and housing them and clothing them, and so would *never* be worked back, not in a thousand generations, but they didn't realise it then because they were not *clever*, like Swef. Not *cunning*, like Swef. Not *evil*.

I was fifteen. I had been the chieftain's son and they made me do women's work. I would have accepted a man's job. I could have been a shepherd, or worked at a trade like smithing. Even being a tanner would have been honourable. But no, I had to feed the pigs their swill and carry chamber pots and scour cooking pans. It was shameful, and I hated them all. Except Friede, because she was kind to me and because her red hair reminded me of home.

My father and my uncle could not stand the shame. They raised their voices and then their hands to their captors and they were punished: the first time a beating, the second time the left hand cut off, the third time death from spearing. 'I will keep no insolent servants,' Swef said in his pride. My mother killed herself that night and took my two baby sisters with her. Because she was a thrall they would not give them a proper funeral pyre. The wood was too precious, Swef said. They *buried* them, like the carcass of an animal gone off in the summer heat.

That was the moment I decided to kill Swef, if I could, when I could; as the clods of dirt covered my sisters' shroud and took my mother from my sight.

I said nothing. I did nothing. I worked hard and made him trust me. When the time came to select the staff for the new steading, there was no question but that I would go, too. He thought I was loyal, but I took no oath except the oath to make his death. That oath I kept.

When Hawk sought me out and asked me to lift the bars on the hall door, I was glad. But I made sure Friede would be safe. She would have been safe, too, if only she'd *listened* to me . . .

I only have one regret. I wish that I had let her kill me, because then I would have had a warrior's death. At a woman's hands, I know, but Friede had a heart as strong as any warrior's, and I am sure the men she killed are feasting with Swith in his Hall.

But mostly I wish that the Ice King had been satisfied before he ever ate my home; before our beautiful valley was crushed and ground in his grasp. While I waited for them to drag me out to Acton, I set myself to remember all of it I could, because I am the only one who remembers. All the others are dead, and when I cease to remember, that valley, green and shining and lovely, will vanish altogether. Hawk's people say there is no such thing as Swith's Hall; that we will go on to rebirth if we have lived well. But I would rather not be reborn. I would rather go on remembering; go on keeping my valley alive, until the Ice Giants eat the sun.

LEOF

LEOF WALKED OUT of the hall feeling like he was going into battle. The feeling was the same: the absolute necessity of not showing others how he felt, in order to save lives. In battle, it was the lives of others he held in his hands; the men under his command, who needed him to be calm and disciplined and rational, or they would die. Now, if he showed how he felt, *he* would die. Any officer who desired a warlord's wife knew the penalty was death.

He had to fill his head with warnings because he could still feel Sorn's pulse leap under his fingers and see the flush sweep up her cheeks as he touched her hand. As he had, all unwittingly, looked into her eyes and wanted her.

He had let it happen because he had thought he was in love with Bramble. Without the memories of her – on the roan, at the inn, in bed, absurdly, terrifyingly, high in that pine tree – occupying his mind and making him guilty, he would have considered whether it was wise to spend so much time with his warlord's young wife. He would have noticed her with his mind, instead of with his heart. Would have appreciated the gentle grace of her walk, the firm curve of her smile. And, appreciating, kept his distance, aware of the danger. Gods knew he would have relished the sight of her in any other circumstances; would have smiled and cozened her into bed in a heartbeat if she'd been just another girl.

As it was, he had been blind, and walked into a snare of his own devising. Worse than blind, because he had snared not only himself but her in the net. At least, he thought he had.

She had been brought up as the lady of the fort, which meant that she was trained to hide her feelings; trained to be calm, serene, unflappable.

The flush on her cheeks when he had unthinkingly touched her hand could have meant any number of things. Anger at his impudence. Surprise. Warmth at simple human contact. Swith knew she got little of that, especially with her lord away. His touch could have meant nothing to her, or been a petty annoyance. She might not even have realised how he felt. It was over in a moment, after all; how much could she have read in his eyes?

The thought should have been a relief, but instead it wracked him with doubt and the desire to know. To be sure.

He went about the rest of the day doing all his duty plus some extra, like inspecting the smithies, and made sure his work was exemplary. He might betray his lord in his thoughts, but he would never betray him in reality. It was a fine, noble thought, but every time he assured himself, he remembered disobeying Thegan's orders to capture Bramble. He had betrayed his lord for a woman once before . . .

He debated whether to have his supper in his room or in the hall with Sorn. If she had not guessed, if she thought his touch a momentary inattention to etiquette, he could still present an unruffled front and they could continue as they had been, with their dignity unimpaired and loyalty intact.

He walked into the hall and up to the high table and saw immediately, from the paleness of her cheeks and the determined way she tilted her head up to face him, that she had wrestled all day with the same snares as he had, and come to the same conclusion. Underneath the tension and the concern, he realised that he felt a kind of triumph – not as pure as joy, not as simple as happiness. They couldn't possibly have joy or happiness, but still, she felt it too, and something in him exulted.

So he sat down beside her, as always, and greeted her formally, as always, and as always she asked him how the preparations for war were progressing. He told her about the smithies and their output of helmets and swords; she enquired if the fletchers needed more feathers; they discussed killing several of the swans for the feast on Thegan's return and harvesting the feathers.

'I have heard that fletchers like swan feathers,' Sorn said, clearly inviting comment not just from him but from the other officers, making the conversation general. She steered the talk between Leof, Gard and Wil onto a discussion of arms and armament and then fell silent, as was fitting for a woman during such talk. Leof carefully did not look at her except when he offered her bread, or salt to season the kid with olives. Carefully, she smiled her thanks and gazed on him and the others impartially. It was a pretence so well devised that he realised she must have been aware for much longer than he had; he wondered how many meals he had shared with her, not knowing that she played this difficult role. How many times had he made it harder for her, unthinkingly blind?

Well, now they would pretend together, and together construct a bulwark against betrayal.

'My lady, would you have more kid?'

'Thank you, my lord, but no. I am satisfied.'

A small ironic curve showed in the corner of her mouth and then disappeared so quickly that he wondered if he had truly seen it. Satisfied was the one thing she must not be, and she knew it. He must resist the temptation to increase their intimacy, even by talking together in public.

'The sweetmeats, perhaps, my lady?'

'Just one, I thank you.'

So, he thought, no great play of denial. She was alert, too, to the desire for secret signals and to the danger they represented. There must be *no* layers to their talk; no secrets shared; no hidden understanding. What is hidden may be uncovered. What is fed, grows. Sorn was far more in control of this situation than he was. Far more practised. She had sat through many such meals, he thought, and not just since I arrived. Meals where what she felt and what she showed were completely at odds.

Leof wondered about her childhood. He had heard that her father had been a hard man and for the first time felt that sudden empathy, the quick wrench of the heart which can herald love, not just desire. *No!* he thought, appalled. Not that. But helplessly, although his face showed nothing, as it showed nothing when he led his men into battle, he conned the way the fire slid shadows across her face, the way her eyelids curved when she smiled, the sudden flash of green when her gaze sharpened on a serving maid who flirted too openly with one of the sergeants in the lower hall. He moved away a little so that he could not smell her scent, rising softly from her warmed skin.

'We will need more heavy drays,' he said instead to Wil. 'But we cannot leave the farmers without a way to harvest, or there will be dearth and death before spring.'

They launched into a discussion of the best way of balancing the needs of the warlord and the needs of the land, and Leof was successful, for a time, at ignoring her. Until she rose to bow goodnight, and the men rose with her and bowed back, and their eyes met – as she met all their eyes, for that was the etiquette, and there must be *nothing*, not even a lack of courtesy, to show that they treated each other differently. But at that moment he saw, behind the calm, behind the courtesy, behind even the hidden desire, fear.

He worried over that glimpse all night. What was she afraid of? Betrayal? Love? Or the thing he did not want to acknowledge . . . was she afraid of Thegan?

Inwardly, he knew she was right to be afraid. Thegan would be unforgiving. No warlord would countenance any hint of infidelity in his wife, the producer of his heirs, even if the woman was innocent. There must be no whisper to taint the rightful inheritance of the Domain. It was only twenty years since the warlord in the Far South Domain, old Elbert, had had his wife garrotted because she danced with another man at the Springtree celebrations. He'd had no trouble getting a second, younger wife, because all the observers had agreed she'd brought it on herself. Though there'd been no children from the second marriage, so maybe the gods thought otherwise.

It came down to inheritance. If Leof cuckolded Thegan – the thought popped into his head unbidden, full of danger and excitement – Leof's sons could inherit the Domain. Which made him wonder why Sorn had not borne children. Thegan had a son – only one, true – and he was an attractive man who had not been celibate since his wife died. Before his marriage to Sorn, he'd had a dozen women that Leof knew of for certain, and no doubt many more. But there were no bastards, none in Cliff Domain, at least, and none that he knew of here. Warlords commonly flaunted their bastards. Not Thegan.

His thoughts turned to Gabra, the son in Cliff Domain who had never had much of his father's love, that Leof had seen. He wondered whose son Gabra might be, and whether Thegan had accepted him unknowingly, cuckolded, or had arranged for his birth. Pimped his wife? No, no, that was not possible. Bramble's warning echoed in his head: Don't trust him. Feverishly, Leof plunged back into memories of Bramble, using her as a preventative against treason. But his memories of her had been leached clean of desire, and they were no use as a defence against desire for Sorn.

Perversely, his lack of desire for Bramble made him readier to
believe her warnings. Or was it just easier to think that betrayal was
excusable if committed against someone unworthy of his loyalty? He
punched his pillow and forced himself to go over the inventory of
spears and slingshots in the armoury until his thoughts grew quiet and
he slept a long time later, then rose in the early light, determined to
continue pretending until the pretence was made real.

That morning he supervised the construction of a drying house, on the
edge of the fort plateau, just inside the walls. By autumn they would
have half a herd slaughtered and the meat drying for winter stews and
campaign food. He skipped lunch to oversee the laying of the founda-
tion stones for the new gate in the southern wall. That had to be done
right. Any gate was a potential breach in a time of siege and if the
foundations weren't strong the fort would be lost.

He approved of all the fortifications Thegan was introducing at
Sendat. In Cliff Domain, not only was the warlord's dwelling fortified,
but most of the towns. There had been years past, when the Ice King's
people had raided, that those towns had been glad indeed that some
warlord, sometime, had put time and silver into building proper
defences. So it might be at Sendat. Soon.

BRAMBLE

HEARING CAME BACK first, but it was dulled. Bramble strained to make out the sound of voices. Then sight returned, but the light was dim. She could see candle flames flickering, or was it oil lamps? There were a dozen of them in a small room, but still her eyes saw vaguely. Everything seemed fogged. But she was seeing through a man's eyes, that was certain.

The man blinked several times and made an effort to see and suddenly everything came clear, although she could feel the strength he was using to pay attention. Only the body lay open to her: she could barely feel this mind. It was opaque, shut off. Not from her, she didn't think. This was a mind which habitually guarded its thoughts. She tried to get a sense of what he was thinking, or feeling, and was disoriented. He thought in intricate layers, convoluted and intertwined, like the threads in a complex weaving. Thoughts linked to other thoughts in endless speculation. She could make no sense of it, catch not even one clear emotion. This mind was alien to her in a way none of the others had been, not even the goat girl on the mountain. This mind was old, and it schemed.

'Oddi,' a voice said respectfully. His gaze sharpened on the speaker – Asgarn, his wiry hair catching the light from the candles and seeming fairer than ever. 'Are you ready, Oddi?'

Oddi, Bramble thought. That was the name of the old man at the Moot, the one who held the Mootstaff, the one who had made Acton into the lord of war. He had been much stronger then. Age had caught up with him.

Oddi nodded, and Bramble could hear the bones of his neck creaking. Very old. But he still held the power in the room.

She wondered about him. He had let Acton make his speech at the Moot. He had made Acton lord of war. But now, as Acton stepped forward to bend one knee in front of him, she sensed no affection in him; no softness. Whatever he had done for Acton, he had done for reasons of policy.

'Acton,' Oddi said, his voice clear but not loud. 'You have served this council well as our lord of war. You have avenged the deaths of our people and secured this territory for our people.'

Agreement rose in chorus. 'Well done,' 'Aye, that's so,' 'A great lord of war!' Bramble realised that the shadows held a big group of men. Chieftains? she wondered. The same men who were meeting in Asgarn's hall when Baluch saw Hawk's attack?

'We are in your debt,' Oddi went on. 'To pay this debt, we are minded to grant you this steading for your own, to hold as chieftain in your own right.'

Astonishingly, Acton was shaking his head. He sprang to his feet and moved back a space so he could look down at Oddi. 'I thank the council, but this is not my desire.'

A murmur of surprise went around the room.

Oddi frowned, but didn't seem entirely surprised. 'You reject this gift?'

'I mean no disrespect, but the steading cannot be mine. There is someone who has a better right.'

Oddi spread his hands. 'Swef is dead, and you were his heir. Surely his steading falls to you, by both right of inheritance and right of conquest?'

Acton shook his head. 'There is still one alive who should have precedence. Wili.'

A buzz rose from the men, half-angry, half-astonished. 'A *woman*?'

'Swef's niece. If he had not adopted me, she would have inherited his steading. Has she not the right to keep it? And if we speak of the rights of conquest, the lord of this steading died by her hand, not mine. Has she not earned it?'

There was silence, as Oddi calculated. He exchanged glances with Asgarn, who looked thoughtful. They nodded at each other, pleased in some obscure way Bramble couldn't fathom.

'Is there dissent?' Oddi asked. Although the men shifted uncomfortably, no one spoke.

'Very well,' he concluded. 'If Wili was Swef's heir, he would have found her a husband to run the steading for her. This council will do as much. We will consider who best might be chosen.' Again he exchanged glances with Asgarn. Hah! Bramble thought. They'd better ask Wili first. She's been through too much to put up with being parcelled off like a prize heifer.

As though catching the thought, Acton spoke. 'I think, honoured counsellors, that you had best consult Wili about that. She is no untried girl, to do as she is told just because a man tells her to.'

A stir went through the room as the men realised what he meant. What Wili had suffered.

'True,' Asgarn said. 'She has earned the right to choose her husband.'

You're sure she'll pick you, aren't you, you arrogant bastard? Bramble thought. But only if she doesn't have Acton around to compare you to.

Oddi looked at the two of them, now standing side-by-side, both tall, both blond, both strong. He pursed his lips, as though wondering which of them Wili might choose.

'There is still the matter of our debt to you,' he said to Acton. 'Is there something you desire?'

Acton nodded, for once intense and serious. 'There is.'

'Tell us.'

'The river outside this steading leads to the sea. To the only port in this land. T'vit, they call it. Along the coast there are only cliffs. T'vit is the one harbour.'

'And so?'

'In the bright days, before the Ice King came, we were a prosperous people. Our prosperity came from the sea. From trading.' There were noises of agreement from the men listening. 'If we are to be prosperous again, we need a port. If you wish to reward me, give me T'vit.'

Oddi sat back in his chair, astonished – and surprised at being astonished. That emotion Bramble could read clearly. Oddi was rarely surprised; he was used to being several steps ahead of anyone else. 'T'vit . . .' he said softly.

'Two boats of men,' Acton said eagerly. 'Give me boat builders and two crews and next summer I will take them down the river and secure us the port. Then our boats can take the dragon's road as they used to. To the Wind Cities and further.'

The audience of chieftains liked that idea. 'Bold thinking!' one said approvingly. 'Trust Acton to see the way clear!'

Oddi looked at Asgarn. Asgarn was smiling, and so was Oddi. What were they scheming? Try as Bramble might, she could not read Oddi's thoughts. Acton, the big idiot, didn't even notice. She could have hit him.

'It is a good request, and a fitting reward. But if you are to take this port for our people, Acton, you must take it as our lord of war.'

Acton nodded, although Asgarn shot Oddi a look of astonishment and chagrin. Oddi smiled sourly at him. So, Bramble thought, Asgarn isn't entirely in his confidence.

'Thus you will act with our authority, and what you annex will be ours to administer,' Oddi added.

Light dawned on Asgarn's face, and he began to smile. He turned it into a smile of congratulations for Acton, but Bramble was not fooled. Nor was Acton.

'But I will be given T'vit, if I take it? That will be my reward?' he insisted.

Oddi looked around the room, checking with the other chieftains. The dark figures nodded, one by one. 'T'vit itself will be yours. This is our oath.'

Acton smiled widely. 'I will take it for you. That is mine.'

This time the sea came to reclaim Bramble; she even smelt its saltiness and heard the slap of waves on a beach, before the waves rolled her away into deeper water.

Her hands were busy, cutting up onions. She could smell the sharp tang and her eyes were stinging. The hands belonged to a woman, and they were familiar. Wili. Bramble relaxed a little. Wili's was a good mind to be in.

'They want to marry me off to Asgarn,' Wili said, and glanced over her shoulder to where Acton was perched on a stool, honing his dagger on a small whetstone.

'Oddi?' he asked. Wili nodded. 'What have you said to him?'

'That I am not ready for marriage.'

He grinned, his blue eyes shining. 'How did he take that?'

'He grumbled. But he can't actually *force* me.' She paused, looking at the knife. 'Can he?' Bramble could feel the fear rise up in her, scalding.

Acton shook his head. 'Not while I'm around,' he said comfortably.

She relaxed immediately, as though his word was solid rock to lean on. 'How are the boats coming along?' she asked.

Acton's face lit up. 'They'll be finished by spring, I think. We're having some trouble getting pitch, but Baluch has heard there's a natural source by a lake somewhere to the east. He's leaving tomorrow to see if we can trade for it with the lake people. Once we have that, we will be ready.'

'More people will die,' she said, not looking at him as she said it, then glancing over.

'Those who die in battle go to feast with Swith the Strong,' he said. 'I feel no sorrow for them. We all die. To give a good death to another warrior is a boon.'

He looked up and met her eyes and Bramble could see that he meant it.

'What about the ones who aren't warriors? What about the women? The children?'

'I will try, Wili,' he said softly. 'I will try to protect them.'

'Hmph. Try hard,' she said.

Bramble wanted to hear his response, but the waters were a solid slap in the face, knocking her backwards into darkness.

The waters were rushing over her, around her – no, under her filling her with the sound. Water splashed in her face and she shook it out of her eyes and held on tight to . . . to what?

'Yeayyyy!' the man whooped as the floor fell out from under him and he crashed down, then pulled himself upright again by the prow of a boat. They were in a boat, and she was with Baluch, unmistakable from the blare of horns in his head, the beating of drums that rose every time the boat shifted. He clung to the high carved prow and peered ahead, one arm above his head. He moved his arm as he saw rocks approaching and the boat turned to avoid them. Bramble realised he must be signalling to the steersman.

It was a frantic race through white water, boulders rising up out of the fast-flowing river like demons, ready to rip out the bottom of the wooden boat. Bramble couldn't help thinking that the reed boats of the Lake People would be much better suited to this river, riding high on the water as they did. This boat dragged too much; had too much of its keel under the surface, where rocks could, and did, grab at it.

On either side of the river, forest crowded the banks, a lush summer green, with ferns and wild roses and blackberries spilling over the

banks to dip leaves in the stream. They poured down the river as fast
as the current itself. Plummeting down small cascades, swinging the
boat wildly around to avoid being smashed to pieces, scraping along
ambushing rocks, wind in Baluch's face, water splashing in his eyes,
bouncing and rocking and jumping over the lip of the rapids like a
runaway horse. It was wonderful – the best thing that had happened
so far.

Baluch laughed and whooped as they went, and behind him she
could hear Acton doing the same. Baluch cast one quick look back and
they exchanged glances, eyes bright with shared laughter and a kind of
joy. Risk, Bramble thought. They love it; and so do I.

It was over too soon. The boat tilted over the lip of the last of the
rocks and swung wide into a shingled pool formed by a beaver dam.
The stumps of the narrow birches they had felled to make the dam surrounded the pool, and further back there was real forest; birch and
beech and oak and alder, rowan and one large, dark holly tree on the
very edge.

Acton called out, 'Beach her here, boys,' and the men, about twenty of them, four to a bench, dipped their oars in the water and rowed
the boat to shore, driving it up onto the shingle with one last huge
thrust. They scrambled out with some relief. One man, a tall red-head
with a slight squint in one eye, grumbled all the way.

'No life for a warrior,' he said to a shorter blond man with very
broad shoulders. 'I want to die with a sword in my hand, not an oar.'

The man clapped him on the back and the red-head smiled at him
involuntarily, as one smiles at a very old and beloved friend.

'There'll be swords enough even for you soon, Red,' Acton called
across to him and grinned. 'They won't give up the port without a fight.'

Red smiled sourly and pointedly took off his jerkin and squeezed a
stream of water out of it into the pool. The men laughed.

A moment later a second boat arrived, a little more slowly. Asgarn
stood at the prow. He raised a hand in greeting and the boat came to
land next to Acton's.

His men dragged the boat up the shingle and Asgarn leapt off. He
didn't look like he'd enjoyed the trip much. 'We can rest here, then.
Good,' he said.

Baluch left them to unpack food and wandered upstream, to a
point above the beaver dam where the forest met the stream. He
stayed, looking into the shadowed green, his mind making music with

flute and pipe, a wistful, calling music that brought an ache up under his breastbone.

Acton joined him and sat on a rock at the edge of the stream, jutting out over the rushing water. 'I still can't get used to it,' he said, looking at the dense forest. 'So many trees!'

Baluch nodded. 'It's a rich land. The forest stretches all the way to the Lake.'

'You'll have to take me there, one day,' Acton said comfortably.

Baluch bit his lip. 'Once you have T'vit, I'll be going again,' he said.

'Going where?'

'Back to the Lake.'

Acton stood up and faced him. 'Something happened there, didn't it?' His face lit with a teasing smile. 'Did you fall in love with one of the Lake girls?'

Baluch ducked his head. Bramble thought he was embarrassed, but his heart was beating in its normal pattern. There were memories moving in his mind, just under thought, but she couldn't catch them.

'Not with one of the girls.' He paused, as though searching for the right words. 'Something . . . calls me. Even now, I can hear it. Like music, or a whisper in the night. The Lake calls me. I have to go back.'

Acton frowned. 'Not by yourself,' he said. 'Come on the first trip to the Wind Cities with me, and when I get back I'll go with you.' Baluch made a face, and Acton punched him lightly on the shoulder. 'You can't trust strange women who whisper to you in the night, lad. You need your uncle Acton to look after you and protect you from hussies and enchantresses.'

Baluch smiled at that. 'You just want some for yourself!' he said. They laughed.

'Come with me to the Wind Cities, Bal,' Acton said, almost wheedling. 'Then I'll go with you to your lake.'

Baluch sighed. Bramble could hear the music in his head grow fainter, as though he had turned his thoughts away from it, but it didn't entirely fade. 'All right,' he said. 'I suppose someone has to look after you, too.'

They went back to the others and ate smoked trout and pickled onions and brown bread. Two of the men had a belching contest. The red-head's friend, whose named turned out to be Geb, won.

'Should have bet on me, Red,' he said, laughing, as the red-head handed coins over to one of the others.

Red grinned and nodded. 'Should have known you were full of hot air, you mean,' he retorted.

The men laughed and joked as they packed their supplies away and launched the boats again. Acton and Baluch watched them from the bank, chuckling, as Red tried to duck Geb in the river. Geb pushed him away, mock-scowling. Red hoisted himself into the boat and held a hand out to Geb.

'Oh, no!' Geb said, standing alone in the stream, thigh-deep, half-laughing. 'You'll let me get halfway up, then you'll let go.'

Red shook his head. 'No, I won't. Truly.'

'Get moving,' Asgarn called impatiently from the other boat.

Geb took Red's hand and began to pull himself up. Sure enough, halfway up he fell back into the water. The others laughed, but Red shouted, 'Geb!' and grabbed for him, pulling on his shoulders. Then Geb started screaming – a high, disbelieving scream like a child in a nightmare.

There was blood in the water. Water sprite, Bramble thought, they're probably in every major stream in this time.

'Pull him up, pull him up!' Red shouted, and the other men rushed to grab Geb's shoulders and haul.

Acton stood to jump into the water, but Baluch held him back. The music in his head was warning, now, harsh and clamorous, full of fear. 'No,' he said. 'There's something down there.'

The men pulled, and pulled again, and suddenly Geb came free of the water. Something was clinging to his legs, but as they watched the water sprite dissolved into air, like mist, like fog dissipated by wind. It cried as it went, a thin mournful cry that set the hairs up on the back of Baluch's neck.

Geb was bleeding hard, the big veins in his legs pumping the life out of him. Red cradled him, trying to put pressure on the worst wound, but there was no hope. Geb gripped Red's jacket and said, 'Meli . . .'

'I'll look after her,' Red promised. Geb nodded feebly, once, and died.

Acton and Baluch climbed into the boat from the shingle, careful not to let their feet get in the water. Red looked up at Acton with accusing eyes. Wild eyes, full of grief.

'You didn't even try to help,' he said. Then he bent his head over Geb's body and began to weep. Acton stared at him, his mouth grim.

Bramble thought he looked older, that the lines in his cheeks showed more clearly than they had a few moments ago.

'Come with me, Baluch, Den, Odda. We'll gather wood in the forest for his pyre,' he said. He leapt from the boat as though glad to leave it behind. The others followed him. One splashed in the shallows as he landed and stumbled, terrified, up the shingle, almost crawling in his haste to get away from the water.

'This land is cursed!' Red said.

Baluch made the sign to avert evil and moved closer to Red. 'Acton tried to help. I stopped him.'

Red glared at him. 'No one stops him doing what he really wants to do.'

Bramble thought that was a fair comment. No one stopped Acton. Baluch turned away to follow Acton.

Red raised his voice. 'When we go on, I'm thinking I'll be in Asgarn's boat.'

Baluch paused. He didn't turn around, but he nodded, then jumped for the shore. In the middle of the jump, in mid-air, the waters came sideways and swept Bramble away in a flurry of foam and bubbles.

She was playing a drum in a simple, repetitive rhythm. In her head, another rhythm echoed and flicked in counterpoint. It has to be Baluch, Bramble thought. Coming back to Baluch at least had the virtue of familiarity; she could relax a little, read his thoughts a little. He clung to the prow with one hand and beat the drum with the other.

He began to whistle, and with the sound her vision cleared and she saw that they were on the river and his drumbeat was keeping the oarsmen in time. The river was calmer here than in the rapids, but its surface was deceptive – the boat was travelling very fast. They were rowing because the river was about to join another big stream and they would need to make their way against the cross-currents and eddies that the confluence created.

Between the two rivers was a sheer clay bluff that came to a ragged point with a tiny beach where several small round boats were tied down. Baluch looked up and Bramble could see a village on top of the bluff; smoke came from drying racks with rows of fish tied to them; some laundry was spread out on bushes to dry.

The bluff was lined with women watching, children crowded between their mothers' legs to peer over at the strangers. Baluch waved to them and a couple of the children waved back. Then the men appeared. Some had slingshots; others carried head-sized rocks.

'Row!' Acton called. 'Head for the bank!'

They bent their backs to the oar as Baluch increased the speed of the drumbeat, marking the time strongly. The boat seemed to pause and then leap away from the village towards the near bank. But stones were raining down on them already. One from a slingshot, about the size of a fist, hit Baluch in the shoulder and spun him around onto the deck. It knocked the wind out of him and for a moment all Bramble could see was the rough-finished boards of the hull, all she could think about was the aching desire to breathe . . . then he gasped and dragged a breath in and hoisted himself up.

The large rocks were mostly falling short but one had caved a hole in the side of the boat, just above the waterline. Several men were bleeding from the ears or nose. One nursed a broken hand. It was clear that the slingshotters could send their stones right to the bank – there was no safety there.

'Back!' Acton called. 'Backwater!'

The unharmed men reversed themselves on the bench and spun their oars around. Baluch sprang down to a bench to replace an injured man and they rowed strongly until they were out of range. The men on the bluff shook their fists in the air and cheered. Their women hugged and kissed them. Bramble wanted to cheer with them. No one ever told this story, did they? About the ones who fought back. Oh, no, the stories were all about massacres, not about brave villagers who repulsed the invaders.

Asgarn's boat, following theirs, was keeping still in the water, rowing against the current just enough to let Acton come level.

'We need to find a place upriver to come ashore,' Acton called to him. Asgarn nodded and ordered his men to reverse oars, then they rowed hard until they came to a sand beach on the far bank of the river.

Careful not to put their feet in the water, they lifted the wounded off the boat and tended them. One man had been hit in the head. There was no split in his skin and he said he was fine, but a few minutes after he sat down on a rock he began to bleed from the nose, and a moment after that he was dead.

Acton looked at his body with tight lips. Baluch's mind was full of mourning music, low and solemn.

'Elric,' he said. 'He was named for my father.'

Looking down at the man, Bramble recognised in his features one of the boys who had played with Baluch and Acton the first time she had come into Baluch's mind. She remembered him, too, as one of the boys who had showed off, trying to attract Acton's attention.

'We would have done them no harm,' Acton said angrily.

'They didn't know that,' Baluch said. 'We're strangers. Maybe they've heard some story about what happened to Hawk and his people.'

Acton was stone-faced. Asgarn put his hand on Acton's shoulder.

'We have to take the village,' he said, 'or we can forget about getting to T'vit.'

'Yes,' Acton said. 'Tonight.'

'Night?'

'Oh, yes. They won't expect it. We land upstream of them and go in, hidden by darkness. We make noise. We threaten. We let them leave, if they want to.'

'What if they don't?' Asgarn said, loud enough for the others to hear.

'Then we kill them all!' Red exclaimed, and the men cheered.

Acton took a breath, and then let it out. Baluch, even Baluch, was nodding.

'They challenged us,' he said. 'They killed first. There are consequences to murder.'

'The women and children will not be harmed –' Acton began.

'Unless they fight,' Asgarn concluded. The men nodded.

'Unless they fight,' Acton conceded.

Bramble really didn't want to be present for the raid on the village. But the gods decided otherwise. She waited with Baluch, feeling his heart beating faster, in the darkness outside the village, until everyone was in bed except the single lookout. She watched Asgarn slit the lookout's throat. She crept with Baluch and the other men until they had surrounded the quiet houses and, as Acton nodded, she felt Baluch's throat contract and release in an unearthly, high-pitched scream. In an instant, all the men were screaming, a terrifying ululation that sounded completely inhuman.

In the houses, there were shouts and cries and clangs as people tumbled from beds and peered out of windows and doors. Acton raised a hand and the men stopped screaming.

'People of this village,' Acton said, in the language he had learned from Gris. 'You have killed one of my men, and for that your punishment is death.'

The cries rose again but now they were human voices, Acton's men cheering, villagers protesting.

'But I am merciful,' Acton shouted over the top of them, and they fell silent. 'If you choose to leave this place forever, taking with you whatever you can carry, I will let you live.'

'Never! We'll never leave!' an old woman's voice shouted back. 'This is our place, you thieving bastards!'

There were shouts of agreement from men and women both.

'I will even let your women and children go before this battle, if you refuse to leave.'

'We'll stay!' a younger woman's voice came. 'We'll fight by our men and we'll see your souls to hell!'

Baluch stood close by Acton, as if worried about him.

'Well, Wili, I tried,' Acton muttered. He turned to Baluch. 'You'll tell her I tried, Bal?'

Baluch nodded. 'They've chosen death. It's their right.'

That seemed to comfort Acton, which annoyed Bramble. He was about to kill a whole village, and he wanted to feel good about it, to feel good that he had given them a choice between losing everything they had, everything they'd worked for, and dying. He had no idea what he was asking! She was angry again, and she welcomed the anger, because it strengthened her against what she knew was coming.

'For Elric!' Acton cried aloud, and his men echoed the cry as they rushed forwards.

There had been men with torches hidden in the undergrowth. Now they threw the torches onto the thatch of the roofs and the houses came alight with a whoosh of air, the sudden heat on their faces, sudden light almost blinding them. The village men came out of the houses waving slingshots, with hatchets, with spears, with staves, but without a sword between them. The women came behind them with anything they could find, from a cooking pot to a kitchen knife. Some of them had babies tied to them with shawls. The children followed them, with little knives, with small slingshots, with bits of wood snatched from the kindling. 'For the River Bluff!' they cried as they attacked.

They fought fiercely, children included, but they had no hope. There was a lot of blood, and Baluch spilt his fair share of it, including a young boy who came at him with a knife. He swiped him away with the flat of his sword, but Bramble heard the boy's neck crack. Baluch paused for a second, but the rapture of battle overtook both him and Acton and he charged villager after villager with real enjoyment, part of him relishing the image of fire against the dark sky, of sparks flying upwards, of flames glinting on raised swords, of the rushing river encircling them with constant music.

Bramble fought against being caught up in the surge of emotion, but it was hard, so hard, to stay separate when Baluch's mind was so close to hers. She pulled herself as far back as she could and made herself think of other things; and then she thought that someone should stand as witness to the slaughter, for the children if for no one else, so she made herself watch it all, and feel it all, the exhilaration and the horror mingling in her until she couldn't split them apart, until it felt that she was drowning in fire and blood.

Was this what it had been like in Carlion, when Maryrose and Merrick had been slaughtered? Had the ghosts felt the same combination of excitement and repulsion? Or were they simply glad to kill?

She wished she could weep.

When the villagers were all dead and the fires had begun to burn down into the stone foundations of the houses, Acton called them together to count their losses. There were none. They whooped and slapped each other's backs and cheered for Acton a few times.

A couple of them went off to look for drink in the sheds which they claimed they had carefully *not* set fire to, because sheds were usually where the beer was brewed. This raised a laugh and a cheer. Baluch was exhausted. He slumped on a bench under an elm tree, incongruously untouched, as though ready for a picnic.

'Women and children,' Acton growled to him. 'Such great warriors we are.'

'Their choice,' Baluch said, his voice flat, his mind suddenly replaying the moment when he had killed the boy. All music emptied out of him and he hung his head between his knees, fighting nausea. Bramble felt a sour satisfaction, all the more so because there had been moments when she had been too involved with Baluch, had shared too closely with his pleasure as his sword had swung cleanly, had killed efficiently.

Baluch sat up, leaned his head back against the elm and closed his eyes.

'We're not going to do it this way when we get to T'vit,' Acton said.

Bramble deeply wanted to hear him say it, wanted him to reject the warrior creed that he had lived his life by. She was surprised by the depth of her desire, the strength with which she silently urged him to put an end to the killing. Perhaps, just perhaps, he was changing . . .

'I don't want any of the houses lost,' he said. 'No fires. We're going to need the houses and boatsheds, and the boats, too. Tell the others. Kill the men, leave the houses alone.'

She should have known. She hated him more in that moment than she had ever hated any warlord or warlord's man. He was as bad as she had always known. She felt as though her chest was being sawn open with a blunt knife. Why should it hurt her so much? She had always known what he was.

Baluch kept his eyes closed as though he didn't want to look at Acton's face. 'And the women and children?'

Acton paused. 'We'll give them the choice. Then it's up to them.'

Bramble could have cried with thankfulness when the waters rose, gently, to carry her away in a deep and silent current.

The current washed her up, again in Baluch's mind, looking at another village by daylight, a whole, undamaged village of about twelve houses lying in a flat bend of the river, untouched, calm, perfect. Except that there were no people.

Acton and Baluch and Asgarn waited while the men went into the houses and searched. One by one, they came out and spread their hands.

'No one. Nothing,' Red said. 'They're all gone.'

Asgarn laughed heartily. 'They must have heard about River Bluff,' he said.

The men began to smile, and then to laugh, too. 'They've heard about our lord of war!' one said. 'Acton the invincible!'

Acton smiled reluctantly and Baluch grinned.

'Let's hope they take the news to T'vit,' Acton said. 'I wouldn't mind taking the port this way!'

His men decided that was the funniest thing they had ever heard. Maybe it was relief at not having to fight. Maybe it was disappointment. But they collapsed in laughter while Acton and Baluch watched, smiling.

Except Asgarn. He smiled, but his eyes were cold.

As cold as the water that came down upon Bramble in a deluge.

ASH

ANIMAL THROATS COULD not talk, but ears could listen, and human minds could understand. Ash kept his counsel about the songs he needed until he could talk with his father in daylight, man to man, but he could at least start Flax on the road he needed to walk. He moved back from his father and pulled Flax forwards.

'This is Flax, whose father Gorham was raised by his mother and never brought to the Deep. Will you teach him what he needs to know?' He hesitated, but it had to be said, or Flax would not be accepted. 'He is a singer.'

The men nodded. Two of them, a deer with wide antlers and a squirrel, whose head looked odd on his large body, came forward and started to strip Flax's clothes off. He exclaimed and looked for help to Ash. Ash grinned at him. He had already started to undress.

'In the Deep, we show our true shapes.' That was true in a way that Flax wasn't ready for yet. But he would be, one day soon.

The badger, his father Rowan in his true guise, put a hand on Ash's arm and led him forward to the cave – or rather, to the caves. The fire cave was only the first in a long series. It was open to all whose blood calmed the waters. Year after year, the boys were taken further in, further down, into the Deep. Ash had been told that before Acton came, each year would add a new scar to the boy's body until he was marked formally as a man. But not now.

'Travellers must travel unnoticed. Scars show, sooner or later, and lead to questions. There must be no questions about the Deep,' he had been told.

In the old days, men wore the masks of their animal in the ceremonies, once it had been revealed to them by the water. But since

Acton came, the River had granted them their true shapes, to be and then wear inside, afterwards.

'This is the River's gift. This is how Traveller men stay men,' his grandfather had told him, in the first year. 'The fair-haired ones look at us with scornful eyes, and a man might come, in time, to believe that he is worthy of scorn. But *we* know that what they see is not what we truly are. The man who knows what he truly is, and accepts it, cannot be diminished by another's gaze. This is the River's gift: when they look at you with hate and disdain, you will think, "You do not know me; you know nothing". Then, though you look at the ground, pretending humility to prevent a beating, you will not feel humbled in your heart, because you know who you are.'

Ash had always felt that it was a great gift, even though, when he went to Turvite, he had forced himself to banish even a stray thought about the Deep. It had been pure superstition; he was afraid then, that he would never return, that he had been cast out of the society of Travellers, forced to Settle, because there was no place for him on the Road. He was afraid that the River would reject him if he had tried to come here without his father.

He was still afraid of that, but there were more important things than his fear. He watched his father who had joined in the testing of the new boy. The demon forms prowled around Flax, growling softly, reaching out hands curled like claws to touch his face, to poke his side, to scratch.

'If you hold still and show no fear, you won't be harmed,' Ash said quietly. It was what he had been told by his grandfather, who had met him and his father here the year before the old man died – the first year that Ash came and had been tested as Flax was being tested now. He believed it was true, but the demons chuckled to themselves disquietingly. Ash wondered what happened to the boys who broke and tried to run.

This was only the first test, but it lasted until dawn, until Flax was swaying with tiredness and fear had passed out of him because he was too exhausted to feel it. As the dawn broke somewhere outside the canyon, the sky lit with rose and orange glory and the demons lifted their heads and howled, a long ululation, then turned as one and jogged inside the big cave.

Ash came over to Flax and supported him to a seat on a flat rock. He brought water in a curved shell from a tiny stream flowing between two boulders, and held it so Flax could drink.

'W-why . . . ?' Flax stuttered.

'That was the first test,' Ash said. 'There'll be others.'

'Demons. One of them was your father?'

Ash nodded. 'You'll meet him soon.'

'That's why he'll know the right songs? Because he's a demon?'

'Ah, no, not exactly.'

'You could have warned me!' With his legs no longer wobbling and his thirst slaked, Flax had found enough energy to be angry.

'No, I couldn't,' Ash said. 'I'd sworn secrecy. I *did* warn you it was dangerous.'

'Yes, but . . . *real* demons.'

Ash laughed. 'Oh, they're not so bad when you get to know them!'

It hadn't occurred to him that Flax would think he was demon-spawned, that he wouldn't immediately understand who the badger-headed figure really was. He couldn't resist letting him continue to think it. The misunderstanding wouldn't be for long, anyway. He collected his and Flax's clothes and they dressed, glad to escape the chill.

Flax rummaged in their bags for something to eat, but Ash moved away, waiting for the sun to come up over the lip of the canyon wall. He knelt by the stream, trailing one hand in the cold water, and wondered what was happening up north, with Bramble and the others. He missed Martine. Oakmere was a long way north of where his ancestors had lived – there were no Traveller songs about it, and right now he was glad. He was sick of songs. Heartsick.

He had held them inside all his life, although again and again they had almost burst his chest with the pressure to sing. But he had never sung, because of the look on his parents' faces whenever he tried. Now he knew that he had sung with the voice of the dead, and his parents' reaction was understandable. But then, when he had been three and four and five years old, all he had known was that his voice was so horrible that even his father could not bear to listen. Yet his father had taught him the songs. Taught the music, on the flute and drum. Taught the lyrics, and heard Ash recite them all until he was word perfect.

All. That was the point – that had *been* the point – that he had learnt all that his father had to teach. That his father had entrusted the songs to him, so that someday he could teach someone else . . . his own son, his own daughter . . . and the songs would continue, as they had continued for more than a thousand years. All of them. If his father had not given him all the songs, then none of them was worth anything.

None.

He wished he could wipe his memory clean of every song he had ever known.

The breeze carried the sounds of the Deep with it; birds, beetles, small animals in the carpet of leaves, and the Hidden River rushing through its banks. He found the Deep disturbing, always, but the sounds of life lifted his spirits. Perhaps – perhaps his father did not *know* the songs Safred was talking about. A small sound came from behind him, a foot on pebble, and he swung around, drawing his knife as he turned.

The men were coming out of the cave, still naked but with their own faces returned to them. Ash stowed his knife hurriedly. His father came first, smiling broadly, and embraced him.

'Ash! You made it!'

Ash knew he should have left his clothes where they were, but embracing his father while they were both naked always felt bizarre, and he'd rather have to strip off again later than experience that oddity.

Flax was looking from one face to another, one body to another, and coming to a conclusion.

'They're *not* demons?' he asked Ash, outraged.

'Only at night.' Rowan laughed. 'When the River gives us our true faces.'

Flax opened his mouth to complain, but Ash forestalled him. 'We have more important things to talk about.' He looked around the circle of faces he knew so well. Friends, an uncle of his mother's, his father . . . They looked at him with welcoming eyes, but would they still look like that after he had demanded to be taught the secret songs? Or would he be cast out, never to return? Would he lose his place in the world all over again? His heart beat faster, but he had to speak.

'There are things happening in the world outside which you must know about,' he said. 'And there is a thing I must ask from you.'

MARTINE

CAEL'S WOUND WASN'T healing. It wasn't getting any worse, and his fever was low, but it was constant. He was losing weight. Zel and Martine had to search further in the Forest to find feverfew and comfrey.

'You have to come out to the island,' Safred said at breakfast. 'I'm sure I could heal you at the altar.'

Cael looked at the lake with loathing. 'I'm all right. I'll last until we get out of the Forest.'

'You look tired,' Zel ventured.

'I'm sleeping fine. Slept like the dead last night. Every night since we've been here.' He sounded faintly surprised.

Safred looked thoughtful. 'So have I,' she said. 'What about you two?'

Martine didn't look at Zel. 'I had trouble getting to sleep last night,' she said truthfully, 'but then I slept soundly.'

'Me, too,' Zel said.

'Maybe there's something in the air,' Safred said.

Something from the gods, Martine thought. Or the fire, safeguarding us. She was warmed by the thought that even in his rage he hadn't lifted that protection. Bramble began to move, twisting from side to side as though in pain. Martine bent over her and smoothed her hair. She tried to give Bramble water, but her mouth stayed firmly closed.

'It doesn't matter if you're sleeping,' Safred said sternly to Cael. 'You have to be healed. Come to the altar.'

He looked resigned. 'All right.'

'Safred,' Martine said, 'I don't think the gods want you to.'

From the centre of the black altar, mist was rising. There had been fog on the water when they woke at dawn, but it had disappeared when the sun hit it. Now, at noon, in full warm sun, mist was pouring off the altar and spreading outwards, across the lake, towards them, as it had the first night, when they had taken Bramble to the altar.

'Dung and pissmire!' Zel said.

'I don't think now is a good time to go out there, niece,' Cael said. But the mist didn't react to this retreat.

'Sit down around Bramble and hold hands!' Martine ordered. Zel grabbed her hand and Safred's and they formed a circle, Cael between Safred and Martine, Bramble in the middle, lying silently, frowning a little. Cael's hand *was* too hot, Martine thought. Then the mist rolled over them and they could see nothing.

BRAMBLE

FOR ONCE, SIGHT came back first. Bright light, sun shining, reflecting off water – water moving, shifting, breaking in brilliance. The sea, Bramble realised. The eyes she looked through were straining to see out past the breaking waves to where a boat with a square sail was making for the narrow harbour entrance. Cliffs reared up on either side, sheer and menacing, making a hazardous corridor to the open ocean. On the left-hand cliff, the northern side, were men, pushing large rocks towards the edge. If the rocks fell as the boat was making its way through the corridor, it would be smashed.

She saw through a woman's eyes. Her hand was at her throat and her heart beat fast, as though she were mortally afraid. She jiggled a baby on her left hip without looking at it. The baby chortled and patted her face with a soft hand, but although Bramble could clearly feel the touch, the woman seemed unaware of it. Out of the corner of her eyes, Bramble could see other people watching the boat's progress. Dark-haired people. After so long spent among the tall, burly men of Acton's world, they seemed small to her.

The men on the cliffs had hair that shone bright gold in the sunlight. They were big, too, and strong. Although the rocks had clearly been piled up ready for any attempted invasion from the sea, they were still a fair way away from the edge, and these men trundled them across the uneven ground with ease. Bramble could see that their hair was in plaits. Acton's men.

This must be Turvite. The battle for Turvite had been fought outside the town, up on the hills that surrounded the city, the stories said, because the men of Turvite wanted to have the advantage of the high ground. The elevation hadn't helped them: they'd all been killed.

Bramble could just imagine Acton laughing as he swung his sword, shouting 'Kill them all!' There he was, himself, unmistakable, standing tall on the cliff edge, shouting down to someone in the boat. There was a woman on the boat who was shouting up. Bramble couldn't be sure why, but there was something about the way she stood and her long white hair that made her think of Dotta. Then Acton motioned his men back from the cliff's edge and gestured to the boat – you can leave, the gesture said. Take the open sea. The old woman waved her thanks.

The woman with the baby gasped and began to cry. There was a mixture of joy and sorrow swirling inside her that Bramble found difficult to experience. This was a woman who felt intensely, far more so than Ragni, or the girl in the meadow. Baluch turned all his feelings into music, and somehow that contained them; Gris had kept control of his through long practice. But this woman had almost no control at all, and it was dizzying.

Next to her, another woman, older, turned and put an arm across her shoulders. 'Now, now, Piper,' she scolded gently. 'He's safe now. They've let the boat go.'

'I'll never see him again, Snapper!' Piper wept.

'Better that than seeing him as a corpse,' Snapper replied. 'At least you know he's safe. Him and the other young ones. You've still got this little lady, Searose, to look after, remember. That tall one with the golden hair said we had until sunset to bury our dead and get out of the town. Lucky to get that much time, I reckon.' She put her hands out to the baby and the baby launched herself happily into her arms.

'Your son is safe on the boat,' Snapper said. 'Time to deal with the dead.'

That quietened Piper, which Bramble was glad of – and then realised that preferring to deal with dead bodies rather than living emotions showed how many dead bodies she'd seen lately. She was getting used to it. She wondered how much more used to it Acton's men were. After all, she merely dipped into their lives, while they kept fighting when she was not observing. Perhaps they were so used to it that death didn't even mark them anymore. Perhaps they just didn't notice it. Was that true of Acton?

That was a disquieting thought, and she pushed it away and made herself concentrate on Piper as she and the crowd of women who had watched the boat leave walked slowly away from the harbour, up the hill which cupped Turvite. This wasn't the place of Bramble's imaginings.

Where was the great and glorious city of Acton's triumph? The songs all talked about Turvite's magnificence – except that really old one, that just talked about the ghosts. There was no magnificence here. Turvite was barely more than a village. Bigger than her home village of Wooding, admittedly, but not by much, and different from it mainly in the number of trees that grew among the houses.

Down by the harbour there were no docks. The boats – small fishing smacks with a single mast – had been drawn up on the narrow shingle beach. There were some timber houses, some huts, a few shanties close to the beach, but no large buildings and seemingly no centre to the town.

Piper and Snapper and the other women walked through an open space surrounded by oak trees. Trees that must have been carefully tended to grow here, in the path of the salt sea breezes. Bramble felt the call of the gods in her mind. The women dipped their heads to an altar in casual familiarity, although one at the back of the group spat on the ground as she passed.

'What shagging good are they?' she asked angrily, when the other women looked askance. 'Didn't keep our men alive, did they?'

'Not their job, Crab,' Snapper said. Bramble felt the attention of the gods centre on Snapper approvingly. 'People die,' she continued. 'Everyone dies. What do they care then? Months and years don't make any difference to them. Their job is to make sure that rebirth happens. That life continues.'

'Easy enough to say,' Crab snarled, and then pushed past them and strode up the hill. The women watched her go.

'She's carrying,' a thin, older woman said. 'And she's lost husband and brother and father this day.'

'So have we all.' Snapper sighed.

They kept walking, passing through the screen of oak trees back into the main street of the town. Some of the women were weeping quietly, others had set faces. Some had the blank look of shock, and were shepherded along by others. Halfway up the hill, a door opened and a woman came out. Dark-haired, of course, and a bit stout, maybe fifty or more. A woman who moved as if surety of her own competence was so deep that she couldn't imagine failing at anything. She had a knife in one hand; a black stone knife that she gripped as if she would never let it go.

'Tern!' Snapper said gladly.

Piper's heart gave an odd kick as she looked at Tern, as though frightened. But she came forwards with the other women, murmuring greetings. Bramble noted that they kept a clear space between themselves and Tern. There were no embraces, no shared consolation with this woman.

Tern raked them all with a glance and moved up the hill, walking briskly. 'Come!' she said. 'It's time to take back what is ours.'

Ah, Bramble thought, the enchanter who raised the dead. Good. I've been hoping for this.

The hill was steeper than it looked and Snapper had to hand the baby back to Piper. Piper began puffing as they climbed higher and the baby thought it was a game. Every time Piper forced out a breath, the baby laughed. Instead of making Piper happier, each laugh brought her closer to tears.

'Searose doesn't know what trouble we're in,' Piper gasped to Snapper as they reached the top of the hill and started down the other side.

Snapper smiled grimly. 'As it should be. Pray to the gods that she keeps unknowing.'

Just over the ridge there was a haphazard pile of bodies. There had been no attempt to lay them out. They sprawled, with limbs askew. Blood was turning brown on their clothes and skin. A couple of severed arms had been tossed on top of the pile, like an afterthought. The smell, of pierced gut and vomit and blood and old urine, was horrible. Crab stood there, staring. Piper gagged, and then ran forwards, pushing past Tern to reach one of the bodies, whose face could barely be seen under another man.

She pushed the body on top away and wailed, 'Salmon,' as she took the corpse's head in one hand. The other still gripped Searose fiercely. Grief rose up in her like vomit, unstoppable, and Bramble was shaken by the strength of it – true grief, untainted by fear for her own future or by anger or confusion. Pure as snowmelt, hot as fire. It seared Piper into scalding tears and Bramble found it almost unbearable. The strength of it brought back all her own grief, every grief she had ever felt, but particularly the newest one, for Maryrose. She almost envied Piper's ability to let it loose; to surrender to it as to a huge wave.

Around her, other women were discovering the bodies of their husbands, fathers, brothers, sons. Sobbing, wailing, choking tears, swearing, praying . . . Bramble felt breathless under the onslaught.

Then Tern touched Piper on the shoulder. 'Sister,' she said, 'hold your tears. Wait, and watch, and listen.'

She drew Piper up and passed her back to Snapper, who held her while Piper blinked at Tern in confusion. The other women moved away also, as though afraid of Tern.

As she passed, Tern looked closely at each woman. Bramble hurriedly drew her attention back from Piper's mind, trying to make herself invisible to the enchantress. Another encounter like the one with Dotta would be too unsettling. Something in her didn't want to be seen by Tern, whom she was rapidly coming to dislike, perhaps because, although she looked again and again into the eyes of women distraught with grief and fear, she showed no sign of compassion.

Tern stopped at last when she reached the woman who had spat at the altar. 'You,' she said. 'Crab, isn't it? I need you. I need your anger. Will you give it?'

'What do I get for it?' Crab asked.

'Revenge.'

Crab nodded decisively, and Tern smiled. Bramble thought, that's what we're fighting. That look. That's the look the enchanter Saker must have, just before he kills. The look that thirsts for blood. Yet, when I was a child and Granda told me the story of the enchantress of Turvite, I thought she was a hero. She felt a great sadness that was separate from her share of Piper's grief; the same kind of sadness that she had felt the first time she had realised that her father was not the strongest, wisest man in the world; that her mother was not the best woman in the village. The sadness of reality intruding on a dream. Of certainties melting.

Tern stood by the bodies, the women in a semi-circle watching her. She held the knife high, and began to speak.

'Gods of field and stream, hear your daughter. Gods of fire and storm, hear your daughter. Gods of earth and stone, hear your daughter.' Bramble knew this incantation. For the first time since she had understood that the gods were translating for her, she was sharply aware of the doubling of meaning, because these were words that she knew. She heard them in both languages, her own and Tern's.

'Gods of sky and wind, hear your daughter,' Tern said. She took Crab's hand in her free one and held tightly. Crab became pale, but she kept her expression of anger and determination. Tern continued to ask the gods for something, but for the first time, the gods failed to translate. It was as though they didn't want Bramble to hear these words, to understand them. Bramble tried frantically to remember, but the words were too alien to her – and to everyone else, she realised, because Snapper was staring in puzzlement. Bramble caught a sound here and there, but understood nothing and was as surprised as Piper when Tern raised the black rock knife and cut her hand open, swinging her arm wide so that the drops of blood fell on all the corpses.

The ghosts rose, stepping up from their bodies to stand unsteadily, confused, next to them. They had died clutching their weapons, so they had them in death: a few swords, some cleavers, mostly hunting spears. They were far clearer to see than any ghost Bramble had ever witnessed quicken. She couldn't see through them. They were solid. Real.

Bramble felt Piper's throat clench, her whole body tense, as Salmon rose and looked around, and saw her. The upsurge of love that poured through her was overwhelming. It shook Bramble. Salmon was an ordinary man, medium height, plain face, pockmarks. He held a sword, and his throat was cut through, the dark gash showing horribly. His eyes were kind, though, and it was in his eyes that Piper searched for something; whatever it was, she found it, because she relaxed and sighed a long, tremulous sigh.

Salmon started to move towards Piper, but Tern waved him back. 'You are dead,' she said. 'I have raised your ghosts to take your city back from the invaders. You cannot die again, but they can. Follow me. Destroy them, and your wives and children can still be safe.'

Salmon reached out a white hand and tried to touch her, but his hand went right through. Tern didn't even shiver, and that was when Bramble knew she was mad. She remembered that feeling, and only someone living completely inside the world in their head could stay unaffected by it.

Salmon looked at his hand in puzzlement, looking questioningly at Tern. 'I will give you strength,' she reassured him. 'My death will give you bodies to fight with.'

The other ghosts were raising clenched fists in the air, shouting words of defiance that no one could hear. Their wounds showed up clearly; some were missing arms, others had guts hanging out of their bellies.

Salmon nodded, then looked across at Piper and smiled, or tried to. His face was full of difficult and deep emotion, and Bramble understood that the same torrent of love was pouring through him. For the first time, she envied another woman. To feel so strongly, and be matched in that feeling . . . Well, she could let that dream go, too. A demon who had stolen a human body had told her that, at an inn in Sandalwood. Thee wilt love no human never, he had said, and she thought she had accepted it. Must accept it. But it was hard, even though she knew that love had brought the great grief she felt still puls-ing through Piper. The baby shifted in Piper's arms and Salmon's eyes went to it and grew soft. Their love had brought Piper the baby and that, too, was no small thing.

Motherhood was not something Bramble had yearned for, but she was no stranger to the appeal of looking after something small and soft and vulnerable – she had nursed too many poddy calves and kids not to understand. Piper looked at Searose and truly saw her for the first time since the vigil on the beach. Bramble felt her fill immediately with a com-plex intertwining of emotions: a softer, warmer kind of love, pity, grief for the father Searose would never know, and a great, bone-shaking fear that the baby would die, too. Which wasn't unreasonable, Bramble thought, remembering River Bluff and the children who died there.

Around them, women were going up to the men they had loved, say-ing things to them in low voices, the things they hadn't had a chance to say before they died. At least Tern had given them that. All the women seemed to care so much that Bramble wondered for a moment whether there were no unhappy marriages in Turvite. But as Tern led the ghosts up over the hill and down through the town, followed proudly by Crab and then the other women and children, she realised that the women who did not care were busy packing their belongings, getting ready to leave. Handcarts stood outside many houses, bags were ready in door-ways, women were ordering children to gather what they could. Only the truly grieving had gone to bury the dead.

As the ghosts went by, the women came out of their houses, snatched their children back from the procession, made the sign against evil and then, as though enchanted themselves, fell in behind the other women and followed. They marched silently up the hill that led to the cliff. Some women walked beside their men, others behind.

Acton saw them coming. Although his men had taken barrels of beer and were drinking freely, he had still set lookouts. He was stand-ing a little way off, talking to – arguing with – Asgarn. Baluch stood nearby, listening. Seeing Baluch gave Bramble a strange feeling – as though he should be aware of her. She knew him well enough by now to tell that he wasn't happy with whatever Asgarn was saying. She had felt that particular frown often enough. When the lookout called, the three men turned as one and suddenly had swords in their hands, glinting in the midday sun.

At first there were shouts and alarms as Acton called his men to order. They sprang up a little unsteadily from where they had been sprawled, but Bramble saw that they were not really drunk, just a bit merry. They were certainly sober enough to kill. They clutched their swords and presented their shields, although they clearly weren't sure what was happening.

Then the first rank of soldiers realised what was facing them. 'Ghosts!' they screamed. 'The dead are come back!' They backed away, their faces white, until they stood at the edge of the cliff, and had to stop. They were terrified. Some crouched to pray, some cast around wildly for a way out.

The women held back, but Tern and the ghosts moved forward. One of Acton's men screamed, 'I killed you, I killed you, you're dead!' and jumped from the cliff. His fellows barely noticed.

As they neared Acton, Bramble was struck by how small the ghosts seemed. Much shorter and slighter. They looked almost childlike compared to the tall, strongly muscled fighting men.

'Who is the leader here?' Tern demanded.

Acton stepped forward. In contrast to the ghosts, he seemed full of colour. His blue eyes were bright, his hair shone deep gold, his skin glowed with health. Even the simple dun and cream of his clothes seemed rich in comparison to the whiteness of the Turvite men. He was vividly alive; more alive, it seemed to Bramble, than anyone else there, even Tern. She felt relieved to see him, which was ridiculous, because she knew the gods always brought her to him, in every time she visited. He wore the brooch on his cloak. Baluch stood at his shoulder; paler hair, paler eyes, but fully there, listening as he always did.

'I am Acton, son of Asa. I am the lord of war,' he said.

'Go from here,' Tern declaimed, 'and you will be spared, as you spared the women of Turvite. Stay and be slaughtered.'

Behind Acton, his men shifted uncomfortably, muttering among themselves. Some were praying. Acton tilted his head, listening to them, and turned to face them, smiling.

'Lord,' one said, 'let us go from here.' It was the man Red, whose friend had been killed by the water sprite. He looked shaken and tired.

The other men murmured agreement, watching the ghosts with terror and fascination.

'We faced these men when they were alive, and killed them all,' Acton reassured them. 'Why should we fear them dead?'

Then, without warning, he laughed, spun, and swung his sword straight at the nearest ghost. Salmon. Salmon raised his own sword, but of course it was futile – Acton's blow went right through his sword and then through him as though he were not there, leaving Salmon unharmed, untouched – and no threat at all. All the women made some kind of sound: gasp, cry, moan. Acton's men whooped and cheered. They yelled, 'Ac-ton! Ac-*ton*!' and beat their swords on their shields.

'You'll never scare our lord of war, bitch!' a man yelled. 'Our lord fears nothing!'

Tern moved aside, towards the cliff. At first Acton let her go, assuming that she was retreating. Then she turned to face him again, and he saw her face. His laughter died, and his eyes narrowed. Bramble, through Baluch, had seen him look at enemies like that. Tern raised her hand and pointed at him.

'I curse you, Acton son of Asa. You shall never have what you truly want.'

Bramble had known what she was going to say, and yet the words cut through her. It was her reaction, not Piper's. Piper was watching, but her attention was mostly on Salmon, who was staring bleakly at his useless sword. She didn't care what Tern said to the blond man. But the curse seemed to drain strength and warmth from Bramble. She felt shaky, as though her own body were close to fainting. She had felt like that a couple of times before, when she had been thrown from the roan and had had the breath knocked out of her; panicky and shaky with shock. She didn't understand it. Why would she react like that to something she had heard in stories a dozen times before?

But Acton clearly felt none of her disquiet. His face lightened and he laughed again, eyes creasing up in genuine merriment. His hand went out, gesturing towards Turvite.

'I already have it,' he said gaily. Bramble felt the shakiness begin to leave her. Acton's strength seemed to steady her as well as his men. His laughter was comforting. She felt vaguely ashamed of that.

Tern shook her head. Bramble felt the gods flow around Tern, but she couldn't tell if they were arriving or leaving.

'Never,' Tern said. 'Brothers of mine, I give you my strength.'

The gods were leaving Tern. Something was missing. Bramble felt that Tern should have given something else – other words, some other action. No – feeling. That was what was missing. Feeling. Tern didn't really care about the dead men, and her words were only words.

Baluch had moved forwards at the first moment that the gods had begun to move, instinctively reaching out for Tern, but he was too late. She stepped over the cliff and dropped out of sight. It was so sudden that even Bramble was startled. Piper and the other women cried out. Acton's men shouted, half of them jubilant, half appalled.

They all crowded to the cliff edge to peer over, but there was no sign of her in the churning surf below.

Piper turned back to watch, eagerly looking for Salmon. The ghosts had been startled by Tern's disappearance, but now they hefted their weapons. One of them, the one Crab had walked beside up the hill, looked at her. She nodded. He nodded back, then threw his spear with all his might at Acton.

Acton raised his shield but the spear never reached it. It vanished in thin air once it left the ghost's hand, melting as the water sprite had melted. Some of Acton's men jeered, but other Turviters gripped their spears and rushed. Acton's men scrambled to meet them, training and experience pushing them to present shields as a solid fence. Acton and Asgarn were in the centre. Baluch took the rear, organising another line of men behind them in case any attackers broke through. Bramble almost expected the clang of spear on shield, all the unholy noise of battle that she had come to know so well.

But the ghosts silently slid into and through the fence of shields, through the line of swordsmen, and out the other side, stumbling to a stop before they got to Baluch's line. Acton's men shivered and made faces of disgust as the ghost chill hit them, but then they realised what had happened and broke ranks, laughing and jeering and whooping with relief.

The women watching cried out in despair. Piper's heart was beating too fast for comfort; too fast for safety. It seemed to swell in her chest as though it were going to burst. Bramble realised that Piper felt like she was going to die – wanted to die, to join with Salmon. No! Remember the baby, Bramble thought towards her. Willed her to look at Searose, to remember that her baby needed her. Astonishingly, Piper did. She turned her face away from Salmon and looked at Searose, clutched her tighter and cried over her wispy black hair. Bramble wasn't

sure if Piper had really responded to her thought, or if it were just
mother love working. It didn't matter. The dangerous moment had
passed.

At least, one dangerous moment.

The ghosts had backed away towards the cliff behind Acton's men,
leaving nothing between them and the women. Acton's men, now the
first jubilation had worn off, were glowering at the women. They were
tossing down their swords and shields. Some of them were smiling, and
it wasn't a smile Bramble liked. Then Acton stepped forward.

'I gave you until sunset to bury your dead and leave your houses. I
think you have just forfeited the right to bury your dead. Clearly, you
don't care if they sleep in peace or not. So I say now: take your things
and go.'

'They've forfeited more than their right to bury their dead,' Asgarn
objected. He came to stand next to Acton, glaring at the women.
'They've forfeited everything.'

Acton shook his head, and smiled irrepressibly. 'Come now,
Asgarn. It was a good try, but it failed. You would have done the same,
if you thought it might work. I would have.'

Asgarn looked exasperated and wiped one hand over his chin as
though buying time to decide what to say. 'The men deserve –'

Acton cut him off, his face for once serious. 'The men deserve to be
treated as though they are men of honour and not rutting drunken hogs.'

'Honour operates between equals,' Asgarn said. He gestured to the
women in disdain. Piper's heart leapt in fear as his glance passed over
her and the baby yelped as she gripped her too hard. 'These are not
equals. Look at them. They're barely human. Runts.' The last word
was spoken with scorn, a contempt that Bramble had heard many,
many times on the Road. 'Shagging Travellers,' were the words usually spoken in her time, but the tone was the same. The men rumbled
their agreement, but Acton wasn't moved.

'I gave my word,' he said. 'Go,' he said to the crowd of women.

Some of them turned to head down the hill, but Snapper folded her
arms. 'Where do we go?' she asked. 'A bunch of women and childer,
with no way of making a living. We know how to fish, but this is the
only harbour from here to forever. Easy to save our lives and feel good
about yourself, but we're still dead by the end of winter, with no shelter and no food.'

Asgarn turned away with a shrug of distaste, but Acton listened, his face growing serious. Baluch said something quietly in his ear, and he nodded.

'There's a village,' he said. 'It's abandoned. You can have it on two conditions. One is that our boats are left undisturbed as they go up and down river. The other is that you accept any other . . .' he searched for a word, but failed to find it, by the look on his face, 'any other people who need shelter. I don't know what the place is named, but it's a few miles upstream of here. Call it Sanctuary.'

'Go on, then,' he added to the women, as though shooing a flock of chickens from his door, 'go on, get going.' Laughter threaded underneath his words and Bramble felt a mixture of annoyance and admiration. He was such a – an *idiot*! He could be as generous as a rich man on his deathbed, but he couldn't see that Asgarn was dangerous. He was too straightforward himself to recognise the point where shrewdness turned to deviousness. That was a point that Asgarn had reached long ago.

The women gazed at their men, gathered on the cliff edge. Acton's men didn't like it. They glared at the women and then one of them started to bang his sword on his shield and shout, 'Ac-*ton*! Ac-*ton*!' Others joined in. Where before it had been a noise of celebration, now it was a threat.

The women hastily gathered their children and turned to go, talking about the new village as if to pretend that they weren't frightened. Some of them knew it. They carefully didn't mention why a village would be abandoned, but after the threats from the soldiers, they were filled with relief to turn towards their houses. Except Piper. She looked helplessly towards Salmon. He pointed to the north, towards a group of large boulders down the hillside about fifty paces away. She nodded and gave the baby to Snapper, kissing her on the head first. Then she walked down with a group of other women, slipping between a gap in the boulders as they passed so that Acton's men wouldn't realise she was there.

Salmon was waiting for her. They came close together, but couldn't touch. He curved his hand as though touching Piper's face, and the tears flowed hot down her cheeks. Bramble was tired of grief. She felt exhausted by it. There had been so many deaths: Sebbi and Elric and Asa and Friede and Edwa, so much grief and so much mourning and so much revenge. She wondered why the gods were keeping her here, now the important part of the story had happened. What use was it, forcing her to see, to feel this, too?

'Herring got away on the boat,' Piper said to Salmon, talking around the lump in her throat, sobbing a little. His face lit with relief. His son then, too, was safe. Bramble wondered how old Herring was. Where the boat had gone, if this was the only port 'from here to forever'. The Wind Cities, maybe. Surely these people had heard of them?

Then Acton appeared through the gap in the rocks, fumbling with his trousers. He had clearly slipped away for a quiet piss, and he stopped in surprise and a little embarrassment as he saw Piper and Salmon.

'You'd better get going,' he said to Piper. 'My men are drinking again. I can hold them a while longer, but after that, I make no promises.'

'I don't understand why you are stopping them,' Piper said. 'I always heard the blond barbarians raped and tortured women.'

Acton's face filled with incongruous enjoyment, as though she had made a joke. 'My mother had strong views about rapists,' he said, his eyes dancing, and even Piper, standing by her dead husband, was warmed by that smile. Bramble felt a stab of irritation with her. He's your enemy, she wanted to say. But he was also Piper's protector, which had not been part of the story. Bramble had never heard of Sanctuary.

Acton looked at Salmon, who was glaring at him, and back at Piper. 'Your man will be fine, you know,' he reassured her. 'He died fighting, his sword in his hand. Swith the Strong will welcome him into the hall of heroes, and he will feast in the company of the brave forever.' His tone was earnest. There was no doubt that he believed it.

Piper looked at him, bewildered. 'What are you talking about?' she said. 'Death is just a door. Afterwards, we go on to rebirth, if we have lived well and justly and pleased the gods.'

Acton's face twisted in surprise.

Astonishingly, this was what the gods had wanted her to see, to hear, because the waters rose up like a breaking wave and smashed her away into darkness.

LEOF

Keeping Arrow, his chaser, in condition was the perfect excuse to get away from the fort. Leof felt ashamed that he needed to, but it had been two days since Arrow had been exercised, and she was getting restive. His groom was quite capable of riding her usually, but in this mood Leof wouldn't trust her to anyone but himself. That was his excuse, anyway. He rode down the valley, inspecting the ditches and stake-traps which were being built in rings around the hill. Every man from the town who could be spared was working there, for all the daylight hours, but even so, it was progressing slower than Leof would have liked. That was another good reason for a ride, to encourage the workers and speed up the work.

At the bottom of the hill he turned aside and went down his favourite path, which led through the valley to a spring-fed pool which flowed out to become the best water source for miles. He told himself he was looking for a way to defend that water, which was crucial for the farmers in the valley. The pool itself was on common ground, and no one's direct responsibility. Which made it his.

The pool was overshadowed by a huge old cedar tree, the fruit of some long-ago warlord's trade with the Wind Cities. The story went that he had swapped his daughter for the seedling, but Leof doubted that. No warlord would give away so great a prize without getting a lot more than a tree back.

Under the sweeping branches the cedar scent was so strong that Leof felt slightly drunk. He dismounted and led Arrow to the pool and waited while she dipped her head to drink, glad of a moment's quiet. It was cool and beautiful here, and it seemed a long way away from the noise and movement at the fort. The pool was ringed with moss-covered rocks and the water spread out between them serenely, with only the faint ripple from the underground spring disturbing its reflection of the tree.

Leof was watching a branch reflected in the water, thinking about Sorn and the way her hair caught the light with sudden fire, when he saw a face appear in the pool.

He jumped back, startled, and Arrow's head came up with a whicker.

There was a man standing on the other side of the pool, smiling at him, his hands raised to show that he meant no harm. Leof relaxed a little, although he was silently berating himself. No one should have been able to sneak up on him like that! He was a warrior, not a love-struck mooncalf.

The man was old, very old, with long white hair braided into plaits around his face and with the back left free. He had a full beard, too, which was unusual. So were his clothes – leggings and gaiters and a long, full tunic, almost like a woman's. He wore a gold arm-ring in the shape of a dragon high on his left arm. His eyes were very blue and he had surprisingly good teeth for such an old man. Leof wished his own teeth were that straight.

He nodded. 'Greetings, sir.'

'Greetings to you also, young man.' The old man looked at him consideringly.

Then a voice seemed to come from inside Leof's head, or from the water, or from the air itself; it surrounded him, it filled him.

'Listen,' it said. It was his mother's voice.

He and Arrow had ridden to this pool a hundred times before, but Leof felt suddenly that he had ventured into an unknown wilderness, where anything might happen. His heart sped up, his hands were clammy, and he felt for his sword.

'The Lake sent you,' Leof said with certainty.

The man smiled. 'Well done! I was expecting you to ask, "Who are you?" Indeed, I am her ambassador. Her mouthpiece, if you will.' He had a beautiful voice, warm and deep and flexible, but there was a hint of an accent, a slight brogue. A voice it would be easy to trust.

Leof set his heart against being persuaded by that voice. 'And?'

'Child, there is great danger approaching, and you will need the powers of the Lake to survive it.'

'*I* will need?'

'Your people. All our peoples. The Lake is not your enemy, but she will not be conquered. There is no living power in this world which could conquer her.'

Leof latched onto that hint. 'What about the power of the dead?'

'If the dead acquire such power as that, your people will be in a sorry state. Convince your lord.'

Leof smiled ruefully. 'My lord goes his own way.'

The man laughed, companionably. 'So did mine, once. But if you are loyal to him, you will convince him. The Lake will resist.'

Leof hesitated, but his inborn impulse to honesty won out. 'He doesn't believe in the Lake,' he admitted.

The man went very still and his eyes widened a little. He whistled in disbelief. Leof was surprised by the purity of the sound – it was like the whistle of a young boy.

'That – explains.' He lifted a hand. Oddly, given the roughness of his clothes, his fingernails were long and well cared for. 'Be resolute,' he said.

Leof blinked. The man was just – gone. Just *not there*. He hadn't stepped away, he hadn't moved. Just disappeared. Leof began to shake. True enchantment. *True* enchantment, not necromancy or trick or potion. He had never heard of such power – and Leof knew that it was the power of the Lake, not of the man. The man had been an ordinary human. Leof forced himself to cross the stream on the stones that ringed the pool and look at the ground where the man had stood.

He felt a great relief when he saw footprints, even though they only led from the pool *to* the tree, and not away from it. At least his sense that the man was alive and real had been right. An ambassador from the Lake. He jumped back across the stream with more energy, and collected Arrow.

The question was, should he tell Sorn about this? He should tell Thegan, no doubt, although Thegan would jump to the conclusion that this man was the enchanter he had declared was his enemy. His shocking ability to disappear would be the proof. Leof paused, reining Arrow in at the end of the river path, looking across the field to the fort on its hill. *Should* he tell Thegan? If he didn't, was that treason? Consorting with the enemy?

He longed to discuss it with Sorn, to lay it all out for consideration by those wise green eyes. But private conversation had to be avoided at all costs. So, what if he said nothing? If Thegan ever found out, it would be the pressing box for sure, and then the gibbet. The sun was going down. He would miss evening muster and inspection of the horses. He clicked his tongue to Arrow and she started off gladly, happy to be heading home. He put aside the decision for now. Or perhaps . . . This would be a good excuse to go to Carlion. He could put Wil in charge for a few days and ride down to tell Thegan personally. It was too . . . odd . . . to put in a message. How could he describe it properly?

Then he could leave Sorn for a while. Let them both recover. Perhaps even persuade Thegan to keep him in Carlion and send Eddil back to command in Sendat. He had at least as much experience as Leof.

He *had* to tell Thegan. The man had even *asked* him to. He ignored a suspicion that it would make the situation in Baluchston worse. But Thegan wasn't going to listen to him about the Lake anyway. He cantered Arrow up the hill more cheerfully. Secrecy wasn't in his nature and he felt much better having decided to take action.

As he went, he saw a local farmer pacing out the course of the next chase. He sighed. As temporary lord in Sendat, he couldn't compete in any of the chases. He had to hand out the prizes if asked. Since Bramble's roan, Thorn, had died he'd gone back to racing in every chase he could, instead of just the ones Bramble wasn't in, and he missed the regular dose of excitement. Missed winning, too. He patted Arrow on the neck and said, 'One day soon, girl,' and she tossed her head in response as he headed her for home.

Leof left the next morning, with no more than a public explanation to Sorn that he needed to discuss some elements of the fort's defence directly with Thegan. She was puzzled, he could see, and so was Wil, but they both accepted his statement. Sorn organised food for him to take and Bandy, his groom, prepared for the trip with enthusiasm. He had a ghoulish curiosity and couldn't wait to take a look at the wreckage the ghosts had caused.

The trip to Carlion was uneventful, although everywhere they stopped he was besieged with people wanting to be reassured that they weren't going to be murdered in their beds. He did the best he could, thinking wryly that they'd never have dared accost Thegan in the same way.

Carlion itself was . . . odd. Leof realised that he'd expected to see the kinds of things he had seen in other towns in Cliff Domain which had been attacked by the Ice King: houses burnt down, or stripped bare of all they had. But ghosts had no reason to loot. It appeared they didn't use fire, either. They just killed.

So the streets of Carlion were the same as ever, aside from a few shattered and hastily repaired shutters and doors. But there were far fewer people on the streets than the last time he was there. He saw fearful eyes peering out at him from behind windows and doors as he rode down the steep streets towards the Moot Hall. But the fearful people staying indoors weren't enough to account for the emptiness of the streets. Carlion was a town stripped bare, but of people, not things. Arrow's hoofsteps echoed forlornly from the brick walls, too easy to hear now the normal bustle of cart and handbarrows and vendors was gone. Leof could even hear the seagulls down at the harbour, and the wash of the waves against the docks.

The Moot Hall, he found with some relief, was bustling as usual, although most of the bustle was provided by men in Thegan's uniform. He was hailed immediately by one of the sergeants.

'My lord's in his office. Top of the stairs. Is there news from Sendat?'

There was anxiety in his voice and Leof remembered that he was a local man, with family in the town below the fort. Leof shook his head and smiled reassuringly. 'Would I be here if there was?'

He handed Arrow over to Bandy and left him to organise their quarters. No doubt there would be plenty of choice.

Thegan's office – once the Town Clerk's, Leof had no doubt – was opulent in a way that sat oddly with Thegan's disciplined style. It was furnished in walnut and rosewood, and every piece of seating was cushioned in yellow velvet. There were golden curtains at the windows and the frieze that ran around the room was of sunflowers and green leaves. Leof remembered that the last Town Clerk of Carlion had been a woman. Dead, now, he presumed. Thegan looked slightly out of place in the office, but it was clear that he was unaware of his surroundings.

'Leof!' he exclaimed, waving away a Carlionite, a small man with a merchant's potbelly and huge moustaches. 'Trouble?'

The small man raised worried eyes to Leof and visibly braced himself for bad news.

'No, no, no problems,' Leof said, smiling at the man. He was so tired of smiling reassuringly. 'But I needed to speak to you privately, my lord.'

The man immediately packed up his papers and bowed himself out. 'Tomorrow, Sirin,' Thegan said. 'In the morning.'

Leof waited until the door was closed and then bowed.

'Well?' Thegan demanded. 'I hope you have a good reason for this.'

'I think so, my lord, or I would not have come.'

Thegan nodded and gestured to Leof to sit down. He lowered himself onto the velvet cushion with some relief. The ride had been a long one. He couldn't resist a quick glance around the room and a smile at Thegan. Thegan smiled back, the real smile.

'I feel like I'm in a bordello,' he admitted, leaning back in his chair. 'But it reassures the Carlionites if I keep changes to a minimum.'

Leof nodded, and hesitated. He wasn't quite sure how to proceed, although he had practised this scene in his head on the way. 'The Lake sent an ambassador,' he said finally. He described what had happened by the pool.

Thegan sat upright. 'So . . .' he said. 'Our enchanter shows himself.'

'Or the Lake –'

An impatient wave cut him off. 'The Lake! It's just water, for Swith's sake! It can't *think*! This man, this old man, yes, he's the one we have to search for. Did you send out search parties?'

Leof gaped. It had not even occurred to him to look. The old man's disappearance had been so . . . final.

'I . . . I searched myself, around the site, my lord,' he said carefully, 'but there was no sign. Not even a footprint of him leaving.'

'Where did he arrive from, then?'

Reluctantly, Leof said, 'The pool.'

'So he came from the Lake by boat –'

'No, my lord,' Leof said firmly. 'That pool does not connect with the Lake. It flows to the Simple River and thence to the sea.'

Thegan paused. 'So he is very powerful, then. Well, you did right to come to tell me. I will consider it. Go and have your meal.'

He turned away to look out the window, but Leof lingered. 'My lord, I hoped . . . I hoped I might be able to stay here and help you. Perhaps Eddil could take over at Sendat . . .'

Thegan stared at him, frowning. 'Bored already? Defending my fort is not unimportant, Leof.'

'My lord, I know that. But the defences are proceeding, the smiths know their tasks . . . I could be of more use to you here. Eddil has more experience than I do at fortifications.'

Thegan's mouth relaxed. 'True. But I wouldn't leave my wife alone with that tomcat for more than an hour.'

'He would never betray you!'

Thegan grinned. 'Some men can't help themselves. At the least, he'd make a play for that holy little thing who waits on Sorn, and then there'd be a real problem! Officers are one thing, but a good sergeant like Alston is hard to find.'

He came around the desk and laid his hand on Leof's shoulders. 'I know it doesn't seem too exciting, Leof, but you are where I need you.'

Leof nodded. What could he say? 'You shouldn't trust me around your wife, either'? A death warrant for both of them.

'Do you have a report of your progress?' Thegan asked, all business again.

Leof handed over the detailed report which he had spent his last night in Sendat compiling. Unless the ghosts attacked again, he thought, I'm doomed to go back. He had a dreadful double impulse, to run as far as he could from Sendat – to take ship for the Wind Cities, perhaps, and leave everything he knew behind – and to ride immediately for Sendat and throw himself at Sorn's feet, declaring his love.

What shocked him most about the thought was that he really didn't know which he wanted more.

BRAMBLE

THERE WAS WATER moving nearby. Bramble could hear the slap and hiss of small waves on shingle, a sound that took her back to a day spent with Maryrose in Carlion before the wedding, when they had wandered over the town and the harbour, down to the small beach, and looked out over the waves. They had talked about their parents moving in to Carlion to live with Maryrose and Merrick in the new house after it was built.

'They'll be safer here than in Wooding, so near the fort,' Maryrose had said, and Bramble had nodded agreement. Yes, Carlion was much safer. So they had thought. But now there were no safe places anywhere, and the dead could rise with axes in their hands and kill, and nothing could stop them. Except Acton, maybe. She forced down the choke of grief and concentrated as her sight cleared. If she had to live every second of Acton's life, she would.

They were down at the beach, sure enough, in Turvite, on a cold still day. Late autumn, maybe. But where before fishing boats had been drawn up on the shingle, now there were boat cradles reaching high ribs that seemed to mimic the cliffs around the harbour. Three of them. They were holding the skeletons of larger versions of the boats Acton had rowed down the river. But these, it was clear, would have masts as well as oars. They were long, flat-bottomed boats with high prows and sterns, a shape much like the reed boats of the Lake People, but bigger. Ships.

She was inhabiting a man, and she was so inured to it by now that when he hitched his trousers to get a more comfortable position for his privates, she didn't even wince. She thought at first that it was a stranger, but then the man reached out a hand past the cradle rib to touch the side of the ship and she recognised the hand. Baluch, but a Baluch so enraptured by the ships that he had not a single part of his mind to give to music.

'You've done well while I've been away,' a voice said. Baluch turned and there was Asgarn, wiry hair bristling with energy, blue eyes bright with admiration. He, too, was entranced by the ships.

Acton's voice replied from behind Baluch. 'We'll be ready by summer.' Baluch turned as Acton slapped the side of the ship as Bramble would give a friendly slap to a horse. 'We're collecting cargo now. I'm sending trappers out during winter for pelts and I've got a lumber crew in the forest picking out fine hardwood. That's scarce in the Wind Cities, the old men say.'

Asgarn nodded. 'Next year we might have grain as well. Bone carvings, too, when our men have more time.'

Baluch added, 'Metalwork, once the forges are set up. I'm sending out a message inviting charcoal burners to come to T'vit.'

Asgarn looked sceptical. 'Why would they leave their steadings to join you?'

Baluch traded glances with Acton, and abruptly the music was back, a low horn note. Bramble was good enough at deciphering his thoughts now to know that the note – and the look – meant warning. But Acton grinned at him. Not reassuring, just shagging cheeky. Acton knew that whatever he was about to say would cause a stir.

'Because here they'll be living in a free town.'

Asgarn frowned. 'What does that mean?'

'It means that T'vit is governed by a town council. Like the Moot, but permanent. It decides how the town is run. The council is elected by the people who live here.' With an air of getting it all out, even the worst, he added, 'Including women.'

Bramble thought Asgarn might have an apoplexy, he turned so red. 'Are you insane? And what do you mean, "is"? Have you set this up already?'

Acton nodded. 'It's going well. I'm the head of the council at the moment, of course, but in time I may be able to hand it over altogether.'

'Did you consult the Moot about this?'

For a moment, Acton looked very much like his grandfather. The same stubbornness. 'They gave me T'vit. I can do what I like with it.'

'Give away your power? What kind of fool does that?'

'One who doesn't want it,' Baluch said.

'Then hand it over to someone who'll use it properly! Not a bunch of traders and . . . and *charcoal burners*!' Asgarn took a step closer to Acton and reached out a hand in supplication. Bramble thought that he really did want Acton's understanding. That he respected him enough to want his support. 'Can't you see the opportunity we have here? This country is *empty*. We needed the Moot before because we were all crowded up ham by haunch and we had to have a way of resolving disputes. But there's so much land here that each chief could rule a vast territory, rule without concerns about how his decisions would be greeted by others. There could be *real* power, not negotiations and bargains and paying compensation because a cow cropped another man's pasture! Can't you *see* what we could have?'

Acton was staring at him with a frown. Bramble tensed. This was the moment, then. This was the time when Acton helped establish the warlords. No wonder she'd never liked Asgarn. Baluch, however, didn't seem to pay much attention. He looked back at the ship instead of at Acton, smoothing his hand over the planks of the keel. Bramble could have hit him. Look at them! she thought. Look!

'The Moot has served us very well,' Acton said. Baluch looked up and nodded agreement.

Asgarn set his mouth. 'One man ruling a large territory would be better. A clear line of command, a clear area of responsibility, each chieftain able to work for his own good and secure his own power.'

So there it was, spelt out. The warlord's creed. Bramble was sickened by it, and yet felt curiously exalted, because Acton was shaking his head. 'Have you discussed this with the Moot council?'

Asgarn hesitated, and Bramble knew what that meant. He'd been sounding out the members of the council, doing deals, finding out what each man most wanted. Acton waited.

'Not in full council, no,' Asgarn said. 'But I am sure they will see the truth of what I say.'

'That may be. But I think I will have a few words to say as well.'

In Baluch's head, the warning music rose sharply at the look on Asgarn's face.

'Perhaps we should go together,' Asgarn said slowly. Baluch put a cautioning hand on Acton's arm. Acton grinned at him.

'Baluch reminds me that we have much more to do here if we want to take the dragon's road in Spring. I will follow you to Wili's steading for the Mid-Winter Moot.'

Asgarn nodded sharply, turned on his heel and headed up the shore towards the houses of T'vit. Acton and Baluch watched him go.

'Don't trust him,' Baluch said.

'I don't,' Acton replied. 'But I didn't think he was mad enough to destroy the Moot.'

'He's never forgiven you for Sebbi's death.'

Acton's eyes clouded. 'I've never forgiven myself.'

'What will you do at the Moot?'

Acton grinned, his eyes gleaming with anticipation. 'It's a different kind of battle. I've watched Harald fight that fight enough times to know how it's done. Don't worry. The Moot will survive.'

Bramble was astonished and elated that Acton had refused Asgarn's arguments, but she was also confused. What had happened to change things? To make Acton a warlord, to have him help set up the warlord system? What had they offered him that had won him over?

She didn't have time to speculate further, because the waves on the beach rose suddenly and crashed over her, tumbling her into darkness.

There was warmth on her shoulder: warm lips, moving, kissing, a tongue touching. Her side was pressed up against something warm, all down her naked flank there was warmth. For one long moment, Bramble simply felt it; heat, comfort, teasing pleasure. Something loosened inside her and relaxed. Then a hand stroked down from her shoulder to her breast and she realised: Acton! That's Acton's hand!

At the same moment sight came back and she saw him, gold head bent to kiss the soft flesh above her breast, hand cradling the breast itself. Get me out of here! she shouted in her mind to the gods, but they did nothing.

Then the woman pushed him away. Bramble felt a combination of emotions from her – affection, unease, a lingering pleasure mixed with revulsion. It was so much like her own emotions that she couldn't quite tell where the woman's feelings stopped and her own began. Acton sat up and looked at her ruefully, as though he were aware how she felt. He had shaved off his beard. She wondered why. It made him look younger.

'Oh, Wili,' he said regretfully, 'was it that bad?'

Wili smiled carefully. Her eyes pricked with tears, but she didn't let them fall. Bramble could sense that she didn't want to hurt his feelings;

but that she wanted to be out of that bed and dressed, securely, with trousers and belt and a good strong knife at her waist.

'Not *bad*,' she said. 'Well, I had to do it, but I don't think I'll be doing it again.'

A light broke on Bramble and she thought, they just made his son. The son of the woman who would have nothing to do with men, except that she tried it once with Acton . . .

He grimaced. 'I'm sorry. I did the best I could.'

She reached out and tousled his hair, making him look like a five-year-old. 'It was a good try. But –'

'It'd be different if you loved me.'

'Or if you loved me? I don't think so.'

His face clouded. Wili drew her knees up to her chest and hugged them. She felt safer that way. Calmer. The feeling of wanting to cry faded from Bramble's mind.

Wili risked letting go with one hand and touched the back of his arm.

'If I loved you the way I loved Friede,' he said, 'it would have to make a difference.'

Wili made a noise of disbelief. 'I doubt it.'

He was offended, but she smiled grimly. 'You didn't love her,' she said simply. 'She knew it.'

He sat up straight in indignation, the blanket falling away to show his muscled chest. 'I did!'

'Ha!' Wili seemed to take some satisfaction in cutting him down to size. 'You liked her. Maybe you were fond of her. Maybe you wanted her. But you didn't love her.'

He looked worried, perhaps sad. 'Did she tell you that?'

'She did. Not that she had to. I could tell. If she'd gone to your bed like the rest of them you'd never have given her another thought!'

'That's not true! Friede was . . . different.'

'Because you thought she needed to be protected. She hated that, you know. She didn't want to be protected. That's why she loved Baluch. He never protected her. Didn't think she needed protection.'

Acton looked down at the bed and stayed silent for a while. 'I don't understand love,' he admitted finally. 'All women are beautiful, even the ugly ones. All of you are delicious.'

'We're not honeycakes,' Wili said quietly, but not to interrupt him.

'Friede was my friend, and that felt different from all the others.'

'So maybe you just called it love, when it was friendship all the time.' Wili patted his hand. 'Friendship's nothing to be ashamed of.'

He looked up and smiled, mischief gleaming. 'Do you think I'll ever love?'

'Not while you go around bedding every woman you meet!'

He grinned, mischief growing, and was clearly ready to tease Wili about being one of those women. Time to change the subject, girl, Bramble thought, and Wili did think a lot like her, because immediately she said, 'What is the Moot saying?'

His face became serious. 'I have ratification for the free towns, to be set up like Turvite, with town councils elected by the people. I have agreement that there will be no thralls.'

'How did you get that?' she asked, astonished.

'Fear. I used that traitor Uen as an example. We are too vulnerable, here in a new land, to have men with us who are not oath-sworn, who do not have a stake in our future here.' He smiled slowly. 'It took some time, but they agreed. Now we just have to re-establish the All Moot and I can go back to actually getting some work done!'

So, Bramble thought, it *was* his idea to get rid of thralls. That was well done. But was fear his real reason, or was it something else? Free towns, no thralls – how could that come from the man who established warlords? Did he simply get voted down? She was tired of being confused about him. She wanted some solid sense of what he was really like. Something beyond fighting and politicking and taking revenge. Or was that all there was to him? She didn't believe that. Mainly because of Baluch and Wili. They didn't think that, and they were not fools.

Wili laughed at him and asked, as she had asked once before, 'How are the boats coming along?'

The gods were not interested in his answer because the waters rolled over her and dumped her down a cascade. Bramble was falling, and falling, with nothing solid to hold on to.

As soon as she came to herself, she knew that she was not with Baluch. This was a much taller man who moved heavily, shifting from foot to foot with a perceptible thump. For the first time she became aware of how lightly Baluch moved, how easily his body obeyed him. She hadn't noticed before because it was how her own body moved, and so she had just accepted it. But this body was clumsy, lumbering. A big man, with big muscles, she thought, and weighed down somehow, not just by the heavy winter clothes he wore against the biting cold.

He was standing in a wood on a hill, a spur of pines on the edge of a much greater forest. He looked down to a steading, a snow-covered collection of houses and barns surrounded by pasture and some fenced fields, although pasture and ploughed ground looked alike under the thick snow. Bramble realised that it was Hawk's – that is, Wili's – steading. She had not seen it from exactly this angle before, but she was sure. There were some figures, well wrapped up, moving between house and animal barns. A woman emerged and shook out a blanket. Bramble recognised her: Wili. Her pregnancy wasn't showing yet, so not much time had passed. Wili had named the child Thegan, she remembered. He had finished what Acton started, the invasion of the Domains, right up to the Sharp River. Wili stood upright and looked up the slope, shading her eyes. Two children raced out the door past her and she called them back.

The sky was grey, but there was no wind. The man Bramble inhabited put up a hand to shake the snow from his collar, and she saw that he had copper hair springing thickly on hand and wrist. Maybe the one who had been in the boat with Acton, whose friend had died? Red. The more she thought about it, the more she was sure, because the only emotions she could sense were grief and fear, combined. It was a familiar grief, constantly refreshed, and it was threaded with guilt, because he was still alive.

Bramble knew that feeling. She felt sorry for him, but she was worried. What was he doing up here in the woodland, waiting, skulking? Where was Acton? Surely it was too soon for him to die? He couldn't be much older than the last time she had seen him, not if Wili were pregnant. The stories all talked about him ruling Turvite, setting up the warlord system, pushing the invasion further and further – surely that would take years more?

Then Red saw Acton, down at the steading, coming out of the main house, talking briefly with Wili, and then going to a barn. A few moments later he emerged, riding one of the stocky little ponies Bramble had come to admire.

He rode up the slope and passed Red, whose breathing came faster as Acton went by. Red reached down and brought a knife out of his boot. Not an eating knife. This was a fighting dagger, meant for killing.

Acton rode further up the slope, his breath and his horse's blowing clouds of steam. He was growing another beard, but it was still short and outlined his face. His expression was hard to read; the set look might just be due to the cold, but she didn't think so. He looked like someone going to do a job he disliked.

Halfway up, though, his face changed. He looked into the wood-land and smiled, as though he had seen someone he knew. Bramble knew that smile, the sideways smile that he cozened women with. Bramble could have hit him. He was courting someone again. Now, of all times! But instead of riding towards whatever girl was smiling back at him, he raised a hand in farewell and continued on.

Further up the hill the forest curved around and continued in a thick ribbon of larch and spruce trees along the lower slopes of the moun-tains. As Acton disappeared into those, Red followed him, skirting the open spaces until his path crossed Acton's tracks just inside the belt of trees. Then he followed the tracks through the trees. Where they ended, he waited. Acton was higher up the steep hillside, near the cliff which showed the entrances to some caves. Dotta's caves? Bramble wondered, and then was sure. It had to be, so close to Wili's settlement.

Acton tethered his horse to a low bush and disappeared inside the cave. Immediately Red started to run forwards, treading as much in the horse's tracks as he could. He fetched up, breathing hard, against the cliff face next to the cave entrance, and peered cautiously around into the cave. The passageway, winding between rough walls, was empty, but Acton's tracks were clear in the dirt, overlaying another set of foot-prints.

So someone was waiting for you, Bramble thought. What a sur-prise. I wonder if Asgarn is man enough to do his own killing.

That was the moment that Bramble understood. Acton never had set up the warlord system. They had killed him first and used his name afterwards to gather support.

She was filled with rage. Asgarn and shagging Oddi. This was their doing.

Red crept along down the passageway as stealthily as he could, and paused at a turn, where the rock screened the cave beyond. There were voices, hard to decipher. Red didn't have Baluch's sharp ears. He edged closer to the opening.

Then Bramble heard Acton laugh in response to some comment. 'Is this what you and Oddi have been scheming about? The Moot has ruled us for a thousand years, would you give all that history away?

The Moot *works*. It has proved itself. That's why I copied it in T'vit. It's a curb on the headstrong and the foolish. The weak are protected.'

'The weak are *favoured*, you mean.' That was Asgarn's voice, of course, bitter and harsh.

Red slid to the very edge of the opening and peered around. Beyond was Dotta's cave, but it smelt stale, of old ashes and grease from the small oil lamp that sat on a rock, giving a wavering and fitful light. Dotta was long gone, and her sacred fire with her. Bramble hoped she was safe.

Acton and Asgarn were facing each other, looking like two versions of the same man. Both tall, both fair, both strong and wide across the shoulders. Only the hair was different, and the way they stood: Asgarn with shoulders hunched and fists clenched; Acton upright and at ease, Asa's brooch on his cloak catching the lamplight like a star. Oh, be careful! Bramble thought. Don't be so sure of yourself.

'The strong are forced to carry the weak,' Asgarn said.

Acton looked at him with curiosity. 'Because we are all one people, of one blood. Should we not help each other?'

'The strong don't need help and the weak should pay for the help they need.'

'Pay how?'

'In obedience. And other ways, if necessary. Labour. Gold. Goods.'

'No,' Acton said. 'The chieftain has a duty to his people. Generosity pleases the gods.'

'A ruler should look to his own interests first, and then give what he can, in return for loyalty.'

Acton paused, as though he could see that this argument could go on forever without either of them shifting position. 'I cannot support you,' he said. 'I think you will find that most of the Moot council is of my view. I have already received endorsement for my free towns.'

'Aye, they're short-sighted, like you. They don't see where that will take us. But uninterested in power? I don't think so. I think enough of them like the idea of being fully in control of their own territory. But it would be just like you to convince them. Just like you to lead us all into disaster, like you always do. Come over the mountains! you said, and so all of them went and died, just so you could feel good. If we'd taken this territory in the first place, Swef and Asa – yes, and Friede, too – they'd all still be alive.'

'That's true,' Acton said quietly.

'Oh, yes, admitting it makes you sound so noble, doesn't it? You're good at that, aren't you? At having grand schemes. You're good at convincing people to die for some stupid noble idea. Like you convinced my *brother*!'

Asgarn sprang, drawing the knife from his belt. Like Red's, this was a killing dagger, not a belt knife. Acton was ready for him, his own knife out and his arm up to deflect the first blow. They began to wrestle for supremacy, kicking and hitting, shouldering each other around the cave.

Bramble could feel Red tensing, getting ready. If only Acton had lived! If only he had swung the Moot his way, there would have been no warlords, ever. How different the future might have been. The future came down to now, to this moment in a cave. To Red.

Because it was clear that Asgarn was tiring. Acton's immense strength was slowly winning out, forcing Asgarn back, step by step. Once he was pressed against the wall of the cave he would have no chance. If Red chose not to help Asgarn . . .

Bramble felt his muscles tense in preparation and screamed into his head: *No! Noooo!* He faltered and she was exultant. She *could* stop him. She *would*, and take whatever consequences that came.

She gathered her strength to shout again into his mind, but the gods flooded into her, overwhelmed her, pressed her back, silenced her, and Red leapt from the shadows and raised his knife high.

He swung the knife down into the middle of Acton's back, and then reversed his grip so he could strike up, under the ribcage, up into the heart. Bramble was straining to break free of the gods, straining to touch his mind again, so as the knife went up, and in, it was as though her own hand guided it, her own arm gave it strength.

Acton slumped down, the knife still in him. Asgarn kicked him as he fell and bent over him to say harshly, 'Before you go to the cold hells, tell my brother from me that I have avenged him.' He glanced at Red, who stood frozen, staring at Acton, his heart thumping and his eyes burning dry. Asgarn's face drained of fury. 'And tell Geb the same, for Red.'

At the name, Red's eyes filled with tears and he took a deep, sobbing breath. He nodded slowly, in a kind of desolate satisfaction.

Acton's eyes had rolled up and his laboured breathing changed to the death rattle. Bramble was almost angry with him. It seemed impossible that he should be lying there. He was so strong! He was too full of life to let a nothing like Red overcome him. Each laboured breath dragged the air from her own lungs, so that it felt like she was dying, too. She needed him to get up. Get up! she pleaded silently. But his breaths were weaker, the rattle more pronounced. Her eyes were full of tears, but they were Red's tears, and his heart, beating fast, and his lungs at last dragging breath into them. She wanted to reach out and touch Acton, to at least ease his passing, but of course Red did not respond to the thought. She had never felt so helpless, not even when the roan was dying in her arms. At least she had been able to comfort the roan in his last moments.

Asgarn reached out and ripped the brooch from Acton's cloak. He gave it to Red, and put a hand on his shoulder. 'That was well done. Keep this in memory of a great deed that must remain secret.'

Red nodded. His heart was slowing, his eyes clearing as he wiped tears away. There was a sense of freedom from pain and pressure, as though Acton's death had lanced a boil.

'You know where to put the body?'

'Aye.'

Asgarn clapped him on the shoulder again. Playing the part of the warlord, Bramble thought bitterly.

'Loyalty will be rewarded,' he said. He shrugged his cloak back into place and strode out of the cave without a backwards glance. Red looked down at Acton. Blood was seeping out of his back and spreading across the cave floor, but he was still breathing, just.

Red bent and took him under the arms. Bramble had so wanted to touch him, but not like this . . . not to take him to his grave. Red began dragging him to a passageway in the back of the cave, the same passageway that Dotta had led Gris down, the one she had told Bramble to remember.

Bramble braced herself for the long, winding path down to the painted cave, but the waters came: as slow and inexorable as funeral music, as strong as winter. The water covered her, smothered her, stopped her breathing as Acton's breathing was stopping. She had killed him, and now she was dying, and that was as it should be. She was content with that; so when the waters receded and left her high and dry under the trees of the Forest, it seemed like a betrayal.

MARTINE

THE MIST WAS so thick that they could barely see each other's faces, but there was movement out there, beyond their circle. From the corner of their eyes, by the prickling on the back of their necks, they knew something, or some things, were out there, circling them, watching, listening. Searching.

Martine opened her mouth to speak, but Safred put her finger to her lips, signalling for silence. They leant close together over Bramble so that their heads were almost touching.

'This isn't about you going to the island,' Martine whispered. She was sure of that, somehow. 'What are they looking for?'

Safred looked down at Bramble. 'We should have left her out there,' she breathed, worried. 'Rigged up a sun shelter or something. She would have been safe there.'

'What do you mean?'

'What she's doing leaves her soul unprotected. Going, she was protected by the gods at the altar. If she is coming back . . . perhaps the mist is their protection against – against whatever threatens.'

'The Forest?'

Safred shrugged helplessly. 'I don't think so. Something beyond life.'

Zel interrupted. 'You don't want to say it, but it's the demons that eat souls, isn't it?'

Safred's face confirmed it. Martine had never quite believed in that story – the demons were supposed to eat the souls of those who had lived badly, without generosity or courage or kindness. The souls of the evil, the petty, the mean-spirited. She wondered if they had eaten Acton's soul. It would be ironic, if all this effort had been for nothing, because his soul was long since dead.

'They're real?' she asked.

'I don't know,' Safred whispered. 'The gods won't answer when I ask. But, there's something out there.'

'Is there anything we can do?' Cael's face was pale. It was the first time he had shown any fear, and that made Martine's gut turn over.

Safred hunched her shoulders, uncertain.

'There is a . . . a spell,' Martine said.

Zel looked at her, shocked. When the old women were at the Autumn Equinox, the young women sang the dark song, the song of protection against evil, to guard their families against the coming winter. Against all demons. But it was secret, passed from mother to daughter of the old blood.

Oh, Mam, forgive me, Martine thought, but I can't leave Bramble unprotected. She began to sing.

There were five notes only, repeated over and over again. The words didn't matter, Martine had been told, but the melody must be precise. Usually, women sang the names of their loved ones, or words like 'safe' and 'protected' and 'life'. Martine sang 'Bramble', spreading the word out over all five notes, repeating and repeating.

After a moment's silence, Zel joined in, her hand sweaty in Martine's.

The moving shadows in the mist seemed to pause as they sang. Then, as though they had been waiting for some sound, something to centre upon, they gathered closer. Gods protect us, Martine thought, I hope I haven't doomed us all.

Then Safred joined in, singing not in the terrible, dead voice she used to heal, but in her own light alto. Cael opened his mouth to begin, too, but Martine warned him with a shake of the head, no. She didn't know what would happen if a man sang those notes.

The mist began to draw back, leaving them in a small circle of clear air. But as it did, screaming began around them. It was the sound of a rabbit screaming as the fox bites down, the sound of the lamb under the eagle's claws, of a child falling over a cliff. Small, defenceless, and totally false, it tried to lure them into breaking the circle, shock them to their feet. Cael jerked as the first cry tore the air, but Martine had him by one hand and Safred by the other, and they held fast, singing louder.

The noises changed into howls, threatening, louder than Martine thought her ears could stand; the sound crept into the back of her brain and urged her to run. Flee! Take cover! It was hard, very hard, to stay still when every instinct said to move, and move fast. Zel was sweating, staring at Safred as though her life depended on it. Cael sat with hunched shoulders, gripping their hands so hard that Martine's fingers were losing all feeling. Safred's legs twitched as if she had started to move and then stopped herself. If only they could *see* what was out there. But perhaps the mist was to protect them from seeing. Perhaps seeing would send them mad.

Bramble jerked and groaned as though she had been wounded. The movement was enough to distract their attention from the howling and bring it back to her. Their song became stronger, and immediately the mist circle moved further outwards, pushing back. They were safe within that circle, Martine was sure, but the howling and shrieking were growing louder and the shadows in the mist darker, clearer.

Larger than humans, moving with cumbersome, swinging movements, the shadows changed as they watched: grew arms and legs, flexed claws, divided one head into three. It was profoundly unsettling – not just fearsome, but striking at Martine's understanding of how the world worked. This was not the world she knew; this lake, this Forest, were connected to the world beyond this one, where humans did not belong. Perhaps rebirth was simply the way humans escaped from the terrible darkness beyond death, if that darkness held these beings.

Bramble shivered, and shuddered, and began to thrash her arms and legs. Her knee struck Safred's and Zel's hands and almost broke their hold. The howling intensified, the shapes throwing themselves at the circle and being stopped by the edge of the mist, their bodies too visible as they flattened themselves against the circle. Much too visible, because they were not animals, nor wraiths like the water sprites or wind wraiths, nor even demons as some storytellers described them. They were human, and yet not. Some elongated, some compressed, some twisted around on themselves like snakes, some wizened away like dried leaves.

Martine sang although her throat was raw, sang with a dry mouth and cracked lips, sang and sang and sang again, the five notes that her mam had taught her, and did not look at the faces of the demons in case she saw her mam's face there, or her da's, or Cob's or any of her loved ones who had gone with Lady Death, because she did not want to know if they had not been reborn, if they had swollen with pride or shrunken with envy or turned awry with greed and become one of these shrieking hungry monstrosities.

Bramble gasped, gasped as though she were drowning, and woke.

LEOF

THEGAN TURNED TO look down at the map spread out over a side table. It showed the Domains in detail, and an outline of other lands as well. It was the largest map Leof knew. He had seen it before, many times, and every time there was more information marked on it – more details about the Wind Cities, about the Ice King's land, about the Wild Shore on the other side of the Eastern Sea, and the Long Coast beyond the Wind Cities. He saw now that the area above Foreverfroze had been filled in – although there was not much to mark in the freezing lands. Leof wondered which of Thegan's agents had ventured so far north.

'We could make this a great country, Leof,' Thegan said sombrely. 'We talk about the Wind Cities with awe because they are so rich, yet the Domains are ten times their size *and* more fertile. But when they trade, they speak with one voice. They play us off against each other and we let them. *We* must speak with one voice.'

'And that voice will be yours,' Leof said. The words came out without thought, and he tensed against Thegan's reaction. But Thegan took it as a compliment, or maybe a vote of confidence, because he laid his hand on Leof's shoulder and shook it gently.

'One day. Soon, perhaps.' Then a sudden gaiety overtook him, as it did sometimes when they talked about the future. 'We're going to need a new name,' he declared, smiling. 'A fitting name for our united country. What about Actonsland?'

'What about Thegansland?' Leof countered, smiling back.

Thegan laughed, but shook his head. 'No, we need something to unite us, not set us quarrelling. "Thegansland" would be seen as a boast, a spit in the face.'

'Sornsland, then,' Leof said, only half-joking. 'She will be a most beloved Overlady, and they would see it as a romantic gesture. Particularly since she will be bearing your heirs.'

Thegan had laughed at the idea of Sornsland, but at the last sentence his brows came together and his mouth hardened. Part of Leof watched him with satisfaction. Yes, there was some problem there that bothered him. But Thegan recovered himself quickly.

'Still too divisive, lad,' he said. 'Actonsland will bring us all together.'

'Except the Travellers,' Leof said.

Thegan shrugged. 'They ceased to matter a thousand years ago. They're nothing.'

'Except this raiser of the dead. He's likely Traveller blood,' Leof reminded him.

Thegan looked at him with puzzlement. 'You've changed. You're more serious than you were. Older.'

Flushing, Leof looked away. 'You shouldn't have put me in charge,' he tried to joke. 'That's enough to give grey hairs to anyone.'

Thegan smiled and nodded. 'But is anything better than being in command?' he asked, not needing an answer, and dismissed Leof to his meal with a gesture as he sat at his desk and began reading Leof's report.

Leof left the office with the last comment echoing in his head. It was true for Thegan – to be in command, to be in charge, was the best thing possible. Power – Leof couldn't quite understand it. Of course, it was a good feeling when your men obeyed you, trusted you to give them the right orders, followed you into battle and committed themselves, body and soul, to supporting you. There *was* nothing like that wave of loyalty and trust, buoying you up so that you were greater than you could ever be on your own. But after battle? Command was the boring part of being an officer, Leof had always thought. Making inspections, reading and writing reports, having to take responsibility . . . Well, his mother had always said he was irresponsible, except with his men. She claimed that he would have been married long since and given her grandchildren if he'd had any sense of family responsibility. Perhaps she was right. He'd worked hard as Thegan's officer, but he'd played hard, too. He smiled at the memory of the chases, the girls, the hunting. Just as well I'm not ambitious, he thought wryly. The last thing Thegan wants is an officer who really yearns to command.

ASH

DAYLIGHT, IN THE Deep, was for sleeping and singing. The other men, with their own faces returned to them, wandered away to curl up on blankets. One older man had even brought a mattress. Ash's father shook his head and laughed.

'Plum says he's getting too old for sleeping on the hard ground. I know how he feels.' He looked at Ash with undisguised pleasure and put both hands on his shoulders. 'It's very good to see you. You're looking well? You've certainly filled out!'

It was a question. Ash smiled. He certainly had filled out over the past two years. He had been little taller than his father for quite a few years, but now he was bigger, too. Stronger.

'Yes, I'm well.'

'What happened with Doronit?'

Ash's face closed in. He could feel it, feel the muscles tense and the jaw set, and he forced himself to relax. 'I've left Doronit. It was necessary.'

His father looked at him shrewdly and, to Ash's surprise, decided to change the subject. He turned to Flax.

'Welcome to the Deep, lad. Flex, your name is?'

Ash smothered a laugh. 'Flax,' he corrected.

Rowan chuckled gently. 'Badger ears are sharp but they don't hear human speech all that well,' he explained. Flax goggled at him, clearly astonished that he would refer so casually to his transformation.

'Oh. Um . . .'

Rowan took pity on him. 'You're a singer?'

Flax nodded.

'Well then, let's hear something.'

This was the moment Ash had been dreading. He took a step back, to have a clear view of both Flax and his father's face. Flax coughed nervously, no doubt wondering what would happen to him if he sang poorly. Then he took a deep breath and let out a single, clear note; the beginning of the most famous love song ever written, *The Distant Hills*.

> *From the high hills of Hawksted, my lover calls to me*
> *The breeze is her voice, the wind becomes her breath*
> *From the high hills of Hawksted, above the settled plain*
> *My lover sings so sweetly, sings the song of death*

The song told of a pair of separated lovers. From the words it wasn't clear whether the beloved was far away or actually dead, and singers differed in their interpretation. The song could have been sentimental, but the music was spare and dignified and it was one of the treasures of Domain culture. The men puzzled over it in the Deep, as they talked over many songs – who might have written it? No one knew where Hawksted was. None of their extensive traditions mentioned the song, but the scale used and the melody line showed that it was very old and probably written by someone of the old blood.

Flax's voice, always beautiful, was taken and magnified by the high walls of the Deep. It took on resonance and depth that sent chills down Ash's spine, but it kept its haunting clarity on the high notes. Rowan's face was unreadable, but the other men came back, slowly and quietly, not wanting to disturb the singer. Halfway through the song there was traditionally a flute solo. Rowan fished his smallest flute, a wooden willow pipe, from his pocket and was ready; he picked up the melody from Flax without a break and when Flax came back in for the last verse he kept on playing softly, so that the flute and the voice wound around each other like the lover's voice and the wind.

Afterwards, every man there had tears in his eyes. Even Ash, although he didn't know if he were crying for the song or for the look on his father's face.

Rowan carefully shook the spit out of his flute and put it back in his pocket. 'Well,' he said. 'Well.' He turned to Ash. 'You did right to bring him.'

Ash nodded. Their meeting had happened just as he had imagined. Rowan would welcome Flax and train him and take him to meet Swallow and they would Travel together and be a family. So, although he felt as though a hole had been scoured out of his gut, he had to remember that this was not important.

'Yes. But I didn't come here because of Flax. I came because I need something from you.' His father turned, surprised, and Ash motioned him away from the others.

'Of course, son. What is it?'

'I need the secret songs,' Ash said.

Rowan went very still. 'I can't teach you those.' His voice was flat.

'Because you don't trust me,' Ash said. 'You told me you taught me all the songs, but you didn't. Because I'm not a singer. Or a musician.'

He couldn't stop the pain from appearing in his voice. Rowan heard it, and bit his lip. But he still shook his head.

'Not for those reasons. I trust you. Truly. But the songs are not for young men. Not for *any* young men, no matter how trustworthy.'

Ash stared at him, wanting to believe him. Rowan took him by the arm and dragged him back to the group seated around the fire.

'Ask them, if you don't believe me.'

'Ask us what, lad?' one of the men said.

'I need to know the secret songs,' Ash said baldly.

The men, just like Rowan, went very still and the atmosphere chilled. One of them got up and stepped forward; a stocky balding man whom Ash had met here before. Skink, that was his name. He glared at Ash, and then around the circle of men.

'What do you know about the secret songs? Who's been talking?' he asked.

'The Well of Secrets,' Ash said.

That astonished them, he was glad to see. Before they could collect their thoughts, he explained everything: the enchanter, the ghosts, the need to find Acton's bones and raise his ghost. At that, they looked at each other and shook their heads. They were going to refuse him.

'I *need* the songs,' he said in desperation. 'Or we all might be wiped out.'

A thin-faced man named Vine pursed his lips. 'But this enchanter wants to take the land back for us, doesn't he? For Travellers? Why not just let him?'

The other men seemed to be considering this. Ash couldn't believe it.

'Let hundreds, maybe thousands of people die? People you all know! Children. Babies. They're killing *everyone*.'

'But not us,' Vine said.

Ash was astounded that the other men were looking thoughtful, some of them even nodding.

'Really? I know they've killed at least one person with some of the old blood in her. How are they going to know who is a Traveller and who not?' He turned to an older man with a bald pate and a fringe of white hair and hazel eyes. 'How will they know who *you* are, Snake? You've pretended to be one of Acton's people often enough. How will ghosts know the difference?'

'Lad's got a point,' Snake said, embarrassed.

'But he can't have the songs,' Vine said firmly.

'Why *not*?' Ash was exasperated.

'Let's sit down and discuss it,' Rowan said, smoothing things down.

Ash sat down in the fire circle. The fire was low, cooking some parsnips in the embers, but it gave a kind of formality to the gathering, as though they were assembling a council.

Ash sat next to Rowan. Flax hovered behind until Rowan pointed to the place on his other side.

'Sit here, lad.' Yes, Ash thought, momentarily distracted. Of course you have to sit next to him. He was surprised that he felt no real hatred of Flax for usurping his place. It felt so inevitable, as though it had been planned by the gods, that he could no longer feel anything but pain and resignation.

When everyone was seated, Rowan cleared his throat. 'So. We have two things to decide, it seems to me. Firstly, will we resist this enchanter? Secondly, will we give the . . . the songs to Ash so that he can resist him by following the Well of Secrets' plan?'

The other men nodded.

Skink leaned forwards and took over. Ash remembered that in other years, it was Skink who ran discussions and gave orders when orders were needed.

'I can tell you one thing. If Acton's people work out *why* this enchanter is loosing the ghosts on them, every Traveller in the Domains will be slaughtered overnight.'

They sat, recognising the truth when they heard it. There had been massacres before, for no more reason than a Traveller man seducing a blonde woman; or a child sickening after a Traveller family had passed by. For a reason, a *real* reason such as this, the massacre would spread like fire through a pine forest.

'We should not only resist him, we should be *seen* to resist him,' Skink concluded.

The other men nodded, even Vine.

'So,' Rowan said.

'So,' Skink echoed. 'The second question. I say, Ash is not ready for the songs. Someone else should sing them.'

'How do you know I'm not ready?' Ash challenged him.

Skink laughed shortly. 'Are you married? Do you have a family? You are not ready.'

Ash was intent on arguing, but Rowan intervened. 'There are seasons in a man's life, son. Babyhood, childhood. Then youth, when a boy first comes here. Then the wild time, when he Travels and lives and is irresponsible. And then maturity, which comes with marriage and children.'

'And then age,' Snake said dryly, 'which comes to us all, whether we like it or not.'

'If we're lucky,' Ash said out of habit. The others nodded and said, 'Aye, if we're lucky,' and spat on the ground for luck.

'I don't understand . . .'

'The songs you're talking about . . .' Skink stopped and looked at Rowan for help.

'Songs of power,' Rowan said. 'They are songs of power.'

'Exactly!' Ash said. 'That's why we need them.'

'Power like that – young men want to change the world, Ash. Just like this enchanter does. So we protect the power from the impetuousness of youth. No man may learn those songs until he has a stake in the future. Until there is a risk to him in changing things.'

Ash was confused. 'I don't understand.'

'Until you have children,' Flax hissed at him. 'Until you're a father.'

The men nodded. Oh, Ash thought. It wasn't me. Father didn't refuse *me*. He would have taught me later. He would have trusted me. But although he was flooded with relief that his father hadn't deliberately withheld the songs, a small doubt remained. He had left the Road, after all, and gone to Turvite. Would his father have ever sought him out again? Visited, no doubt, when they were in Turvite, but that only happened every decade or so. Would his father have come to teach him the songs when the time came?

He couldn't brood over it; there was too much at stake to let his attention wander.

'You have no stake in the future yet,' Skink said. 'One of us will sing the songs.'

'It won't work,' Ash said.

'Oh, only you can sing?' Vine mocked him. 'Hah! I've never heard you sing a single note ever.'

There it was, the moment he had dreaded. He opened his mouth to try to forestall it, but Flax got in ahead of him.

'You don't understand!' he said. 'He has the prophet's voice, like the Well of Secrets when she heals!'

Ash was surprised by this championship. Flax's voice was full of awe, and it impressed some of the men, but Vine was still sceptical.

'A prophet's voice? What does that sound like?'

Flax opened his mouth to explain, but Ash put up a hand.

'It's not a prophet's voice. Is it, Father?'

Rowan shook his head. The other men looked at him. 'It is the voice of the dead,' he said.

There was silence. Then Flax spoke, his brow furrowed. 'The dead don't speak. *Can't* speak.'

Rowan explained reluctantly, not looking at Ash. 'Some people have the power to compel the dead to speak. When they do . . . "from the grave, all speak alike, and it is not easy to hear".'

'But that saying means that the dead are silent!' Snake objected.

Rowan and Ash both shook their heads. The movement was identical, and as Ash realised that his heart contracted inside him.

'No, it doesn't mean that,' Ash said. 'It means that the voice of the dead is terrible.'

'You didn't think to share this with us, all these years, Rowan?' Skink asked quietly.

Rowan flushed. 'It's not one of the secrets of the Deep,' he said. Ash knew that it would have been his mother's decision to keep the information within the family. He was almost certain that he had inherited the ability from her.

'I was told,' Ash said, to distract the men from his father's discomfort, 'that only one in a thousand thousand can compel the dead to speak.'

'And that's you, is it?' Vine asked.

'Yes.'

Skink was still gazing at Rowan as though he had betrayed them all. Rowan cleared his throat.

'It is a great blasphemy to compel the dead to speak. It is a power best left unused.' His voice was urgent, utterly convinced. 'That is why we did not teach Ash about his . . . ability. Blasphemy must be avoided.'

Ash remembered the shame and excitement of standing next to Doronit at Mid-Winter, compelling the ghosts of Turvite to speak. He remembered the ghost of the girl he had killed, and the stonecaster's ghost, anxious to help his son and go on to rebirth.

'To compel a ghost to speak is blasphemy,' he said. 'But if a ghost wishes to speak, the power can be a blessing.'

It was the first time in his life he had disagreed with his father. Rowan looked at him in surprise.

'I still don't believe he can sing the songs,' Vine said.

Ash stood up, trying to relax his throat muscles. He knew how he was *supposed* to sing; knew about breath control and pitch and phrasing. But he had not sung aloud since he was a small child, and the ring of faces was hostile, except for Flax and his father. He felt his gorge rise, and forced it down. Then, deliberately making it as bad for himself as he could, so there could be nothing worse waiting for him, he chose to sing *The Distant Hills*.

As the first note left Ash's throat, he saw them all flinch. His father kept his head bowed; Flax and the others stared straight at him, mouths agape. Except for Vine, who looked away and then back again, over and over.

He sang the first two lines, which was more than enough. The grating, stone-ripping-stone sound was magnified by the rock walls, just as Flax's voice had been, but with Ash the sound became unbearable, unthinkable, the howling of demons. He watched their faces. They were horrified. Repelled. Just as he had known they would be.

At the end of the second line Ash fell silent and stood there, waiting.

'So?' Flax said eventually, running out of patience.

'Mmm,' Skink said. 'He was on pitch.'

Ash gaped at him. The last thing he had expected was a critique. 'I —'

'That's a voice to make a man's balls climb up into his gut. But the phrasing wasn't bad. He was in tune, though it's not an easy melody line.' Skink spoke as if Ash were any young singer, come to the Deep to learn the old songs. He had seen the older men do this, time and again — take a young singer and groom him. He had never expected it to happen to him. He felt a warm ball of gratitude to Skink grow in his belly.

Vine looked sour. 'I don't care if he can hit the highest note in the scale. He's a child. He has no stake in the future and he shouldn't be taught the songs. That's the real issue.'

'He doesn't even know his true self yet!' Snake added.

Ash could see what was happening. Better to keep things the way they always had been. Better to be in control; especially when the alternative was to give away power to someone strange, like him. Someone incalculable. What he had to do was to make himself unthreatening: to meet their demands in a way they could accept.

'I have a stake in the future,' he said softly.

They looked at him, puzzled.

'Got some girl pregnant in Turvite, did you?' Vine snapped. 'Might have known.'

'No,' Ash said, controlling his impulse to slap Vine backwards onto the hard rock. 'No, not that. But friends of mine had a baby last winter. He's being raised in Hidden Valley, and I have sworn to protect him and his family. He is my stake in the future.' He paused for a moment, trying to look them all in the eye, one by one, to convince them. 'His name is Ash.'

Skink considered, pulling at his lip while he thought. 'I will ask you some questions. If the answers are sufficient, then we will think about the next step.'

'What's that?' Flax jumped in.

'No man may learn the songs unless he knows his true nature. If we accept that Ash has a stake in the future, he must find his true shape. Only if the River accepts him can he learn the songs.'

Ash breathed out, hard. Another step, and another step. Fighting was a lot easier.

'When the child was born, what did you feel?' Skink said. Ash knew by his tone that the question was more complicated than it appeared.

'Well . . .' he said, trying to give himself enough time to think it through, then realising that all he could do was tell the truth. 'Firstly, just thankfulness that everything was all right; that his mother was safe and he was well.'

The men nodded.

'Then, when I saw him, I felt . . .' Ash paused. What had he felt? 'I was surprised, because he was so little and so . . . red and scrunched up.'

Some of the men laughed, but it was the laughter of recognition.

'Then he was named for me, and I held him for the first time and I felt . . . joy. But later, when I thought about it, I felt afraid. Afraid for him. Afraid of all the things that could happen to him. Like the ghosts. That was when I swore to protect him.'

His answer poured out of him, each emotion vividly alive again. He was still afraid for little Ash, and it showed, he knew from the looks on their faces. Rowan had tears in his eyes. But it wasn't enough.

'Have you sung to him?' Skink asked, putting him in his place.

Ash felt his face harden. 'No,' he said.

'And you have left him.' There was condemnation in Skink's tone. Traveller children were few, and cherished. Rowan placed his hand on Ash's shoulder in support and warning. Be calm, he meant. Ash could almost hear the words. He took a breath and let it out slowly, then answered.

'The gods willed it. Go to the Well of Secrets, they said, and she sent me to find the secret songs.'

'There is one last question. Is the child of the old blood?'

'His mother was a Traveller.'

'Was?'

'She has Settled.'

Skink, Vine and Snake exchanged glances. Vine shrugged, and the other two nodded.

'It is enough,' Skink said. 'We declare that Ash, son of Rowan, has a stake in the future in the form of the boychild Ash.'

'When the time comes,' Vine added, 'Ash, son of Ash, son of Rowan, will be admitted to the Deep and meet the River.'

'As you will do, tonight,' Skink said, 'when you make your climb.'

BRAMBLE

FOR A MOMENT, Bramble wondered whose body she was in. Whosoever it was, it was achy and cold, with sleep-encrusted eyes. She wanted to open those eyes and see, and astonishingly, they opened as soon as she thought it. There were faces staring down at her that she knew, looking scared and relieved at the same time.

She was back.

Her eyes closed again for a heartbeat, in a mixture of thankfulness and loss, then opened again.

They weren't on the island any more, but under the trees. They were holding hands around her, which seemed strange. She was half-naked under a blanket. As she struggled to sit up, they sprang into life, supporting her, getting her water to drink, pulling up the blanket which threatened to slip down.

'Are you all right?' Martine asked.

Bramble nodded and swallowed more water. Her mouth was as dry as a Wind Cities' river in the hot season. 'I have to go to the Western Mountains near Actonston,' Bramble said. No sense wasting time. 'That's where he . . . where the bones are.' She turned her thoughts firmly away from Acton's death to consider how she was going to get there. Forget him, she told herself. Think about it later.

'I need Zel,' Bramble continued. Her mind was crystal clear, as though she had thought through this plan for days. Perhaps she had. She had no idea how long it had been since she left Acton.

'I'd rather stay with Safred,' Zel said quietly.

'Maybe. But we're going to the Western Mountains, and I am not going through Thegan's territory to get there.'

Safred frowned, pleating the crown of her hat in her hands. 'So? How will you go?'

'The sea ice will be breaking up about now. By the time we ride to Foreverfroze it should be free and we can take a ship for Turvite, then ride up the southern bank of the White River to Actonston.'

They were all silent, surprised.

'So I need Zel,' Bramble repeated. 'She's the only one of you who knows enough about horses to help me on board ship.'

Zel nodded slowly. 'You'll need help, sure enough, if we take those chestnuts. But why will you need more than your own horse?'

'Because I need Cael, too,' Bramble said.

Safred started to argue, but Cael held up one hand. 'Why?' he asked.

Bramble hesitated. 'The bones are in a cave; maybe thrown down a shaft, I'm not sure. We might need some muscle.'

'We'll all go,' Safred said.

'How are we going to afford a trip like that?' Cael asked. 'We don't have enough for even Bramble and Zel, let alone all of us.'

'If we wait a day,' Safred said, her eyes unfocused, 'we will meet someone on the Road who will help with that.'

Bramble thought it odd, that she could never feel the gods coming and going from Safred, the way she could with Baluch. Maybe they didn't come and go. Maybe they were there all the time.

Then Cael moved away so she could put her breeches back on in privacy, and she became consumed with thoughts of food. She was starving.

In the middle of the night, after the moon had gone down, Bramble woke with a sudden jerk. Had she heard something? She drew her knife and rolled out of her blankets, glad to be disturbed from a sleep choked with dreams of Acton's blood. It was a cloudy, flickering night, with a wind high in the sky sending the clouds streaming in tatters across the stars, so that the light varied from faint to none unpredictably. An unchancy night to meet something vicious in the dark.

The others had told her about the mist, although she had a feeling they were leaving out the details. Since then, they had set a watch. She had thought it was Martine's turn, but she could not see her anywhere on the perimeter of the camp, where she was supposed to be. She didn't wake the others. Not yet. Just in case the noise she had heard was Martine making her rounds.

She prowled the border of the camp closest to the Forest, but heard nothing but the sough of the branches. Then she realised that something was moving down at the water. She paused, her heartbeat increasing. That mere . . . They could probably cope with wolf or bear, but a creature from the depths of the lake . . . She forced her imagination away from the thought.

She walked down towards the water, which was lying still even in the increasing wind. There was a figure at the water's edge, pacing backwards and forwards – Zel. It must be later than she had thought, if it was Zel's watch. She felt adrift in time, where before she had always been securely anchored.

'Sorry if I woke you,' Zel said. They moved closer together so they would not disturb the others.

Bramble shrugged. 'No matter.' In the past, she would have just turned and gone back to bed, but in the moonlight she could clearly see the little tell-tale signs that Zel was worried, or upset, and somehow she didn't want to just leave her to her troubles.

'Are you all right?' she asked, although it went against all her habits and felt like prying.

Zel fiddled with her belt and half-shook her head. 'Just thinking about Flax.'

'Mmm.' Well, Bramble could understand that. When Maryrose had left for Carlion, Bramble had worried about her every day, too. I was right to worry, she thought, grief clutching her throat. She should say something comforting, like, 'He'll be all right,' but with Maryrose's death so fresh she couldn't bring herself to say a well-meaning lie. He was abroad in a world where ghosts killed the living. Who knew if he would be all right or not?

Zel looked down at the ground, and then out at the mere, then back, as if it were hard for her to talk. 'Um . . . I wanted to ask . . . what was he like?' she said finally.

'Acton?'

Zel nodded.

Bramble shook her head, not to refuse the question, but to clear her thoughts. 'He was very alive. It's hard to believe he's dead.'

'Are the songs true? Did he really laugh during battle? While he was killing people?'

Bramble hesitated, then shrugged. 'Yes,' she said. 'He laughed.'

'Did he really say, "Kill them all"?'

'Yes,' she said. 'He said that.'

'And that they should keep the houses intact so his people could use them?'

'Yes.'

Bramble could see that Zel was somehow eased by the knowledge that Acton was as bad as she had imagined – that the songs didn't lie. Bramble stared out at the lake. Her eyes filled with tears. Why did it feel like betrayal to tell the truth? Acton *had* done all those things. He had killed and massacred and taken this land for his own people, he had *enjoyed* battle. He had. But he was not what people thought he was. She thought that even now she didn't really know what he was. No – what he *had been*. She mustn't forget that he was dead, even though it seemed to her that she could take the brooch in her hand again and swim through the waters to find him; to watch him; to perhaps finally understand him.

'He was a man of his time,' she said, and blinked away the tears before they fell. She sat on a rock at the edge of the mere and stared at the still water, trying to find calmness in its serenity.

'Do you want company?' Zel said.

Bramble stiffened. 'No. No, with thanks. I've slept too long, I think, and now my body doesn't know when to rest. Go back to sleep. I'll keep watch.'

'Good night, then,' Zel said.

Bramble watched all night by the mere, trying not to remember. The silent water should have been soothing, but it wasn't. It reminded her too much of the waves that had risen up, over and over again, to take her away from Acton's life. She knew she couldn't sleep. She kept seeing Red's arm – her arm, it had felt like – strike at Acton. Kept feeling the knife go in.

If she had been told, before she grasped the brooch, that she would have the chance to kill Acton, she would have rejoiced. But all she felt was horror. How could she be lamenting his death – the death of the invader?

It was because of the future that had been killed, she decided. The future where all towns would have been free towns, where every person, Travellers included, would have had a say in how things were done. The gods had stopped her from creating that future, and no doubt they had their reasons, but she mourned for that world, for the nation the Domains could have become, for the freedom lost.

She still had a chance to save *this* world. Maybe, afterwards, there would be a way to create the future she had seen, if only briefly, in Acton's eyes. She put that thought aside. There was no use thinking about it now. Now they had to stop Saker.

But walking by the lakeside, she kept wondering what she could have replied to Zel's questions. 'Yes, but he wasn't that bad?' He *was* what Zel believed: a killer, an invader, a destroyer of too much. He *had* laughed as he killed, in the battle light-heartedness that all his people seemed to share. He *had* said, 'Kill them all'. The provocation didn't matter, did it? Had Hawk and his men deserved to die? Maybe. But their women and children? No. And yet, he had been upset about that . . . Oh, it was too much to think about, Bramble told herself. It was over, and she had to get on with things.

She went to the privy before she woke the others, and was returning to the camp when the trees shimmered in front of her eyes and her hunter appeared next to a huge oak, its gold eyes gleaming in the shadow as though reflecting light from some other place or time. She controlled her shock instinctively. Show no fear, she thought.

'Kill Reborn,' it said, 'you are in haste.'

She didn't care how it knew, only what it might be able to do.

'I need to get to the Western Mountains quickly,' she said. 'Can you help me?'

It tilted its head as though listening to the Forest. Then it nodded.

'It will not be easy.'

'What do I have to do?'

'Trust me.'

Bramble laughed. This was better. No more discussions or plans or arguing. Just a leap of faith.

'I have to tell them, get my saddlebags.'

'Just come,' the hunter said. 'Or not.'

She paused. Just walk away? Oh, that was tempting. She would have done it, too, except for Trine.

'I have to make sure my horse is looked after,' she said. 'That's my duty.'

The hunter understood duty, and the husbanding of animals, even if its way of husbanding was to cull. It nodded.

'Be quick,' it said. The hawks' feathers in its hair caught the light as it shifted backwards into the undergrowth and disappeared.

Bramble ran back to the camp. Her saddlebags were by her bedroll. She grabbed them. Her last memory of Maryrose was wound up with these bags, and she wasn't going to leave them behind.

Zel woke immediately when she touched her shoulder.

'Look after Trine for me,' Bramble said softly. 'I've found a quicker way. I'll meet you in Sanctuary.'

Zel barely had time to nod and no time for questions, before Bramble was racing for the Forest.

She found her way back to the oak and stood on the same spot as before. 'I'm ready,' she said.

The air shimmered and the hunter appeared.

'Then walk with me,' it said.

MARTINE

SAFRED WASN'T HAPPY, with Bramble or with Zel, and Martine felt increasingly annoyed with her as they rode single file back through the Forest and she maintained the sulk. Trine was sulking, too, lagging as much as she could on the leading rein Zel had secured to her own saddle. Zel already had bites on both hands from bridling her. Martine thought that Safred and Trine had the same expression, and the horse had more cause.

Nothing happened to disturb them. They crossed the stream without incident, they weren't even bothered by the strange panic that they had felt earlier. It was all easy – too easy, Martine felt, as though the Forest wanted to see the back of them and was urging them on.

At the point where the trail into the Forest crossed the north-west road, they dismounted so that Safred could heal Cael.

'Out of the Forest,' she said, smiling. She placed her hand on his chest confidently, and sang a high chant in her terrible voice. When she took her hand away the wound was as bad as ever. She tried twice more, with the same result, until her face was white with effort and she swayed on her feet.

'Enough,' Cael said. 'Let it heal on its own.' His face was solemn and wary. 'Don't kill yourself for something impossible,' he added gently.

Safred's eyes filled with tears. 'I can heal everyone else, why not you?'

He shrugged and helped her to mount. They all settled back into their saddles, while Safred recovered a little. Martine could see that she was getting set for a long, involved discussion of why and why not and what could be done about it, and she was thankful, at first, when they were interrupted by a party of riders cantering down the north-west road. Then she saw they were a warlord's men and she felt the familiar tightening in the gut that armed men always brought, anywhere in the Domains. But Safred smiled for the first time since she had woken to find Bramble gone.

'Arvid!' Her voice rang with pleasure. 'It's you!'

She was calling to a man with light brown hair, dressed as the others were in simple green uniforms without emblems. No crossed sword and spear here, as there was on Thegan's uniforms. Arvid. The warlord himself. He was about forty, maybe a bit older, with a smiling, open countenance that invited trust. With very shrewd blue eyes. Martine felt another jolt in her gut, but this one brought heat with it, fire licking along her nerves and into her bones. She wanted to melt into her saddle, but she stiffened her back and kept her face impassive. The week after Equinox, she thought with resignation. All the body wants is to be satisfied, and it doesn't care who does it.

'They didn't tell you who to expect?' he asked, smiling.

Safred laughed too, ruefully. 'No. Just that we would meet someone.' She looked quizzically at him. 'Someone who would give us silver.'

He laughed. 'Oh, yes, that's all I'm good for, I know,' he said with mock humility. 'Just the treasury, that's me.'

He was easy to like, but he was still a warlord, Martine reminded herself.

Safred introduced her companions by name, but with no other information. Martine nodded at him, and received a nod and an assessing glance in return, which warmed into admiration.

'You travel with beautiful companions, Saf,' Arvid said, nodding politely to include Zel, but looking at Martine. She felt the colour rise in her cheeks. The fire was getting entirely too strong for comfort.

'I am riding to the Plantation, and then to Foreverfroze,' Arvid said. 'There is a question of markets, of sending food to Mitchen for sale. The Valuers and I are combining to hire a ship, to trade down the coast.'

'As far as Turvite?' Cael asked, edging his chestnut forward.

Arvid looked surprised. 'We hadn't *intended* so,' he said with a question in his voice.

Safred answered. 'We need to get to Turvite. We were headed for Foreverfroze, to find a ship to take us there. The gods said we would find someone here today to help. I *thought* they meant with silver, but a ship would be even better!'

Cael laughed at her enthusiasm and at Arvid's long-suffering expression.

'It seems to me that the gods use me like a banker!'

'At least you have some use,' Martine said quietly.

His gaze lifted quickly to meet her eyes, and this time he was the one who flushed. 'Not all warlords are useless,' he said.

'So they say,' Martine replied. She wasn't going to give in to the fire, no matter how hard her heart beat when Arvid looked at her. This was just backwash from the ritual, and nothing personal.

One of his men moved his horse closer, as though Martine might be a threat, and scowled at her with ferocious loyalty. 'My lord is the best warlord in the Domains!' he declared. Martine saw with surprise that it wasn't a man but a brown-haired woman of about thirty, strong and tall and flat-chested. The woman continued, 'My lord shares his wealth and his power. He's even set up a council of all the Voices in the Domain to guide his laws!'

'Does he abide by their advice?' Martine asked, looking at Arvid.

He smiled and answered her directly. 'He does, when he can. When he can't, he explains why and gets their agreement.'

'Always?'

Arvid nodded. 'So far. The Voices are usually reasonable people. And an increasing number are Valuers, which makes coming to an agreement easier.'

'A warlord who values Valuers?' Martine's tone was sceptical, but her eyes never left his. That would be more than unusual – it would be extraordinary. Could he be that extraordinary?

'My mother was a Valuer,' was all he said.

Martine nodded, once, and looked away. If she maintained that gaze any longer she would drown in it. Valuer mother or not, he was a warlord and no concern of hers. The thump her own heart gave at the thought surprised her.

'Let's get going,' she said.

Arvid nudged his horse into a walk and somehow managed to get it next to Martine's chestnut. 'The Plantation for the night, and then Foreverfroze,' he said companionably. Martine turned to look at him, making her eyes as unreadable as she could. He smiled, nonetheless. 'I'm not a despot,' he said quietly. 'Don't condemn me without evidence.'

She sniffed in exaggerated disbelief, but her hand went to the pouch of stones at her belt for comfort. She wished that she could cast the

stones for herself, to see what he would mean to her. The last time her
heart had beaten this fast for a human man was when she was a girl,
with Cob. That had led to heartbreak, and he had been one of her own
kind. No good could come of encouraging Arvid. But she let him ride
beside her, with Safred, Cael and Zel behind, and she was aware of
every movement of his thigh against the horse, every shift of his hands
on the reins. She was glad when Trine took a dislike to Arvid's horse
and surged forward to kick it, because it made Arvid give a rueful
shrug and move up the column to get away from her.

Martine had heard about the Valuers' Plantation all her life and had,
as most Travellers had, imagined living here in comfort and beauty. But it
was just a farm. A very big farm, admittedly, with quite a number of houses and sheds and barns, and dairies and forges and one big meeting hall.

A tall, solid woman named Apple, with greying yellow hair, met
them with a smile and arranged for them to have lunch in the meeting
hall with the Plantation council, but there was no special banquet
organised. The councillors came from the fields in their work clothes,
and Arvid was treated the same as the other guests. Children ran in
and out of the hall constantly, cajoling food from their parents and
from other people, including Arvid, who sat up one end of the table
with the councillors, engaged in serious discussions.

Martine noticed that the children looked up into the adults' eyes,
instead of down at the ground in respect as they did in other places. She
mentioned it to Apple as she passed a plate of ham and pickles to go with
her bread.

'They're taught that they are the equal of all. To look up, not proud,
or cheeky, because that means you are more important than the other
person. But of equal value.' The words came easily to her, and it was
clear this was a lesson she had recited many times to her own children.

'*Thinking* you're equal won't stop the warlords' men from beating
you if they think you're disrespectful,' Martine said.

Holly, Arvid's guard, laughed, unoffended.

'Aye, in other places, that's so, and we've all had cause to know it,'
Apple answered around a mouthful of ham. 'But Arvid is a Valuer himself, or as good as one.'

'His mam was raised Valuer, just like mine,' Safred said unexpectedly.
'But she stayed with her lord. She's still alive. Almond, her name is, but
they named the baby Arvid after his grandfather, instead of Cedar, like
she wanted.'

There was a brief, uncomfortable silence. Safred grinned.

'The gods didn't tell me that. Almond did.'

Cael laughed and had to cover his mouth to stop crumbs flying out. Then he winced, and his hand went surreptitiously to his chest, as though to ease the pain of the wound there. Safred noticed and her face tightened, but she said nothing.

Martine turned to look thoughtfully at Arvid, who was smiling courteously at an older man as he laid down the law about something, poking Arvid in the chest with one bony finger as he spoke. She couldn't imagine a warlord like Thegan even sitting at the same table as a farmer in dirty boots. Anyone who poked him in the chest would be poked back with a sword through the heart.

They were parcelled out amongst the cottagers for the night, and Martine was placed with Apple. She was grateful when Martine offered to cast the stones for her, but refused.

'There're questions which shouldn't be asked, and there're questions which aren't worth asking, and those are the only two kinds I've got,' she said, smiling, but with a tightness behind the smile that told Martine she'd seen some pain in the past.

Apple sent her son, Snow, over to stay at a friend's place, and Martine slept in his bed, in clean sheets scented with the rosemary bushes they had dried on. The Plantation wasn't paradise, and no doubt they had a long, cold winter of it so far north, but Martine thought as she drifted off to sleep that it was the best life she had seen so far in a warlord's territory.

She dreamt of Arvid. They were naked, encased in flames that did not burn, but sent impossible heat through every nerve. Her hair floated about her as though they were in water, and he tangled it in his hands and brought her head towards him, seeking her mouth as though frantic for her, as she was for him. She woke the moment before their lips touched and lay, aching, staring at the window, wanting him to climb through like a lover from a story.

I must be mad, she thought. This is more than the normal backwash from the Equinox. Perhaps it's punishment from the fire. Lord of Flames, she prayed, forgive me and set me free from this. But her skin was tender as though exposed to too much heat, and every movement of her breath rasped the sheet across tight nipples. She had to curl up in a ball, like a child, for hours before she fell asleep again.

She dreamt of Arvid.

APPLE'S STORY

WHAT GOOD WAS it? Where was the use? I had served, worked, been loyal – for what? An empty alleyway. Yet now they expected me to go on. To serve, as if nothing had happened. As though the alleyway still led home.

I stood with the tray in my hands, looking over at the glass table.

'You're lucky to still have a job,' the cook said gently, 'Go on. The lord is waiting.'

Let him wait, I thought. Let him wait until the giants eat the sun.

I put down the tray and walked out of the hall, straight out of the fort enclosure and down the hill to the gibbet and the pressing box. The guard on the gate called out as I went, 'I'll be closing up in a few minutes, girl,' but I ignored him. I was not coming back.

I went to the gibbet. The crows had had three days at Lidi already, and I didn't want to look. I watched the gallows instead, and I was ready when his ghost quickened.

Lidi came back not in mid-air, where I'd been expecting him, but on the platform, which meant that he hadn't had the quick death I'd thought. He rose, slowly, knowing where he was, knowing what had happened, and I went forward so that he could see me.

He reached out to me, and I to him, but what good was that? His hands and mine passed through each other with a chill that went to my bones. It's a cruelty of the gods, that they let us see our dead, but not touch them.

'They will not offer reparation,' I said, and only as I said it did I realise that I was crying, hiccuping with a tearing grief. 'They never do. But don't let them condemn you in the next life as well. Cheat them. Go on to rebirth.'

He reached for me again, his face bereft. I put my hand up near the side of his face. He pointed at me and spread his hands as though asking a question.

'I'm leaving,' I said. 'I'm going to the Plantation.'

He stilled and nodded, and then tried to smile. He raised his hand and blew me a kiss, and that was the hardest moment of all, I remember, because it was a thing he never did. I used to do it to him as I left for work every morning, but it was a joke between us, that he would never copy me. 'It's a girl's thing to do,' he'd say. So he blew me a kiss and smiled and faded, gone before I could return the kiss, and I sank down at the foot of the gibbet, my legs unsteady. His body hung above me, laced in chains, three days' dead.

I couldn't touch his ghost, but I could touch his body, for the last time. So I reached out and put my hand on his foot, still in the shoes he had made himself. I didn't mean to, but I set him swinging and his chains rattled. It was like he was sending me a message, and the message was: *Run!* So I ran. I ran back through the alleyway to the rooms we had called home and I packed everything I could carry into his old backpack and I left, right then, no thinking about it, no planning, I just left and headed north. I spat on the road that led to the fort as I passed. They said he had withheld taxes, but the truth was that he had not bowed low enough. That he was disrespectful.

So he was, and so he should have been. What was there on the hill to respect? I'd always said, 'No, love, don't anger them, just look at the ground as they pass by,' but now I was filled with the anger that had filled him, the anger that had pushed him too far, pushed him right to the gallows.

So I went to the Valuers. We'd talked about it, Lidi and I, in the winter nights, snuggled under our thin blankets. We'd talked about making the trip north, to the Plantation. But I was still in tax bondage, from the bad summer when Da's crop failed, and they would have chased me and brought me back and branded me too, like as not, if not condemned me to the pressing box. So we stayed, and worked, and saved until I had worked out my tax bondage. We were planning to go that summer. It was Lidi's dream, not mine, but I would have gone anywhere with him.

Now there was just me, and I was going for him.

Well, it's a long trip and it took me a good long while to do, and made no easier by the fact that a month out of Whitehaven I found I

was carrying. I sat by the side of a stream, my road-sorry feet in the
water, and took a moment to count the days. Then I realised – understood that my tiredness wasn't just from walking so far. Lidi's baby.
Oh, gods rest him, he'd wanted a child so much. I didn't know whether
to laugh or cry, so I did both. I was more determined to get to the
Plantation, so that Lidi's baby would grow up without any overlord,
free in mind as well as body.

But it took a long time, and I had to winter over in Pless. I got work
as a maid in the clothier's on the market square. One of the women
spoke up for me, said that I was just travelling, not a Traveller, that
they should let me stay long enough to have the baby and recover. I
don't know why she did it, but it was life itself to me. Maude, her
name was, she was kindness itself. Had no children, she told me, and
always wanted one to fuss over, so she helped as though she'd been the
aunty. She was a seamstress for the clothier and she made a whole set
of baby clothes for me. So beautiful. Fit for a – I was going to say a
warlord's child, but sackcloth would suit one of those better. Fit for a
prince from the Wind Cities.

My own little prince was born in the middle of a winter storm,
when the wind howled against the shutters and the snow blew sideways down the city streets. So I called him Snow, and it was a good
name for he was as fair as Lidi had been. I was glad of that. I'm red-
blonde myself, but my great-grandmother had been a Traveller, and
they say the dark hair can skip generations and appear at any time. I
knew it would go harder for a child with black hair, and it had been
worrying me – one of those silly worries a pregnant woman gets, yet
real for all that. Life is harder for a dark-haired child, there's no doubt.
But my Snow was a tiny blond scrap with long fingers that clung to
mine and a cry that went right through your head and out the other
side. Oh, he was a cryer, that one! Just as well I was living at the back
of the workshop and not in someone's house, for he would have woken
the dead with his bawling. But it was just colic, and he got over it after
a month or so, though for that month I walked around like one dazed
and the seamstresses were lucky if they got anything to eat or drink, let
alone what they'd asked for. But they paid me, and I saved every sker-
rick.

When spring came, I decided to head north again. Maude tried to
get me to stay. 'It's a free town,' she said. 'He'll be as free here as on
the Plantation.'

Maybe she was right, but I'd promised Lidi's ghost. So I went on, through the spring and summer. I made it as far as the North Domain just as autumn was closing in, through a small pass that the stonecaster who came to cast for the seamstresses had told me about. It was harder but faster than going all the way around to Golden Valley. I climbed steep goats' trails that I would never have dared if I had not needed to get Snow safe to the Plantation before winter set in. I saw no one.

On the evening of the second day after I cleared the pass, I came down from the foothills into a small wooded valley, no more than a dale full of upright birch trees, where the first autumn colours were late appearing so that the trees seemed like green pillars with a faint veil of yellow fire at their tips. It was a beautiful place. I was glad, because I could hear a stream trickling nearby. I had slung Snow across my chest in my shawl, and now he woke and began to cry for his feed. I drank from a cup made of birch bark, and I was so thirsty I forgot to ask the tree for permission to strip the bark. I drank and sat and fed my babe and was smiling at his tiny fingers kneading my breast when I realised someone was standing before me.

My heart thumped in surprise. I hadn't heard any sound. I looked up but there was no one there. A trick of the light. I looked down to Snow and again, the figure stood in front of me.

I had known terror, when they came for Lidi, when they killed him, but this fear was different. A holy fear. I have never had the Sight, or heard the gods, but I knew that whatever I had seen was from the other world that they inhabit.

Snow finished and burped, loudly. I flinched and looked down at him without thinking, and again I saw the figure. This time I kept my head down. The edges of the figure were shimmering, moving yet anchored, as leaves move but the trunk stays still. It was not green, though, or any colour I knew. More like a lack of colour, like heat haze over rocks in the summer. I couldn't see through it. It was solid, but – not there. Not wholly here, in this world.

'Greetings,' I whispered.

The figure bent and picked up the bark cup I had torn from the tree. It cradled the cup in its – were they hands, or something else? I couldn't see, couldn't quite make it out. It hissed, a strange sound like wind through leaves.

I was certain that this was the spirit of the birch tree, come to punish me for stealing the bark.

'I'm sorry, truly, truly,' I stammered. 'But the baby needed to be fed and I was so thirsty, I acted without thinking.'

The figure reached a hand towards Snow and I jumped up and pulled him away. As soon as I stood it disappeared from my sight, but not from hearing. The hissing continued.

'It's not his fault!' I cried. 'It's mine!'

I lowered my head to look at the ground and I could see it, faintly, before me, its hand stretched towards Snow, but stopped, considering. Its head turned up and I realised it was smaller than I was, but its arms were much longer and, perhaps, there were more of them. I couldn't see, and not being able to see frightened me more than I would have thought. To have the threat to my son disappear when I raised my head . . . It could be anywhere, go anywhere, spring out from anywhere . . . I kept my head down and watched it as close as I could.

It looked at me and the hissing increased, until it sounded like a forest in a gale, an ocean of trees tossing in the wind. The hissing came in waves and, although I cannot understand the gods, I understood this. This was not the spirit of one tree, but the guardian of many. And it wanted retribution.

'It was my fault,' I said, 'and I will pay the cost. But not now, I beg of you.' My voice broke on the words and I bit back a sob. I didn't think this thing would understand tears.

'Let me get my son to safety, let me raise him, and then I will pay.'

The spirit hissed more softly, but still not pleased.

'What are a few years to you? Just a few seasons, that's all. Then I will pay the forfeit.'

I stared at the ground as if it were my beloved's face, praying to all the gods that were. The hissing dropped away to a faint shushing noise. It understood, I felt. It accepted. Then it reached one threatening hand to my son and poised its long fingers over his throat. The meaning was clear. If I did not pay, Snow would.

'I understand,' I whispered. 'When he is grown, I will come.'

But it was not satisfied. It wanted something else. I thought frantically, and remembered the old stories, about bargains between humans and spirits. There were certain words that were always used. I had thought it was just a storyteller's trick, but perhaps it wasn't.

'I am Dila, daughter of Sarni. I swear by my blood that I will return to pay the forfeit.'

The spirit fell silent, accepting the bargain. Then it disappeared into

APPLE'S STORY 387

the earth, sank into it as one sinks into a bog, but the earth was firm where it had stood.

I went from that place as fast as I could, and I made it to the Valuer's Plantation the next day. They took us in, just as Lidi had said they would, in those winter nights when we'd planned this trip together. They gathered us in like lost lambs, and I felt a bit like a lost lamb, I was so shaken by my meeting with the tree spirit.

But then there was just life – working in the dairy was my main job, milking and cheese-making, although I helped with the sowing and the harvesting, like everyone else. And like everyone else I voted for the council members and said my say in the open meetings, which was one thing I would not have had in a free town, where only people who own property can vote. We had some fights in those meetings, I can tell you! Everyone helped me build a little cabin and I planted a circle of rowan trees around it to safeguard Snow while we slept, and under-planted them with larkspur, which protects from illusion. But nothing happened, except winter turning to summer and back again.

Until the evening of Snow's fifteenth birthday, when I had to pay the forfeit.

I had known it was coming. Every new moon I marked his height on the back of the cabin door, and it was three months since that mark had changed. He'd reached his full growth. I had promised to return when he was grown, and that was now. How I wished I'd said it some other way: when he was an adult, when he was settled in a home of his own – anything but this, which had come so soon.

For the last three days, every time I had walked outside the wind had risen, whipping my cheeks and tearing my hair out of its plait. Even the rowan trees seemed to hiss at me. When I walked out to empty the evening slop pail in the pig trough and the larkspurs were lain flat under the rowans by the wind, I knew in my gut it was time to go.

I'd never told Snow about the forfeit. No need to grow up knowing a thing like that. He was a happy soul, a lot like his father, and the Plantation was the safest place in the Domains – maybe in the world – so he'd grown free and wild like children should; grown up to look everyone in the eye and respect only those who'd earned it. He was best friends with a much bigger family – four boys and three girls – who lived a stone's throw from our cottage. He spent more time there than with me, and I knew they'd take him in, if he wanted it, and cherish him as I would. So early the next morning I went to talk to Cherry, the mother and a good friend of mine, and told her the story.

'I have to go tomorrow,' I concluded. 'Or the forfeit will fall on Snow.'

Well, she was troubled and a bit disbelieving, but I'm not one for fancies or telling tall tales, so she took me at my word after the first surprise.

'Do you think you'll be coming back?' she asked, looking down and pleating her skirt with her fingers so she didn't have to meet my eyes.

'I doubt it.'

'That's a high price to pay for a bark cup!' she said indignantly. 'We could get the men and go and chop those trees down! That would sort it out.'

I laughed. It was so like her, to fire up in defence of someone she thought was being hard done by. Cherry was the loudest voice for justice in our meetings, and I loved her for it. 'More likely sort us out. No. I made a bargain, Cherry, and it was a good one. I got to raise my Snow, didn't I?' My voice broke a little on that, and she hugged me. I hugged back, glad of the comfort.

'I'll look after him,' she said.

'I know.' I collected my thoughts and smoothed my skirt. 'I'm not going to tell him where I'm going,' I said. 'Just in case I do come back. No need to worry him. It's a hard thing to ask, but will you tell him, if I'm not back in a day or so?'

She made a face, but she nodded. 'He can come and stay with us while you're gone,' she said.

'You're cramped for space here,' I said, looking around the small house as I stood up to leave. 'After I . . . afterwards, why not let the two eldest move in with Snow? They could still come back for meals, but they'd be out from under your feet.'

'Time enough to think of that later,' she said quietly. 'Gods go with you, Apple.'

Apple was the new name they had given me, my Valuer name, taken to show my connection to all living things and my respect for the people of the old blood and their ways. It was a good name. Homely, ordinary, but useful and sweet on occasion. I had liked the idea of being Apple, and I liked it still.

I kissed her cheek, which was not a thing we did, normally, and went to find Snow.

It was hard to pretend that I was just going on a trading trip to Oakmere, when what I wanted to do was grab him and cry over him and make him promise to be a good man, a man like his father, and promise to look after himself and eat properly and clean up after himself and to choose a kind, sweet girl to marry – oh, and all the rest of the things a mother worries about. But I just hugged him and kissed his brow, as I had done other times, when I went trading, and he noticed nothing, because what fifteen-year-old boy notices anything about his mother?

Somehow that was comforting, that he was so – workaday. So unknowing that danger could lurk unseen in the wild. That he was safe here.

Then I went. I took just enough food and drink to get me there, because I didn't expect to come back. I didn't take Lidi's backpack, just a potato sack. I wanted Snow to have the backpack.

I was surprised by how much I remembered about the way, considering how upset I had been fifteen years ago. I slept under the same holly bush I had sheltered under then, and next morning found the trail easily enough, but though I had worked hard and was still strong I wasn't as young as I had been then, and the climb was hard. I was breathless when I reached the ridge that rimmed the little valley where I had seen the tree spirit, and I paused a moment. It was mid-morning, with the sun gilding the young leaves and the birch trunks shining brightly in the shade, almost glowing, it seemed, with the stream chuckling between ferns as though it laughed.

I thought then, and I still think, that it was a place worth protecting. That if I were a tree spirit, I would act, too, to save it from desecration.

I went down the slope and stood by the stream, where I had seen the spirit before, and put my sack on the ground.

'I have come to pay my forfeit,' I said. Nothing happened. No figure, no change of sound, nothing. Then I remembered, and looked at the ground.

There it was, waiting. Silent. It raised its arms, the long fingers wavering as it shimmered in the sun, looking both real and unreal at the same time.

In the old stories, the words had to be said again, almost the same as when the bargain was made. So I took a breath and said, 'I am –' and then I stopped, because I did not know what to say. I had made the bargain as Dila, but now I was Apple, and glad of it. I stared at the figure in confusion, and of course it vanished as soon as I lifted my head.

I looked back down at the ground. 'I don't know what my name is,' I said. I must have sounded daft, but it was the truth, and maybe it could hear the truth in my voice, because it hissed – to my surprise – in laughter, like a spring breeze playing in the branches. That gave me confidence.

'I was Dila when I made your bargain. But now I am Apple.'

The spirit hissed again, and this time it was like the wind that rises before a storm.

'I don't know what to tell you,' I said. 'I'm here to pay whatever forfeit I have to, to keep my son safe. But I can't say to you, "I am Dila," because I'm not, anymore.'

It tilted its head, considering, and I considered, too. Was there nothing of Dila in me? Just my love for Lidi, I thought.

Its hissing increased, and now it was a question.

'There's a little part of me that is still Dila,' I confessed. Should I tell it what? It was growing impatient, I could tell. The wind was rising around us, the trees beginning to shake and the stream had small white waves. 'My love for my husband. He's dead. He died while I was still Dila, so that part of me is her.'

It was a poor explanation, and sounded sentimental to me, but the thing paused and the wind died. For a moment, the glade was silent, waiting. The back of my neck was getting sore from staring down for so long. Then the spirit reached out a hand and placed it on my chest. I thought, goodbye Snow, and I hoped – I remember hoping – that Lidi had waited for me so we could be reborn together.

Then I felt . . . Oh, I can't explain. A kind of tearing, in my heart, in my mind, all through my body. There was blood flowing, but not from any wound, just out of my skin, out of my eyes, out of my ears. It hurt. But not unbearably. The pain was not as bad as giving birth, not nearly as bad. The strangest thing was that the blood did not sink into my clothes. It flowed over my skin and down into the ground, disappearing as the spirit had disappeared the first time I had met it.

The spirit took its hand away.

There I stood, whole, unmarked, the blood leaving not a trace on my hands or anywhere that I could see, the pain fading, and me still alive.

The spirit hissed with satisfaction, and disappeared. That was it.

I stood there stupidly for a while, expecting something else to happen, but nothing did. The golden day went on around me and the stream chuckled its way along its bed, and I stood like a booby on the grass with tears running down my cheeks, because I had expected to die and now I was alive.

I climbed back out of the valley slowly, relishing every moment, and it wasn't until I had reached the ridge and was looking back at the valley that I thought of Snow, and how now I would be able to tell him the story, and I thought of Lidi, who would have to wait for me a bit longer. Then I realised what the spirit had taken. The last bit of Dila. The part that loved Lidi.

I could remember him. I could remember loving him. I could remember my grief when I lost him. But the feeling itself was gone. The part of my heart that had been full since the first day he kissed me was empty. He was just a memory, as though I'd heard about him in a story.

I felt the empty part of my heart every day, as I went about my milking and my sowing and my cooking. I felt both lighter and less solid, as though I had been hollowed out like a gourd. I had no grief, but nothing came to take its place, and I did not think anything ever would, because that was the nature of the forfeit, that that part of me should die.

It was a fair bargain. Blood and love and pain, for the life of my son. I would pay it again. But this was the thing: I knew that Dila badly wanted for Lidi to wait for her, so they could be reborn together. I knew that Dila, that *I*, thought that it was more likely he would wait for her because she continued to love him so much. So I wondered: I was Apple, wholly Apple, and Apple did not love him. So would he wait? Did I want him to?

I didn't care. It seemed to me that I would greet him after death merely as someone I once knew, with no more feeling than I have for the weaver in Oakmere who made my cheesecloths. But perhaps the part of me that had died already, the part that was Dila, will come back when it is time for me to go on to rebirth, and make me whole in death as I was not in life. Perhaps I will love him again, and greet him with joy.

I will have to wait to find out.

LEOF

THEGAN CAME WITH him to his horse the next morning, a great mark of favour. He handed Leof the stirrup cup himself, and said, 'Keep me informed. You are doing well, but don't forget to keep the officers on their estates up to date. We will be calling the levies in soon enough, I suspect.'

Leof nodded, feeling like a traitor because his heart was leaping at the thought of returning to Sorn. He was determined not to betray Thegan, but the image of her, waiting in her hall, that shaft of sunlight gilding her autumn hair, her green eyes wide and welcoming, made his heart turn over. And there was betrayal, right there, whether he did anything about it or not.

He had opened his mouth to say a formal goodbye when a shriek like a cold demon dying deafened them. Arrow and Bandy's horse, Clutch, reared and Thegan stood back, swearing. Leof fought with Arrow and got her under control, but Clutch bolted down the main street, straight for the harbour.

The shriek came again and this time Arrow stood, feet planted, head down, shaking uncontrollably. Leof looked up. Thegan was staring at the clear blue sky, his face pale. Leof followed his gaze and saw . . . something. A ripple in the sky, like a shadow on water; not quite a cloud, not quite anything.

'Wind wraiths,' Thegan said, tight-mouthed.

They were hard to see, but now he knew what was there, Leof could make out vague figures, misty and curving through the sky, long arms out as though reaching for the ground. He expected them to pass over the town.

'Where is he?' one of them screamed. The sound scraped over

Leof's nerves and Arrow trembled so hard he thought she would collapse. He dismounted and went to her head, soothing her. She turned her face into his chest like a child seeking comfort.

'Where is the enchanter who will feed us? Find him!' The voice was neither male nor female; it was high and low together, as a storm will have a deep voice and yet wuther high at the same time.

Thegan stared straight up at them, his face stern. 'There is no enchanter here. Begone! You are forbidden in this realm.'

'Hah!' The shriek rose high and passed the border of hearing, but Leof's ears still hurt as though the sound continued. 'Soon!' it declared. 'He will feed us spirit and body! Find him! Find him!'

The wraiths swirled out over the town, for all the world like hunting dogs looking for a scent. They shrieked and screamed and laughed so sharply that every dog started howling, or hid in terror, and every horse they passed panicked.

Thegan turned to Leof with sudden urgency. 'Quick! Follow them. If they find this enchanter for us, so much the better!'

Leof mounted Arrow, who was still trembling. He bent low over her neck, patting her and murmuring reassurance. Bandy had regained control of Clutch and was trotting up the street from the harbour.

Thegan watched the wraiths intently. They were gathering around the town's southern gate. It was hard to see them, but it looked like there was a local mist there, or a low cloud. Then it disappeared and the shrieking died away.

'South,' Thegan said. He slapped Arrow on the rump and she jumped forwards and then began trotting up the slope to the gate. 'After them, Leof! Find me this enchanter!'

Bandy clattered behind them, but Arrow was already picking up the pace. They swept through the gate at a canter and on the level ground of the cliff plateau Leof urged her on.

She responded to his hands and knees and began to gallop. Not her best pace, but one that she could sustain, if need be, for some time. He thanked the gods that he'd lost weight recently, having had so little time to sit down for meals and so little appetite when he did. Bandy was already far behind. Leof allowed himself a fleeting thought of Sorn, and then settled in the saddle.

He kept his eyes on the horizon, where a flowing mist, a ripple in the sky, showed where the wraiths were flying. As he watched they began to veer inland, following a minor road towards the farmlands of

Central Domain. This was his chance to catch up with them. They were following the way the enchanter had taken, and he had clearly kept to the roads. But Arrow and he weren't bound to marked routes. They could go cross country and perhaps even get ahead of the wind wraiths.

Leof headed Arrow at a low stone wall and she pricked her ears with pleasure. Like all chasers, she loved the sport and had missed it in Sendat. She took the jump flying and landed with precision on new hay. Leof couldn't bother, this time, about wrecking farming land or crops. Too much was at stake.

'We have to win this one, sweetheart,' he said to Arrow. 'This is the chase of chases.'

ASH

After Ash had learnt the truth about the demons of the Deep, he had been wild to discover his true shape, his animal nature. Now, with the truth promised to him, he had to wait, and wait, and wait . . .

'I am so hungry!' Flax complained for the sixth time.

'Well, you can always walk out of the Deep and take Cam and go back to Gabriston and eat,' Ash said, annoyed. Flax looked sheepish.

'I don't know what you're complaining about,' Ash added. 'You only have to fast until after the ceremony. I've got two more days to go.'

'Stop talking, you boys!' Vine ordered. 'We're trying to sleep!'

Ash and Flax exchanged glances of mutual long-suffering. They were in a group with three other young men who had arrived with their fathers during the afternoon. Each of them was at a different stage of his journey to the Deep, but each had to fast the day through before he could go to the appropriate cave and learn what he had to learn. Ash had been through all this preparation in previous years, but he was about to skip over the last couple of steps and go straight to the final test, the climb to discover his true shape. For that, he had to fast for three days, taking only water, and staying silent for the last full day.

The first day went slowly. At sunset, the men disappeared into the caves and reappeared a little while later in their true shapes. Individually, the boys were chosen and led away. Flax was last. Rowan came for him, with Skink, whose true shape was a fox. Flax made a nervous face at Ash and stood, half-unwillingly, and began to strip off his clothes. He seemed both attracted to and uneasy with the Deep, which was not a bad thing, necessarily. Ash just hoped he was trustworthy. Tonight he would have the demon warnings, the threats about keeping silent, the solemn vows of secrecy. They made an impression, as they were meant to.

Once Flax was naked, the demons led him to join Ash at the mouth of the cave. Ash patted his shoulder reassuringly. Rowan the badger led them forward, around the leaping fire, to the first of the chasms, a split in the rock that blocked the exit from the cave. Black as pitch, it was a couple of paces wide. From below the sound of water thundered up. Rowan gestured to Ash. He nodded, remembering. This warning was usually given in daylight, when the men could talk. The youngest boys were shown this cave on their third day in the Deep, to prepare them for the night, which was hard.

'This is the beginning of the Deep,' Ash said, echoing what he had been told precisely. 'This is your first glimpse of the River. This is not the Hidden River, which flows from the Lake for all to see. This is the Dancing River, the Lake's little sister. She flows throughout the land, underground, never seen except by us, here, where she reveals herself to us that we might know who we truly are. She flows from cliff to cove, from sand to snow, binding the Domains as no man ever could, making this all one country. Our country, given to us by water and fire and never taken away, no matter what the fair-haired ones think. But beware! The River is not the Lake. She is wild, not tame; she is joyous and terrible; she is lover and she is Death herself. Beware. Do not betray her, or her punishment will be unthinkable. Do you swear allegiance to the River, to finding your truth?' Gently, he added, 'You don't have to, but if you don't you can't go any further. You'll just have to wait in the clearing until morning.'

Flax gulped and glanced back to where the demons waited in the shadows made by the leaping fire. 'With them?' He shook his head and opened his mouth. 'I –'

Ash cut in quickly. 'Don't say it if you don't mean it. This is for life, Flax. There's no going back.'

Flax met his eyes, uncertain. 'Doesn't everyone want to know who they truly are?' he asked.

'No. Not everyone,' Ash said. 'Some are afraid. Some are so happy in themselves they don't need it. And some . . . some think they already know, and don't want it confirmed in front of others. Not everyone comes to the true Deep.'

Around them, the men waited patiently. No one moved. Ash could feel the pull of the River, feel its power flowing up from the slit in the rock. It was a different power to the gods; wilder, happier, more grief-stricken. It *felt* more, as humans feel. The River desired them to go forward. He sensed that desire, the desire to know and be known, to accept and be accepted, which lay at the heart of the River mysteries. He had always found it irresistible, but Flax was not him.

Flax stared down into the dark, listening. 'I swear,' he said suddenly.

As one, the men took in a deep breath and howled triumph to the roof of the cave. It was the sound they had heard the first night, but this time it buoyed them up instead of chilling them. Ash felt himself grin, and Flax smiled widely, puffing his breath out in a long sigh.

'Now what?' he asked.

Ash flicked him a glance full of mischief, and backed away. 'Now you jump,' he said.

'Over *that*?'

Ash nodded. The howling grew louder and Rowan ran and leapt, high and long, over the black chasm, over the pounding waters, landing in a crouch and waiting there for Flax.

'You next,' Ash said. 'Come on.'

Flax blew out his breath again and then backed up as far as he could go, until the fire was almost licking at his legs. Then he ran forward and leapt.

It wasn't a high leap, and for a moment Ash had a terrible fear that he would fall, and he would be left to explain his death to Zel. I promised to look after him, he thought in a quick panic, but then Flax was over safely and half-collapsed at Rowan's feet, panting much harder than he should have been from the jump. Yes, Ash thought, we learn about fear here. Rowan helped Flax to his feet and thumped him on the back in congratulations.

They went down the passageway and Ash returned to the clearing and settled down to wait. Tomorrow Flax would be taken to within touch of the River for the first time. The night after that, she would touch him. That was the night that Ash would climb.

All night he tended the fire and tried to ignore his rumbling stomach. The hunger would get worse, he knew. He had seen other young men go to the climb stumbling, light-headed with hunger. Fasting made the climb more dangerous, but cleansed the spirit and opened the heart to the River. It was necessary.

As he fed the fire, Ash realised that there was music building in his mind; a complex kind of music which he had no words for, no way of describing to anyone. He brooded over Skink's words after he had sung. He had been on pitch. His voice was true, even if it was horrible. If he could find someone willing to listen, he could share his music at last. But he doubted, as intertwined patterns of flute and drum and harp and voice ran through his mind, that simple singing could convey what he wanted. Perhaps this music simply wasn't meant to be heard by others. Perhaps it was only for the gods.

He resisted the temptation to take out the casting stones and ask. Casting for oneself was notoriously unreliable. But he decided to ask Martine, the first chance he got.

Because he was determined that there would be a future; that they would defeat this Saker; and he would not be a safeguarder in that future. Returning to the Deep had rekindled his love of music. He thought about Flax and the beauty of his voice. But it was the song that displayed that voice, and Flax was only a singer, not a maker of songs. Ash felt that, perhaps, he might be able to make songs that could rival the beauty of *The Distant Hills*. If he could find a way to teach the songs to others.

The young men came back just before dawn, exhausted, and ate cold meat and greengages and cheese. Ash sat away from them so he couldn't smell the food. Then the dawn lit the red rock walls as though drenching them with blood, the men came back from the caves in their true shape, ate breakfast, and all of them, Ash included, fell asleep in the early morning light.

He dreamt of water, running, endlessly running; of waves that took and carried him away; of Bramble smiling at someone out of sight; of fountains. Underneath the constant water sounds was music.

LEOF

OVER THE POST and rail fence, around the big willow tree and splashing across the stream, up the slope beyond, around the herd of dairy cows. The bull took objection to their appearance and put his head down to charge, bellowing defiance. Arrow scrambled out of the way and leapt over the dry-stone fence beyond. Leof leant low over Arrow's neck and grinned. It was like the best of chases – he felt like he was out alone, leading the field, the way Bramble used to do on Thorn.

Ahead of him the Kill raced, but this was one Kill he didn't want to catch. He shivered at what might happen if the wind wraiths realised he was following them. Then he grinned again and urged Arrow on. She was tiring, but her heart was so big that whenever he asked her for more she gave it.

Leof thanked the gods that he had spent so much time at chases when he first arrived from Cliff Domain. He knew most of this countryside, had ridden over a great deal of it. It was a mixture of pasture and crops, intercut with many, many streams and small rivers. One of the most fertile areas of the country, this farmland was the reason Thegan had wanted Central Domain so badly. Leof thought ruefully of the crops he had trampled since he left Carlion, but it would have wasted too much time to avoid them. The mixture of animals and crops meant that the fences were frequent and sturdy, and that the ground beyond them was usually firm and reasonably level – perfect chasing country.

In the next field, Arrow soared over the post and rail fence, took long low jumps over three streams that divided the field, cantered for a moment to catch her breath, then gathered speed again across the pasture, scattering ewes and lambs as she went. Leof stood in the stirrups to ease her back for a while.

The wraiths were following a winding route among villages and small towns. They had stopped twice to investigate something, the second time for so long that Leof had a chance to spell Arrow. Without that respite, she would have foundered. He might have been able to catch them, but that wasn't his task. He had to let them lead him to the enchanter.

He would very much have liked to see what had interested them so. They had swooped close to the ground, over and over, and seemed to be *smelling* it. But they had taken off so fast afterwards that he had no time to look. He had to take the straight line after them. He noted the locations and left them for another day. Right now, all he had to do was chase.

It was a glorious chase: over walls and streams, under shade trees and around coppices, over logs and through new hay that brushed his boots and smelt of summer. He felt vaguely guilty about enjoying it so much, when the safety of the Domains was at stake.

By the time the sun was overhead, out of his eyes, Arrow was tiring badly. He cast about for somewhere where he might get a change of horse, but the last village had been tiny and would have no messenger horses stabled there. He eased Arrow to a walk, watching the wraiths streak ahead of them, knowing he had probably failed, but clinging to the hope that they would keep going in that straight line and he would be able to find them again.

Then they stopped, in mid-air, hovering like hawks before a kill. And like hawks they stooped, shrieking. Leof wasn't close enough to see exactly what they had found. They were over a small grassy hill just outside the next village – Bonhill, that was it – and when they stooped they disappeared behind the hill.

He dismounted and walked Arrow slowly towards them, hoping that they would give her time to recover before speeding off again. Then he got close enough to hear a man's voice, speaking to them, and realised he had found the enchanter.

SAKER

ROWAN'S SONGS HAD been so precise. Saker gave thanks for the musician who had taught him all the old songs, the invasion songs which told how many of the old blood were killed in each place, and where they were buried. He wondered, briefly, where Rowan was now, and Swallow his wife, and Cedar their drummer. He had Travelled with them for months, learning the songs, and it had been the happiest time of his life.

Until now. Saker smiled as he turned over the ground and the spade revealed the graves. They had been shallow when made, but the centuries had covered them with layer after layer of dirt. He had had to dig deep. These bones were not in such good condition as others he had found. They were much browner, and soft, crumbling as he touched them. It was the damp. Water was a great destroyer of bones. The grave here was in a hollow which must have collected rainwater for untold years, making a lush patch in an otherwise scrubby field. Fed by the blood of his ancestors, Saker thought, and watered by the friendly rains of their home.

This was the fourth site he had excavated since Carlion, and it was almost routine. He sorted through the bones until he had taken fingerbones from each skeleton. Sometimes it was hard to decide which bone belonged to which body, and then he took extras just to be sure. After he had the fingerbones he laid them out on a piece of cloth and called to them, going over his litany of names. When he felt the twitch in his mind that told him the spirit had not gone on to rebirth, he placed that bone into the sack with the rest of his collection, and made a note of the name on his scroll. He had amassed quite a collection of names, now. He felt both triumphant and sad to read them over. So many, ready to fight. So many lost to Acton's greed.

He had sorted through almost two-thirds of the bones from this site and had gathered another dozen names when he heard the shrieking. He froze, immediately remembering the sound from terrible nights with Freite, the enchantress who had trained him. Wind wraiths. He began to shake with fear, as though he were still a child.

She had used the horrible spirits to cow him into obedience – had threatened to give him to them to be eaten, or worse. She never said what the worse was, but she didn't have to. The sight of them, their long clawed fingers, their sharp teeth and, most frightening of all, their hungry eyes, filled him with terror. He had given up his strength to her, holding nothing back, rather than be delivered into their hands. She had lived so many extra years because of that, but he had been much older when he had discovered what she was doing with his power.

They came over the hill and swooped down into the pasture, crying out, crying triumph. He had never seen them in daylight before. They were barely visible, merely a suggestion of movement in the sky, like a ripple in water. But their harsh voices were as strong as ever, and he shook at the sound.

Then he set his mouth. No. He was not a child to be terrorised anymore. Never again. He was an adult, and more powerful than any sorcerer had ever been, even Freite. He had seen her tame them. He could do the same.

Except that Freite had tamed them with music, with whistling and fluting, and Saker was as deaf to music as he was indifferent to dancing. He could not use her spell, the five repeating notes. But if he could find the right words, the right sounds, that would work as well. He thought frantically, quicker than he had ever thought in his life, while they swooped and jeered above his head.

'Feed us, enchanter!' they screamed. 'Feed us flesh and spirit!'

Saker paused. Feed them? That was what they had asked of Freite, and she had fed them, he knew, on vagrants and unwanted children. He had been excluded from those ceremonies as part of her obsessive desire to keep her secrets safe, but he could guess what had happened there. Perhaps he did not need to fear them after all.

She had told him, once, that they could not take what was not given. 'At least, it's so in the settled lands,' she had said. 'A prohibition was put on them by an enchantress. My tradition says it was done by a woman named Tern, but where she lived and how long ago I don't know.' She had smiled, the smile that she used to terrify him. 'They cannot take, but they can be fed. Beware, child.'

He shook off the unease of memory.

'Not yet,' he answered the wraiths.

'When? Whennnn?' they screeched.

'Soon,' he said, 'soon.'

He was disturbed, and unsure. Flesh he could give them in abundance. They could have all they could eat of Acton's people's flesh. But spirit? Now he realised what the 'worse' was that Freite had threatened. To have the spirit eaten . . .

Should he set them loose on the warlord's men? Should even justice go so far? He did not know. He did not know how to decide.

But if he wanted to restrain them, he had better find a spell that would work. Or they would turn on him and his ghosts, too. The ghosts' bodies might be unassailable, but what of their spirits? It might be that they were even more vulnerable to the wind wraiths than the living. He could not risk it. The warlord's men would have to lose their chance at rebirth as well as their lives. Unless he could find the right spell.

MARTINE

THEY LEFT THE Valuer's Plantation early. Apple rousted them out of bed before dawn and they set off as soon as they had eaten breakfast.

Travel with a warlord was easy, Martine discovered. No one looked sideways at a dark-haired woman in the warlord's party. Food just appeared out of inns as they stopped to water the horses; carts pulled to the side of the road to let them go past. Even with Arvid, who was probably as good as warlords got, there was still the forelock-tugging and the curtseys and the obsequiousness that all sensible people show to anyone who travels with a party of armed guards. She got angrier as the day went on, and noticed Zel felt the same.

Martine manoeuvred her horse next to Zel's chestnut, and they dropped back a little so they could talk. Trine came up next to them, still on a leading rein, but to Martine's surprise she didn't try to bite or kick. Perhaps she was beginning to accept Zel.

'It puts a bad taste in my mouth,' Zel said, nodding to where a goose girl was bending double, she was curtseying so hard. Martine discovered a desire in herself to defend Arvid. Which was ridiculous. She had to change the course of this conversation. 'The Valuers want to do away with warlords,' Martine said. 'Will you join them?'

That silenced her. Zel wasn't a joiner by nature, that was clear. She leant over to pat Trine, perhaps taking as well as giving reassurance. Trine snorted at the touch, but didn't bite. It might do her good to be with Zel, someone else she could learn to trust. Martine thought they were all having a lesson in trust, herself included.

It was two long days' ride to Foreverfroze, so they stopped overnight at an inn which did nothing but service the traffic to the port. There was barely a village surrounding it, and the countryside around was pure forest. The road here was only a cart's width, although the ground on either side had been cleared for a bow-shot by Arvid's orders to prevent bandits ambushing trading parties.

They ate in the inn parlour. Martine sat as far from Arvid as she could, but the fire was still disturbing her, still churning at her every time she looked at him, every time she heard his voice. Her hand shook with desire as she poured cider into her cup, and she put the jug down abruptly to conceal it. This was worse than her infatuation with Cob, when she'd had the excuse of youth. The fire was taking a difficult revenge. She went to her room early, ignoring Arvid's attempt to catch her eye.

What was she doing here? Martine wondered. She stood in the inn chamber and stared at her empty bed, too restless to go to sleep.

When she and Ash had left Turvite, she had meant to go to the Hidden Valley, to visit Elva and Mabry. She had done that, and the winter she had spent with them and the new baby had been a golden time, despite the shadow of the ghosts hanging over them. But since leaving the valley – since the gods had told her to leave – she had just moved from one place to another without a plan, without any idea of what she was supposed to be doing. Finding Bramble, bringing her to the Well of Secrets, the journey into the Great Forest, sending Bramble on her mysterious journey, even taking horse for Foreverfroze, had seemed to make sense because she felt some responsibility for Ash, and then for Bramble.

But now, with Ash gone to the Deep and Bramble gone gods knew where, what was she doing here? Her gifts weren't needed – Safred could do all the future sensing anyone could ask, and more. Any part she might play in this gods'-driven attempt to stop Saker was probably over when she gave Acton's brooch to Bramble.

Martine was used to being in control of her own life. Now she felt adrift, and she didn't like it. She sat down on the side of the bed and took off her right boot, then noticed the sole. All around the edge it had been nibbled away, as though rats had got to it, and the bottom was pitted with holes that went almost all the way through the thick leather. She stared at it in puzzlement, then suddenly understood. She had walked in these boots out on Obsidian Lake, not once but six times, and the water of the lake had done this. Eaten tanned leather, hard leather, like vitriol did. She shivered, remembering the sting of the

waters as she and Zel had cowered away from the fire. If the fire had-
n't burnt off the water so quickly, she and Zel might look like this
boot, or worse.

Martine felt a sudden desire to go home, back to Hidden Valley,
and protect her daughter and grandson. But she had promised to meet
Ash, and she would keep that promise.

They rode on the next day into increasing cold. Although it was
summer, the Foreverfroze peninsula was swept by winds that blew
across the never-melting northern ice. Yet the country teemed with life
under the horses' hooves. As they turned north and began the journey
up the peninsula, the trees grew sparser and more crooked, bent like
old women toting loads of kindling home. Under the trees, though,
there was lush grass and blazing wildflowers, and a constant scurrying
of small animals making paths through the long stems. In the distance
they saw elk and deer browsing. Birds were everywhere, and ignored
them as if they had never seen humans. Terns, swallows, herons in the
hundreds of low-lying pools, hawks high above in the vaulting pale
blue sky, flocks of geese and ducks, waders and moorhens and cranes,
even an albatross sailed above them and went on, riding the wind further out to sea.

The wind made Martine glad of the felt coat Drema had made for
her in Hidden Valley. It seemed a long time ago, although it was less
than a month since they had left. She spent a while wondering how little Ash was and how Elva was coping with motherhood. She realised
with amusement that she *had* turned into a grandmother . . . at least in
her thoughts.

With some determination, she forced herself to think about the present place and time. At least the wind kept the insects at bay. She was
sure that in the lee the midges would attack furiously.

As though he had been waiting for her to finish her thoughts, Arvid
brought his horse next to hers and smiled at her. The smile seemed to
split her mind in two. One part was full of the suspicion of a lifetime:
what would a warlord want with a Traveller woman? That had an easy
answer! The other part came from deeper down, the part that had been
brought back to singing life by the fire. The easy answer was the
answer it wanted. The fire inside her urged her to simply drag him
from his horse and take him there, on the ground, in front of everyone.
No, the fire's voice seemed to whisper to her, it would be better in private, where he would not be distracted. She was increasingly sure that

this was her punishment from the fire – to be tormented by desire that could never be fulfilled.

His smile was tentative and he looked like a boy of sixteen approaching his first Springtree dance partner. There was a sweetness in that smile that disarmed her. Sweetness wasn't a quality she associated with warlords.

But he was also an experienced negotiator, and he was too canny to begin with anything personal.

'Safred is still upset with your friend who has gone,' he said, a trace of the smile lingering at the corner of his mouth.

She smiled involuntarily. 'Bramble's hard to predict,' she said.

'You know her well?'

Martine considered. 'I've not known her long,' she said. 'But I have some understanding of her, I think.'

'Safred has told me about your undertaking,' Arvid said, his face completely serious.

Martine was shocked, and then wondered why she should be. They would need all the help they could get – this was a problem for the whole of the Domains. They were not spies, on a secret quest for their lord! Of course Safred had told him. No doubt all the warlords would know soon enough anyway. They kept each other informed of any threats to the Domains.

'Do you think Bramble is committed to her task?' Arvid asked.

That was the warlord talking, and Martine resented it. 'Oh, no, I think she's gone off on a holiday,' she said.

He winced. 'She is young, and perhaps afraid,' he suggested.

'Hah! That one's never been afraid of anything in her life,' Martine retorted. 'She says she's found a quicker way. She'll meet us in Sanctuary. Well then, we should go to Sanctuary.'

'"We"?' Arvid asked delicately.

'Safred and Zel and Cael and I,' Martine said. She didn't look at him. Would he offer to come with them? It was unheard of for a warlord to enter another warlord's territory without formal invitation: an act of war. He could come as far as Turvite, but after that . . .

'And Trine?' he asked with a smile, then paused. 'I could come as far as Turvite, if you think it would be helpful.'

She paused, struggling with herself. The two halves of her mind were in conflict. One wanted nothing to do with him. The other craved his company. Then her Sight reared up and swept all personal feelings

aside. It was one of the strongest sensings she had ever had. Her hands
shook with the power of it and the chestnut she was riding skittered a
little. She clutched at the reins, still unsure on horseback.

'Yes,' she said, eyes staring blindly at the stream they were passing.
'Yes, we will have need of you in Turvite. Great need.'

He nodded silently, but then let his horse fall back as though unsettled by her. She felt a flash of an old bitterness. She had lost her first
love because he couldn't accept her gifts. Elva's father, Cob, had turned
to Elva's mother instead, but fathered a babe far stranger than Martine.
It was so long ago that most of the time she rarely thought of Elva as
anything but her own child, but their relationship was the result of a
man rejecting the uncanny twice over, in her and in his own flesh. With
no excuse, because he was of the old blood. The oldest blood.

She shook her head free of the thoughts. Time she accepted that no
man wanted to lie next to a seer, in case she could see into his soul and
perceive the small, grimy secrets that lie in the centre of all human
hearts. Well, that rejection had given her a daughter, and now a grandson, so she should thank Cob instead of resenting him.

But when they stopped for lunch and to water the horses, she kept
a distance from Arvid, all the same. There was no use inviting hurt. Or
thwarted desire.

In mid-afternoon they passed a long train of ox-carts lumbering
along the track, piled with high, canvas-covered loads. This was the
merchandise the Last Domain was shipping to Mitchen, no doubt. A
party of Arvid's guards protected them, although what bandits would
attack them out here Martine couldn't imagine.

'Go on,' Arvid said. 'I'll just have a word.'

They rode around the carts, raising their hands to the drivers who
sat hunched against the wind and who occasionally lifted a whip to
their oxen. The drivers nodded back, staring at Safred, whom they
clearly recognised. Martine wondered how often Safred had visited
Arvid at his fort, and why. Well, no doubt the gods had given her reasons, but consorting with warlords still seemed strange to her. It was
disconcerting, after so many years spent avoiding warlords and their
men, to be riding with them, part of their group, as safe as if she were
among friends.

Arvid consulted briefly with the group's leader and then cantered
up to rejoin them. 'They'll be in Foreverfroze tomorrow, maybe the
day after if the wagons get bogged down again. It happens a lot in this

season. Easier on sledges in winter, really, but then the harbour is ice-locked.'

He spoke absently, as though mentally computing the oxen's speed and endurance against a private timetable.

'Do all warlords concern themselves with trade?' Martine asked him, trying for a normal conversation with him.

He grimaced. 'They don't have to. They have the free towns to organise trade for them.'

'And you have no free towns?' Despite her intentions, the comment came out accusingly.

He glanced shrewdly at her, and smiled a little. 'All our towns are free towns,' he said. Martine shut her mouth firmly. Enough talk. No matter what she said, he would twist it. That was what warlords did. But Arvid went on. 'Unfortunately, there are not enough people living in them to take all the goods that we produce. The things worth the most, the furs and the sapphires and the timber, those are worth more in the southern Domains, so it pays us to ship them down, but no one town is big enough to hire a ship for itself. So I do it.'

'And take a cut!' Safred said.

Arvid laughed. 'Of course! I have to support my people, after all, and that takes silver. Better a tax on exports than on grain, or cattle, or houses. This way, only the people that can afford it pay.'

Safred sniffed. 'You don't need so many guards.'

'Tell that to the people on the borders of the Ice King's land. We have repelled two attacks this year already.'

'Why aren't you there, then?' Martine asked. It struck her as odd that a warlord would leave a battlefield. It went against their whole code.

'*Because*,' Arvid said, provoked at last and glaring at Safred, '*someone* told me the gods forbade it. So my men have to face the enemy alone and I am here, counting wagons like a merchant, instead of leading them as I should.'

Ah, Martine thought. There's the warlord. He's been hiding, but he's there. The thought gave her some satisfaction, but also brought pain, as though a needle had slid into her heart.

Safred shrugged. 'Complain to the gods,' she said. 'It's not my fault.'

Involuntarily, Martine exchanged a glance with Arvid, both of them amused at Safred. It was hard not to smile back. She had never thought of blue eyes as being warm before.

To distract herself from the heat spearing through her, she said a prayer for Elva and Mabry and the baby. The gods don't pay much attention to humans, she thought, but sometimes they do; sometimes they take a liking, and they liked both Elva and Mabry. Loved them, even. So perhaps the prayer would work. She said none for Ash or Bramble. They were already in the hands of the gods, and no prayers of hers would change the outcome.

BRAMBLE

WALKING WITH THE hunter was like stalking deer. Bramble had to move stealthily but also quickly. The hunter was entirely silent; no footfall, no rustle of grass or branches. Bramble had roamed the woods all her life, but still, inevitably, she brushed aside grass stems which sighed, or occasionally placed her foot on a twig which groaned under her. Each time, the hunter flicked her a look that was impossible to decipher. Scorn? Disbelief? Astonishment?

They moved through the darkening Forest so fast they were almost running. Her skills came back to her, but she would never equal the hunter in stealth. It seemed to realise this and slowed its pace, just a little.

Bramble knew they were travelling further north, but she asked no questions. She had taken the leap and was in mid-air; she just hoped there was firm footing on the other side.

As the night grew darker, the hunter realised that Bramble was having more trouble following it. 'Soon,' it promised, and went more slowly. They came, after a while, to a space where a huge tree grew. Some kind of conifer, that was all she could tell in the darkness, but enormous, its trunk larger around than Gorham's house in Pless. Much larger. The tree looked almost as wide as the Pless Moot Hall, and its upper branches disappeared into the stars. As they ducked down to pass under its branches the faint light disappeared altogether. Bramble stood still, her head just below its lowest limbs, lost in a sighing black that moved around her as the wind soughed.

She wanted to ask where they were, but knew it was a foolish question. They were in the Forest, they were underneath an old tree. Any other answer was a human answer, one the hunter would not know.

'Come,' it said. It took her by the arm and led her to the trunk of the tree, a journey that took some minutes.

They stood between huge writhing roots and the hunter said, 'Do you remember where you want to go?'

'Um . . .' Bramble thought about it. She had to be very clear about this. 'I remember it in the past.'

'Soooo,' the hunter said, and listened to the Forest. 'Do you remember it clearly? Tell it to the Forest.'

'It's a cave,' Bramble said. 'In the Western Mountains. A cave with drawings on the wall from long, long ago.'

The hunter sniffed. 'All times are long ago,' it said. 'But we cannot go to a cave. That is the domain of the stone-eaters. I cannot take you there.'

'But –'

It ignored her interruption. 'Do you remember outside the cave?'

The memory flooded back: being in Red's body, watching Acton ride up the slope towards the cave. Watching him disappear into the trees. Into what had been the Forest, in those days when the Forest had covered the whole country. The hunter hissed with satisfaction.

'So. You remember. The Forest remembers. It will take you there. The journey will take much time and no time.'

'How?'

'The Forest remembers. We will go to your memory and then come back to your moment, this moment you are tied to so strongly.'

Bramble half understood, but only half. I'm still in mid-air, she thought. She felt, immediately, the exhilaration of the chase. The hunter smiled, showing sharp teeth, as though it too felt the surge of excitement.

'Put your hand on the tree, prey,' it said. 'Its roots go back far. Very far.'

Bramble reached out and placed her palm on the crinkled bark. Just as before starting a chase, all her senses seemed more alert. She felt the faint breeze on her cheek, heard owls and, high above, a flock of smaller birds. The small songbirds were migrating to their summer breeding grounds. They always flew at night, to avoid the hawks: black caps, warblers, swallows. Their wings flurried the night air, there were so many of them. Bramble could feel the tiny shiver along the tree as the owl launched itself from the upper branches in pursuit of the flock. Was it possible that she had really felt that? The night shifted and seethed around her, full of life. She could smell something: cedar? A strong, heady scent that dizzied her.

'Take a step forwards,' said the hunter. She did, and it was broad day.

She stared at the hunter. It leant casually against the tree, its elegant bones jutting in the wrong places. She had been right, it was a kind of cedar tree, although a type she had never seen before. Her instinct told her never to show weakness to the hunter, so she disguised her disorientation.

'I thought cedars needed warm places to grow,' she said.

The hunter shrugged. 'Not this one.'

They stepped away from the trunk. More than the light had changed. The tree seemed much smaller. It was, surely, only a young tree. Even allowing for the magnifying effects of night, Bramble was sure it had been huge before.

'We're in the past,' she said.

'Not in *your* past yet,' the hunter said reprovingly, as though she had been stupid. 'There are more steps to that memory. Come.'

It set off through the Forest at a slower pace than the night before. Almost strolling. 'No hurry now,' it said.

'Why not?' Bramble was concerned that the question might sound like a weakness, but she had to know. The whole *point* of this was that she didn't have any time to waste.

It listened to the Forest, and lost the disdainful look on its face, as though it had been chastised. 'We travel in the past,' it said as though explaining to a child. 'So no time is lost in your *moment*. Then we return to your moment. I told you.'

Bramble wondered how far back they had come. A hundred years? Five hundred? She felt light-hearted and light-headed. There was no task waiting for her here, and no grief. Maryrose was not yet dead. There was no one being slaughtered – at least, not more than there had always been, as the warlords extended their territory. The thought sobered her. She had seen too much death recently to be flippant about it, even five hundred years in the past.

The hunter slipped through the Forest and Bramble took off her boots and followed it, barefoot as it was barefoot, treading where it trod, trying to see with its eyes. There was no difference between this Forest and the one they had been in last night. It renewed itself eternally and time, to it, Bramble realised, was a matter of concentration, of where it put its attention. There was no *present*, no *past*, perhaps no *future*. Just the Forest.

The sense of timelessness was a gift from the Forest, she thought, as keeping the mosquitoes away had been a gift from the Lake. A gift to the Kill Reborn. Bramble wondered fleetingly if they would have done as much for Beck, if he had made the same journey. Then she thought, with a little satisfaction: the hunter would have killed Beck. She knew that she had been saved from fear because she had already been dead, had experienced the death-in-life for so long before becoming the Kill Reborn. Beck would not have had that toughening, and he would have feared, and died. It was all the roan's doing.

For the first time since his death, she could think of him with simple gratitude untouched by guilt. Perhaps seeing his death reflected in the eyes of the Well of Secrets was responsible, but she thought it more likely because of all the death she had seen, all the grief she had shared, while watching Acton's life. Everyone dies. What matters is the life shared beforehand.

But, just as she had learned acceptance through living other people's grief, she had also learned fear. Her body had learnt what it felt like to be afraid; had learnt how fine the line was between excitement and terror. So here she was, with a creature not human, who yearned to kill her, who *needed* in some way to kill her, in a landscape full of wolf and bear and sudden dangers, in a past she had no way of escaping. Her body wanted to be afraid, as Elric had been afraid, as Baluch had, waiting for Sebbi to die. But she refused. To understand fear was a good thing. The knowledge might make her kinder, she thought. But to let it fill her, let it take over, would lead to more than death at the hunter's knife. It would mean losing herself, the self that would survive death and go on to rebirth.

So she looked at the unfamiliar Forest, at the undergrowth which could conceal anything, and laughed, and the hunter laughed with her, a deep belly laugh.

The days went past as they walked the Forest, and Bramble let them go without counting them. They had not come back exactly in the year; it was full summer, and the best time to be wandering under the green shade.

They stopped occasionally to find food for Bramble. The hunter didn't seem to need food, only a sip of blood from each creature it killed, but it did need that, although not, perhaps, the way she needed to drink. It showed her how to stand so still that the deer would come up and surround her and she could reach out and plunge her knife into a throat.

'A moment,' it said. 'Just pause a moment for the fear to come before you thrust. Then you will be cleansed.'

But she wasn't cleansed, just the opposite, so she left that to the hunter, after the first time, because it seemed calmer, happier, after a kill. Although it might be covered in blood afterwards, the blood vanished immediately, with a little shiver in the light so that the hunter became momentarily hard to see. A ripple in time? Bramble wondered, but didn't comment on anything except the excellence of the hunt.

'It is my purpose,' it said simply, gutting and butchering the carcase of a fallow deer for her with swift, beautiful strokes of its black rock knife.

She asked it no questions about its name, or its life, or anything not directly related to their path. The need to know would be seen as a weakness, she was sure. An indication of fear. She remembered too well the feeling of its knife at her throat. Then, she hadn't been afraid; now, she had a task to complete, which made it harder to face death without regret. She owed it to Acton to find his bones. Let him be a hero in death the way he had wanted to be in life but wasn't, quite.

Although she guarded always against showing any fear, Bramble was happier than she could remember being except for when she was racing the roan. This was where she belonged.

She found blueberries and raspberries as they walked, collected greens and wild carrots and onions, found tiny sweet plums and small black cherries. The hunter could find anything Bramble wanted, but she was determined to feed herself. She had done it hundreds of times before, after all. As the days went past, the hunter seemed to acquire some respect for her knowledge of plants. They seemed irrelevant to it; not needing to eat anything except death, plants were known but not important.

The hunter did not need to eat, but it did need sleep, as she did. At night they found soft grass to cradle them. Bramble offered to share her blanket, but the hunter refused. 'Cold and hot are the same,' it said, lying easily on its side.

Bramble watched it sleep and saw that it simply closed its eyes and was still, stiller than any human sleeper. Although that stillness was strange, it was real, and she was reassured by it. The hunter was not tricking her into vulnerability. She closed her own eyes and fell into slumber as easily as it had.

Four days after they left the tree – or was it five? Bramble couldn't remember, and was warmed by the thought that it didn't matter – they arrived at a ridge, and Bramble realised that they were looking down into what would become Golden Valley. The valley was wild, still, although the bottom was studded with the poplars that still grew there. But the rest of the valley was pure Forest.

She smiled at the sight. 'I like this time,' she said.

The hunter gave a small puff of laughter. 'All time is the same,' it said, shaking its head at her.

They travelled through the Valley for some days, then headed west from the bluff at its mouth, going south-west on a long diagonal that would bring them to the foot of the Western Mountains, near where Actonston would lie. On a cloudy day which threatened storm, in a sparser, drier section of the Forest that favoured pines and larches, they found themselves at the edge of a cleared area of ground that led down to a farmhouse by the side of a river. It looked primitive. Not like the solid timber halls of Acton's time, nor the stonemasonry of her own. This farmhouse was slab construction, flung up in a hurry in summer to make sure there would be shelter by the time winter came. A short line of skinny cows was heading for a shed which no doubt doubled as the milking barn. In a pen near the barn, a scurry of calves bellowed for their mothers.

They stood looking down on the scene in silence. From a distance, the sound of axe blows cut through the late afternoon. The hunter and she both winced, then looked at each other in a kind of comradeship.

'Come,' it said. 'There are too many humans here.'

It led her through the edges of the Forest towards the mountains, until they could no longer hear the axe or the lowing of the cows. The hunter went into a deep defile in the hillside, a narrow valley that raised its sides high above their heads in minutes. At the end of the valley, where it could gather all the water that run off the hillside, stood a lone chestnut tree, dominating the valley.

'Its roots do not go far enough, but it will take us some way,' the hunter said. 'This is a good place of remembrance, this. The tree remembers strongly.'

This time, the step forwards, hand on the bark of the tree, took her to early, early morning, a winter morning which lay ice still, frost covering the ground, tiny icicles edging each bare branch. Bramble looked up. The chestnut branches were dark against the pale, cloudless sky. As she watched, the sun crested the rim of the valley and lit the tree: each icicle flashed rainbows of colours, the whole tree flickered with brilliant light, with sparks and flames and ripples of cold fire.

This is what rebirth must feel like, Bramble thought. Shivering, she stood transfixed until, only a few moments later, the sun had warmed the icicles enough so that droplets hit her face and shocked her out of the reverie. She turned to the hunter, who was watching her with approval and a slight unease, as though her appreciation of the tree worried him somehow.

'Come,' it said, 'we must cross the river.'

Unnervingly, although her breath was making steam, the hunter's did not, as though its breath was as cold as the air. She tried to remember the moment when its knife had been at her throat. She had been close enough to feel its breath, but she didn't remember feeling it at all.

Bramble fished her boots out of her saddlebags. Barefoot was all very well for the hunter, who seemed not to notice the cold, but frostbite was something she'd rather avoid. She wrapped her blanket around her shoulders as well, but even so she was very cold. She followed the hunter across snow dotted with the tracks of hare, followed by fox tracks.

The hunter chuckled. 'The fox seeks its prey. Good luck, little brother.'

She smiled, too, until she saw that the hunter left no tracks in the snow, although she saw its feet sink in. It saw her looking back at the single line of footprints in the powdery snow.

'I am here, in truth,' it assured her. 'I just allow the snow to remember what it was before I passed. I will show you.'

It took a few steps and suddenly there were tracks behind it. Then it turned and waited, and the snow smoothed itself out. Bramble couldn't see any movement of snowflakes; it was just, suddenly, as though the tracks had never existed. It was a much smaller manipulation of time than the one which had brought her back to this moment, but it unsettled her more, because it was done so casually. As though time was infinitely malleable.

She needed to control her upset immediately, before the hunter sensed it and saw it as fear. She grabbed for the first thing she could think of: Acton. If time *was* so malleable, did that mean she could journey back again? Change things? Stop Red plunging that knife down, and up again? She shivered, and it was not just the chill air. What if he lived? What if he lived *while she was there*? Her heart beat faster at the thought. She could guide him; warn him. If she went back far enough, she could even prevent Hawk's massacre of Swef's steading, and the resettlement from over the mountains would have been peaceful. She longed for that; remembered the lightness and joy she had felt when she had thought that the invasion was not going to happen.

But like a shadow over the too-bright snow-covered landscape, the memory of Dotta's warning came back. She had said that if Acton didn't invade, others would. Nothing could save the Domains . . .

'How far back can you take me?' she asked the hunter as they trudged down the slope to the frozen river.

'Far.'

She left it at that, but she kept thinking about it; wondering which was the right moment to go back to. Where could she do the most good? It kept her mind off the cold.

In this time, the steading they had seen did not exist; the Forest reached all the way to the river. They crossed by sliding on the ice like children, laughing and falling and making faces at the water sprites who stared up, impotent and hungry, from beneath the ice. These moments of gaiety came on and off to the hunter, and its laughter was infectious.

It led her through several more seasons, finding places of remembrance every few days. One was a vast holly thicket, which seemed exactly the same in the earlier time. Another, a shaded clearing full of mushrooms.

'They go deep,' the hunter said, smiling.

Although she left her boots off unless it was very cold, by the time they came to the mushroom glade the soles were almost worn through. They had travelled a very long way, and not by the shortest route. The hunter diverted them often; to hunt, to investigate the health of a herd of deer, sometimes simply to see something it considered significant, although there was no pattern to what was important: a single leaf, a spring, a small grouping of rocks. It never took her near a black rock altar, and she didn't ask why not, but she noticed that the gods left her alone. The whole journey was free of their presence; she felt liberated and forsaken at the same time.

MARTINE

THEY REACHED FOREVERFROZE at mid-afternoon. Martine had never been there, not in all her wanderings, and she stared as openly as Zel.

The town was sheltered by a ridge of light grey rock to the north which ran down to the sea, forming one headland of the huge harbour. The other was a flat tongue of land to the south, which curved like a fishhook. The long, long wharves for which Foreverfroze was famous ran out into the curve of the fishhook but were still in the lee of the ridge. The town looked exposed, compared to the high-cliffed ports of Turvite and Mitchen, but it offered the best harbourage available in the north, and had prospered as the southern cities had grown – there was always a market for smoked whitefish.

There were no houses, as such – most of the buildings were underground, or at least dug in to roof level, so that the town looked like a collection of hats left lying on the ground by careless giants. Some were roofed with straw, some with turves. They were spaced in a series of circles, surrounded by gardens, so that no one was far from a neighbour's door, but each household had a green space around it. The gardens were full of vegetables but there were no flowers except the ones which bloomed casually along the side of the street.

Foreverfroze was a casual place overall. Green-eyed, fair-skinned children ran by their horses, calling up at them in a sweet, singing language, their black hair cut short, boys and girls alike. Martine realised that she was among people of her exact colouring: the pale skin, the green eyes, the black straight hair. A wave of excitement rose in her. There were still places, then, where the old blood lived together. Survived. Thrived. The last time she had been in a village of her own kind seemed a lifetime ago. Was it twenty-two, twenty-three years, since the twin villages of her birthplace had been destroyed by the Ice King's men? She had thought that the old blood was permanently scattered, flung in droplets across the Domains, harassed and driven and cheated and spat upon. She had thought there was no resting place for her people anymore. But here they were, just living. Tears rose in her eyes and her heart felt hot and tight. She was grateful that the town itself was different from her home. But the people were so similar, she almost expected to see Cob, or her mother, or one of her many aunties, come around the side of one of the roofs.

Instead, men sat in groups by the small doorways of their houses, weaving baskets; or tended the gardens; or nursed a baby. One lifted a hand as the party rode by. Occasionally an old woman mending a fishing net nodded to them as they went past. They saw only one younger woman. She was heavily pregnant. Otherwise, Martine knew, she too would have been out on the fishing ships.

On the horse, looking out across rooftops, it struck Martine forcefully that there was nothing in the town taller than an adult human. She felt like a giant, and was reminded of stepping back across Obsidian Lake with Bramble in tow, when she had felt immense, like one of the old gods.

The road curved through the circles of houses until it came to a half-circle set back from the wharfs, which were the only things that looked like their equivalent in the south. There were no large boats tied up, although there were quite a few small skiffs with blue sails out in the harbour. Martine noticed a few nets spread to dry. The largest building in the semi-circle was a big hall with an entrance held up by pillars of carved wood – precious in this landscape of sparse and stunted trees.

A few men and two older women ambled across to meet them at the doors. They dismounted and Holly took the reins, being careful to avoid Trine's teeth. One of the men beckoned her to bring them around the back of the hall. Arvid looked at Safred and then at Martine. He seemed to be debating whether or not to take the lead.

'Skua, Fox, greetings,' he said to the older women. It was hard to tell them apart, they were both so wrinkled and bent and white-haired, although Fox had a more determined mouth and Skua's eyes were so creased with good humour that they almost disappeared when she smiled.

They nodded at him and then at the rest of the party, examining Martine with interest. She smiled at them, and Skua came forwards and patted her cheek and said something, something she could almost understand. It was as though the language of her childhood had been taken and twisted back onto itself. The rhythm was right, some of the syllables were right, but the meaning eluded her.

'Skua says, you look like one of them,' Arvid said, surprised as he took in the resemblance.

Fox said something seriously.

'Fox says the old blood will never be gone from the land while you are alive.'

Martine shivered a little. That seemed too much like a prophecy for her taste.

'Let's hope I live forever, then,' she said lightly. From their reaction it was clear they understood her, because both women firmed their mouths in a wry half-smile, and Skua patted her on the shoulder, as though she read her thoughts as well.

'Come to hall,' Skua said, pronouncing the words with difficulty and some pride. She pushed Martine in the back to get her moving.

That simple touch, full of authority, made Martine feel young and vulnerable. *I am a grandmother*, she reminded herself, but with the two old women next to her, taking an arm each and shepherding her along the path, she felt like a child again, being taken by her aunties to see the village Voice because of some naughtiness. It had happened, once, when she had Seen the villages being attacked and raised a false alarm. She had been belted well and truly by Alder that day. He had a hard hand and her parents hadn't spoken to him or his family ever again. She had tried to forget the whole thing. Now, as she was being chivvied along, she realised it had not been a false alarm. She *had* Seen the attack which eventually destroyed the villages. She had just Seen it too early. Although, in her vision, the attackers had been warlord's men, not the Ice King. That memory pulled at her for the first time since the beating, and she wondered what her Sight had truly meant. When she had some time and solitude, she would try to remember it more clearly.

ASH

O N THE SECOND night, when the men went into the caves to
become their true selves, Rowan stayed behind with Ash. He did-
n't say anything until Skink came back and took Flax away, naked and
scared but eager, too.

Rowan nodded towards the cave entrance after they were gone.
'He's a fine singer, that one,' he said.

Ah, Ash thought. That's why he's stayed with me. To have the 'Flax
will join us' conversation. He was a little light-headed with hunger and
he found it vaguely funny.

'Yes,' he said. 'Mam'll be pleased as a bear cub with a honeyfall.
You'll be able to perform all the duets, now.' He waved expansively.
'All the difficult stuff that needs more than one voice.' He found he
was avoiding the word 'song' as he would avoid using a sore finger.
That made him both sad and angry. 'All the *songs* you couldn't do
while I was with you.'

Rowan looked down at his hands, fiddling with the flute he carried
everywhere. 'I won't say that hadn't occurred to me,' he said. 'But it's
not what I wanted to talk about.'

He paused, as though waiting for Ash to prompt him with a question. Ash kept silent. Rowan sighed. 'We've missed you,' he said.

'I've been gone two years,' Ash said. 'You know where Turvite is.
You could have visited.'

'We did,' Rowan said. 'We went back this winter past, but you were
gone, and Doronit wouldn't answer any of our questions. If it wasn't
for a man named Aelred, we wouldn't have known if you were dead
or alive. He told us you'd left with a woman named Martine.'

It was a question.

'Yes,' Ash said. What could he say? Tell the whole story – Doronit's use of him, the attack on Martine's life, his decision to reject everything Doronit stood for? That was past, and no sense going over it. 'She's Elva's mother. Little Ash's grandmother. That's how I met Elva and Mabry.'

At the word 'grandmother', Rowan had relaxed, no doubt imagining some white-haired old dodderer instead of the brazen seducer he had feared. Ash smiled, thinking of Martine's calm beauty and the times he had forced himself not to desire her.

'When you leave here,' Rowan said quietly, 'to sing the songs . . . do you want me to come with you?'

Astonishment kept Ash silent. This was one thing that had never occurred to him. He had imagined, when he first felt the power in his casting stones, joining his parents back on the Road. But he had never imagined his father joining *him*. He didn't know what to say.

'Will I need you, to sing them?' he asked finally.

Rowan went very still, and then shook his head. 'I doubt it.'

'Well, then,' Ash went on, suddenly sure. 'I'll be going into the middle of this fight. Better for you and Mam to be a long way off. Where I don't have to worry about you.'

Rowan looked rueful. 'Where you don't have to safeguard us?' he asked. 'No, don't answer. You're right. You have more to concern you than us, now, and that's as it should be.'

Ash wasn't sure if he'd offended his father or not. He never did anything right, it seemed.

'Your mother wanted you to go to Doronit. She said it would be the making of you. I wasn't so sure, but she was right.' As usual, Ash thought. You always think she's right. 'From what you're not saying, it may have been unpleasant,' Rowan added, 'but it's made you grow up.'

That's a good thing, isn't it? Ash wanted to shout at him. Why look so sad?

Rowan stood up and clapped him on the shoulder, then started to undress, getting ready to join the others in the caves. He hesitated, his eyes unreadable in the firelight. 'Did you find anyone to love, since you've been gone?' he asked.

Ash thought of Doronit, Martine, Elva, Bramble . . . 'No,' he said. 'Other things have concerned me.'

He hadn't intended it as a rebuke, but his father stiffened.

'It's a hard road, when the gods hold the reins,' Rowan said. 'Take care of yourself.' Then he walked into the cave, disappearing behind the entrance fire like a spirit.

Ash sat for a while, staring into the narrow sky above the clearing, and wondering why he felt both loved and lonely at the same time.

BRAMBLE

GRADUALLY THEY APPROACHED the mountains and their path grew more difficult, over ridges and through steep valleys, down into chasms and up the other side, climbing with fingertips and toes. Halfway up a cliff face, barely hanging on over a sheer drop, they looked at each other and laughed, united in joy.

Then the hunter led her to an oak tree and said, 'Take a step forward.'

When she did so, it was winter. The air bit at her cheeks and hands.

'You are in your moment, now,' the hunter said. 'Your place is over there.'

It pointed west of south. Bramble's mouth went dry. She had stopped thinking days ago; had relaxed into the rhythm of walking and climbing and hunting. Acton had retreated in her mind; now her need to make a decision surged forward. Her breathing quickened, and that was a mistake, because the hunter's hand went to its knife in anticipation.

'Are you afraid?' it said.

'Look,' Bramble said, finally exasperated, 'I'm not going to be afraid of you, all right? Just accept it.'

It smiled, painfully. 'Until I kill you, I am in your world,' it said. 'Bound to share your time. Your death will free me. Return me to what I was.'

'Fine. Later. I'll try to be afraid of you later, after all this is over, and then you can kill me.' It nodded, seriously, as though satisfied, and she thought wryly that she might regret that promise. 'Can you take me further back?' she asked. 'Can you take me back another five years?' If she warned them, then, of what was going to happen, surely she could divert history's path?

But the hunter shook its head. 'The Forest told me to bring you here. Nowhere else. No other time.' It looked at her suspiciously. 'Why do you want more of the Forest's time?'

'So I can change things,' she said. 'Make them better.'

The hunter took a step back in shock. 'No, no, no. Do you not understand? These are places of *remembrance*. They are not to be changed. Never. Memory is sacred.'

'But –'

It drew its knife. 'I would kill you uncleansed first,' it said, 'and die.'

'Why?'

It searched for words, its face troubled, like a child who had been asked too hard a question. 'Time is knotted together with memory. With the places of remembrance. Make a change, and the knots come undone altogether. Not only the future unties. The past, too.'

Its voice was earnest, and she knew it told the truth. Her shoulders sagged. She might have known it wouldn't be possible. Over and over the gods had put her in a place where *if only* she had changed things, the future would have been better, and over and over they had prevented her from acting. She supposed it was time to accept it. Her role was to watch, and to retrieve. To witness, and to remember. Just like the hunter.

It was watching her with concern, an expression she had never seen before on its face.

'You don't want to kill me,' she said, wonderingly.

It flinched and looked away, then lifted its chin and stared her in the eyes. 'You are too like one of us,' it said. 'Fearless and joyful. But you are still my prey, and one day you will fear, and I will be there and claim my kill, and then I will be a true hunter once again. One who has not let the prey escape.'

She nodded. 'That will be a good death,' she said. 'I forgive you for it, and release you from reparation.'

The hunter paled. 'What is it that you have done?'

Bramble smiled and touched its shoulder, just once, lightly. 'It is how we cleanse each other of killing.'

That troubled it again. It stared at her, golden eyes unblinking, like a hawk's. 'I do not know if that is a good thing or a curse,' it said.

She didn't know either, so she shrugged and grinned. 'That's a risk you'll have to take, then,' she said, and it caught her gaiety and chuckled, suddenly full of energy.

'Come,' it said. 'This way.'

She followed it, expecting another long trek, but within a few minutes they were standing at the edge of the woodland, looking down on Wili's steading. It was very cold and her breath – but only hers – steamed in the air. The view she had of the steading was very much like the view Red had had. Startled by the thought, she looked around quickly and saw him, concealed from the steading by a large tree but clearly visible from their vantage.

She took a step forward into the shelter of a juniper tree so that he would not be able to see her. The hunter was already concealed there. She watched Red closely. He *was* a big man, shambling, looking uneasy and excited. He looked subtly different from seeing him with Baluch's eyes, although she wasn't exactly sure how. She saw him more clearly, saw the details of his clothes, the shape of his head. Perhaps it was just the difference between a woman's gaze and a man's, or perhaps Baluch's attention was so often on the music inside his head that he noticed little.

She had watched Red, wondering, for too long. With a shock she heard the puffing breath of a horse trudging through snow behind her. She wheeled around, and there he was.

Through her own eyes Acton seemed bigger than ever, particularly on the small horse. Tall, so broad across the shoulders that he reminded her of a blacksmith. His hair was uncovered and the new beard lit his chin with gold sparks in the winter sunshine. It was different, profoundly different, from seeing him through Baluch. Emotions roiled through her and she couldn't separate them. She had hated him for so long, and then learnt not to hate him, and then to hate him again. He had killed so many people . . . But here she was, standing in the past, and seeing him in the flesh made it real to her that he came from this time, as she did from hers, and he carried its strengths and weaknesses as his own. He was a killer because he had been trained to be, encouraged to be by everyone he respected. What excuse did she have? At least he tempered his killing with generosity and kindness and a great, encompassing enjoyment of life.

Her heart thumped wildly. He was so *big*. She had seen him, most often, through the eyes of a man as tall as he was, almost as strong. In her own body she was sharply aware of how much larger he was, how male.

As he came abreast of her, some instinct made him glance over. She couldn't move. The gods would have to witness for her that she was frozen in shock. She was so used to being an unseen observer that it just hadn't occurred to her that he could see her now. Surely this was tampering with memory; with history? Would all the past and future come unravelling around them because she had made a stupid *mistake*?

Then he smiled at her, that crooked sideways smile he used for courting, and she realised that she had seen this happen before, through Red's eyes – that she was already a part of this time, this history. Relief hit her, but it wasn't relief that made her smile back. It was him. His glance seemed to invite her to share joy in the day, the trees, the crispness of the air. It was a look full of celebration and invitation, and she could not resist it. Any more than any other woman ever resisted it, she scolded herself, and schooled her face into composure. But he had seen that first, irrepressible reaction, and he winked at her.

She wanted to pull him down from the horse and shake some sense into him; to take him by those broad shoulders and drag him away from the path he was riding; to drag him to safety. He was so reckless! To go riding off to who knew where without even Baluch at his back. She was reckless herself, and she understood why he took risks; had gloried in them with him. But this time, just *this* time, she desperately wanted him to be careful . . . If only he had been careful!

He smiled wider at the frown on her face and raised a hand in farewell, then rode on. There was something in the gesture that implied, 'I'll see you some other time.' The movement cut to her heart and reminded her where he was riding to. She regretted frowning. The last woman's face he saw should have smiled at him.

'Are you done?' the hunter asked.

Bramble watched Acton ride into the apron of trees; watched Red leave his position and follow; and watched them both disappear behind evergreen. She thought of the burial ceremonies of her youth: the pine sprigs placed between the fingers, the Wooding Voice saying, 'In your hands is evergreen; may our memories of you be evergreen'. Her eyes filled with tears, and she blinked them away.

'Yes,' she said. 'I'm done.'

'I must touch you,' the hunter said. She realised that it wanted her to know that it wasn't attacking her and understood that it must rarely touch. She reached out a hand, and it took it, its palm dry and rough, like a dog's paw. They had been through the shift in time often enough for her to know what to do: she took a step.

Instantly the world shifted and tilted around her. The earth under her feet moved; instead of a slope, she was standing on level ground. Trees vanished. Buildings appeared. Men, turning, shouting, 'Ghosts! The ghosts have come!' They raised weapons to their shoulders and one ran in and swung straight at Bramble.

'No!' the hunter cried. It leapt in front of her and the weapon – a pickaxe, the end wickedly sharp – pierced its body. It fell.

'Stop!' Bramble yelled, pushing and shoving the man away. She didn't even have time to find her knife. She was defenceless. But the attackers jumped back, as though she had stung them.

'They're talking! They're talking! Ghosts don't talk!' The men started to babble, the one with the pickaxe looking sick. He sank to his knees, the handle loose in his grasp.

'Gods of cave and dark,' he whispered. 'I've killed him.'

The hunter was spouting blood from the big vein under the heart. Nothing could stop it, Bramble knew. Except perhaps enchantment, or the power of the Forest. She looked around wildly, but there were no trees here. They were in a place of grey stone and nothing else: stone buildings, flagstones, a great gash cut into the side of the hill. A mine. That's why the men had the pickaxes ready. They weren't an army, just men coming home from a shift in the pit.

Bramble gathered up the hunter, supporting its head. 'I thought you lived forever,' she whispered.

'In the Forest. As a true hunter. Me, neither, now,' it gasped. It looked at the man who had killed it. 'I fear,' it said. 'You must taste the fear and be cleansed.' It dipped one finger in its own blood and held it out to the miner, who stared at it in confusion.

'That's not how we do it,' Bramble said.

'No . . . I remember.' The hunter's words were coming harder now, and weaker. It coughed; there was blood on its lips. 'I remember . . . Forgive. I forgive . . .' Its head drooped but it turned its face to the miner. Its voice was hardly audible. 'I forgive and . . . and release from reparation.'

Bramble was crying. The tears she had held back all these weeks in case they had made her seem afraid were pouring down her cheeks and dropping onto its face, its hawk-feathered hair, its body.

'Why did you save me?' she said.

'You are *my* prey.' Its voice became stronger for that one sentence, then faded away. 'No one but me should kill you.'

'In our next life,' she said, trying not to laugh, because surely there was nothing to laugh at. 'I promise. In our next life you can kill me.'

'Too late,' it said, smiling with an echo of its old joy. The slitted pupil in the hawk eyes narrowed and disappeared until the eye was entirely golden. Then its flesh grew insubstantial in her hold and vanished away like a water sprite pulled out of water. The wind blew away only a mist, a scent of pines, a whisper. Bramble bowed her head over her empty hands and wept.

LEOF

Leof turned Arrow to the road and trotted sedately into Bonhill like any normal traveller. It wasn't a large village, but it had an inn. He called up the ostler and handed Arrow over to her with strict instructions about water, feed and grooming. Before he let her be led away he patted her and told her how marvellous she was. She knew it – tired as she was, she tossed her head and flirted with him.

Then he found the innkeeper and ordered a message be sent to . . . He hesitated for a moment. The enchanter had moved in a serpentine route. Although finding him had taken many hard riding hours, they were not that far from Carlion. Sendat was further, but he was sure that Thegan would not want to take the garrison out of Carlion. Two messages, then, one to Sendat and one to Thegan. While the best horses the inn had – sturdy little cobs which usually pulled the wagon – were being saddled, he wrote quick notes to Thegan and Sorn.

This was the first time he had written to her, and he reflected that he should take a lesson from the circumstances – the only communication between them should be like this, an officer's note to the warlord's wife. He signed it formally: 'Thy willing servant, Leof son of Eric'. He wrote with truth that he would be her servant, if nothing else.

Sendat was a day's march away, and they couldn't wait for the foot soldiers to catch up. He asked her to send the mounted troops, and to double each trooper with a pikeman. Hard on the horses, but it wouldn't be a long campaign and the roads were good.

Thegan had put a lot of silver into repairing roads when he first came to power in Central Domain, as he had done in Cliff Domain, and for the same reason. The people thought it was to improve trade and connection between towns, but Leof knew it was in preparation for moments like this, when he needed to move large numbers of men quickly.

Once he had sent the messages and checked on Arrow, he grabbed a piece of cold roast chicken from the flustered cook in the kitchen and went out the back way, taking a threaded, concealed path to where he had seen the wraiths hover.

Farmland wasn't ideal for stalking, but Leof had been well trained in scouting and by the time he had finished the chicken he had managed to worm his way to the side of the hill near the enchanter. He kept well back, away from the circle the wind wraiths were endlessly tracing above the rise.

He had been half-expecting Thegan to be right: to see the white-haired man from the pool. In any event, he was expecting such a powerful enchanter to be old. Perhaps very old. But the man who was digging and sorting out the bones he unearthed was around the same age as Leof: twenty-five, twenty-eight, no older than thirty.

Leof was tempted to simply kill him before he could raise more ghosts. He didn't look like a warrior – he was tall but had no muscle, and his mannerisms were nervous. Leof suspected that confronted unexpectedly with a sword, the enchanter would have no defence.

Two things stopped him. If he failed – if the enchanter had protective spells of some kind, or if the wind wraiths protected him – Thegan would have lost any chance of surprise. And the other thing: he just didn't know enough about the spell on the ghosts. Maybe the enchanter kept them under some kind of control, and if that control disappeared . . . Leof shuddered at the thought of the Carlion ghosts let loose on the rest of the Domains.

So he just watched. The enchanter was afraid of the wraiths. Leof had assumed that the wraiths were his servants. But judging by the looks he cast over his shoulder as he worked, he didn't trust them any more than Leof did. They were circling and calling to each other in a language he had never heard; half wind noise and half speech. Occasionally, they darted at the enchanter and laughed when he flinched. But they seemed to respect his right to work, and they were interested in what he was doing.

He worked without pause, following a strict routine. He dug a new section, taking the turf off in squares with a sharp spade and laying it aside, then digging deeper until he found bones. Then he put the spade aside and took up a spoon, loosening each bone carefully and laying

out skeletons. From each skeleton, he took a bone – a fingerbone, usually. He bent his head over this bone for a moment. Sometimes it was
a long moment, sometimes short. After this, he either put the bone and
its skeleton carefully back in the earth and buried it, or he put the bone
even more carefully into a sack, and then buried the rest of the bones.
The work was painstaking, and for a while he seemed to become
unaware of the wind wraiths.

After a couple of hours, Leof realised that he urgently needed to
piss. He eased back from his vantage point, losing sight of the
enchanter, and retraced his path step by careful step until he was hidden in a dense coppice of willow trees and it was safe to relieve himself. He stood in the green shadow for a while, trying to decide what
to do. The enchanter was so caught up in his work and, from the size
of the hill, had a lot more digging to do. Leof decided he was better off
going to meet Thegan and guide him to the spot.

So he left the willows and made for Bonhill, not sure whether he
was deserting his post. The wind had risen as the sun began to lower;
every gust or wuther made him look behind him, in case the wind
wraiths were following.

BRAMBLE

THERE WERE FAR too many questions and too much exclaiming and explaining by the miners, particularly explanations to the mine boss, a middle-aged man named Sami whose brown eyes trusted no one. Sami insisted on knowing who she was and how she had got into the mine.

Bramble was sick of talking, and disconcerted by the appearance of a group of young boys who poked their way in to the centre of the circle and listened, their eyes wide. She bit back a curse as she met the eyes of a pale child surely not more than nine or ten.

'Enchantment, all right?' she snarled at Sami.

He took a step back and then recovered his authority. 'You've got no right here.'

'You've heard about the ghosts?'

'One of our buyers told us,' Sami confirmed. 'The news is all over the Domains.'

Bramble wondered how long it had been in this time since the attack on Carlion; since Maryrose's death. 'How long ago did it happen?' she asked.

Sami shrugged. 'Three, four days. We haven't heard anything else yet.' His eyes narrowed. 'What's it to you?'

She didn't have time for this. She didn't have the time *or* patience. 'My sister was killed there.'

There was silence. Bramble used the moment of shock to take charge. 'I need to find the animal cave,' she said, gesturing to the mine. 'There's something in there that we need to defeat the enchanter who set the ghosts on Carlion.'

'Are you an enchanter, too?' The miner who had killed the hunter stepped forward, his pickaxe still in his hand. She could see that he wanted to feel justified; to not be guilty of murder. He didn't look like a murderer: he was strong enough, but his face was gentle and his voice quiet. She felt sorry for him. If she had heard the stories about Carlion and then had seen two figures appear out of nowhere, what would she have done?

She shook her head. 'No, it was the hunter who had the power, not me. I'm just ordinary.'

They looked sceptical, and she supposed she didn't blame them. But she was wound up with tension and grief and purpose, and she couldn't baby them.

'I need the animal cave,' she said again. 'Then we might be able to stop the bastard who raised the ghosts.'

'Why should we trust you?' Sami asked.

'Oh, shag it, I haven't got time for this.' Bramble drew her belt knife, grabbed Sami by the collar and put the knife to his throat. She was faster than she had been, she thought. Hunting every day had made her more dangerous. She grinned at his frantic eyes, pretending to enjoy his fear. Her stomach roiled in disgust.

'Because I could kill you right now. But I won't.' She let him go, and only then thought of the right thing to say. 'Because the Well of Secrets sent me.'

These were truly powerful words. Each man there relaxed, as though everything had been explained.

'What animal cave?' the miner asked.

'The cave with the animal drawings on the wall, from the very old times,' Bramble explained. 'The aurochs, and the elk and deer.'

The miners exchanged glances and shook their heads.

'Never seen ought like that,' one said. 'What about you, Medric?'

The miner pushed out his lip and shook his head, too. 'No,' he said. 'I don't know it.'

Bramble felt her guts cramp. The cave *had* to be there. She had been sure the miners would have found it.

'There's another cave,' she said. 'I could find my way from there . . .' She looked up at the mountainside, trying fruitlessly to spot any familiar landmarks. She had seen this mountainside only a few moments ago, as Acton rode up. Surely she could remember? That big peak, yes, but that was miles away . . . a thousand years of mining had altered the side of the mountain beyond recognition. The area where

Dotta's cave had been – that was where the entrance to the mine was. Inside were not caves but tunnels, wide enough for carts to be pushed up and down.

Despair began to creep over her, but she pushed it down. 'Who knows the caves best?' she asked.

There was silence, but everyone looked at Medric. He rested his pickaxe on the ground and stared at it, as if unwilling to meet their gaze.

Sami cleared his throat. 'Think you'll be able to find him, Medric?'

Medric took a breath, and let it out again as if unsure what to say. He shrugged. 'If I call him, he might come,' he said eventually, in a voice that gave nothing away.

'Who?' Bramble asked.

'A friend. Fursey. He, uh . . . he lives in there.' Medric indicated the mountain with a jerk of his head.

'Human?' Bramble asked.

A couple of the men looked at the ground as though unsure of the answer. One shorter man grinned and said, 'Well, we've had our doubts,' and then shut up as Medric glared at him.

'Human,' Medric confirmed.

She was glad of that confirmation as she followed Medric and his lantern down the tunnel and felt the weight of the earth above her, encountered the absolute darkness of underground for the first time with her own body. The dark hadn't seemed as bad when she was looking through Gris's eyes.

He led her down a long way, through tunnels that sometimes required her to crawl, and sometimes took them through caverns where the roof echoed high above her head. They stopped, finally, in a small cave – no, a tunnel. She saw the marks of pickaxes and chisels on the rock walls. This was the bottom of the mine, but there were fissures in the rock, passages like the ones Dotta had shown her, leading further down. Medric put down the lantern and stood for a moment, as if gathering courage.

'Fursey,' he called softly. 'Fursey! I've come back!'

He waited a few moments, and then called again, and then again.

There was silence. The earth seemed to grow heavier above them. Medric checked the candle in the lantern – it was more than half gone. He tightened his lips and sighed. 'Fursey,' he called again, but this time reluctantly. 'I need your help.'

Nothing.

He raised his voice in frustration. 'There are people dying, Furse, and I need your help!' Echoes rang along the tunnel walls, so that the whole mine seemed to be whispering, 'help, help, help . . .'

Medric turned to Bramble and shrugged. 'If he doesn't want to help . . .'

Behind him, from the thinnest of the fissures, a slight figure appeared. A man. Yes, human, Bramble was sure, although there was something about the way he moved that reminded her of the hunter. He stood staring at Medric for a moment as someone might stare at a picture of devastation. Then Medric realised where Bramble's eyes were staring and whirled around.

'Fursey!' He took a step forward and clasped the man to him, but the slight figure slipped out of his grasp and stook looking at him, head to one side.

'I thought,' he said in a soft voice, 'that if you came back, you would come alone. Is this your *wife?*' There was venom in his voice.

Medric flinched. 'Of course not. I only just met her. She needs help, and you're the only one . . .'

'So you came back for her, not for me? How was your family?'

The question threw Medric. 'They were fine. Da's dead. Mam's remarried. My sisters're fine. So I came back to find you.'

Somehow, the words took the tension out of the cave. 'But you hate the mine,' Fursey said.

'Yes,' Medric confirmed. 'I hate the mine.'

'Then you should not have come back.'

Medric bent his head, as he had after he had killed the hunter, and stared at the floor of the tunnel.

Bramble had had enough of all this melodrama. 'I need to find the animal cave, the one with the paintings on the wall,' she said directly to Fursey. 'Will you help?'

'That's a sacred place,' Fursey said.

'I know.' This man might have been human, but he was strange. Well, she had dealt with stranger things than him. 'I need to find some bones,' she said.

'Are they calling you?' he asked.

Very strange. But in a way, they were.

'Yes,' she said. 'They have called me for a thousand years.'

He nodded. 'Then I will take you.'

MEDRIC'S STORY

THIS IS HOW it was.

It's cold and windy. Da's hand is the only warm thing in the world, and there won't be that much longer.

The man from the mine is not too impressed; this one's too skinny, his look says, too bloody hungry. My boys'll eat him for breakfast. But he clinks some coins in his pocket.

'Five silver pieces.'

Da's hand tightens. Too much, or too little? It's hard to tell. What's five silver pieces worth, anyway?

'He's worth more than that,' Da says. 'He's a good boy, obedient. He's a hard worker, aren't you, Medric?'

Oh, yes. Da's strong enough to make sure of that. He's got a hard hand, has Da.

'Say something, why don't you?'

The man interrupts before Da does more than raise his voice. 'Five and a half. That's it.'

'It's robbery.' But he takes it.

The man from the mine is called Sami. He's from the north, with fair hair but brown eyes. Traveller blood in there, somewhere. A middling-size man, running a little to fat. But a man with a hard hand. It's not difficult to pick them, once you've known one.

'Come on,' he says. 'I'll put you in with the pushers. They'll start you off right.'

He leads the way to a long stone building with a slate roof. It'd be impressive in a town, but stone's cheap here, after all. All it costs is the labour of getting it out of the ground.

A chill strikes off the stone as he leads the way through the doorway. Inside, the floor is packed dirt. The little windows are so high up that at this time, late evening, there's almost no light at all. There are wide wooden bunks in rows on both sides of the room. In the closest bunks are boys, two or three to a bed: every age from ten up, and all of them asleep with the sleep of exhaustion. They sprawl uncaring, arms hanging out, legs uncovered by the one blanket. The mine whistle blew an hour ago, as Da hurried up the steep path to the mine, saying, 'By all that's holy, hurry up.'

An hour from leaving the mine to this oblivion.

Da said, 'Forget your bloody big words and your bloody airs and graces, boy. You're here to work, and don't you forget it.' Good advice. The only good advice Da ever spoke. Maybe not such a good farewell, though.

Sami gestures to a bunk in the far corner where there are only two boys. 'Nav and Fursey. Bunk in with them tonight and they'll show you around tomorrow. You'll be pushing. Get some supper over at the kitchen.'

He points northwards, through the stone wall, then considers. 'You'd better give me your duffel. This lot'll steal anything that's not nailed down. Don't worry, I'll look after it. You can get it back when you leave.'

Right. In seven years, at nineteen. Those clothes are going to be really useful then.

Sami grins. A clip over the ear is clearly his normal way of saying goodbye. It could be worse.

The kitchen is bright with firelight but there's not much food left. The cook grumbles as he fills a bowl with lentils and scrounges around until he finds a crust to go with it. The food's not too hot, but it's good. Solid. Sustaining. After all, you have to feed boys if they're going to hew out a mountain for you the next day.

Nav and Fursey both grumble about having to train a newcomer, but only Nav means it. Nav's a city boy from Turvite, mean-eyed and suspicious, sold to pay his 'uncle's' gambling debts. His mother let him go without a word, he says, scared that if she objected his 'uncle' would leave her.

'She'm a twitty bitch,' he says, 'no shagging good on her own. I's well off without her.'

Fursey's an orphan, with nowhere to go and no one to complain about. He's yellow-haired and blue-eyed, so his folks must have come from the south, but that's all he knows. He's been here since he was five; he doesn't remember before that.

'I was somewhere else,' he says. 'I don't care. Now I'm here.' He smiles, sweetly.

Fursey's the smallest of the pushers, but the others let him alone.

'Go easy with him,' Nav says quietly. 'He looks like he's a soft one, but if he takes against you he'll kill you. He don't never forget nothing; and he don't never forgive.'

Fursey looks people in the eye, even the hewers. He smiles like a much younger boy, but his stare is too strong for even Sami to bear for long. So Sami doesn't look at him.

'Get moving,' Sami shouts at all of us. 'You think it's a holiday?'

Fursey leads the way. Pushers don't really push — they pull the ore-laden carts out of the mine, up the steep, stony ramps. The traces go around the chest, and a long strip of leather rests against the forehead and is attached to the sides of the cart. A trained twelve-year-old boy who leans into the leather headband and puts his whole weight into it can haul a fully laden cart up a mile of mine ramps in twenty-two minutes. That's how fast Fursey is, but Sami doesn't know it. Fursey stops halfway up, every time, in the darkest part of the ramp, and just looks around.

The leather strap cuts. The ramp is stony and sharp on bare feet. The mine's not cold, exactly, not like up above, where the wind cuts through clothing like it was paper. But it's dark. By the gods, it's darker than anything. A darkness that settles down, heavy, like thick cloth over your mouth. The pale yellow of the candles at the turning points of the ramps can barely be seen. There is only the great bear of the dark. The roof feels like it's caving in.

'Look for the gold,' Fursey says urgently. His hand is warm. The boy-smell of him is comforting.

'What?'

'Look for the gold. There's always sparks of it, even here. That's why I stop, to see the gold.'

There are sparks. Tiny, flickering at the corner of your eyes. Barely there.

'There's a reef behind there,' Fursey says, pointing at the wall. 'But those fools up top don't know it. They've passed it by.'

'How do you know?'

'I know,' Fursey says, and settles the leather strap onto his brow. 'Back to your cart, Medric. Follow me. I'll go slow.'

With the strap around your forehead you have to look down and the dark doesn't seem so heavy. But it's a long, long way to the top of the ramp. To the sunlight. There are four more trips to make before mid-meal.

Well, you get used to anything, they say. Even to unending work, eat, sleep, work again. Not every day is pushing. The mine closes down at the dark of the moon for two days, and the free hewers go down-valley, to their families, those who have them.

'Dead unlucky to be underground at the dark o' t'moon,' Nav explains to me. 'That's when the delvers come out.'

'Delvers?'

Nav looks quickly over his shoulder, and makes the sign against hexing. 'The dark people, the little people, the eaters of rock, the owners of the blackness,' he says, and it's clear those aren't his words, that he's learnt them off by heart. But from whom, he won't say.

Even with the mine closed, the pushers don't stop working. There's always work: scything the grass around the barracks, cutting wood, weeding the kitchen garden. That's not so bad, with the sun warm on your back and the smell of fresh earth; living earth. Different from the dark, dead smell of underground rock.

These two days, Fursey is twitchy as a cat. Snapping at everyone. His wide-eyed stare has become a glare.

'He just hates being out o' t'mine,' Nav says. 'I told you, he'm crazy.'

It's true. Back in the mine, Fursey sings as he pushes; and stops to look at the gold twice as long.

In bed that night, he talks about it, whispering. 'I know none of the others understand, but you do, don't you, Medric? It's so beautiful down there, with the gold shining all around me. The gold calls to me, I can hear it, I know where it is underneath the rock. It wants to be taken out, to be melted down and made into beautiful things. It wants to be admired and treasured. It yearns for the pain of the pick cutting through the reef.'

His hand is warm. He is the only warm thing here.

'I don't really understand. But I suppose . . .'

'You'll see,' he says with confidence. 'You'll get to love it, too.' He snuggles closer. His hair smells of dust and leather.

In time, pushers become hewers. Hewing is better. Striking hard at the rock face, choosing your spot so the whole slab falls away with just one blow. There is skill in hewing, and responsibility. It's easy to make a mistake, to bring down a section of wall on your fellows.

That's how Nav dies, when a new hewer takes out part of a supporting wall and the tunnel collapses. The mine closes for a day. The free hewers walk down the valley to the gods' altar stone to pray for him and for once the bonded hewers and pushers are allowed to go with them, under Sami's watchful eye.

'Why don't they have a proper funeral? Why don't they dig him out?'

'The delvers will have taken his body,' Fursey says matter-of-factly.

He is right. Expecting the worst, it's hard to go down into the dark the next day. But Nav's body is gone and the tunnel floor partly cleared.

'No one knows where the bodies go, but nothing bad could happen. They only eat rock,' Fursey says. 'I think gold is like dessert for them.' He pauses. 'I'd like to meet them some day.'

'Don't say that! You might meet them the way Nav has.'

He smiles. In the pale light of his candle his eyes have no irises; they are wholly black, like the dark of the mine halfway up the shaft. The flickering of the candle puts gold into his eyes. Sometimes it is there even in daylight.

'There are worse places to die.'

The bed is bigger and colder without Nav. At home, the night seemed dark. But after the heavy darkness of the mine, even the blackest night is full of light. Fursey's head shines in it. Now there is some privacy, but Fursey thinks it's best to wait until the others are asleep.

They know anyway. All the boys who share beds share pleasure as well. What else is there? Where else can warmth be had? But Fursey is like that; secretive, solitary.

'Except with you, Medric. I'd never keep a secret from you.'

When Fursey finally becomes a hewer, months behind the other sixteen-year-olds, it's a relief to everyone, even Sami. Fursey was like a chained bear, sullen and dangerous, those last two months.

'If Medric can start hewing, I can too,' he argued. 'I've been here longer than anyone. You know I know the mine like no one else. I can pick a reef better than you can!'

But Sami was firm. No one becomes a hewer until they reach the height mark on the kitchen doorway. Not even Fursey, no matter how he argued and cursed.

His first day, Fursey fairly races down to the rock face, laughing and swinging his pick. He chooses a completely different part of the wall to work on. Ignores the foreman.

'Here, Medric,' he calls. 'This is where the reef is thickest.' He talks to the rock. 'I can hear you,' he says. 'I'm coming to get you out. Fall to my left,' he says. He swings his pick as though he's been doing it all his life. The pick head hits the rock and a whole section falls off, to his left. The way only the best and most skilled hewers can do, after years of practice.

Underneath there is pure gold. The full seam, shining so bright in the weak candlelight it looks molten, glowing. The hewers gather around silently. Even the bonded ones, who have no choice about being here, even they sigh a little, looking at the gleam of it. Fursey reaches out and touches it, traces the broad river of it down the wall.

'Hello,' he says.

That's the way it goes. Fursey chooses where we hew. Each time, he talks to the rock, tells it where to fall, how to split. And it does. The mine production triples. Fursey is Sami's pet. He gets new clothes, the best food. No one minds because, with Fursey telling them where to lay their picks, and talking to the rock face, no one dies. There are no more tunnels collapsing.

At night, he lies staring at the ceiling, smiling.

The other hewers in the barracks whisper to each other of the girls down in the valley, whisper and touch and groan. They talk about what they'll do when their bond time is up. Where they'll go. Sandalwood. Carlion. Foreverfroze. Who they'll shag, and how. Then they touch again.

Fursey talks about gold, and then touches.

'Gold and you, Medric. What else do I need?'

Only three months until the seven years are up. Fursey was sold in for fourteen years. He has another nine months to go.

'I'll work the nine months with you, Furse. Then we can leave together.' It's a faint hope. There's no chance.

'Leave?' he says, not understanding.

'My bond is up in three months. Yours is up in nine. I'll work the extra six months with you, get a bit of pay in my pocket. Then we can both leave together.'

He stares. '*Leave*?'

He's right, of course. It would be crazy for him to go. As soon as his bond is worked out, Sami will hire him back at three times a normal hewer's pay. He's worth twice as much again. He could have a house in the valley, live a good life doing what he loves. Why should he leave?

'I never chose to come here, Furse. I've got family, somewhere to go.'

'Your own da sold you!'

'Not my da. I wouldn't spit on him. But I've got two sisters. I want to find them. Make sure they're all right.'

He relaxed. 'Well, you can do that and then come back. No need to go for good.'

No need. Except the dark and the cold and the flickering of gold at the edges of vision like madness, waiting.

Except the hard slog of the walk up the mine ramp. Except the ugliness of the barracks and the dirt and the smell. Except having to watch the young pushers heave their hearts out and no way to help.

Except the girls in the valley. And the girls in the world beyond the valley. And the idea of children, some day. Children to be loved. To be cared for. Not hit, not terrorised. Loved. Never, ever, sold.

Nine months can seem longer than years put together. And shorter than a day.

Three days to go, Sami tries a recruiting talk. 'You're a good hewer, Medric. You've got a real gift for it.' That's true. 'Why not think about staying? Fursey's going to have his own house up here, you know. The two of you could have a good life.'

He's frightened that Fursey might desert the mine. He can't afford it.

'It's not such a bad life, when you're not a bondsman,' he says confidentially, leaning close. 'The valley girls like a free hewer.' He winks, then thinks again as he sees Fursey's face. 'Course, there's no need for you to go anywhere, really. Nice house of your own, good food, good company. There's many a man in the outside world would cut off his right arm for a life like that.' He chuckles. 'Course, he wouldn't be any use to us then!' His hand descends in what he means to be a friendly pat on the back. But he's a heavy-handed man, like my da, and it hurts.

'Don't go,' Fursey says when Sami leaves. It's the first time he's said it straight out.

'I can't take the dark any longer than I have to, Furse. I'm not like you. I've never loved it. There's a whole world out there. Don't you want to see it?'

He shakes his head. 'And the valley girls?' he asks bitterly.

'Oh, gods, Furse, I don't want them like I want you. But don't you want a family? A real home?'

He looks up with his eyes full of tears. 'You're my family. You and the gold.'

'Well, you'll still have the gold. I hope you enjoy it.'

Maybe that wasn't kind. But he talks always like gold is human. Like it has feelings.

On the last day, he stays at the rock face until after the mine whistle, until the other hewers have gone up the ramp and there is no one else around. No one will come back. They let him make his goodbyes in private.

'Don't go, Medric,' he says.

'I have to.'

'No, you don't. You can change your mind and stay here, where you belong. With me.'

His eyes are as black as always, down here, but they are shining gold, too. Strong flickers of gold. Nav's warning comes back to mind, from the first day. 'He don't never forget nothing; and he don't never forgive.'

Love is not a word that's ever used at the mine, and it's too late to try it now, anyway. But it's true. Even when he's acting like a madman.

'I only stayed in the world because of you,' he says. 'I never wanted to go up into the light. You know that. I went up there for you.'

'I know, but –'

'I'm not going back again. Not without you. I'm staying down here.' He pulls up the pickaxe, hoisting it casually, as hewers do, and I'm suddenly aware of the muscles in his shoulders and arms, the broad hewer's chest. The pickaxe can hew rock — it would go straight through blood and bone. Who knows what he's going to do, but he has to be stopped.

'You won't be able to help the gold anymore. What will it do without you?' It's a forlorn, stupid argument, but it makes him frown, considering.

He stands at the tunnel mouth and smiles, fair hair shining in the candlelight, just like gold. The only warm thing in the world.

'The mine will still go on,' he says. 'A little slower without me, that's all. But I'll be here forever.' Then he walks right up to me and kisses me, the pickaxe held between us so that all I feel is soft lips and rough wood and cold steel against my neck. Then he walks past me, down into the darkest part of the mine.

As he walks, he whispers to the gold, 'Show me where they are, the delvers, lead me to them, honeyfall, bright stream, sweet gold, you're my only love now, lead me to the people of stone . . .' And he disappears into the darkness.

The only warm thing. How could I help but go back?

MARTINE

THE PEOPLE OF Foreverfroze had gathered in the open space before the hall, examining the strangers with interest. Fathers hoisted their children onto shoulders so the little ones could see the warlord and his companions. Larger children wormed their way to the front. There was a holiday atmosphere, cheerful and expectant. Martine felt that she was as much a focus of interest as Arvid – the strange woman who looked like one of them.

Skua and Fox led her through the crowd, following the others. Safred, Arvid, Cael and Zel reached the hall steps first and turned to watch Martine come through. Men and children and old women touched her lightly as she passed: on the arm, the shoulder, the back, patting, saying 'Welcome', a word that sounded exactly as it had in her own village. Tears rose in her eyes and a woman clucked gently at her, 'Now, now'. She felt overwhelmed by the sense of family. She wondered if she could come back here to live after . . . afterwards. Perhaps, finally, she had found somewhere she could belong. Then she looked up and saw Arvid.

He was staring at her as though she were a miracle. She flushed, the lingering cold of the wind banished by pulses of heat, by a deep blush that swept through her, from head to foot, the fire spreading as though she stood before the altar in the middle of the ritual. She kept walking, trying to control her face, but she could see from his expression that he had seen her reaction. His breath was coming faster, his eyes darker than normal. As Martine reached the group, trying to focus on Safred and Zel instead of Arvid, Skua gave her a little push so that she stumbled and landed in his arms.

Skua said, 'Hah!' and Fox slapped her hand, mock reproving.

Martine was only just aware of them. One of Arvid's hands was under
her elbow, the other on her back. Her own hands were spread across
his chest, fingers splayed. Every point where they touched was alive,
warm, intense. She didn't dare look at his face, although they were
almost the same height and all she had to do was raise her eyes to his.
She could feel his breath, warm on her cheek; fast breaths that comforted her because it was clear that whatever was happening, was happening to both of them.

'She's cold! Better warm her up, lad!' Skua said. The crowd cheered
and laughed and Martine broke away from Arvid and turned, glaring
at Skua.

'I'm too old for these games,' she said sternly, and Fox, for the first
time, laughed.

'Never too old,' she cackled, digging Skua in the ribs. The two of
them chuckled and made some clearly lewd comments to an old man
standing behind Skua, speaking too fast in their own language for
Martine to understand. He took it with a private smile buried under a
long-suffering air, and exchanged a glance of sympathy with Martine.
She had forgotten this part of having a family – the lack of privacy, the
assumption that the aunties knew best, the interference. She *was* too
old for this, too old to get accustomed to it again. Her vision of a
future homecoming wavered.

Then they took pity on her and chivvied everyone into the blessed
warmth of the hall, and fed them fried whitefish and salmon roe,
mushrooms and greens, snowberries and smoked eel. Martine made
sure she wasn't sitting next to Arvid, but she ate the whole meal with
every sense tingling, aware of each move he made.

Towards the end of the meal, Arvid spoke directly to Skua. 'The
ship?' he asked.

'Tomorrow,' she said.

He nodded, satisfied, then said, 'There may not be room for the
horses.'

For a moment, Martine didn't realise what he meant, then she and
Zel and Cael all spoke at the same time. 'Trine's coming!'

Arvid was perplexed. 'It's just a horse.'

'Bramble's horse,' Safred said quietly.

He shrugged. 'Very well then. The wagons will arrive tomorrow, we
can load and sail with the next tide,' he said. He grinned at Martine
and she had to bite her tongue to stop herself smiling foolishly back.

'One thing about Foreverfroze, there's always lots of strong men around to help load ships!'

'Why is that?' Martine asked Safred.

'The shipmasters prefer women fishers,' she said absently, picking over a platter for the last of the mushrooms.

'But why?'

Arvid turned towards her. 'Because the shipmaster has to pay a levy to the family if a fisher is lost at sea, and when a ship is blown far off course and has to limp home, women take starvation better than men and are more likely to survive,' he explained seriously.

Martine smiled grimly. 'So it's a matter of silver,' she said, leaning forward so she could hear him better above the hubbub in the hall.

'Silver and gold,' Arvid agreed. 'A ship that loses its crew will bankrupt the shipmaster and he will lose the ship.'

'Shipmasters are men?'

He shook his head. 'Not always. But to steer a ship in rough weather, you need a man's strength, so the shipmaster is either a man or has a steersman as a husband.'

'You know a lot about it,' Martine observed.

'They are my people,' he said simply. 'It is my job to know them.'

She realised abruptly that she had been lured into private conversation with him, and sat back, trying to seem calm. The memory of the moment outside rushed back and to cover her embarrassment she spoke with severity. 'And to make sure they know you,' she said. 'And your guards.'

'Of course,' he agreed gravely, but with a hint of a smile, 'they must know their warlord and the people who protect them.'

She sniffed with disbelief, and he laughed.

'Don't judge me so swiftly, stonecaster! Things are different up here in the north.' Heads had turned as he laughed, and indulgent glances were cast at them.

Martine couldn't wait to get out of Foreverfroze, and preferably without Arvid. She pushed herself back from the table and stood up. 'If you'll excuse me,' she said.

He let her go, but called after her, 'Go breathe the northern air,' he said. 'It clears the head.'

She threw him a withering look, but he looked back without a smile, his guard down, eyes dark with emotion and desire. For her. The fire flared up inside her again.

Martine went out the door fast and into the bracingly cool air. She turned away from the houses and made for the ridge, where she might find solitude and time to reflect. The climb was a stiff one, but there was a path and she ploughed up it, glad of the movement after the day spent riding. At the top, she had used up enough energy to stop and appreciate the view. The sun was setting and the light had changed quality, losing its brilliance and becoming misty and golden. The moon was just rising, huge over the dark, moving sea. She stood on the ridge and reached out her hands, one east and one west, until the sun and the moon seemed to sit in her palms, and felt herself and the world come into perfect balance, poised on the ridge as if she were riding some great beast, one of the giant bulls of the Ice Giants, or a sea serpent, and she a hero out of the legends of her people: Mim, or the Prowman, or old Dotta herself, saviour of the fire.

For the first time since the fire had roared and rejected her, she was herself again. Whole. Calm. Back where she ought to be. Her breathing eased and grew slow as the sun slipped out of her hand and disappeared, and the moon swam slowly aloft, turning silver as she swam, and laying down the gleaming hero's path on the shifting sea. Martine lowered her arms.

Arvid's footsteps below her came as no surprise. She half-smiled, expecting to find that this, too, had returned to normal. That now the fire was gone, she would be able to look at him as she looked at any other man.

Then he reached the top of the ridge and she met his eyes.

ASH

Boys were not allowed to take the risk of finding their true shape until they were fully grown. On the third night of his fast, the thought returned to Ash with some comfort, watching Flax strip uncertainly in the forecourt of the big cave, that he himself was now fully grown, and strong enough to risk it.

They jumped the chasm and proceeded to the inner cave, much smaller than the first, and lit only by the glow worms and the faint flicker of light from the first cave. Here, a small stream sprang from the wall and flowed across the floor of the cave, spreading itself into a shallow pool and then flowing out another crack in the rock to fall to the River below. The deer and squirrel took hold of Flax and made him lie down in the pool, his face just clear of the water. His teeth started chattering immediately. Ash remembered that sudden chill, the freezing water clinging to his skin.

'This is the third test,' Ash said. 'Lie still and trust the River. Listen to her voice. Learn her. Love her. If you trust in her, you will be safe.'

That was all he could do for Flax. He had been told the same, the first time he came here, by an older boy who had not yet found his true shape. Now it was up to Flax. Ash walked towards the next passageway, where his father waited for him.

'Where are you going?' There was a note of panic in Flax's voice.

'Not far,' Ash said. 'But you must meet the River alone.'

Flax stared at him. Ash could barely see him in the dimness, but he could hear his breathing, fast and shallow.

'Trust her,' he said gently. 'But don't drink any water from anywhere in the Deep unless you have been given leave.'

He followed his father down the passageway, leaving most of the men behind with Flax. A wolf and a fox followed them: Vine and Skink. His excitement built further, and with it came apprehension. Was this the night when he would find his true shape? Outside the Deep you did not think about the Deep, but you couldn't stop yourself from dreaming. After his first visits here, he had dreamed again and again about becoming truly himself, about finding his animal self. His dreams had ranged from the grandiose – wildcats, bears – to the ridiculous – moles, water-rats, shrews – to the disturbing. He didn't want to be a weasel. Truly, he didn't want that.

They took him ever deeper, through dark caves without a single green star, through passageways which were rough underfoot, down and further down until they came at last to a place with another small fire.

They were on a broad platform which ended in a cliff. Beyond was darkness. There was no way to tell how large the cavern was, but the river roared loudly and echoed through the darkness. There was a large pool to one side which reflected the light of the fire in a perfectly still surface.

A man came from behind the fire, and unlike every other man in this place, he wore a human face, and was clothed in leggings and tunic. Ash had never seen him before, and wondered why. He was very, very old, his skin hanging in wrinkles and folds, his hair so white that it was impossible to tell what colour it might have been in his youth, although Ash felt sure it would have been jet black. He wore his hair in braids that reached past his shoulders, tied off with threads and feathers and beads. Immediately, Ash felt that his own short hair was out of place. He wondered how this old man managed in the world outside; only warlords' men were allowed to wear their hair long. Any Traveller who did so risked a beating or worse from warlords' men.

The man, surprisingly, had bright blue eyes, so his blood was not purely Traveller blood. This was a person with a complex past, a long and convoluted history that took in both Traveller and Acton's people. Ash found that reassuring, somehow, although he didn't know why. He put the thought away to examine later, and stared into the man's bright eyes.

'Will you meet your true shape?' he asked Ash. His voice was beautiful, the voice of a singer born and trained.

Ash felt a sharp stab of envy, but pushed it down. He nodded. The small movement made his head spin. Fasting cleansed you, but it left you weak. 'I will,' he said.

'Then climb, and drink, and know.'

The man led him to the edge of the cliff which descended into blackness, the small light from the fire making it seem even darker. Rowan came forward and placed both hands on his shoulders. He hissed. Ash could tell it was a blessing. He tried to smile at his father, but managed only a tight grimace. The fear was climbing up his stomach to his heart.

The old man came forward and placed a hand on his head. 'Take our love to the River,' he said. 'Climb, and drink, and know.'

Ash turned and backed over the cliff in the place the man pointed to. At least he was strong, and fit, thanks to training all winter with Mabry. He felt cautiously for toeholds and handholds. He didn't like heights; had always felt a treacherous desire to throw himself off. The darkness made it a little better, but it was impossible to see where his hands and feet were. As his head went below the edge of the cliff, he closed his eyes. Better to trust to his sense of touch than strain his eyes uselessly.

He didn't know how deep the cliff was. The last two years he had come with his father to the Deep, he had been brought to watch, as youths a little older than he was had made the climb. Not everyone survived the climb itself. Not everyone survived the knowledge of who they were. Some went mad. Some, when they returned up the cliff and were shown their true self in the reflecting pool, jumped off the cliff. Ash had seen it happen to a boy who found himself in a field-mouse shape.

As a watcher, the climb had always seemed a long time. Now it seemed endless. Fumbling in the dark, knowing one misstep, one bad handhold, could send him plummeting, screaming perhaps, into the dark, thundering river . . . He controlled his breathing as Doronit had taught him to, concentrating on only the next movement, the next shift of weight. This was a test of patience and self-control as much as skill and strength. Not to hurry, that was the main thing. Take it slow and sure, think of nothing else . . . He tired faster than he expected to and realised that strength wouldn't get him through this, but determination might.

The wind from the water below dried the sweat on his bare skin and made him shiver. His fingers were bleeding and his feet were cut. Why did a stubbed toe *hurt* so much? He had never understood that. The thought worried him. He was becoming light-headed. When he next had a foothold which would bear his whole weight he stopped and breathed deeply for a few moments, calming down before starting again.

The noise of the river was getting louder. He began to feel splashes on his legs: small droplets of water hitting and tickling as they rolled down. Then larger splashes, small waves flung up from the surface over his feet. The rocks grew slippery and he moved more slowly. There was no bottom to the cliff, he realised. Nowhere to stand. He would have to cling precariously to the rock and lean down to drink.

He decided that the safest way was to keep climbing until his knees, at least, were under water. Although the current might tug at him, he wouldn't have to bend so far down. He wasn't sure if he was being brave or foolish, but perhaps the River favoured fools, because as he carefully edged his feet down into the chilling water and waves slapped against his thighs, he found a ledge to stand on. The current was much faster and more turbulent than he had expected: he teetered and grabbed for a protruding knob of rock to steady himself. He could hold against it, just, but not for long.

He bent to the water, and then paused. It didn't seem polite to just drink, as though he had a right. He didn't know what to expect, but he felt he had to ask first.

'Lady,' he said quietly, 'may I drink?'

Immediately the water began to flow more quietly; the current stopped tugging at him, the waves grew still. The River seemed to pause in its course.

'Lady, I thank you,' he said, and scooped a palmful of water to his mouth. It tasted of chalk and iron, sweet and harsh at once, strong. Dizziness swept over him and he clutched at the cliff face in a panic. Then he felt the power of the River reach up to him, steadying him.

Trust me, it said in a voice unlike any he'd ever heard; a woman's voice, for certain, but with harmonies no human voice could carry, as though many voices spoke in rhythm with each other; and behind the voice was music so intricate, so complex, that it was almost unrecognisable as melody. He was ravished by it. His heart swelled with it until he felt it would burst with emotion. But there were no echoes from the voice and that was when he understood that she spoke inside his head.

'I do trust you,' he answered aloud, and it was true.

She laughed, bells and nightingales and waterfalls of laughter, and then was silent. He was left to climb the cliff again, his dizziness replaced by a wild curiosity. What had he become? He hadn't felt his face change, but perhaps that moment of dizziness had been the shift

to his true shape. He knew not to touch his head, and that it was forbidden to guess the shape before he saw it in the reflecting pool.

The climb up was quicker but just as physically demanding. The
cold of the River had leached strength from his muscles and he had to
force himself upwards by sheer will. Eventually, he became aware of
the light growing brighter, the flames flickering. His eyes were almost
blinded as his head crested the cliff edge and he pulled himself up onto
the platform.

His father was there, helping him over the lip and then standing
back to stare at him, open-mouthed. Oh gods, Ash thought. I'm a vole.
Or a weasel.

The old man was staring, too, and the fox and the wolf, all staring
as though they'd never seen anything like him. What if I'm a *snake*? he
thought wildly. Or a tame animal like a sheep? Please, not a sheep.

He walked forward, stiff-legged, to the reflecting pool, and the others followed behind him. He bent over its still surface, its perfect reflection, and saw himself.

Just himself. His own face, his normal face, a little pale but just the
same as always.

A great grief rose in him and he hid his face from his father, from
the other men. The River had rejected him. Why? *Why?* When it took
squirrels and voles, yes, and even field-mice men, why would it reject
him? He was worthless, he had always known it, useless for anything . . . No wonder his father hadn't taught him all the songs. Not
just because of tradition, they had said that to put him off. He was
flawed deep inside. The River had probably told his father not to share
the deep secrets with him. He fought back tears because he felt that if
he started to cry he would never stop.

'Ah . . .' the old man let out a great sigh as he hid his face, and came
forward. 'My son, welcome. I have waited a long time for this.' He
laughed a little. 'You don't know how long!'

He took hold of Ash's hands and pulled them away from his face.
Ash wanted to look away, but a last remnant of pride made him meet
the man's gaze, expecting scorn and derision. The blue eyes were full
of joy and comradeship. The man put his arm around Ash's shoulders
and turned him to face the others. Ash looked away, down at the
ground, anywhere but at his father.

'Rejoice with me,' the old man said. 'The River has found another
lover.'

LEOF

THEGAN ARRIVED BEFORE sunset, with a small body of men – all sergeants, except for his personal groom. Leof smiled to himself. Any old campaigner knew that when you used oath men in battle, you'd better have some good sergeants keeping them in line and making sure they didn't break and run for it.

'My lord,' Leof said as Thegan sprang down from his horse.

Thegan clapped him on the back and looked out over the landscape, which glowed golden and rose from the setting sun. It was a scene of perfect peace: dairy cattle wound their accustomed way to the milking sheds, birds settled to their nests, a sheepdog barked in warning at an errant ewe as it herded her into the fold for the night, and down the street mothers called their children in. Bonhill was full of the best possible reasons for resisting the enchanter.

'Where is he?' Thegan asked.

Leof pointed out the hill and described the work the enchanter was doing. 'I'd say he'll be there several days, if he wants to make sure he gets all the buried bones. It's a big area for one man to cover.'

'The bones . . .' Thegan brooded. 'You think that's what he's using to raise the ghosts?'

'What else would he want them for?'

Thegan nodded, his face dark. 'Is it the enchanter you met?'

'No. He's a young man, under thirty, I'd say. Not a warrior.'

'Hmph. If he were a warrior he wouldn't have resorted to tricks and spells.' Thegan nodded in decision. 'Well done. When will the Sendat troops arrive, do you think?'

'Depends if they march through the night. If they do, we might be in place before sunrise. If not, then mid-day.'

Thegan called his groom. 'Sandy, take the road to Sendat and tell whatever officer you find leading my troops that I want them to take no more than two hours' rest tonight. Tell them we have to be in position before it gets light.'

The groom nodded and ran for the stables.

'There's no guarantee that the wind wraiths won't smell us out anyway,' Leof cautioned.

'We'll deal with that if it happens,' Thegan said. 'Come, let's eat and rest while we can.'

It was good advice, and Leof took it. He and the sergeants ate and lay on the inn benches, jackets under their heads for pillows. Thegan lay more comfortably in the innkeeper's bedroom. They were all experienced men, so they slept, waking quickly as Thegan's groom barged in through the inn doors.

'They're almost here!' he called. 'My lord! My lord! They're coming!'

Leof sprang up and pulled his jacket on, feeling the familiar sense of tension and excitement he always felt before battle. This time, there was no unease. These were no innocents, like the Lake People; this was a monster aided by monsters, and he would hew the enchanter's head off with great satisfaction, if Thegan didn't get to him first.

Thegan appeared from the bedroom looking, as always, pristine. Leof retied the combination of leather thong and brown velvet ribbon that kept his hair back and pulled his jacket into shape over his hips, then followed Thegan out into the dark. On the eastern horizon, the sky was just beginning to grey.

The road leading to Bonhill curved around a series of hills, so that they could make out glimpses of movement and shadow, and hear the sound of horses hooves and harnesses clinking. Wil and Gard were at the head of the column, with Alston behind leading the first group.

'Privy break!' Alston called as they came to a halt two lengths away from the first village house, near an orchard. It was a well-practised routine. The men swung down from their horses and helped their pillion passengers, the pikemen, off. Then three out of four riders handed their reins to the fourth and disappeared into the coppice, followed by their passengers. When they emerged the fourth man went, too. Then they stood by their horses, waiting for orders. Leof could smell the piss from the inn door, and the nervous sweat. Thegan always

ordered a privy break before a battle; the men knew they would be
fighting soon.

While the men relieved themselves, Wil and Gard dismounted and
came for orders.

'The enchanter is on the hill, over there,' Thegan said. 'There's no
chance that we will completely surround him before he hears us, but I
want to get a small force up close and hidden before the main charge
starts, so that if he sets a spell loose we have a surprise up our sleeve.'
They nodded, nervous as the men. Neither of them liked the idea of
fighting an enchanter.

Leof put an arm around Wil's shoulders, and shook him slightly.
'I've seen him. He's a scrawny bastard, and he doesn't look too brave
to me. He'll probably run when he sees us, and then we'll have him!'

Thegan nodded approval at him. 'Twenty pikemen, Leof, under
your command. Take them to your observation post and keep them
there until you get my order. Use your own judgment if he sees us and
starts to fight. I'll give you a count of three hundred to get into position before we move.'

Leof nodded. He went to Alston and relayed the order. Alston gathered the twenty men and gave them a brief speech about keeping low
and staying silent. He had chosen experienced men, not the oath men.
Leof paused. He knew Alston liked to pray before he went into battle,
but this time he just motioned the men to start moving.

'No prayers?' Leof asked curiously.

'No need to ask for forgiveness from the one we are about to kill,'
Alston said. 'He has forfeited any rights to life or to rebirth.' His voice
was flat with a kind of hatred that Leof had never heard from him
before. 'This is a blasphemer of the worst kind,' he added. 'He will rot
in the cold hell for eternity.'

The words sounded so unlike his normal sensible self that Leof was
troubled. Could anyone forfeit their right to life or to rebirth? That
was one of those questions that had never worried him before he knew
Sorn. Her belief had made an impression on him without him realising
it, just as she had herself. He felt a quick, aching yearning for her; to
be sitting calmly with her, gazing quietly at her beauty. Although he
knew that if he were there, there would be no quiet inside him, only
raging desire and desperation. He shook off the thought and concentrated on leading his men quietly through the convoluted path that led
to the willow coppice.

They only just made it within the count of three hundred. Once there, Leof led the men under the trailing curtain of willow boughs, to the hard task of waiting. They heard nothing from the hill of bones except the wuthering of the wind, which might have been wind wraiths or might have been merely air. From beneath the trailing willow branches they could judge the quiet onset of day. The light grew brighter until they could see each other's faces, then eyes. The men listened hard, pikes clutched in sweaty hands.

Leof alone peered out, trying to make out any movement from the hill. He fancied he could hear the soft noises of Thegan's approach, but he knew how easily imagination magnified every sound before a battle. Thegan would not have had time to get everyone into position yet.

Then, as the highest leaves of the willow trees were lit into bright yellow green, they heard the wind wraiths crying, 'Ware! Ware! Master, beware of men with iron!'

Leof looked out to see Thegan still some way away, and the enchanter springing up from sleep. Frantically, he grabbed the bags of bones and poured them out in a circle around him. Leof realised it was the first step in making a spell, and he charged out of the screen of leaves, yelling, 'For Thegan!'

'Thegan! Thegan!' his men shouted. The enchanter faltered as he saw them, then he grabbed his knife and gabbled some words, holding the knife over his palm.

Leof ran up the slope at full pelt, but he was too late. The enchanter drew the knife down as Leof grabbed for it, scattering blood over the bones around him. He spun around, showering as many bones as he could before Leof grabbed him and pressed his hand against his own jacket to stop the bleeding. But it was too late. Around them, a circle of ghosts was forming. The first one, a short man with hair in beaded plaits, was the leader. The ghost aimed a sword at Leof's head. Leof let go of the enchanter and brought up his own sword in defence. He was stunned by the strength of the blow. For the first time, he understood to his marrow how dangerous the ghosts were.

The enchanter was backing away, terrified, protected by a phalanx of ghosts. The ground shook as Thegan's men charged the hill, horns blowing the attack. Leof's men had reached the hill just as the ghosts appeared and were now engaging them as they had been taught.

'Aim for the arms!' he heard Alston shout, and the men shouted acknowledgment.

Leof was fighting bitterly. The ghost wasn't a warrior, that was clear, but it didn't have to be when it didn't have to guard against death. It attacked furiously but without trying to defend, so that for a moment Leof had to put all his energies into protecting himself. The strangest thing was that the ghost was not breathing. Leof had often fought at close quarters, and he knew the interplay of gasp and breath and grunt as each man gave or took blows. This time only he breathed and gasped; it was disconcerting; strangely impersonal. Yet the hatred in the ghost's eyes was very personal. After a flurry of blows he manoeuvred the ghost around until he could take the blow he wanted. As he raised his sword for the cut he was aware of Thegan's horse arriving, of the riders bringing axes down on ghost after ghost, targeting the shoulders and arms and legs, as they had been instructed.

He grinned and brought his sword down on the shoulder of the ghost's sword arm. He had done this before, to one of the Ice King's men. He knew how much effort was needed to actually cut someone's arm off. But he did it. The ghost's arm fell to the ground. Astonished, the ghost looked down at it and Leof used the moment to bring his sword around and up for a backstroke that cut off its head. The head tumbled to the ground.

The ghost itself did not fall. The body swayed and then, sickeningly, the head and arm disappeared from the ground, and reappeared on the ghost's body. Complete with sword in hand. Leof stood watching in shock, his mind racing, his hands trembling. He and his men were all going to die. The Domains were going to die. There was no way to fight this – none at all.

The ghost twisted its head slightly, as if testing the surety of its neck, then looked down at its sword hand. It looked slowly up at Leof and smiled mockingly, then raised its sword again and struck. Leof blocked it but it drove him to his knees.

'Regroup!' Thegan shouted. 'Withdraw!' He spurred his horse closer to the hill and reached down to hoist Leof up behind him just in time to avoid the ghost's killing blow. Thegan wheeled the horse and hacked with his own sword at a group of ghosts, giving his men time to get away. Leof spun from side to side, guarding their backs.

All around them, men were screaming and running as they realised that the ghosts were not being harmed by even their worst strokes. The horns sounded the retreat, a pattern of notes Leof had only ever heard in training. Thegan had never retreated before.

'Abandon it!' Thegan yelled to the remaining men. 'Barricade your-selves in the houses.' He pulled his horse away.

A few of the men were down, lying dead or dying, and as the horns rang out the wind wraiths appeared as though summoned by them. They descended towards the battlefield with shrieks of joy, like enor-mous ravens. The ghosts stopped still to watch them, their faces dis-torted by fear.

'Feed us!' the wraiths shouted. Thegan checked his horse as the wraiths hovered over the enchanter, safe in his circle of ghosts.

'You may feed,' the enchanter cried and the wraiths dived on the dying. The men screamed, long bubbling screams that made Leof's gorge rise. The ghosts backed away, except for those around the enchanter, and then turned and ran, streaming down the hill, heading for the village and beyond. Leof blanched at the likely outcome; he hoped the inn had stout doors and a good strong bar. If the past pat-tern stayed true, they had all day before them. Sunset seemed a very long way away.

The ghost Leof had fought stood beside the enchanter now, and it raised its sword and shook it threateningly, grinning with satisfied mal-ice.

'Archers!' Thegan shouted. A rain of arrows left the trees, where archers had been concealed, all aimed at the enchanter, who was just within bowshot. But as the shafts hissed through the air they were overtaken by the wind wraiths, who snatched them up in mid-flight and cast them down to the ground, shrieking with glee.

Thegan tensed and leaned forward, staring at the enchanter, clearly considering whether he could reach him and drag him out, or perhaps rescue some of the men.

'Don't do it, my lord,' Leof said. He put a hand on Thegan's rein, and dragged his horse's head around, heading him back to Sendat. 'It's useless. No army alive could stand against them.'

BRAMBLE

Fursey led them. He needed no lantern, finding his way with uncanny ease up and down and up again, past walls through which they could hear the rushing of water. The sound reminded Bramble too vividly of the many times water had seemed to sweep her out of Acton's life and back into it again. It was only an hour or so since she had seen him, vividly alive. She smiled despite herself as she remembered that sideways smile, the promise and admiration it had held, the energy of every movement he made. She was going to miss that energy.

In the darkness it was easier, somehow, to think about all the people she had come to know through Baluch's eyes, and Ragni's, and Piper's – all dead and gone. She remembered her mother telling her about a man whose whole family had been killed in a fire. 'Never really got over being left alive,' she had said. 'Hung himself on the first anniversary.' At the time, she hadn't understood how anyone could regret being alive. She didn't, she *didn't* regret it. Maryrose had told her to live, and she would live, as long as she had to. But she understood, for the first time, how lonely that man must have been, when everyone he loved was gone and he was left to carry on. She thought that, after all this was over, she would find her parents and maybe stay with them for a while.

After that she would find a song-maker, and tell him or her the truth about Acton and the past, and set the record straight. Damn Asgarn's name for eternity. The thought made her slightly more cheerful.

Then Fursey turned a corner and suddenly she was in a passage she recognised, one Dotta had led her down. Her heart beat faster. Not far now. She recited the turns in her head as Fursey took them – yes, he did know the way. Finally, they made the turn into the cave, and Medric raised his lantern high, looking at the walls in amazement. The painted animals seemed to leap and buck, as though they were still alive. Fursey stood for a moment with bowed head, as if praying.

The lantern candle was almost burnt out. Medric took another from his pocket and replaced it. The new candle burned with a whiter light, allowing Bramble to examine the corners of the cave. She searched thoroughly, but there were no bones, not even animal bones. In the furthest corner, however, was a shaft, and the smell from it was dry. No murmur of waters, no sense of damp. If the bones were in there, they might be retrievable.

'The bones must be down there,' she said. 'We'll have to bring tackle and try to fish them out.'

'No.' Fursey's voice was adamant. 'That is a place sacred to the stone-eaters. We can't go there. We can't *fish* there.'

'We need the bones,' Bramble said, equally adamant. They stood, glaring at each other.

Medric cleared his throat. 'Um . . . can we ask the delvers?'

'No one can summon them!' Fursey said indignantly.

He was wrong. Of course, Dotta had known. Bramble realised with shame that Dotta had warned her about this, and she had forgotten. She remembered another thing Dotta had told her: 'The prey must be called with love, though, or it does not come. Remember that.'

Were the delvers her prey, or was she theirs? It didn't matter. She was moving once again in a bizarre world where the impossible was necessary. She touched the images of the earth spirits which someone had painted thousands of years ago and sent out the call, as the hunter had taught her, as the hunter had done, with love. Come to me, she said silently, as she had been silent in the Forest when the deer came and nuzzled her before their deaths; as she had been silent when the hunter had his knife to her throat; as she had been silent when Red had brought the knife up. Prey or hunter, it was the same thing. Come to me, for I have need of you.

Medric's gasp alerted her. She turned to see Fursey kneeling, separated from her and Medric by a river of dark rocks. They were slow moving but inexorable, filling the cave not from the outer cave or through fissures but from out of the walls themselves, sliding through the rock as easily as she moved through snow, but leaving no trace of their passage behind. They were half her height, and glinted in the light from the lantern as polished granite glints, but they were rough, not smooth.

They were far more strange than water sprites or wind wraiths; dangerous and alien. Bramble grinned at them in the darkness, feeling the familiar lift of excitement, and moved forwards, slowly, giving them time to get out of her way. They made an aisle for her and she reached the shaft at the edge of the cave easily – but now she was alone, in a little island surrounded by earth spirits.

'There were bones,' she said clearly, 'thrown here a thousand years ago. The bones of a man. I need them. I am sent by the gods to recover them.'

She had no idea if they would understand her, and when they spoke to her in grating rock-sliding-on-rock voices she knew that they hadn't. She looked at Fursey.

He lifted his shoulders. 'I don't understand them, either,' he said.

The delvers edged forwards, pushing Bramble closer to the shaft. Medric sprang forward too, shouting, 'No!' but he was too late. They pushed suddenly, hard and impossible to resist, and she felt herself falling. The sensation was like the waters sweeping her away once again and she forced herself to relax, as she had then, to let the current take her where it willed.

She landed with a thump that knocked breath and thought from her body and lay for a while in darkness so complete that her eyes made light for her, peopling the cave with specks and fireballs, with colours and sparks.

There was something sharp under her. She moved with difficulty and edged it out. If Acton's bones had broken her fall – she laughed silently. That would be rich. She drifted off into semi-consciousness.

'Bramble! Bramble!' Medric's voice roused her.

'Mmm,' she said. 'I'm all right.' That was a lie. She hurt all over.

'The delvers have gone,' he shouted. 'I'm sending down a candle. Do you have a tinderbox?'

No, of course she didn't have a tinderbox. What a stupid question. 'No,' she managed to say.

She dragged herself up and sat with head hanging. A moment later a thin cord with tinderbox and candle came snaking down through the shaft and hit her on the head.

'Oh, dung and pissmire!' she said. The box had bounced off her head and fallen somewhere nearby. She felt for it cautiously. The rock beneath her was covered with bones. Whether they were Acton's or animals', she didn't know.

Then at the same moment, her left hand touched the tinderbox and the right one found a smooth surface . . . rounded, with holes. Oh, gods, it was a skull. She grabbed the tinderbox but her hands were shaking too much to undo the knot. She put it on the rock next to her foot and reached out again for the skull. His skull. The bone was silk covered in dust. She rubbed it on her trousers to clean it and held it in both hands, leant her head down until her forehead was on his.

He was dead. He had been alive, smiling at her, only a few hours ago. But he was dead. He had been dead all this time, lying here, flesh withering away to dust, to nothing but bone. He was dead and she would never see him again.

The grief rose in her overwhelmingly; worse than for the roan, or the hunter, or even for Maryrose. The strength of it burned her as it rose, choking her, stopping her breath so that she thought she would die, racking her with so much pain that her eyes could not fill with tears, and at last she recognised it for what it was. She had felt this grief before, when she was Piper, looking at the ghost of Salmon. This was the grief of love.

Alone in the dark, she cradled his skull to her and rocked backwards and forwards and remembered him, because all she would ever have was memory, and she would love no human never, because he was no longer human, because they had never been human together except for that one moment on the hillside, where he had smiled at her with such promise, such delight. She remembered him vividly, gold hair shining in the sunshine, flecks of gold glinting on his jaw from the new beard, blue eyes bright and mischievous, mouth curved with desire. For her. Her, not Wili or Freide or the girl on the mountain. He had smiled at her, only two hours ago.

And now he was dead, and his bones were as dry as her eyes.

SAKER

INVINCIBLE. THEY WERE invincible. All day the warlord's men fell before them, or ran before them. They cowered behind locked doors, they pleaded for mercy before the killing stroke came. Nothing could save them.

Saker himself was invulnerable – guarded not only by undying men, but by the wind wraiths as well. Safe against archers, safe against blades, safe against blows. Invincible.

He was buoyed by victory, elated and exalted and set free from all fear, at last. He had thought that the wraiths were a terror, but they had saved his life. The gods were truly with him, supporting him. *They* had sent the wind wraiths.

He left the cart behind on the hill and took only the casket of bones and the scrolls with him. Now that he had been discovered, he must hide until the next time. They would keep a lookout, to stop anyone digging for bones. This army was all he had, and probably all he could get, for now. It was enough.

Enough for Sendat. Enough to raze the warlord's fort and kill everyone within. Enough to gather all the weapons they would need.

Then, Turvite. He would raise Alder, his father, to participate in that great fight.

As the day ended, he found an abandoned water-mill whose course had run dry, and hid the bones and scroll under the decaying wheel before holing up himself in the mill loft. Owl went with him. They looked out the window slit across what seemed peaceful, prosperous country lying golden in the last light of the sun. Owl smiled ferociously and gestured wide, then began to fade, still smiling.

'Yes,' Saker confirmed as he disappeared. 'Yes, we will have it all.'

He ignored his empty stomach and settled down, smiling, to plan for massacre and conquest.

extras

www.orbitbooks.net

about the author

Pamela Freeman is an award-winning writer for young people, and is best known for the Floramonde children's fantasy series and *The Black Dress*, an inspired biography of Mary MacKillop's early years, which won the New South Wales Premier's History Award in 2006. Pamela has a Doctorate of Creative Arts from the University of Technology, Sydney, where she has also lectured in creative writing. She lives in Sydney with her husband and young son. *Blood Ties* is her first novel for adults.

Find out more about Pamela plus other Orbit authors by registering for the free monthly newsletter at www.orbitbooks.net

why i hate the olden times

Do you ever get the feeling that most epic fantasy is set in the same time? Olden times – vaguely pre-industrial, vaguely medieval, vaguely Dark Ages . . . often a bit of each. One example I read recently – a society which had tailored jackets but no socks!

Do you ever get the feeling that most epic fantasy is set in the same time? Olden times – vaguely pre-industrial, vaguely medieval, vaguely Dark Ages . . . often a bit of each. One example I read recently – a society which had tailored jackets but no socks!

So often, fantasy authors stick technologies from widely different times together as though every culture prior to the invention of the steam engine was the same. The point of history is that things change – and this includes technology.

Technology! I hear you exclaim. They didn't have technology then!

But they did. It didn't use electricity, but it was technology nonetheless.

Just look at boats. It was the development of the Viking longboat in the 700s that allowed the Norse invasion of Europe. The Vikings, over a couple of hundred years, developed a shallow-draught vessel which was seaworthy *and* which could carry a reasonably sized raiding party up any navigable river (the Seine, the

Thames . . .). It differed from the Roman galley (which was larger and with a deeper draught) in its ability to go far inland, in its manoeuvrability and in the ease with which it could be beached or launched on any shelving shore.

You can see the development of this technology quite clearly in the remnant vessels we have. Once the boat was big enough and strong enough, Viking trade blossomed – and so did Viking raids. Europe shifted radically as a consequence. The Normans were originally 'Norsemen'; they invaded mainland Europe well before they invaded England.

Boat-building technology was the basis for a civilization – and for the destruction of others. But it didn't freeze in place – the longboat gave way to the cog, the barque, the galleon . . . and the clipper, the paddle steamer, the steamboat, the ocean liner, the aircraft carrier . . .

Boat-building is just one example; every trade could be discussed in the same way. Boats are in my mind because I've just finished the second book in the Castings Trilogy, *Deep Water*, and in that book we go back a thousand years in 'story time' and we see boats like these being built. In the third book, a thousand years later, other characters will be on a trading ship, and I am being very careful to show that boat-building technology has changed.

And also clothes, saddles, horse-breeding, hearths and chimneys, weapons, living quarters, hairstyles, boots, drinking-cups, glassmaking . . .

This has two purposes: first, it helps with world-building. I want my readers to feel that a thousand years has indeed passed. That this place, this particular culture, has shifted over time in a believable way. Secondly, I want to do it because I get very annoyed by stories where the passage of time somehow has no effect on ordinary life – as though the fabulous ability of human beings to invent new stuff just doesn't operate in fantasy worlds.

That's why I hate the 'olden time' where so much fantasy takes place. It spits in the face of every craftsperson who worked hard to improve their techniques. It ignores the sweat and toil of thousands of unnamed people, men and women, who improved everyday life incrementally over our history. Each one of them was a person of their time – starting with the technology of their day, and adding to it.

I'm not saying that technology in fantasy worlds should slavishly ape our own – those worlds have different histories, and their technologies will be different as a result. But there are some things which shouldn't – *wouldn't* – exist in the same culture at the same time, and to stick everything pre-industrial in together, willy-nilly, is bad world-building. A culture with tailored jackets would have found something better to protect the feet than strips of rag. Maybe not knitting, as our culture did. Maybe something else, like fur or sewn tubes of cloth – or the elastic skin of a fabulous animal, now bred for just this purpose, its wonderful magic debased into keeping humans blister-free. (If anyone wants to run with that story, be my guest.)

In a world based on ours, there are some good bets you can take. There will be rope of some kind – even if they have to make it from human hair! – because every human culture has invented twine at the very least. Clothes usually reflect the current technology – the finer the spinning, weaving and sewing, the more advanced the base technology (think about the difference between the ivory needle and the bronze needle, the spindle and the spinning wheel, blunt shears and carbon steel scissors which can keep an edge . . .) In every horse-riding culture, saddles have been invented before stirrups. (Come to think of it, inventing a world which had stirrups but no saddles would be very interesting . . .) A culture which can make very good swords (that is, is experienced with iron and steel working) will probably make iron rims for their cart wheels, because they work.

But while it's reasonable to assume that any culture will find a solution to common problems (keeping clothed, transporting goods . . .) at the level they are capable of, not all cultures follow the same route of technology. What they use (like the Romans using clay amphorae for transporting trade goods instead of wooden barrels) is influenced by their history, what is easily available to them and by their contact with other cultures, which also has to be taken into account. In other words, if you are going to create a believable culture with believable levels and types of technology, you have to think about it in some detail, and make sure it is internally consistent.

I feel similarly about the food in fantasy worlds. Not just because, as Diane Wynne Jones points out in *The Tough Guide to Fantasy Land*, everyone seems to eat nothing but stew, but because so often the food depicted in a setting based on medieval Europe bears little relationship to the food which was actually eaten in medieval Europe. Potatoes, for example, which abound in fantasy worlds. A New World food, not seen in Europe until the sixteenth century. Also tomatoes. Pumpkin. Chillies. Chocolate. Coffee. The word 'corn' in ancient writing refers to a kind of hard maize used to make flour, not to sweetcorn, which again comes from the Americas. Pasta or noodles are from China via Marco Polo, so no earlier than the thirteenth century. Ditto tea. Even carrots are a trap for the unwary! You didn't get orange carrots in Europe until the eleventh or twelfth centuries – before then they were white or purple. Without all these ingredients, European food looked a lot different. It's startling to realise how much of 'traditional' European cooking, like spaghetti bolognaise or spicy paella, is quite recently invented.

I know I haven't got all the technology or the food right in the Castings Trilogy. I'm not sure anyone could get *everything* right and actually finish a book by the time they died. But we could do it better, I think.

if you enjoyed

DEEP WATER

look out for

FULL CIRCLE

by

Pamela Freeman

ASH

LIKE HARP music, the sound of the river rippled far below them. It sounded calm, now. Soothing, as though it had never leapt high, never threatened. The old man smiled, his long white hair casting a shining circle around his head in the firelight. Ash was aware of the other men, his father included, standing in the shadows of the cave, but he couldn't bring himself to look at them. Desperately, he stared into the old man's intense blue eyes.

'She calls you,' the man said. 'She calls your name. Close your eyes. Listen.'

Bewildered, hoping that he was not beyond acceptance, that the human face which had reflected back at him from the pool did not mean that he was worthless, Ash closed his eyes. He had so hoped to find his true shape when he climbed down to meet the River. Every other Traveller man did so, after all. Why should he be different? Did he *have* no true shape? No animal spirit deep in his soul which the River could call out? What did that make him?

Ash shuddered with a combination of grief and horror at the thought and felt the old man pat his back in comfort.

'Listen,' he said gently. 'She will speak to you.'

The river was growing louder. Ash concentrated. He had heard the River speak only minutes ago, when he stood in her waters and asked permission to drink. She had laughed, and granted it. Now there were no words, only sounds, like music, like the music he carried in his head, day after day.

The music built in his mind, speaking of emotion deeper than thought, deeper than words, stronger than time. Love was only a small part of it, on the edges. Desire ran through it, but was not the centre. That was . . . he strained, listening harder, and felt it slip away.

Be still,' the old man said gently. The hand on his back was warm and reassuring. Ash let out a long breath, forcing his muscles to loosen, and found the centre of the music, the rhythm that controlled everything. *Welcome*, it said. *Belong*.

He began to cry. He had yearned towards homecoming when he lived with Doronit, hoping past sense that she could give it to him. He had seen belonging like this and envied it, watching Mabry and Elva hold their baby, his namesake. He had dreamed of returning to the Road with his parents as a stonecaster, earning a place with them as he had not been able to do as a musician. Each dream had withered, sending him back onto the Road, and finally pushing him here. Perhaps he had been Travelling towards the River all his life.

Yes, said the music. *All your life*.

Ash raised his face to the old man, who was smiling.

'She has been waiting for you for a long, long time, child,' he said, as he had said once before. 'And so have I.'

Ash found his voice with difficulty. 'Who are you?' he whispered.

I am the Prowman.'

It was a term Ash knew from old river songs – the

Prowman was the one who stood at the front of the boat and signalled to the steersman which direction to take, to avoid the rapids and treacherous currents. He found the name reassuring; he could certainly use some guidance himself.

Ash's father, Rowan, came forward hesitantly. His head was a badger's; each of the men there wore his true nature in the form of an animal, revealed to them through the power of the River. The sweat on his naked skin reflected the torchlight in slabs of gold and red.

Rowan put a hand gently on Ash's shoulder. The dark badger eyes searched his. And then Rowan let Ash go, turned to the other men and lifted his arms high in a gesture of victory. He howled triumph and the other men joined in, dancing and shouting, the animal screams and yowls echoing off the cave walls until Ash was nearly deafened. It was a terrible sound: harsh, cacophonous, wonderful. It lifted him up into a kind of exaltation. He still didn't understand what had happened, or why he had not been given his true shape like the other men, but he did understand that they accepted him, honoured him, just as he was. The moment was over too soon. Rowan and the other men gave a last whirling leap and ran off into the darkness which led to one of the other caves. Some of them carried torches, the flames and smoke flickering behind them as they ran.

They left one torch behind, stuck in a crevice in the rock wall. The dark closed in around, making the cave seem even bigger, the echoes sharper and more eerie. Ash was aware of his wet feet and calves, suddenly cold where the River had splashed him as he climbed.

The Prowman went behind one of the large boulders near the passage and came back with a blanket and pack. He threw the blanket to Ash, who hesitated.

'Am I allowed . . .?' All the other men were naked, except for the Prowman, who wore leggings and a tunic. The old man shrugged, the beads at the end of his long braids clicking softly.

'Animals go naked,' he said. 'We are not animals.'

'What are we?' Ash said.

The Prowman gestured to the floor and they sat, cross-legged, Ash pulling the blanket around himself. The pack held food: cooked chicken, bread, apples, dried pear. Ash fell on it thankfully. He hadn't eaten in three days.

'Slowly,' the Prowman said. 'Or you'll just throw it all up again.'

It was good advice, but it was hard to follow. Ash forced himself to start with the bread and chewed it thoroughly instead of wolfing it down.

'What are we . . . well, that's a little hard to say,' the Prowman said, smiling. 'We are . . . hers. I can tell you some things about yourself, although I do not know you. You are a musician.'

Ash shook his head vigorously, glad his mouth was full of chicken so he didn't have to say the disappointing words out loud.

'No?' The Prowman paused, surprised. 'You *don't* make up music?'

Ash stilled, his hand over the chicken. *Did* he make up music? The moment seemed to stretch for hours.

'In my head,' he said finally. 'Only in my head.'

'Ah, well,' the Prowman said comfortably, reassured. 'That's where all music starts.'

'But I can't sing!' Ash said. 'Or play anything.'

The River doesn't care about that. She wants what's inside you, not what you do outside.'

'What? What's inside me?'

'The thing that makes the music, that *thinks* the music. The centre of you. It's why she chose me, why she chose you.'

'Chose us to do what?'

For the first time, the Prowman seemed unsure. 'Different things. Be her voice, for one. Be her eyes in the world. Be her . . . life.'

'Her lover, you said,' Ash prompted. He wasn't sure how he felt about that, except intensely curious.

'Mmm . . . you'll find out about that in time, although it won't be what you expect.'

'Nothing ever is!' Ash exclaimed, tired of being told only part of things, tired of always being at the beginning of understanding. Enough of this mysticism. He had a job to do. 'I need to learn the secret songs.'

The Prowman shook his head, and Ash jumped to his feet, infuriated.

'Don't tell me there's *another* shagging test!'

'No, no, don't worry,' the Prowman said, laughing sympathetically. 'You don't need to learn the songs because when you need them, she will give them to you. How do you think the men learnt them in the first place? She gave them to me, and I gave them to the men. She will be your teacher, lad, when the time comes.'

But Ash had a better idea.

'*You* can sing them!' It was a relief, to hand over the responsibility to someone he was sure could fulfil it. But the Prowman put up a hand in refusal.

'No, lad. This is your job. Your time to be active in the world. I have had my time, and it was more than enough.'

There was a note of sorrow, of loss, of relinquishment, in his voice.

'So there is nothing to keep you here,' the Prowman said.

'Go where you need to go, and she will be there waiting for you.'

'Sanctuary,' Ash said without thinking. 'I have to go to Sanctuary.'

The Prowman's face became shadowed; tears stood in his eyes. With their bright blue clouded, he looked very old, the torchlight showing hundreds of wrinkles, his hands browned with age spots, his hair snow white.

'Sanctuary,' he whispered. 'That is a name I have not heard in a very long time.' He looked up, tears disappearing. 'Good. That is the right place. Why do you go to Sanctuary?'

Ash hesitated, but only because he was overwhelmed by how much he had to explain. Keep it simple, he thought.

'To raise the ghost of Acton,' he said. 'So that Acton can lay this army of ghosts to rest.'

The Prowman went very still.

'Acton,' he said. 'She did not tell me that. I wonder why.' He sat for a long moment and then stood up, as supple as a young boy. 'If you go to raise Acton's ghost, lad, I think you will need me with you.'

Relief washed over Ash.

'You'll come with us?'

'I will take you the River's way,' the Prowman said.